PRAISE FOR TORI WHITAKER

A Matter of Happiness

"*A Matter of Happiness* is a thrill of a ride and a beautiful read. Violet and Melanie are connected across generations by blood, bourbon, cars, and a great need for independence. Tori Whitaker unfolds the narrative with a deep sense of history imbuing every sensational page, weaving the women's stories until the inspiring conclusion. This is a compelling story of women who understand that we can choose our happiness and we can choose our lives. A story about strength, fate, and choice, Whitaker crafts a riveting read you will not want to put down until the very last page."

—Patti Callahan Henry, *New York Times* bestselling author of *Surviving Savannah*

"*A Matter of Happiness* will take you on a wild ride to remember, from the modern-day bourbon distilleries of Kentucky to the speakeasies and parties of Detroit in the twenties. With astute attention to historical detail, Whitaker tells the tale of two strong-willed women, Melanie and Violet, determined to make it on their own terms. You'll find yourself rooting for these two young women, connected by a cherished 1923 Jordan MX, as they attempt to navigate modern womanhood and what it really means to be happy."

—Nicola Harrison, author of *The Show Girl*

Millicent Glenn's Last Wish

"This touching story of the love and forgiveness between mothers and daughters will win fans."

—*Library Journal*

"This tenderly written, fast-moving tale of marriage, women's friendships, and family reconciliation is satisfying and extremely moving."

—Historical Novel Society

"A heartwarming and affecting novel centered around the love between mothers and daughters, of what we share and the secrets we keep . . . Whitaker brings us back to the 1950s, highlighting the old gender norms and the cost paid by those who tried to shake them . . . an engaging and illuminating walk through the not-so-distant past . . . with a worthy heroine to lead readers through a life full of loss, love, heartbreak, and, ultimately, of forgiveness."

—Karen White, *New York Times* bestselling
author of *The Last Night in London*

"A novel about the legacies women pass to their daughters—and the price of the secrets they keep. Millie is a heroine to cheer for as she makes her journey from . . . working wife and mom to grandmother seeking forgiveness for her decisions—made because of jaw-dropping challenges you will never forget. You'll miss her long after the book's cover is closed."

—Jenna Blum, *New York Times* bestselling
author of *The Lost Family* and *Those Who Save Us*

"Tenderly told and full of heart, *Millicent Glenn's Last Wish* is a deeply satisfying story that hooked me from the first page. Tori Whitaker's debut offers a fresh and poignant perspective on motherhood, loss, and, ultimately, forgiveness."

—Lynda Cohen Loigman, bestselling author of *The Matchmaker's Gift* and *The Two-Family House*

"*Millicent Glenn's Last Wish* is a delight of a book that explores how one long-held secret can shape a family. Tori Whitaker's characters sparkle with warmth and humanity, especially ninety-year-old Mil, whose voice rings clear and true throughout these charming pages."

—Tara Conklin, *New York Times* bestselling author of *The Last Romantics*

"Written with compassion and grace, Tori Whitaker's *Millicent Glenn's Last Wish* is a nuanced debut illuminating the multigenerational strength of love, loss, survival, and the limitless power of family. I dare you to read without shedding a tear. Readers will think on these characters long after turning the last page."

—Sarah McCoy, *New York Times* and international bestselling author of *Mustique Island*

"Tori Whitaker explores the depths of mother-love with insight, care, and heart-wrenching honesty in this post–World War II story brimming with exceptional historical detail. A moving and emotionally charged debut by a writer to watch."

—Susan Meissner, bestselling author of *The Nature of Fragile Things*

"I loved this story. Tori Whitaker has created characters who are irresistibly real and hard to leave behind! A meticulously crafted debut."

—Lynn Cullen, bestselling author of *Mrs. Poe* and *The Woman with the Cure*

A MATTER OF HAPPINESS

OTHER BOOKS BY TORI WHITAKER

Millicent Glenn's Last Wish

A MATTER OF HAPPINESS

A NOVEL

TORI WHITAKER

LAKE UNION
PUBLISHING

This is a work of fiction. Names, characters, organizations, places, events, and incidents are either products of the author's imagination or are used fictitiously.

Published by Lake Union Publishing, Seattle

www.apub.com

ISBN-13: 9781542038072 (paperback)
ISBN-13: 9781542038065 (digital)

Cover design by Laywan Kwan
Cover image: ©ABCDstock / Shutterstock; ©Leonid Zarubin / Shutterstock; ©Spaarnestad Photo / Bridgeman Images; ©Jack Hearld

Printed in the United States of America

SOMEWHERE WEST OF LARAMIE

Somewhere west of Laramie there's a bronco-busting, steer-roping girl who knows what I'm talking about.

She can tell what a sassy pony, that's a cross between greased lightning and the place where it hits, can do with eleven hundred pounds of steel and action when he's going high, wide and handsome.

The truth is—the Playboy was built for her.

Built for the lass whose face is brown with the sun when the day is done of revel and romp and race.

She loves the cross of the wild and the tame.

There's a savor of links about that car—of laughter and lilt and light—a hint of old loves—and saddle and quirt. It's a brawny thing—yet a graceful thing for the sweep o' the Avenue.

Step into the Playboy when the hour grows dull with things gone dead and stale.

Then start for the land of real living with the spirit of the lass who rides, lean and rangy, into the red horizon of a Wyoming twilight.

Advertisement for the Jordan Motor Car Company's 1923 Model MX Playboy

Saturday Evening Post, June 23, 1923

PROLOGUE

Violet

Detroit, Michigan
August 1923

He has a highball with whiskey. And me? A bee's knees with lemon and gin. I don't drink whiskey smuggled from Canada over the river; it reminds me of what Prohibition did to Kentucky. Gone are distilleries in the bluegrass with their smells of bourbon evaporating from barrels—the "angel's share" as it's called. But I adore this splendid elliptical bar in the fastest-growing city in America. The crowd is affluent: automobile types vie with those of old money. The Confectionary has no address and sells no candy, but there are Tiffany lamps and green velvet sofas. A pianist plays the hit "Dreamy Melody" on a Vose baby grand. Photographs of federal agents hang on the walls in gilded frames as if they're priceless art.

My boyfriend lights my cigarette in its long silver holder, and then he lights his own.

"Had we known our friends would be late," he says with the cleft of his chin prominent, "we might've had time for—"

"There's always later tonight," I say.

I had enjoyed our romp the night before. But it'd taken me an hour to do my Marcel hair wave, and I hadn't wanted to mess it up before this evening began. No denying it, though, my man looks dashing. I slide my palm along his worsted jacket of midnight blue with its matching satin lapels. I peer up at him from the corner of my eye, my lashes thick and black from mascara.

"Your dress," he whispers now in my ear, "looks delicious enough to peel like fruit."

"Well, designers do call the color cranberry crepe." I grin.

It's a stunning gown falling just to my shins with bugle beads of blue, gold, and red. Its sash of gold lamé rides low on my hips and glimmers in the bar's mellow light.

His fingers drop now to my crossed leg. I had dabbed Tabac Blond—with its whiff of carnation and leather, a fragrance designed for women who smoke—in the bend of my knees. As his fingertips tease my skin, it tingles. My thighs are bare, and I lift my hems up higher. I'd rolled my stockings to below my knees on elastic garter bands. Then I'd rubbed a hint of rouge on my kneecaps, too, to make them look a tad rosy.

After a few minutes' more flirtation, I twist to face the door. For a second tonight feels too frivolous. Where are Lela and Gil?

It's unlike my best friend to be an hour past due. That very afternoon, she and I drove to Grosse Pointe in my Jordan MX. My sporty scarlet-red car is less sumptuous than Lela's powder-blue Packard, of course. Her Runabout Roadster convertible is the most head-turning model Packard makes. I put my car's top down for a ride past vast green lawns, rows of pink flowers, and shimmering blue water with frothy white tips. We laughed as we rode, with the lengths of our scarves blowing behind us with the wind. Just two girls having fun.

Now at the bar, I check my wristwatch: fifteen past ten. Perhaps Lela and Gil had had some merrymaking of their own before leaving her parents' estate?

I take up the cool stem of my glass and sip my cocktail slowly as the pianist begins a tune my sister, Evelyn, used to play.

Then people I don't know storm into the Confectionery, shouting. All heads turn to the man in black tails and a flapper in sparkling sequins.

My own man's blue-eyed gaze locks with mine. He secures his wallet inside his coat.

"What's the matter?" I ask him under my breath.

Then the strangers yell, "A tip-over raid down the street."

Bartenders start stuffing bottles in cabinets and pulling out large jars of licorice twists and long, colorful candy sticks. A waiter rushes from patron to patron whisking our glasses into a bin.

"Violet, doll, looks like we've got to get out of this place. But we'll make our way out as though nothing's amiss."

There's no urgency in his voice, so I'm not too afraid. Not at first.

"As long as we're gone before they charge in with sledgehammers," I say, suddenly having a vision of glass shards flying everywhere.

I squeeze his arm and walk more quickly in my T-strap heels than I had when we arrived. I feel quite frightened after all. Detroit's "tip-over raids" don't require search warrants; enforcement officers can't arrest a soul. But they put owners out of business by smashing everything from chairs to booze bottles—yes, they break the laws to stop the lawbreakers.

Outside in the dark, the streetlamps flicker and I feel a little less anxious. We'll catch the next streetcar back to my place and try to call my friend. But a speakeasy on the next block is in chaos—a confusion of cars and patrols and people angling to get away.

"The Apothecary is the one that got hit," says a woman with a purple feather in her headband.

I hate to think the Apothecary might be destroyed. It's another speakeasy we frequent. More people like us in their evening attire have gathered on the sidewalks in clusters, despite the presence of police nearby.

But as the mass disperses, the scene a block over emerges more clearly—in the way a master painter's floor-to-ceiling oil reveals itself when one enters a gallery.

I cover my mouth with my hands, but this doesn't suppress my scream.

"At eighteen our convictions are hills from which we look;

at forty-five they are caves in which we hide."

F. Scott Fitzgerald, "Bernice Bobs Her Hair," 1920

CHAPTER 1

Melanie

Frankfort, Kentucky
July 2018

I wasn't supposed to be here. Not *here*.

I was supposed to be working—working for my real job, that is, instead of my mother's pet project. I could've taken my laptop to the courtyard at my Louisville loft apartment and sat in a lounge chair on this sunny Saturday morning while marking off my to-do list. The Bourbon Craft Cocktail Bash was coming up, and the distillery where I worked was a major sponsor. At twenty-eight years old, I would be helping to pull off the leading bourbon event of the year . . . which might earn me the biggest promotion of my career. I'd devote seven days a week, if that's what it took. I had more riding on this than a director's title and raise.

Yet here I sat, almost an hour from home in a rented U-Haul pickup truck.

I was parked in front of my great-great-great-aunt's old Victorian house. Violet had lived to be 103 but had been gone for fourteen years. She left this place to my mother, Angie, her nearest relative in Kentucky.

Now Mom's last tenants were gone, and she was set on selling and diversifying her investments.

I promised Mom that today I'd help her clean out the 124-year-old garage—the one my aunt had called a carriage house. Maybe that sounded too romantic, like calling a burger a filet mignon. But if that was Violet's way, it was fine by me.

Then three days ago, Mom sprained her ankle while walking the dog and had to stay off it awhile. Appraisers were coming in two weeks, and next weekend was worse for me than this one; a big bourbon event didn't just happen like "poof," even if it was three months out. I had to stay on deadline. Dad was on a golf trip with a bunch of accountants—not that Mom would let him help do the job anyway. Years before, he'd inadvertently tossed her signed first edition of *The Feminine Mystique*, and Mom was out three grand. She worked full-time and as self-proclaimed "CEO of the Home," too; Dad didn't even unload the dishwasher without her grumbling that forks must face up and knives must go down. Couldn't she just be happy that he always pitched in?

I would try to come through for Mom today, though. She was counting on me.

I cut the engine on the truck. I removed my sunglasses, tightened my ponytail, and made sure the carriage house key was in the pocket of my yoga pants. Two crape myrtle trees, their branches heavy with fluffy pink blooms, stood in relief against the pale-gray paint of the house. It was built in the Queen Anne style with a white balustrade around the covered front porch. The balustrade was fairly well preserved with not too much paint chipped off. No spindles were missing. The single offset gable had looked much bigger to me when I was a kid. The house wasn't a mansion—there were no towers or turrets—but it must've been much admired in its day. I was fourteen when Grape Aunt Violet—that's what I called her when I was three, and somehow it stuck—stood on the covered porch, her cheeks sagging and her back hunched over, waving at me the last time. That was before her round-the-clock nurse moved in. I waved back as Dad honked the horn. We never pulled away in a car from a relative's house without Dad giving a few beeps. It was his tradition.

Now, even though it'd been forever since I was here, an ache swelled within me. When Mom sold this place, Violet would be more gone to me than she already was. I hated to see this last vestige of where we'd all spent time together go.

My affection for Violet was cinched years before when she played the card game Go Fish with me one Christmas when no one else would. I was four or five and had no siblings. Then during my summers, I visited for a week. I got all her attention. We plunked out tunes on her piano, baked cookies together, and built tents with her hand-knitted afghans while she told stories of the olden days. In her midnineties, she was slow but never boring. A week with her was unlike vacations with my folks—where Mom made minute-by-minute itineraries for her parental bucket list of places to go. Never did she take a week just to play or to see how the days unfolded.

Mom is a C-suite marketing exec at a global fast-food corporation—one with famous chains for fried chicken, pizza, and tacos. She is petite whereas I, like Dad, am tall. But I share her dark-brown eyes and dark-brown hair with amber highlights the color of bourbon. When I was growing up, she instilled in me: *Everything is marketing, Melanie. From perfume to pro football, from politics to toilet paper*. I listened well. There would always be work in marketing.

To her consternation, though, my marketing career didn't follow her path with a Fortune 500 company.

I followed Aunt Violet's path into whiskey, but joined a start-up distillery. Distilleries made bourbon from New York to Texas to Oregon. And in our state, distilleries dotted the verdant rolling hills with their tours and tastings and visitors' centers. The Kentucky Bourbon Trail was the Napa Valley of the east.

After Prohibition, Aunt Violet supervised thirty women on a distillery's bottling lines—a prestigious role for a female then, especially during the Depression. In her forties, she was instrumental in WWII, too, helping design a new bottle with recycled glass. But what she impressed upon me much later was how bourbon had been more than her job. Her elderly voice grew lively when telling me stories.

We had cypress wood vats big enough for giants to bathe in, she said, her eyes dancing with magical light. *I still smell the mash bill of corn, rye, and barley fermenting with yeast. I hear the thunder of the barrel run at another distillery, with barrels filled with "white dog" rolling on the rail to the rickhouses.*

She taught me how the "white dog" would change into its rich caramel color as bourbon aged over years in barrels of charred oak. I'll never forget her last words to me about bourbon. She was in the rented hospital bed by then with a nurse at home, already well past one hundred. I had her brittle, bony fingers in mine as she said, *Bourbon is the balancing of temperature, humidity, the right grains—and time. Bourbon is our history. Bourbon is the earth. It's an art. Don't let anyone tell you otherwise, Melanie.* She died a week later.

Mom, on the other hand, was all about sales quotas, mass media ROI, and new point-of-purchase displays. While Violet drank one finger of bourbon on Friday nights clear up to her final months, Mom didn't even eat fast food. But I liked to think my job combined some of Mom's marketing savvy with a passion for bourbon like Violet's.

I unloaded the flattened U-Haul boxes from the bed of the truck now and hauled them to the backyard.

I dumped them beside a standing Grecian birdbath filled with rainwater and leaves. At the end of the terrace edged by orange canna lilies, I used to jump rope on flat stones, and I kneeled in the grass to hunt four-leaf clovers—like young Violet and her sister had done. This place held family memories that went back over a hundred years. I hated to see it go.

The carriage house was two stories high, gabled, and as wide as the two bayed doors with raised panels and narrow rectangular windows lining their top edges. A couple of the glass panes were busted out. The roof was sagging slightly on the left side, too, like a hammock tied between oaks. It and the main house dated from 1894, seven years before Violet was born in 1901.

I removed the key from the pocket of my pants—my oldest, least fave yoga pants, so that if I ruined them it wouldn't be tragic. Time to clear out things like the old clay planting pots, holiday lights that never got strung, rakes and hoes and the old lawn mower, the kind where open blades revolved on two wheels. Mom said to keep my eyes out for anything good we might salvage, though she doubted there would be much of value. I approached the overhead door on the right. It was the kind of door that lifted all at once with no folding hinged panels. I squinted as I wrestled the key into the rusty old lock and cranked the handle until it released. Click.

I bent at my knees and swung the door over my head.

The smell was the first thing that hit me. I'd call it some caustic combination of heat, sawdust, mildew, oil, age, dirt, and cat pee. Maybe a dead squirrel or two. I sucked in a big breath of the fresh outside air before going in, praying I'd get used to the stench.

There it was. Violet's old car.

I let my eyes adjust to the imperfect light, and with the door open wide to the great afternoon, my nose was growing accustomed to the stink. The car faced me, its two huge round headlamps attached to the body like a bug's eyes, but not built *into* the body. Each flat tire was as narrow as a motorcycle's. The black axle that connected them was exposed. Years' worth of grime layered the car's body. I ran the tips of my fingers along the door's surface, making a trail in the dust. The original color must've been a brilliant red, but now it was washed out, almost a smoky rose. I twisted the handle and opened the door exactly as I had as a girl.

When I was twelve, Violet let me climb up into her car. She grasped its cloth roof to steady herself as she watched with an indulgent smile, the wrinkly skin of her underarms jiggling in the short sleeves of her white blouse. She wore baggy pants, too, with an elastic waist and thick-rubber-soled shoes. I wrapped my hands around the steering wheel. I'd never seen one so big. It was made of polished wood, and I pretended to steer it way far to the right and then back a hard left, my arms wider apart than my shoulders. I pushed the round button in the center, but the horn didn't work. There was no back seat and, oddly, no windows in the doors. The cloth top was frayed at the seams, and though I was a kid, it wasn't that high above my head. I stretched my flip-flop-clad foot to the pedal and pressed. I squealed like I was swerving around tight corners.

Violet roared with laughter. Then she said, "Scooch over."

She wiggled her way into the driver's side and took the wheel herself. She quieted. It was as if Amelia Earhart had ascended into the cockpit of her first airplane a gazillion years ago. Violet held the wheel with reverence and tears in her eyes, surprising me.

"You know, this is a girl's car," she said, facing me.

What did that mean? "A girl's car?"

"Yes," she said, and then she clammed up as if she'd said too much.

She unlatched the flap of a small panel in the driver's door that I hadn't noticed was there. A short metal chain secured the flap on this, the first of what she called her "secret compartments."

"See here?" She removed a miniature hammer. There was an array of hand tools like what Daddy had in his toolbox, only smaller: a screwdriver, a wrench. "For fixing the car in case it broke down," Violet said.

"That's cool," I said. "Grape Aunt Violet, did you used to drive this old car? Why do you keep it stuck in the carriage house?"

"That's a story for a different day. Maybe when you're old enough to drive yourself?" She grinned as if she'd turned this into a game.

"I have to wait till I'm sixteen?"

"Let's hop out now," she said. "There's one more compartment you might like to see."

~

Climbing into the filthy driver's seat now, the stench of the carriage house all but forgotten, I let my gaze sweep over the car's interior. A dried-up bird's nest lay on the passenger-side floor.

Grape Aunt Violet had left this 1923 Jordan MX Playboy to me in her will. I never got to hear the car's story, because she died well before my sweet sixteen. I hadn't known what to do with the car ever since.

Now Mom was adamant: *Before the house sells, get rid of the old jalopy.*

I jumped out of the Jordan and went to the rear. With some difficulty, I unlatched the trunk handle and pulled up on its hefty lid, just as my aunt instructed when I was a child.

There, on the left side, Violet said, aiming her knobby forefinger while I stooped over. *See the buttoned compartment?*

I examined it now, with its wood-paneled door. The jack to fix a flat tire that'd once been stored there was lying out in the open. Careful not to knock my head on the trunk lid, I leaned in and unbuttoned the storage latch, and the door dropped down. The space wasn't empty—and my whole body buzzed as if I were a newbie archaeologist finding something poking up from the dirt. The compartment was deeper into the side of the car than I recalled. I pulled out two objects. No, wait, there were three. I ducked back out and shifted the stash to the light. A vintage magazine, a small cloth pouch, and a leather-bound book. What was all this? I climbed back into the car seat to explore the pieces more closely.

The magazine was protected in a clear plastic sleeve—a faded issue of a *Saturday Evening Post*. From 1923? Whoa. Its cover art was classic

Rockwell with an illustration of a rural boy just let loose from school. I had no clue as to its significance.

I set it and the book aside and examined the small cloth pouch. It was sewn from a remnant of shiny gold cloth, the size of a sandwich baggie with a drawstring closure. Something hard was inside. I unraveled the delicate cords at the top and pulled the mouth of the pouch apart. I turned the pouch over in my hand and let its contents slip: a key on a short metal chain. The silver of the Jordan emblem was tarnished and scratched. To think, Violet had held this key nearly a century ago. I brought it to my lips.

I secured the key back in its pouch, eager to unveil the book. What I wouldn't have given for a breeze right then. I blew air up my face.

The book was more like a journal, I guessed. Two suede ties secured the weathered brown leather. I pulled on the long, slim ropes and bent back the pliable cover inside which an ivory card of stationery lay loose:

To Melanie. With love, Grape Aunt Violet

My heart skipped a few beats. Had this book waited for me, hidden, for fourteen effing years—since I was fourteen? Something my aunt had intended for me to read as soon as she died?

I should never have waited so long to return to this car.

Why didn't I guess that Violet might've hidden something for me inside it? She often hid things, like chewing gum in the cubby of her desk where she stored coloring books and markers.

I sifted through the journal's pages, their deckled edges turned yellow-brown, and her beautifully written script with scrolling capital *M*'s and *D*'s. I landed randomly on one page, held it up to the daylight, and read:

Detroit, August 14, 1921

Detroit, as in Detroit . . . Michigan? There was a city in Kentucky called Paris, and a Versailles, Kentucky, too—the latter pronounced not in the French form like *Ver-sigh* but rather *Ver-sails*. But I'd only ever heard of one Detroit.

The ink on the page was faded, and there was a blotch like a stain from a spill. The pages weren't ruled, yet the words flowed across in fairly even lines. I directed my cell phone's flashlight at the words to make out the tiny text:

The jazz was divine. Those horns!

I traced my finger down a few lines of her hazy text . . . *He was blotto. Well, so was I after passing around hip flasks filled with gin. I slid my hems higher up past my knee at my leg that was crossed and then idly swung my foot to give a better show . . .*

I covered my mouth and suppressed a grin. Was this really a journal penned by my grape aunt Violet? Never in all her stories had she mentioned Detroit. Now that I thought better of it, I recalled no tales from the 1920s at all. There were a few from when she was a child. And those from the Depression and war years. This journal suggested she had a more colorful past than she let on.

A text sounded and jarred me. Even now, I often jumped at the notification, half hoping it would be Jason. But no, of course it wouldn't be my ex-fiancé. I'd made sure of that the last time we talked.

This text was from Cora, my boss. Hey Melanie. I'll be out on Monday but if you get a sec, give me a buzz. No emergency.

I'd definitely have to call her back, no matter how I had the work of two women to do here today—and after the distraction of this journal. If I wanted to advance at the company, I'd maintain my 24-7.

"Hey, Cora! Got your message," I said when she answered.

"That was fast," she said. "Listen, just giving you a heads-up before you go in the first of the week. I know you're working hard, especially with my director's spot coming open this fall."

With growth from our distillery, she would be taking over the sales and distribution side exclusively, leaving open my group for marketing and publicity. But I wondered what sort of heads-up I needed. It made me feel uneasy.

"Mitchell Fox stayed late last night to talk to me." She paused. "Says he's throwing his hat in the ring."

Shit.

"Oh," I said, trying not to sound down. "Guess you'll have two strong candidates then."

Shit.

I had assumed that she and the higher-ups would interview at least a couple of candidates from outside. That was good business. But Mitchell Fox was lateral to me on the org chart. He handled PR. He had two more years of experience since college, but I had seniority here. I'd started at Goldenrod Bourbon Distillers when I was twenty-three. Truth was, he'd already stepped on my toes a time or two—not that I'd ever told Cora. I didn't whine to my boss about coworkers.

"Thank you for the advance notice," I said.

"You're an amazing marketer, Melanie. You've got a few more months. Make 'em count."

Shit.

After we hung up, I sat immobile. Now I wanted this promotion more than ever. I didn't wish to be humiliated by a company-wide memo announcing my rival had risen to director. I could always find a job at another distillery, but I didn't want to pack my bags to go somewhere else, either. We were soon to launch a new whiskey product—one I'd had a part in from the start.

But there was another reason I wanted this promotion, one I hated to admit even to myself. Despite all the differences Mom and I had—and despite how I'd been "adulting" since college—I hoped that my heading up marketing would finally make her proud of me.

How would I get everything I had to do done? There was so much work ahead at the distillery, and I still had to figure out what to do with "the old jalopy." But today I was stuck here for hours, hauling junk to the truck bed, scrubbing ancient windows, and clearing out cobwebs older than me.

So what were the chances of my getting time to read Violet's journal anytime soon? Not high. But before closing its cover, I flipped to the journal's first page:

Frankfort, Kentucky

August 1919

Violet would've been in her late teens then. I turned over the card tucked in the jacket, the one that she had inscribed in ink. Its reverse side read:

Take from this story what you will, Melanie, and you can bury the rest.

CHAPTER 2

Violet

Frankfort, Kentucky
August 1919

I was addressing an envelope with one hand and putting a stamp to my tongue with the other when the telephone rang in the sales office. This was how mornings began: bustling with so much activity, I could use two extra arms. There was only one clerical employee, though, and that was me. I dropped my pen and picked up the receiver.

"Labrot and Graham Distillery. May I help you?"

It was another merchant calling to check on available stocks of bourbon—bourbon that'd been aging for years in barrels or was being bottled each day. It was the third inquiry I'd had in ten minutes. The rickhouses where bourbon aged were all out in Versailles, some miles from here. It was in this office where bills of sale stacked up on my desk halfway as high as my elbow.

I wouldn't think to complain. I'd just turned eighteen, and this job was important to me. I got to use my mind: doing numerical calculations and drafting letters for the manager. Thank goodness Mother had taught me to type. This job set me one step closer to becoming a modern, independent woman. Afternoons tended to slow down, but

I'd gladly scurry around every hour of the day like a hungry squirrel in fall if that's what it took.

But a feeling of dread spilled over me when I thought of how this all might soon end. Prohibition was coming in January.

The "ill-advised, short-sighted, do-gooder temperance marchers," as Mother had once called them, had won. Not that she didn't believe in doing good; Mother did plenty with her charities, church, and women's club. She just knew how hard a ban on the sale of liquor would be for our state.

Indeed, distillers were scrambling to sell off bottles and barrels before the government locked them up. There was one hope for Labrot and Graham's survival. This distillery—named for two founders who were long deceased—might earn one of a few coveted licenses to sell medicinal alcohol. There were two hundred distilleries in Kentucky, but perhaps no more than six licenses. My manager, Mr. Baker, got more jittery by the day. A long rut had formed across his forehead as deep as a split on the crust of fresh-baked bread.

My poor father's forehead had been the same right before he died last fall. A shadow came over me now, like it often did when I thought of him. It was as if inside my body there was an eclipse of the sun—the saddest blackening out of my heart that could cause tears to stream for hours. How did a body do that? It was grief, not something Mother had covered in her lessons on biology. She always said that Father's second-generation dry goods store had survived the flood of 1883 and the panic of 1893. But the day he heard Woolworth's was planning a move to Frankfort was the day his heart gave way.

"Who's next after Woolworth?" Father bellowed that last morning. "That upstart James *Cash* Penney and one of his damnable stores?"

Department stores and five-and-dimes had sprung up like epidemics. I'd not forget the sound of Father crumpling the newspaper. When I kissed the top of his head goodbye, it was the last time I saw him alive.

Now the distillery was threatened, too. Such was the price of the era's "progress and reform."

I wanted more for my life. As a modern woman, I would keep up with the times and not lag behind. Even when I was sixteen and the war was full on, I knew I'd one day live independently. No one would tell me what to do. Not Mother divvying up chores. Not my bossy big sister, Evelyn, who, before she married, used to shush me while she read or needle me to do her hair. Not even my beloved father who wouldn't let me drive his car. It was unclear whether his concern was solely for my safety or something "women just shouldn't do." Mother never drove his Model T, either. And despite my protestations, she sold it for cash when he passed.

One day, decisions would be mine alone. I would earn my own keep, go on adventures, travel to far-off places. And purchase a car of my choice.

I had started at Labrot and Graham in the spring, earning and saving for my future. What was I supposed to do the day I flipped over the office sign in the window to Closed for the last time?

I rubbed my temples with the strain of the question. I'd have to be strong and clever—like the heroines of westerns and other films I watched as a girl. Yes, like the star in *What Happened to Mary*. Mary, trapped in a seventh-floor bedroom, tied bedsheets together to form a rope and lower herself out the window. As a twelve-year-old, my palms went clammy and I gritted my teeth until she landed safely on the ground.

I'd have to land myself safely, too.

By late afternoon, the flurry at work died down. I was reading a novel to occupy my mind between calls when the bells on the heavy door jingled. Two smartly dressed men entered and removed their straw boaters.

"Mr. Adams," I said and stood from behind my desk in the small wood-paneled lobby. "How are you?"

He supervised the motorcar dealership down the way, but I had to steel myself from staring at the stranger beside him, one who was a good head taller and had the widest smile with straight white teeth.

"I'm as cheery as the day is warm," Mr. Adams said. "Let me introduce Robert Neumann. And Robert, this is the lovely Miss Violet Bond."

I felt the prickle of a blush rise high on both cheeks.

"A pleasure to meet you," the newcomer said as he removed a chamois summer glove and extended his hand.

His accent was from up north. He shook mine with his whole hand—not the mere tips of his fingers as if he were full of himself—yet his grip was gentle enough for a lady. He was a man to be trusted, my father would've said.

"Are you here to see Mr. Baker?" I asked them, checking the scheduling book.

"Yes, an impromptu visit," said Mr. Adams.

"I'll go let him know you're here."

When I returned to the lobby, I felt the appraising stare of two pairs of male eyes and became more aware of my attire. I wore a daytime skirt of brown with a high ruched waist and oversize pockets, paired with a pale-yellow blouse. It was practical for my job—though with the more modern hemline, my ankles and a hint of a curve of my lower calves showed.

Part of me liked the men's attention. The bigger part would stay strictly professional.

"Mr. Baker begs only for a few minutes' time while he wraps up some orders," I said.

I noticed the automobile the visitors had arrived in was drawing a crowd of men outside. Mr. Adams winked and said, "Prospective customers," as he headed out the door.

There was nothing inappropriate about me being alone with Mr. Neumann. But while he was quite handsome, I wouldn't give him any "ideas." Not like other girls my age might—those whose top priorities in life were marriage and motherhood. I never led on Billy Probst in high school, either. He'd been nothing more to me than a puppy wagging his tail, a partner at community dances.

"I couldn't help noticing what book you're reading," Mr. Neumann said with a glint in his eye. "*Treasure Island*?"

Was he teasing me? Perhaps I should be reading my more mature *House of Mirth* or *Anna Karenina*—or *Pollyanna*—instead of a tale for boys.

"I'm afraid I've left my other books at home," I said to match his teasing tone, "those more suited to the weaker sex."

The man looked taken aback. Then I perceived a spark of humor and smiled sweetly. If I had my copy of *Sons and Lovers* in a drawer, it'd be fun to pull it out and shock him. But if word got to Mother, she'd be scandalized. She had let me read the "obscene book" for its artistic value alone, but I was never to tell anyone. As for the book I was rereading today, I enjoyed its story of sailors and pirates of the high seas. As a child, I'd also longed to be like Peter Pan—to fly away to Never Never Land.

"Stevenson's book," Mr. Neumann said, "is good for girls who crave adventure."

Now I was the one taken aback. It was as if he had seen right through me. And that was somehow unsettling, like he might be someone to stay away from—or someone I had to learn more about.

I guessed him to be a couple of years older than me. He was impeccably dressed—perhaps not in hand-tailored clothes, but still, neither a wrinkled seam nor puckered dart showed. His hair might've been towhead blond as a boy but with age had grown strands the color of brown barley. His smoothly shaved jaw was what a magazine would call chiseled. Did I detect a scent of Bay Rum, too, as he stood closer to my desk? His aftershave with hints of citrus and spice oils? And those eyes. They were of a blue so pale they seemed to soak in the light.

"What brings you to Kentucky's capital city?" I said.

"Ford Motor Company," he said with pride. "At age seventeen, I joined the assembly line—helping build trucks and ambulances for the doughboys. Three years later, I happened to be at the right place at the right time. I recently started as a roadman."

"You're from Detroit?" That explained his accent. "And what's a roadman? Like a drummer?"

"I do drum up business," he said. "I'm a traveling salesman, helping dealerships in several states and meeting with men like Ben Adams. We make calls on prospective Ford owners."

That's why they wanted to meet with my boss. "It must be great to travel," I said, a little envious. "And the automotive industry is such a sensation."

A redness crept up his neck, a humbleness, I thought.

"You wouldn't believe how the industry's booming," he said. "A new car rolls off the line every ninety-three minutes."

I gasped. "A whole car built in ninety-three minutes?"

"I assure you it's true."

Long gone were the days when some believed automobiles would be a passing fancy—or too dangerous with their gasoline tanks to last. And Ford made sure almost any man in the country could afford one. Maybe a Ford is what I would one day buy.

Then Mr. Neumann said, "Have you ever been on an adventure, Miss Bond?"

I was unused to a man surprising me so with his questions. If only I had a more interesting answer. I'd never been farther north than Cincinnati with family nor farther east than Philadelphia.

"Well, when I was a Camp Fire Girl," I said, "I went on many a tramp through the woods. I once cooked an entire meal over an open fire—potatoes baked in ashes, and bacon wrapped around green sticks I'd found in the trees. But I long to tour Chicago and New York someday."

He quirked an eyebrow. "Why not Detroit?" he said. "It's become the fourth-largest city in America, you know. There's a world-class museum of art. Glorious parks. And a new orchestra hall that's soon to open. It'll be the cat's meow."

"Hmm," I said, never having given a thought to a city in Michigan having all the entertainments. "Why not? I'll add it to my wish list. Though with Prohibition headed our way, I may have to find another means to save up for my travels. I might be out of a job soon."

"Women have jobs in industry in Detroit as well as men," Mr. Neumann said without letting a beat go by. He tapped my desk with two fingers. "Not only in clerical posts, but in making automotive parts."

"Really?" I said. "I thought that once men got back from the war, women had to give up their factory jobs."

"Not everywhere. Especially where the skill of deft fingers is required," he said. "Everything from assembling spark plugs to rolling cigars. It may not be as prestigious as office work or retail. But hours are regular and pay is better."

I'd never heard of spark plugs, but I felt my breathing pick up as I pondered this news.

I once worked out at the distillery in Versailles where a tall boiler stack had Labrot and Graham's big L&G emblazoned on it. One of the best gals on the bottling line fell ill. It took special skill to place a label on a bottle just right; women's nimble fingers had proven best across the industry. The line supervisor told me I did a great job, and I would've enjoyed staying—with its higher pay—if it were as close to home as the sales office.

Perhaps I should open my mind to new possibilities and move north. But no, surely the idea of my going for an automotive position in Detroit was silly. My sister would call it far-fetched. I'd find something else here if Labrot and Graham closed forever. I had to.

“You are a fount of information, Mr. Neumann,” I said. “Thank you.”

He smiled that dazzling smile. “Robert,” he said. “Please. Should you ever decide to come,” he continued, “my aunt operates a clean and comfortable boardinghouse. You could check if she’s got a room.”

Did he personally want me to come? Or was he just being kind?

His eyes scanned my desk. “Have a piece of paper handy?”

I gave him my pad and pen. But it was a waste of energy. It’s not as if I’d ever move to the automobile capital of the world. Besides, how could I even think of going anywhere while Mother was still mourning? She’d be left all alone. I couldn’t do that to her.

Robert ripped a page from the pad and handed me the note. It contained the name and address of his aunt and her establishment.

“You can say her favorite nephew referred you.” He smiled as the bells of the door jingled, and his colleague returned.

My boss came out to greet the men.

“Good day, Miss Bond,” Robert said as the men moved toward Mr. Baker’s office.

“Violet,” I said as he passed.

CHAPTER 3

Melanie

Louisville, Kentucky
July 2018

It was ten thirty Saturday night when I returned from Violet's, nearly comatose after cleaning the carriage house that was built when Grover Cleveland was president. Mom liked the video of it I texted her, though; she only snipped at me once.

"You didn't mess with the AC controls in the house, did you? Forgot to mention that. I don't need the energy bill spiking."

"No, Mom. I peed in the half bath with its suffocating ninety-five-degree heat. Just for you."

"Ha ha," she said.

I showered and met my college friends Casey and Nicole at the Post, our staple for pizza near the Germantown Mill Lofts. The original Louisville Cotton Mill was built in 1889 and was now our metro industrial living complex with a fitness center, a coffee bar, and a courtyard with a pool, grills, and umbrella tables. The girls yapped at me to start dating again, as usual. It'd been five months since I broke my engagement with Jason Levy. I'd thought we had a future—and a mutual respect for each other's careers. I'd been wrong. And I didn't need a new man.

Back at home, I flopped on the blue velvet couch in my living area with exposed brick walls and splashes of weathered yellow paint. The boot camp–like burn settling into my muscles wouldn't stop me from diligently preparing on Sunday for my upcoming report at work. Tuesday's meeting was going to be huge.

Goldenrod Bourbon Distillers was in downtown Louisville in a renovated elevator factory from the turn of last century. The brand borrowed its name from the Kentucky state flower—yellow wildflowers known for bearing sweet pollen and symbolizing luck. The five of us in our marketing group circled a table in the small conference room for a midyear meeting.

I felt energized to begin. And a bit queasy. Stakes were high not only for me, but for Mitchell wanting the promotion.

I scanned Cora's agenda between sips of strong coffee pumped with hazelnut. She would open with an update on her other team, national sales accounts—the crew working with distributors to get product in liquor stores, bars, and restaurants—and where she was slated to take over full-time come fall with its growth. That would leave the group in this room to a new leader. Hopefully me.

Bourbon's a tricky business, Cora once said.

Our signature product took time to craft and then at least four years in the aging process. Most industries' products, like cars, didn't sit in stock that long before seeking buyers. On the up side, bourbon was America's sole native spirit—in much the way champagne was tied to a region of France or scotch was native to Scotland. By law, since 1964 under President Johnson, the United States was the only country that could claim the bourbon name on a bottle.

While the industry had its challenges, one thing I shouldn't have had to worry about was a coworker. Our company had a new product launching this fall—our first rye whiskey, meaning it was a bit spicier than bourbon that's made with more corn, and hence was a sweeter pour. Some months back, I had suggested the name Goldenrod 105 Rye—a specific nod to its slightly higher 105 proof, its alcohol content. I also liked how Goldenrod 105 Rye sounded off the tongue. It looked good in the mock-ups of label designs, too. Then recently, a friend in the cube next to Mitchell's overheard him bragging to someone in media that *he'd* suggested tying the name to its proof.

How dare he? The seeds of my passion for this industry were planted when he was still sucking his thumb. I had taken a quick peek in Violet's journal on Sunday after finalizing my report and got inspired all over again by her pre-Prohibition days at a distillery. Bourbon was in my blood. Would Mitchell have pretended he came up with the red wax seal that dripped down the bottles of Maker's Mark? Marge Samuels drove that marketing innovation in the 1950s. Not that my idea remotely compared to hers. But I've been on guard with Mitchell ever since.

Cora finished her report and said, "So with that good news on package store expansions, we turn to events and sponsorships. Melanie?"

Start strong. Lead with a win. That's what Mom always said.

"I'm super excited," I began, "that Goldenrod will be a big player in this year's Bourbon Craft Cocktail Bash. We'll be the major sponsor of the popular Celebrity Mixologist Cocktail Competition. I was able to lock in the fourth star mixologist for the panel. She's from Louisville Kitchen and Bar." I named the remaining panelists.

"Great job," Cora said. "And it's good how your panel brings gender and racial diversity."

"Thanks," I said, smiling.

Helping to advance diversity in the industry was a company-wide goal. I took a lead in embracing it, inspired by Violet. In 1964, she helped organize a civil rights march on the Frankfort capitol—where Martin Luther King Jr. spoke to ten thousand citizens who protested peacefully for the removal of segregation. African Americans were beginning to get a long-overdue limelight in the broader whiskey industry—such as a Tennessee brand headed by a Black woman and that honored an enslaved man from the 1850s. Nearest Green had taught one of the old-time distillers—a white man with his name on a label—how to distill. Research was unearthing more all the time about the historical significance Black people had in Kentucky bourbon.

I continued to the next bullet in my report. "And our gifts for the VIP reception are on target, too. We've got a lot left to do before October, but *we're where we need to be as of this moment*." A chuckle emerged from the others, who knew this was one of Cora's mantras. "Besides branded T-shirts and coasters, our premium custom glassware sets should be done on time." Distilleries had marketed with glassware as early as the 1800s, but ours would be special.

"What's included in a set?" That was Mitchell. He stroked his goatee and wore a long-sleeved blue polo shirt.

"Two Glencairn glasses for nosing and tasting," I said, "two lowballs, and two short-stemmed coupes. All etched with our logo. Our research shows that no competitors offer full sets, and we'll add some to merchandise in our online store after that, priced to be the most profitable item we sell."

"Nice," he said.

"How are registrations looking?" Cora asked.

"Tanisha is doing an amazing job promoting the cocktail competition. I'll let her chime in."

Tanisha was a rising star. I'd brought her in as a summer intern from Kentucky State University, and she'd so wowed us, we hired her on full-time after graduation.

"Thanks, Melanie," said Tanisha. "Our targeted eblasts and selective advertising are paying off. In assessing registration numbers, we're fifteen percent ahead of where we were this time last year."

"Yay!" Cora interjected, tapping her hands together.

Tanisha grinned and went on, "And it's still early. Feedback suggests attendees love how their entry fees now go toward the winning mixologist's charity of choice. And Melanie's other idea to collaborate with the Women's Bourbon Alliance has been a win-win."

"Brilliant," said Mitchell with an actual note of enthusiasm.

"Thanks, Tanisha!" I said.

I reported on the VIP reception where members of our Connoisseur Club would be treated to a daylong private hospitality tent at the Cocktail Bash. "I've confirmed that burgoo from one of Kentucky's top five picks will be ladled up en masse." Another chuckle. Burgoo was Kentucky's specialty, a stew made of hickory-smoked meats and vegetables such as corn, potatoes, lima beans, tomatoes, and okra.

"The last thing I'll mention is our company's contribution to the educational sessions." I summarized the workshops our brand ambassadors would teach, ranging from An Insider's Look at Distilling to How to Pair Bourbon with Cuisine.

"Excellent update," said Cora, and I felt good.

"Mitchell?" Cora said. "What's up in PR and visibility?"

He massaged his goatee again before speaking. "The media are lining up for the launch of our new 105 Rye. I didn't want to get anyone's hopes up, but yesterday the *Bourbon Review* confirmed: we're getting the December cover."

"What? That's amazing!" Cora said. Her green eyes flashed. "Wonderful news!"

Tanisha was wide-eyed as well and said, "Our distillery's first-ever cover. Way to go!"

Mitchell had led with a win, all right.

I was thrilled for the brand, so despite a twinge of jealousy, I said, "I can envision magazine issues now, displayed in newsstands nationwide and on coffee tables of subscribers."

"Thank you," Mitchell said, a bit glib, I thought, as though that's the kind of media hit he pulled off every day.

He covered the rest of the year's media plan. And then, like Columbo used to do in a TV series my paternal grandfather watched, Mitchell said, "Oh yeah. One more thing."

"Sure," Cora said, checking her watch. "I've got three minutes before my conference call with buyers."

"Melanie," he began. "What do you think of adding a sponsorship next year for the National Whiskey Fest? My buddy says they just set the date." Mitchell eyed Cora. "I think we'd get good visibility out of this one."

My cheeks burned.

I said, "I'd definitely love for us to be there. My research two years ago suggested it was another power event. When Tanisha and I checked it out again last February, the investment was still too high for our budget, even if we got them to whittle it down." I turned to our boss. "What do you think? Will accounting loosen up the purse strings for 2019?"

"Won't hurt to ask."

Mitchell jumped back in. "My buddy said if we move fast, he'll hold us a sponsorship spot at the silver level. Of course, I can hook him up with you, Melanie, since sponsorships are your expertise."

And that's where he'd like me to stay put, I was certain.

"Sure, Mitchell. Shoot me his contact info."

Cora's cell phone rang to a Kenny Chesney country song. "There's my call."

If Mitchell thought that just because he had two more years' experience than me, he would get promoted from manager to director, he would be sorely disappointed. Goldenrod had taken a few years to source some barrels from other producers, age the bourbon, and make its own barrel blends before ever opening its doors. But I'd been here since the distillery's grand opening five years back.

If my company promoted from within, I expected a fair shot. I expected to win. I'd already had an idea for a new series of events that wasn't even on my report.

CHAPTER 4

Violet

Frankfort, Kentucky
Six months later, February 1920

I departed Olson & Son Attorneys at Law where Mr. Olson Jr. had presented a sympathetic demeanor. But I couldn't help feeling as if the door hit my backside on my way out. It was the last of four law firms I'd tried, toting my clerical credentials and character references on my lunch hour from work. My sister Evelyn's husband, a lawyer, had referred me to them all himself. There I was bundled up in the cold, cutting air, trudging back to my office in what everyone hoped was the last deep breath of winter.

I had begun searching for a new job before Prohibition hit in mid-January. But nothing.

Now almost a month had passed, and Mr. Baker motioned me into his private office as soon as I returned. I slowly removed my coat, hat, and gloves as if to prolong the inevitable. This was it. I knew what was coming as I lowered myself into the chair across from his big, heavy desk.

"Violet, I deeply regret to inform you that Labrot and Graham Distillery did not secure a license to sell medicinal alcohol. I'm afraid we have no more need of your services." His face turned red, looking genuinely remorseful, but I could feel my own skin blanch.

"Thank you. I'll not forget your kindnesses," I said. He'd kept me on far longer than necessary.

Though I'd expected to be let go in this circumstance, I struggled to put one foot in front of the other as I left. But as I walked with the wind whipping my face, I determined I would not let myself feel defeated. I would be the heroine of my own story, like the stars of the films in my youth.

I caught a bus straightaway to the George T. Stagg distillery, the largest distillery in the area—the one on the river just minutes from home. They'd received one of the six coveted licenses in the state.

"I understand, Miss Bond," said the busy but kind superintendent Albert Blanton, who oversaw bottling and warehouses there, "that you've had both clerical and bottling experience."

My optimism soared. I had two chances to secure a position here.

"And I know these are difficult times," he went on. "But I'm afraid our employee roster is full, as is our list of backups."

I left the building feeling as if my lungs had fully collapsed even as I smelled the angel's share of the bourbon in the air. To be so full of hope only to have it dashed. By now, the line of applicants shivering in the cold could've circled Frankfort's capitol twice. Each of their faces, mostly men, must've reflected my own. Lost.

During the next week, I scrounged this city's insurance agencies, the real estate and accounting firms, the stationer, the bank, and the hat shop. I tried two physician partnerships and the library to help shelve books. I offered to clean or cook at the hotel.

But nothing.

Back at home in my warm upstairs bedroom, I took out my journal, hidden under my mattress. Mother had given it to me for my birthday in July, and I'd started making entries the day Robert Neumann told me about the automobile industry. And there on the scrap of paper was the name and address for a boardinghouse far away in Detroit. I hadn't looked at it again since that day. But I pulled the scrap out now and traced the words he'd jotted: Mrs. Sturgeon's Boardinghouse.

Old people often said that time flies, and it goes faster with the years. I was only eighteen, but I felt that way now. Time was wasting. I wanted to earn and to save to get out on my own. If I didn't begin to achieve my dreams, it could be too late. I'd miss my chance.

And I'd be relegated to becoming a young wife—the opposite of what I wanted.

The following morning, my sister was soon to arrive for a mother-daughter day—an afternoon tea for her, Mother, and me. It had been Mother's idea. She knew the struggles I was facing, having just lost my job. No longer was I the sprightly girl whose biggest problem was a scraped knee from climbing trees, roller skating, or riding down our great walnut stairs on a pillow toboggan and cackling.

I wrestled with whether to bring up the subject of Detroit. Was the idea of my leaving too soon after Father's death sixteen months ago? What would Mother and Evelyn think of my even considering a move? But I couldn't help feeling buoyed by thoughts of making my way in the world, even if it meant somewhere else.

Mother and I gathered in the parlor, a comfortable room with shelves of books, a card table and chairs, cheery yellow-papered walls, and a blue rug and drapes. Framed family photographs lined the mantel and the top of the piano. So many pictures included my father. If one could smile sadly, that's what I did at seeing the picture of my parents as newlyweds. That was a happier time for Mother.

Now, at least she no longer wore black for her mourning. Today's brown day dress with burgundy trim in itself lifted my spirits.

"You look beautiful," I said, and I loved the crinkly smile that reached up to her eyes. She smelled of perfume Father had bought her, too—April Violets by Yardley.

Father used to say that in Mother's youth, suitors would announce themselves in twos. Her waist was thicker now than in the photograph. She hadn't had children until they'd been married five years. Of course, she'd worn corsets then, too. But her friends these days said she looked years younger than her age, forty-five. She had the prettiest hands, no matter her pulling weeds or crimping crusts for berry pies or beating rugs outside.

Mother had been educated at the Normal School in Louisville and loved to teach before she wed. I never understood why male teachers could take a spouse but female ones could not. It wasn't fair. When we girls were growing up, she supplemented our educations with everything from art to science.

Once I became reestablished in the workforce, I would not give up my position unless it was *my* decision.

I loved my father with an intensity that could rival that of Cordelia in *King Lear*. But he did hold me back and set a yearning in me to break free. Mother intervened when I wanted to cut my hair to my shoulders. And it took an age for him to let me raise the hems of my dresses. Besides not letting me drive his car, he also pressed me to work for free at the dry goods store in summers when I was in school. Not because he sought my help with window displays that were vastly inferior to those of Isadore Davis Dry Goods. Not because he wanted my help with the books—despite how I was top in my class in arithmetic. Father merely wanted me in a position to see and be seen by prospective mates—his colleagues in the Chamber of Commerce and such. Or their sons.

It was Mother who encouraged me to follow my heart after he died, to seek out paying work I'd love. I found that at the distillery.

"Evelyn's here," she said with glee.

My sister, two years my senior, set her packages down, and we all hugged before she even got out of her winter wraps.

"You look radiant," I said.

Marriage suited her. She had a style right out of a women's magazine. She wore a cobalt-blue coatdress with a fabric belt at the base of her ribs. Her ever thick and wavy hair was darker than mine, and she had Father's brown eyes, not blue. People often remarked on the resemblance of those two, and Evelyn thought it gave her an advantage. She always curried favor with Father most of all. Now, her life revolved around Charles Weber the way the planets circled the sun. Mother wanted her to get a college degree in literature. But Evelyn did just as Father wished: went to the University of Kentucky for one year, met her man, and quit to get married the next summer. These days, when the legislature was in town, Evelyn entertained her husband's law school alumni with dinners in their new home. In the afternoons, she toured their wives through Frankfort, where the house designed by Frank Lloyd Wright on Shelby Street was a highlight.

Mother had been the same way with Father. She cooked *Father's* favorite meals every night. Decorated the rooms in the colors *he* preferred. Laundered and ironed *his* clothes. Entertained the guests *he* brought. Deferred to *him* on all things financial.

Were the tender moments that I saw between them enough? Maybe. But I couldn't foresee it for myself. Why would I rush into marriage so young? Why would I scrape and earn to succeed on my own and then give up my autonomy?

Love was not on my wish list for being a modern woman.

To Mother's credit, she stood firm with Father at times where her girls were concerned.

She taught me about Darwin—and survival of the fittest. She taught me that one day, I'd have a chance to do things she never could; it would begin with women getting the vote. Without her insistence, my sister and I would not even have gone to the Nickelodeon. Some thought it immoral for girls to sit in a dark theater, and Father had fussed. And perhaps he should've. There I dreamed of riding on horseback, letting my hair blow in the wind, and living a life without curfews. Some friends dreamed of becoming a star of the silver screen. Not me. It wasn't about the stunts or danger or fame. It was about independence.

"I brought chocolates," Evelyn said, removing a Rebecca Ruth's candy box from her bag.

"Oh, how I will devour those," I said. I had a sweet tooth for milk chocolates. "And look at those lovely relishes."

She'd brought a small platter of pickled red beets that she'd cut into fancy shapes—diamonds, half moons, and clovers—and garnished with olives and parsley. I had sliced some marmalade ham, and Mother had rolled out her buttermilk biscuits for making little sandwiches.

They sat at the settee and I in a wing chair around a low table. Mother poured some steaming tea in cups from my late grandmother's Liberty Blue Transferware tea set—the one for which I'd lost the lid to the sugar dish when I was six, but thankfully Evelyn had found it. It wasn't the only time she'd rescued me.

"I have some news," Evelyn said.

I thought she might announce she was expecting. Evelyn had been married a year and a half, and she loved babies. Even as a child, she constantly played with dolls. She had a buggy to stroll them in and dresses of white lace. I envisioned her offspring looking like children in the book that began "'Twas the night before Christmas"—with their round elfin cheeks while dreaming of sugarplums, and gentle spit curls in hair dark like hers. News of a baby would brighten Mother's life with Father gone. There were still days that she'd hole up in her room, asking to be alone in her grief.

"There's an employment opportunity for you, Violet." Evelyn beamed.

"Really? Where?"

"Charles's law office needs a secretary. You won't work under him, but with his partner whose staff is moving to Kansas. It's only two days a week, but you can start on Monday."

"Wonderful," I said. "Thank you." A little money was better than no money.

Mother joined in. "Working part-time, you'll still be able to seek other employment."

"Yes," I said, and I suddenly felt the pluck of nerves as if tight strings were tweaked on a violin. This was my opening.

"Sometime back," I began, and then I sipped my tea. Could I do this? "Mr. Adams from the Ford dealership stopped at the distillery sales office with a colleague from Detroit. We got to talking about the thriving automotive industry. Ford produces one car every ninety-three minutes." Mother and Evelyn gasped just as I had when I heard it, but I rushed on before they could speak. "You know, of course, how women have flocked to big cities for work for some time."

"Yes," Mother said evenly, though Evelyn stared at me, mute.

"Women find all kinds of work in Detroit. It's the fastest-growing city in the country." It gave me a thrill just to say it. Detroit.

"Are you thinking you'd consider leaving here?" That was Mother.

"I'm thinking I need *full*-time work. Steady, well-paying employment." I wanted to add, *And I can't live off you forever*, or, *And I have my dreams to break free.*

Evelyn's face registered a cross between confusion and alarm. "You would climb on a train and cross the country by yourself? Like Phoebe Snow or some such?" She let out a skeptical laugh.

Phoebe Snow had been a fictional character in a massive advertising campaign in magazines when we were girls. Phoebe was single and gorgeous and rich and traveled by rail extolling the virtues of a new clean form of coal. She wore a long white gown with a corsage of purple lilacs. Never did the train's smoke muss her dress.

Mother opened her mouth again to speak—and Evelyn did, too—but my lips were faster.

"Mother, before you married, you attended the World's Columbian Exposition in Chicago. You were only eighteen when you traveled there by train alone."

It was 1893, and she toured the Woman's Building that housed artworks from more than a dozen countries. She taught us of its wondrous array of women's arts—from sculpture by Blanche Nevin to paintings by Mary Cassatt.

"Yes," Mother said, though the word strung out more like a question.

"But, Mother," Evelyn said. "You didn't go to Chicago to *live*." Perhaps it'd come out harsher than she intended, because she lightened back up with, "Women don't wear hatpins in their hats anymore anyway."

That brought a chuckle, even from me. Mother had shared how in her day, solo female travelers had their sharp, nine-inch hatpins ready to stab a male passenger if he overstepped his bounds on the train.

I set down my teacup and began to rattle off the virtues of the automotive industry, the growth of Detroit, the opportunity for clerical work or more lucrative manufacturing. Then I said, "You don't think it's the remotest possibility for me?"

I heard the catch in my voice, but this time I would stay quiet, let the question hang.

Evelyn spoke first. "Prohibition will never last. You're only eighteen. Why not sit it out awhile longer? Then you can return to the job you loved."

"I'll be nineteen this summer," I said, "the same age you were when you married." It came across as defensive, and I suppose it was. "Besides, Mother's friend at the market last week said, 'Oh my Lord, who knows how long this drought imposed by the government will last? Could be a few months or could be forever.'"

I went on about how the effects of Prohibition kept getting worse. Mother's friend's husband owned a cooperage, but now, who needed new barrels made to age bourbon? Farmers in the state were angry as well. Their best customers for grains had completely dried up.

"And smaller towns," I said, "that dot the counties where a distillery fed the lives of many? They're becoming ghost towns."

Evelyn couldn't deny it. Mother parted her lips to speak, I thought, but my sister jumped back in. Again.

"Father has been in the ground scarcely a year. Would you have Mother stand on the porch waving goodbye to you? Alone?"

She might as well have shot a bullet through me. Did she wish to make me bleed? And Mother's face suggested this was not the light-hearted afternoon she'd hoped for. She would rather we sat listening to Evelyn play a peppy tune on the piano.

What had I started? And why was Evelyn being so vehement? She had been growing much more full of herself these days—the wife of the rising legal star.

"Mother?" I said. I wasn't sure if I sought her to take sides or sought out her wisdom. Or I just needed to hear her voice.

But Evelyn cut in yet again. "Mother, how are you getting along? With expenses, I mean?"

Where did that come from? Mother was doing fine. She had no mortgage. Monthly bills were paid out of proceeds from Father's life insurance and the sales of inventories when closing his store. Her bonds from the war were soon to mature. She led the Liberty Bond Drive herself. Of course, since Father passed, Mother stopped spending on frivolous things like hair combs and candies. She cut back on coal and kept our house cooler in winter. She stretched our meat budget and didn't buy as many clothes, but then, she was in mourning. I shared in all her means of conserving, from turning out lights earlier of an evening to buying fewer records for the phonograph. Mother was not poor. *We* were not. I saved my earnings for my nest egg.

But was there a question of an income further out in Mother's future? Would her funds deplete?

"You girls don't need to worry about money where I'm concerned." Mother brushed biscuit crumbs into her napkin.

"Mother," Evelyn said.

What now?

"But are friends asking if you'll remarry? They're asking me." She fiddled with her napkin in her lap.

How dare she bring up such subjects? Had Evelyn heard something, a rumor? I hadn't seen her so intrusive, but were these matters that needed discussing? A tug of worry worked its way to my shoulders.

I knew there was Dr. Keller from church who'd also recently been widowed. Women who were alone often needed to be cared for. But I hadn't thought our conserving on expenses as a burden. Under no circumstances could I imagine another man taking Father's place at the head of our dining table.

I had to get out on my own and earn. If Mother's money was a problem, it would actually help her—one less mouth for her to feed. Or was Evelyn meaning to suggest I pay more for my share of the household while here? That Mother needed it? Maybe I could earn enough income to help her.

But not on a secretary's wage two days a week.

"No," Mother said adamantly. "Friends are not suggesting marriage. Not to my face anyway." A frown scrunched her brow. "Please don't bring it up again, Evelyn. Anyway, I can go back into teaching if needed."

I said, "Are you thinking about that?"

"I'm to begin tutoring for a start. I've already lined up two students. For algebra. I was going to tell you both today."

I lightly clapped my hands. "Bravo."

This was what I loved about Mother. Her strength. Her fortitude. She recently said that, come November, she would be the first local woman in line to vote for US president.

"I'm glad you'll start tutoring," Evelyn said more softly. "You have so much to give."

"Thank you."

"Violet," Evelyn said, and I braced for her attention back on me. "I'm sorry I reacted so severely at first—to your idea of leaving." She leaned in and put her hands on my knees. "If you move away, it's I who will suffer. I'll miss you."

And just like that, my angst over all she had said dissipated. A lit match snuffed. I liked this sweet side of Evelyn much more than the pesky one. But would a day ever come—no matter how I fancied myself independent—that I'd stop needing my big sister's approval? Her affirmation?

"I love you, too." I lifted her hand and kissed her knuckles.

"Violet," Mother said.

With one word, she could signal with her tone that what she was about to impart must be heard. Uninterrupted.

"My dear daughter," she said directly to me. "I know you have dreams. And Evelyn has had hers. As Father had his. And, I have had mine, too—when I taught for a time, with my philanthropies, and most of all, with the honor of raising two daughters."

She smoothed the pale-blue cloth napkin on her lap and with it further smoothed our temperaments. Tears welled in my eyes no matter how I wished it weren't so. After all I'd been through—we'd all been through, with Father and then Prohibition—I needed her voice of affirmation as well as my sister's.

"I want you to do what will make you happy," Mother said. "And perhaps that's going to Detroit and finding your own way."

She looked to her hands, her beautiful hands locked in a steeple in her lap. I held my breath as my vision grew of skyscrapers and streetcars and plumes of factory smoke filling the skies with prosperity.

Then Mother's gaze bored straight into mine again.

"But I ask you to wait. For one year. That's all. Be sure this is what you want." Mother lifted her chin. "And then if you go," she added firmly, "you will do so with my and Evelyn's unyielding support. Our blessing."

My spirits at first lifted and then plunged but then soared again—like an eagle swooping down to the water with its wings wide and then flying back high to the sun.

I understood.

My mother needed me to wait, and I would. For twelve months. I'd sacrifice for her. Tears dampened her eyes now, too, and she added five simple words I would never forget . . . words meant to capture her feelings on everything.

"You have only one life."

CHAPTER 5

Melanie

Louisville, Kentucky
July 2018

Wow. Violet was so cool to broach the subject of heading to Detroit with her family. I loved sneaking in a few minutes here and there to read her entries. She was a go-getter. I wanted to be like her. And it would be nice if Mom were more supportive like Violet's mother, too.

Today was Saturday, and I was being proactive. I'd lined up a full schedule for my day off to explore my idea for a new series of locally-based events: Bourbon and Books. It would pull together a cross section of two groups—bourbon enthusiasts and book clubs. The program would be low cost for our distillery and get customers in the door at some favorite haunts. If the program really took off, we could expand to markets nationally with social media and starter kits—another step toward my promotion.

By midafternoon, I'd already had an appointment with the manager at Bourbons Bistro downtown. The well-stocked bourbon bar was five shelves high. Kentucky bars displayed whiskeys the way libraries stacked books. They had an awesome covered porch, too. My idea was met with lots of enthusiasm. Our marketing group would provide flyers to post outside the window or to leave with a hostess. We'd promote dates on social media.

I had also connected with heads of the Exchange, the coolest kitchen and pub in southern Indiana—worth the extra fifteen-minute drive north across the Ohio River from Louisville. When my friends and I ate there, Nicole would say, *Bring on the green leafy vegetables, girls. I only eat healthy*. We'd laugh and then devour kale braised in bourbon and bacon. Again, this pub was on board if Goldenrod launched the program.

I met with a couple of more hot spots and then got impulsive. I'd not gotten time to visit BOM—Bourbon on Main—last weekend in Frankfort, so I made the trip back.

Downtown Frankfort was everything quaint. Couples with dogs and families with children strolled the walks. Repurposed old buildings of brick or wood, mostly Italianate in style and dating back 150 years, lined each block. In no time, BOM was also "in" for letting groups gather for book talk and bites to eat. They had space upstairs and a breezy deck overlooking the Kentucky River.

I mingled with folks everywhere I went—good people having a good time and drinking responsibly. We chatted up their tastes of the pours. Bourbon was not just a beverage. It'd come from the land and our state's limestone water. It was to be mixed in a favorite cocktail or savored like fine wine, without pretentions.

Today had been a success. Take that, Mitchell Fox.

After leaving BOM, a sign caught my eye on the next storefront.

CAPITAL CITY CLASSIC AUTO CLUB
CRUISES EVERY 3RD SATURDAY OF THE MONTH

That was today. It ran from six o'clock to nine. There were labeled thumbnail pics of cars in full color—a 1934 Ford, a 1940 Buick, a 1957 Chevy, and a 1963 Corvette. They all looked like relics to me but were in pristine condition.

Mom's directive had been clear. I had eight days before real estate appraisers would show up, and the car had to be gone when the house sold. How was I to know exactly when that would be? A day? A month?

If I ran over to the cruise for an hour, I might meet an expert to advise on my own classic car. A quick google search had shown a Jordan recently going for $29,000. But it was a different model year and looked rougher than mine. How did I really know how much mine was worth? Maybe I'd even find a buyer.

I swung by Violet's house to snap a few pics of the Jordan. I spruced it up with the hose and towels after I cleaned the carriage house windows. Then I hit the bathroom in the hot, stuffy house.

I'd be sure not to mess with the AC, or Mom would have a fit.

The cruise for the Capital City Classic Auto Club was at the Frisch's Big Boy out on Highway 127. The main lot was full of spectators coming to gawk. The classic cars themselves were parked at an angle in rows. The evening was midseventies with low humidity, perfect for shorts and a T-shirt. But all I had was the jeans, cute top, and flat-soled sandals I'd worn all day.

Exhibiting cars lined up bumper-to-bumper waiting to find a spot to park. Some just arriving had their windows open or their tops down and owners waved at me as they passed. A DJ played oldies from the 1950s like "Rock Around the Clock" and "Puppy in the Window." Dad listened to golden oldies in his garage sometimes, too, so I knew a few of the songs.

Cars were teal colored or two-toned beige and brown. There were yellow and navy and silver ones, too. Lots of chrome—chrome wheels, chrome bumpers, shiny chrome decorations on the sides—with evening sunlight dancing off it all.

Many car owners sat in woven folding chairs beside their pride and joys. One guy had a handlebar mustache, waxed and curled into loops three inches out. Several cars had their hoods up, so onlookers could get a peek at the engine.

I stopped to examine one car on display.

"It's a 1955 Chevy," said a man with a thick southern accent. His drawl reminded me that I wasn't in Louisville, where even we natives sounded midwestern. His hands were in his jeans' pockets. "My daddy bought it new."

"He handed it down?" It still looked brand new.

"Yep. Painted her myself," he said as bystanders admired his work. The body was immaculate in what he called candy-apple red. "Ain't easy keeping them whitewalls clean, either." He laughed.

Whitewalls?

"It's my first time at a cruise," I said as if this were my first slumber party. "How many cars come here?"

"Sixty to seventy-five. From Maysville, Lexington, Bardstown, and more."

"Impressive," I said. "Thank you."

He lifted his cap in a grandfatherly way, and I moved on.

Firefighters at a red fire engine had a table collecting money for clothes for underprivileged children. I rolled some bills together and pushed the donation into the slit on the lid of a plastic cup.

I twisted right to find a young guy with amazing eyes also making a donation.

"Having fun?" he said.

"Yeah, this show is great."

"You got a vehicle displayed?" he asked, friendly.

"No, but I am here to check out antique cars."

"Cool," he said.

This guy's height didn't reach six feet, but he was so good-looking, he could play a movie double for Chris Hemsworth—brown hair with goldish highlights in a style that looked just combed but also mussed up; sculpted pecs beneath a tucked-in black T-shirt; and eyes that squinted at me just enough to make their blue bluer below thick, dark lashes and well-shaped brows. With his short-whiskered beard, too, my girlfriend Casey would call him a total smoke show, meaning he was hotter than hot.

I hadn't been attracted to anyone since breaking up with Jason.

My ex and I were together for three years and engaged for three months. He worked in information technology. We were to have gotten married later this year. And despite Mom's pressuring for a grand affair at the storied Seelbach hotel, Jason and I planned a casual, intimate ceremony and reception on the grounds of a farm venue, where the sun set behind a restored barn in the country.

We first met at a football tailgate party, in line for barbecue. It was during a University of Kentucky homecoming game when I was twenty-five. We both bled Wildcat blue. We liked Iron Man movies and bourbon tastings and eating out for brunch on Sundays. There were times I thought we were perfect. He was *the one*.

Until he wasn't—when recruiters pegged him for a job in Silicon Valley.

"Listen, babe," he said one night at my loft. "I just want to play it out. You'll have input the whole way."

"What's the position?" I could not believe he was thinking of relocating. *Us* relocating.

"Program engineer. With a huge pay increase. At Apple."

It did sound like a dream job. And part of me was really excited for him. Over the next couple of weeks, he got the offer and pressed me to move to California. This was during a period of my own career growth. I already knew of the future organizational change at work and promotion opportunity. And a commuter marriage was not my bag.

In a way, it felt as if he'd been unfaithful; I thought he would be my forever rock . . . when we first told each other we were in love, when we spent holidays with our families, when he proposed. What a day that one was. I still got tingly thinking about it. But it just never occurred to me that he'd let me down over something so fundamental as my career.

The hotbed of IT was in Silicon Valley. The hotbed of bourbon was in the bluegrass. There was no mixing the oil and the vinegar. I didn't beg him to stay, to give up a chance at stardom in his chosen field. I just decided to put my career first for me.

Sometimes love wasn't enough.

Some days I felt like I was in mourning. But the end of our relationship wasn't just the end of us. It was the time I learned that a man wouldn't watch out for me. Only I would watch out for me.

"You've come to the right place," the cute car guy said, bringing me back to the cruise. "Want to see mine?"

Did I want to see his— Oh yeah, he must have a car. "Absolutely," I said, following him to his car. "I want to see it."

"It's the prettiest I've seen here, but I must confess," I said, "I don't know what kind of car it is. I'm new to all this."

"No worries. And thank you," he said, crossing his arms. He had serious biceps. "It's a 1932 Ford, three-window coupe, customized," he said. "I could talk your ears off all night."

"Forewarning accepted," I said.

To call his car's main color maroon would be an insult. I didn't know the color, but that car was *hot*. Like, if the metal and lines and curves and shine and proportion of a car were art, this car would be a master's painting of a nude.

"Exactly what color is that?" I asked.

"Pearl burgundy, not counting the transparent black flames," he said, squinting at me again. The flames reached from the front fenders to the doors.

"I'm Brian, by the way."

"Melanie." Our handshake went on a bit long. There might've been a time I'd welcome that, before my outlook on relationships changed. "What does 'customized' mean?"

"One example is here. See how the windows look shorter than usual? The roof is lower to the car. I had a three-inch chop done."

"Oh!" I did see that now.

"Down here, air bag suspension so it rides low to the road, too. Let's just say I don't take it out in the snow," he said with a laugh. "It's a full-fendered car as well—gives it this scrolling curve effect here." He used his hands as if he were an artist.

"Ah. Very nice."

A week ago, my eyes might've glazed over at this shop talk, a language from Mars I didn't understand. But this was actually interesting.

"Did you notice there's no door handles?" he said as men and women hung around hoping for his attention.

"That's ridiculous," I said.

"I shaved the handles off. It's a thing."

A shapely woman in tight jeans and a red tank top stepped up, beamed at him, and asked, "Who painted your flame-job?"

Brian crooked an eyebrow at me as if to say, *Sorry, I'll try to make this short.*

I poked around between Brian's car and the neighboring showpiece, making idle chitchat, as a couple of more people stopped Brian. Soon he caught my eye again.

"Your car is very popular," I said as more groupies circulated. Or maybe it was just him?

Then, with a twinkle in those heavily lashed eyes, Brian said, "It does seem to draw a crowd, doesn't it? Or maybe it's just *you*."

He grinned a teasing smile, and I blushed all over.

It wasn't quite dusk, but cars were starting to leave.

"Hungry?" Brian asked. "Some club members gather in the back of the Big Boy for a late supper."

I was starving. And I always enjoyed a triple-decker burger and a chocolate shake served in a cold metal container. But to tag along with a bunch of strangers?

"Or, I could treat you to a bite at Capital Cellars. I'd throw in a bordeaux or a bourbon while we talk cars," he said. "You haven't even told me why all this newfound interest in the classic car scene. You a reporter?"

"Ha! Not at all." I chuckled. "I have a personal interest. And, candidly, I could stand to pick your brain." Maybe he could help me find a buyer. "Might be easier to talk if we get away from your fan club," I said. "But I'll drive myself."

"That's cool. Meet up at the Cellars in twenty minutes?"

"Sure."

"Great," he said. "It's a date."

I winced. This was a plan. Not a date. This was personal business.

CHAPTER 6

Violet

Frankfort, Kentucky
Seventeen months later, July 1921

Mother teased that my jaw might get stuck because I smiled so much. More than a year had come and gone, but I was on my way to the train station at last.

Evelyn twisted around to peer with her big brown eyes over the back of the automobile's front seat. I wiggled my fingers in a small wave. Her husband drove his four-passenger touring car, and Mother sat in back by me. I gazed right out the window unencumbered as the sun rose and we crossed the miles from Frankfort to Louisville, the land I'd known all my life. I would miss the fertile green grass of Kentucky. As I walked out of Bond House that morning, I knew it wouldn't be the last. I couldn't bear for it to be the last. I'd be back to visit. But it felt as if the house was hurting to see me go, too. It was silent. Cold in the midst of summer.

This was the classic example of *bittersweet*. Wasn't it? Happiness at the possibilities ahead and terror of the rest. I relished the vision of progress and industry I'd find in Detroit—and the monetary security and adventure it'd bring. I hadn't slept for days, given all my excitement. I had a room and a job already waiting.

In the more than a year since I voiced my desire to leave, the country's economy had declined beyond problems with Prohibition. The Federal Reserve played with interest rates in a fight with national inflation. The government sliced its budget, pulling money out of the economy. It hadn't occurred to me that a fallout would hit the burgeoning automotive sector like a boxer's uppercut punch. But orders for cars lagged when the recession spiked last summer. Americans adored their automobiles, but when it came down to Sunday drives or food, especially as winter approached, food won. Detroit's thriving industry had never before dipped. For his company's part, Henry Ford responded by pushing all of its inventory and stocks of replacement parts to the dealers.

Ford dealers normally ordered automobiles as their sales demanded. But the roadmen worked with frenzied dealers who were forced to take out loans to absorb all the inventory. Henry Ford's directive was clear: take the cars, or lose your dealership. They took the cars.

I'd thought now of Robert Neumann, as I had periodically over time. It'd been nearly two years since we met in the distillery office. Was he getting on well? Things were flourishing again. Production was high in Detroit. The country was prospering, save for the brewers and distillers and their chains of suppliers. I couldn't help but wonder if our paths would cross again—not for a liaison, of course. Just so that I could thank him for his help. Besides, after all this time, he might be married for all I knew.

"Oh," I said now, craning to see up front. Was that steam or smoke curling up from the hood of Charles's car? The car was sputtering, and he was maneuvering to get to the side of the road.

I can't miss the train.

"What's the matter?" Evelyn asked, the back of her neck reddening.

"Don't worry," he said. "I've used everything from chewing gum to paper clips to get a car going again. I'll fix it."

He jumped out, lifted the hood, and waved steam away from his face. When it dissipated, he stood at the side to bend over the engine. He clunked something and rose his elbows as if he were twisting something else. He slammed the hood back closed. He brushed his hands together and hopped back in the car.

"We'll let it cool a bit here in the shade," he said. "It's a journey to Louisville, but we're over halfway there. We'll make it."

"That's why we left early," said Evelyn, glancing back to me, optimistic. "Right?"

"Right." Besides the fact that my train would depart at eight thirty a.m.

I fiddled with my pocketbook. I checked my watch. I bit my lip. Mother patted my knee. If we didn't make it on time, I'd take it as a sign I wasn't meant to go. But with my nerves, my body felt thick and hard as a stone. Was this why Father wouldn't let us women drive his car? We'd get stuck with no idea as to how to fix it?

Charles got back out and hand cranked the car to start it. Nothing. Tried again—something close this time, a sputter, but nothing. A third time and this was it. It fired up.

As he pulled the vehicle back onto the road, Mother said, "Magnificent job, dear."

My shoulders eased. We spoke little the remainder of the trip. I was never so happy as when the city came into view.

The rail route to Detroit would be circuitous: fifteen hours with three stops before arriving—including changing trains at one station. I couldn't miss my first boarding. I stretched my neck of its tension.

At last Charles rounded a corner, and before us stood the celebrated Louisville Union Station.

"There it is, Mother," I said.

She smiled at me. She once toured us girls here for a study of its Romanesque architecture and limestone ashlar, its immense clock tower, and its barreled vaulting. My parting with her and Evelyn weighed heavily on me. Tears blurred my eyes, but I wouldn't let them spill. I wouldn't.

Once inside, I was glad to have Charles, a seasoned traveler, guide us through the maze of crowds. The smell of men's cologne and steam from coal mingled with the voices of chatty women and grinding locomotives echoing in from the terminals.

"Charles," Evelyn said as Mother had done long ago, "don't you love the ceiling's skylights and stained glass? I do."

She was putting up a strong front. But I saw the shifting light in her eyes. Seemed to me, she was taking my departure harder than Mother was.

The month before, Mother came to me in the rear yard on one of my days off. There she had a garden and room for playing croquet. It was sweltering hot outside, but we took to the shade for a while with sweet tea.

"I have something for you," she said.

An envelope? It wasn't time for my birthday card. I would turn twenty next week.

I opened it. "Money?"

"A small sum," she said. "I know you've got your nest egg. You've saved for a long time."

She touched my cheek with the backs of her fingers.

"Go to Detroit. Get a job there. Make new friends. Be independent. I know it's what you want. And you've waited patiently." She rubbed her own cheek then. "It's time. You shouldn't grow old without having tried."

A feeling overtook me, like a filly ready to burst through a gate at a derby.

"Thank you, Mother." I wrapped my arms around her and inhaled her floral perfume Father bought her. When we parted, her eyes scoured my face as if to remember its every bend and pore.

"But you have to promise me something," she said.

"Anything."

"Keep this money on hand at all times to afford a train ticket back. If things there don't work out—if they go miserably for any reason at all—or, if they do work out well but you just want to come home, come."

Her voice cracked as she emphasized *come*.

"I promise."

And the weight of the promise felt light, not heavy. I had everything I'd dreamed of ahead of me.

Now in the station, Evelyn and I took hands and dodged the mass of travelers exiting the terminals. Some fifty trains came in and out of here each day.

I wore a two-piece day suit in navy blue and a wide-brimmed hat. My skirt hit at midcalf, and Evelyn especially loved how the hat's brown trim looped through a smart buckle in front. I'd get good use of the outfit in the city—and I prayed that despite July's weather, no one would open their windows on the train. I didn't wish to arrive in Michigan looking like I'd just come from the furnace in the cellar. The cleaner coal of Phoebe Snow hadn't survived due to the Great War's needs.

"Two bags?" the railway employee asked.

"That's right."

I already shipped a huge trunk. With luck, it would be at the boardinghouse when I arrived. I spent three days preparing my wardrobe alone—selecting, cleaning, folding, and carefully packing the garments. I wished I could've brought more.

"This is it," Charles said, "where we leave you." He needed to return to Frankfort for a client's court date. "I'll wait over here," he said, "so you girls and your mother can make your farewells."

I gave him my heartfelt thanks. I might even miss him. He'd been kind to me at his law firm. My sister had married a good man.

I swiveled toward Evelyn. Her solitary dimple sank deep into her cheek whenever she pressed her lips together so, trying to remain composed. I silently prayed for her happiness always. I sniffed as tears clung to my lashes. We hugged as we never had before, except for when we lost Father.

"Take care of yourself," she said.

Then there was Mother. We embraced so warmly, I knew this must be how it felt when I was an infant in her arms, rocking in a chair near a fire. How could I leave and do this to her? To myself? A lump of remorse rose up in my throat and it hurt.

I peeped over her shoulder at the hordes of travelers, while the sounds of announcements rang out and a baby's wails faded into silence.

Was it too late to turn back?

Mother maneuvered her hat around mine and pulled away from me a few inches. She put on her cheery air. "You have only one life."

Tears filled her eyes now, too, but I'd come to know her tears. These were happy ones.

"I'll miss you so much," I said. "I'll telegram when I'm settled. Thank you for being so good and understanding and brave. I love you more than anything in life."

"Violet," she said, her voice quavering. "You're following your dreams. You're doing it for us both." She tilted her hat and kissed my cheek. "Remember your promise."

I gulped back a sob. She and I and Evelyn clumsily dabbed each other's tears with our handkerchiefs that Mother had embroidered. Birds. Blue jays on mine and red cardinals on my sister's.

Charles gave us a nod.

After taking a few steps away, I looked back at my sister and mother, and they hadn't budged but for Evelyn to bring her gloved hand to her cheek. We waved.

"Write me!" she called. And I blew her back kisses.

I snaked through the throng toward the designated platform where the train bound for Detroit awaited. Steam whistles blew. Plumes of steam rose all around. People jostled in twos and threes to find their right lanes.

My ticket was in coach. I'd not be in a Pullman car, of course. Some had Cuban mahogany, marble showers, and gold-plated lamps for the wealthy. They were the cars farthest from the coal-burning steam locomotive to get away from the cinders and smoke. A sign said which passenger car was designated for Black people; they were sectioned off in the car closest to the smoke. I hoped life would be different for them in the North, too. I knew many were making their way to new ground to find work.

"Watch your step, miss," said the conductor.

As I climbed the last metal step up into the passenger car, a peculiar sensation overcame me. I was acutely aware that I was entering a whole new world.

My life was about to change.

The aisle between the train's seats was narrow. And I'd never given the two-passenger seats a thought on the trips I'd taken with family. But I had a stranger beside me. A middle-aged woman who wasn't a conversationalist. She read and grunted and that was about it. The train picked up speed with a rhythmic *cha-chunk, cha-chunk*. Off and on, her arm brushed mine. I tried to keep to my half, but it would be a long ride. At least I had a window. I had new places to see—even if that only meant farmland and cornfields through Indiana and Ohio.

The thing that gave me the most angst was knowing my purse contained my life's fortune. I had dared not pack it in a suitcase that would be jumbled with others in the baggage car. I kept the strap laced around one arm so that if I drifted off, someone couldn't remove it.

By the time the train made stops in Jeffersonville, Indiana, and then Seymour, Indiana, I was hungry. I'd left early in the morning and hadn't had a bite. All my dining and napping would be done in this seat. Except for the switch of trains later on where I might afford something hot. My back was already stiff, and I hoped nourishment would help.

A man a couple of seats away said, "Here comes the butcher boy."

The butcher boy was all of fourteen, I guessed, neat and friendly, carrying a basket of magazines and newspapers, cigarettes and snacks. "What would you like, miss? Exact change appreciated. A homemade roll?"

"Yes, that looks tasty. Coffee, too." I counted out his due to the penny. While I would enjoy the new *Red Book* magazine to catch up on beauty and fashion, I resisted. I would be frugal. I'd paid for the train ticket myself. And the rest that I'd saved would be my nest egg.

When I wrote to Mrs. Sturgeon that her nephew recommended her establishment, she wrote back quickly that she had a room coming open—the smallest in her boardinghouse, but that was perfect for me. As awkward as I assumed it would be to live with complete strangers, especially with men, society accepted such arrangements. Boardinghouses dotted block after block in Detroit, New York, Philadelphia, and Boston. Those that housed only women were suspect. The landlady would not risk a rumor that hers was a house of ill repute. Mrs. Sturgeon's respectable home would be mine for now.

I got giddy thinking of my new job. Mr. Adams in town had given me a directory of Detroit's automotive manufacturers and suppliers. I'd pored over it for days. When I saw the spark plug factory, it resonated. Robert Neumann had mentioned that it was one where women with nimble fingers worked.

Two more letters to Detroit later, and I had my wish. Today was Friday. I would have orientation at the Jubert-Dufour Spark Plug Factory on Monday. I felt like I had as a girl on Christmas Eve.

My foot kept bouncing on the floor as fast as my thoughts. The lady beside me glared.

CHAPTER 7

Melanie

Frankfort, Kentucky
July 2018

Brian the car buff lifted his glass in a toast, and so did I. "To classic cars," he said.

"To automobiles as *art*," I said, and that drew a grin.

We clinked our glasses of a nice cabernet, but I'd have only a few sips. I had quite a drive ahead. The evening was perfect for a sidewalk café table. We ordered a cheese and charcuterie plate—something Jason had never been into. He was more of a nachos guy.

But why was I thinking of him? I exhaled and focused on the present.

"Why your sudden interest in old cars?" Brian asked.

"How about some visual aids?"

I unzipped my purse for my cell and swiped through the few pics of the Jordan I'd taken that afternoon. Brian's fingers grazed mine when he took my phone.

He tilted my phone to the light. "Whoa." His eyes shifted up to me without moving a muscle. "This is, whew. Early 1920s. It's yours?"

"Yup. A 1923 Jordan MX Playboy."

"Ah," he said, nodding approvingly. He checked out some more pictures. "You know what you got here?"

"Actually, I'm not sure. What do you think I've got here?"

"A collector's piece."

"Oh! Can you tell me more?"

Maybe a collector would buy the car from me. But as the words crossed my mind, I wished I didn't have to get it out of Mom's hair—part of me didn't want to sell Violet's precious car at all.

Brian glanced to the moonlit sky. "Sales for this car were strong when it was made, but it didn't roll off a major automaker's assembly line by the hundreds of thousands, you know? There were over a couple hundred auto manufacturers of various sizes in the early 1900s, many outside Michigan. Jordans were produced in Ohio."

Consolidation wasn't so unlike the bourbon industry. There'd been some two hundred distilleries in Kentucky going into Prohibition, and we had around forty here now.

The more I learned about cars tonight, the more it seemed the Jordan was rare. Maybe it was worth more than $29,000?

"How'd you come by the car?" Brian asked.

I was noticing a merest hint of a twang in Brian's words that had long *i*'s. *By. Tonight. Mine. Try*. They held a hint of short *a*. He looked like he might've looked when he was a little boy, asking his daddy how Santa delivered presents when a house had no chimney. He was a nice guy. And he had cute crow's-feet when he smiled.

"My great-great-great-aunt left it to me." I felt a warm swell of pride in saying it.

"Very cool. Ford produced almost half of all cars made in that era, so there's still many thousands of those left with collectors. But I'm guessing there might be a hundred Jordans, total, of all the years and models combined, surviving anywhere. Maybe less."

"Wow," I said. I was ready to probe him about the car's value when he scrunched his forehead as if trying to grasp a memory. I might be a fool not to sell it, even if it pained me.

Then he said, "The Jordan make of car was considered quite sporty in its day. F. Scott Fitzgerald even named a character after it in *The Great Gatsby*—"

"Stop it." I leaned forward. "You kidding me? Jordan Baker. The flapper who was a professional golfer."

"That would be her."

"Totally. Amazing." I picked up my water, tingling. My car was part of history.

"What are you gonna do with it?" Brian asked.

"Huh! That is the big unknown. I'd thought I would sell it."

Maybe, I thought now, *I should keep it as an investment instead. Maybe I could get it "customized" in honor of Violet, after my promotion? What would that cost? Maybe I won't have to do away with Violet's last memory.* *No*, I thought, thinking better of it. *As much as I hate putting Violet's prized possession down the road, selling it makes the most sense in my life.*

The server set down a rustic wooden plank and described an array of delights—from a Genoa salami to a soft camembert cheese to a compote of fig and clover honey.

I popped a Marcona almond into my mouth and then plucked a dried apricot from the display.

"I seriously can't believe I'm sitting with a girl who owns a small production Jordan."

My lips bent into another smile. "Any idea what the car is worth? Or what it would take to fix it up?"

He broke a poppy seed lavash into halves and shared. "I really couldn't hazard a guess," he said, "until I view its condition in person. And then maybe do some digging." He smiled. "When do you take me to see it?"

"Did I forget to mention I live in Louisville? And I'm driving home tonight."

"Are you inviting me to go home with you? To see the car before the clock strikes twelve and we both turn into pumpkins like in a fairy tale?"

I laughed, a bit embarrassed at his Cinderella reference. I'd already learned that glass slippers from Prince Charmings meant nothing, especially where their own careers were concerned.

"The car is here, actually. In Frankfort. My mother's selling the house where it's stored, so I've got to get it out quick. But I'm afraid it plays much better in the natural light of day, not under the glare of one bare, fifteen-year-old bulb."

His eyes widened and I realized what that sounded like—like I was suggesting we spend the night someplace.

"Maybe you can see the car one day," I said and quickly moved on. "So are you in the car biz? Or what's your jam?"

"My dad owns a small custom restoration shop. I know lots of people who know cars." He dug into his jeans pocket for his wallet. "My card. I'm happy to help you. I could try to estimate its value. Help find a buyer. Or connect you with somewhere to store it while you figure everything out."

"Oh, that sounds great. Thank you so much."

I glanced at his card. Vice president? Hmm. He had looks and brains and was certainly nice. He had a great title and position, too. He must have girls lining up to snag him.

But I wouldn't be one in line.

A few days later I had an evening event for my job to attend. I hadn't contacted Brian because I didn't want to lead him on; having a relationship was not in my plan. Not now. Not later.

But the car had been on my mind. I wondered when in Violet's journal she would buy it. It was her dream to own a car, and I looked forward to seeing her accomplish that. We Bond women were goal-driven women.

The fact was, though, I needed help, and Brian was an expert. I didn't expect him to consult with me for free. He'd said there were insured places to store cars. If it wasn't too expensive, it would give me peace of mind to have it out of Mom's way—and buy me more time to decide whether to sell or keep it as an investment. I was torn. The Jordan was a vestige of Violet, and her goal. I'd be home by nine tonight and email Brian.

The Sidebar at Whiskey Row was this month's destination for the gathering of the Women's Bourbon Alliance's local chapter. Tonight, Goldenrod was sponsoring—another initiative of mine to show my company my dedication. It was the kind of event I most enjoyed, too. Thirty or so women would network and share nibbles and tastes of our products in a laid-back environment. My budget would absorb the tab. Servers already knew what to bring to our jovial group.

"Hi, I'm Melanie," I said to the first three women to arrive, and I stuck out my hand.

One of the things Mom had taught me was to always be like the host, even when you're the guest. I was the host tonight, but it would be no different if I weren't. There was always someone who didn't know anybody or was shy to start conversation.

By six thirty, the happy hour was going strong.

"I love their pimento cheese fritters," a woman named Kathy said, and I had to concur.

We also had hummus and dippers and a couple of other snacks. Women were chatting in small groups, mingling and laughing and discussing my bourbon. That's what word of mouth at these gigs was all about.

"Is this your first WBA event?" I asked Kathy.

"It's my second," she said. She was an engineer at a local manufacturer. She said she was still learning how to nose and taste a bourbon.

We walked through the process, beginning with giving our glasses of bourbon—served neat, no ice—a swirl and observing the color. The darker, rich-copper color meant it'd aged more years in the charred oak barrels. Then we dipped our noses to the rims and sniffed with our mouths slightly open to enhance the scent.

"I smell butterscotch," she said. "Maybe a hint of vanilla?"

"You know what you're doing," I said, and she grinned.

Then we took a short acclimation sip to let our palates adjust to the heat—and then sipped again. For me, it was sweet on the front and spicy on the back with a cinnamon note.

"Did you hear we've got a rye coming out?" I said.

Two other women joined our conversation, a mother-daughter duo.

"Caroline and Jennifer," I said. "So nice to meet you both."

Caroline, the mother, said, "Thank you for hosting tonight."

"Mom here happened to ask for a bottle of Goldenrod for her birthday," Jennifer said.

"Awesome!"

I reveled in programs like this, with people talking bourbon. This was it to me—and it made working toward the promotion more fun. I scanned the crowd: PhDs, older women, younger women, women with tattoos, writers, lawyers, and veterans. No matter our backgrounds, we all had at least one thing in common: bourbon.

Caroline pointed her thumb at her daughter. "This one got me into bourbon. I grew up here, but I used to be a vodka gal."

Jennifer laughed and said, "Now she likes a good Kentucky hug." And the two hugged each other.

"How sweet!" I said.

A *Kentucky hug* referred to the fire going down your esophagus with a sip of bourbon. But their spontaneously real hug was something Mom and I never did.

Maybe more hugs would come after my promotion, when Mom was proud of me.

CHAPTER 8

Violet

Detroit, Michigan
July 1921

The Michigan Central Station was said to be the tallest in the world—my first sign of Detroit's industrial might. I navigated through the crowds in my low-heeled shoes at a slower pace than I had in Louisville. This was all new, and I didn't have Evelyn's husband to guide me. I'd have to find my way to claim my baggage. My abdomen tightened with anxious excitement as I tried to shake the light dust of coal from my outerwear. Wearing dark clothes helped.

I was here.

The smell of roasting sausages wafted up from a vendor, but I wasn't hungry. I had my purse with my money securely wound around one wrist, and with my other hand I held the crown of my hat as I glanced to the ceiling or dodged other passengers. There were sharp businessmen in suits of fine cloth; immigrant families speaking in foreign tongues; and a band of girls about my age smoking and laughing and wearing man-size coats with sleeves that bunched up on their arms. Strangely, these girls plodded in oversize unbuckled galoshes, too. With every step, their open boots flapped and flapped about their shins.

I'd definitely arrived in a new place.

"Oh," I said, bumping into someone and turning to offer an apology.

"Pardon me, ma'am," said a man quickly. He had a southern drawl thicker than mine. I'd place him as a Georgian by birth. He said, "I didn't mean to—"

Two well-dressed women scowled at the man, backing up and visibly clutching their pocketbooks tighter.

"Silly me," I said. "Not watching where I was going."

His eyes flickered with surprise. In seconds his gaze shifted side to side.

"The fault was all mine," I said to him. "I'm sorry."

The stranger tipped his hat and walked off through the crowd with his suitcase.

The women stood glowering at me, apparently for apologizing to a Black person. But bumping into the man was my fault, after all. I hated how they treated him. I might've grown up in the South, but Mother had taught that everyone deserves respect.

I shifted my attention to the decorative ceiling, this time without running into anyone. The vaults soared three stories high—though I'd overheard on the train that part of the structure held offices for thirteen stories. There was magnificent marble and tons of brown brick and tall pillar after pillar all around us. Two hundred trains came through every day, four times as many as where I departed. But as glorious as this concourse was—and though the architect who designed New York's Grand Central Terminal designed this station, too—I would write Mother that in its finest details, none outdid ours in Kentucky.

After getting my suitcases and asking for directions twice, I went outside for the interurban. While it was almost midnight, the light and people made it feel more like day. I clumsily boarded the train for Mrs. Sturgeon's neighborhood. I had much to view on my way to Saint Aubin Street. I gazed through the dark upon streets lined with shops and small factories and car dealerships. I imagined that afternoons would have men in uniform directing traffic at intersections as we passed, holding up posted signs. Horns would blare.

I felt pride in making it this far without getting lost. I was doing this. I had traveled on my own and done well.

Now I saw houses speeding by one after the other, the lights growing dimmer. They were closer together and with fewer trees than where I had lived before. And there were more cars than I'd ever seen in my life. They lined the curbs of the streets and cluttered the drives as moonlight beamed on my new city.

Had I expected everything to look the same as what I'd known? I realized, then, that I hadn't known exactly what to expect.

My hands clenched my luggage because I needed something to hold on to. This newness of discovery thrilled me; at the same time, I didn't want to misstep. I had to keep sharp.

Evelyn's voice echoed. *Take care of yourself.*

"Mrs. Sturgeon? I'm Violet Bond." I smiled and extended my hand. I stood on the small covered porch of the clapboard house painted blue.

The landlady's brow scrunched. Was she angry? Maybe she had difficulty understanding my accent.

"You're expecting me? Violet Bond."

She was a medium-framed woman, younger than I would've guessed. "Come in," she said.

She wasn't exactly a warm hostess. But then, I wasn't her guest; this was her business. Or, did she think ill of me because her nephew was the one who referred me? There was nothing inappropriate about the referral I received. Not that I would mind seeing Robert again.

I lifted my suitcases and entered the hall. "Something smells good," I said to be kind.

Some sort of soup? A roast? Though with my nerves over all the newness, I'd not be able to eat. I had to orient myself to this place.

She swiveled. "Thank you. Beef stew day. But I'm afraid you missed that meal. We dine promptly at six o'clock, six nights a week. Never on Saturday."

"Of course."

I hoped she wouldn't begrudge me a glass of water. Such rules. So much for my getting to make all my own decisions in my newfound independence. But this was a start.

"I'll show you to your room," Mrs. Sturgeon said. She had the faintest hint of a German accent, like my late maternal grandfather.

I needed sleep. I was tired as a bear in hibernation after traveling fifteen hours sitting straight up.

"Breakfast," she said as we passed the dining room, "is promptly at seven o'clock each morning."

I was used to structure, but schedules were of Mother's or my own making. Would I adjust to Mrs. Sturgeon's regimen? What if my job conflicted with the landlady's times? How would I eat? And what if her menu was not to my taste? I'd rather eat cheap soda crackers and canned beans with my sister.

"Your room is here," Mrs. Sturgeon said with an outreached hand for me to enter.

I'd known it would be small, but the room was at the head of the stairs. It would have the most noise from heavy boots and heels marching by my door. I fretted that I'd made a mistake by coming here.

I stepped inside.

I set down my suitcases and saw my trunk. A piece of my home. My gaze darted about the space that seemed scarcely larger than our pantry at Bond House. Perhaps a larger bedroom had been divided to accommodate more paying residents.

Yet the room was sweet in its effect—with a small, neat rug, dainty white curtains, and an embroidered square pillow for accent.

"Very nice," I said, looking my landlady in the eye so as to be on her good side.

She warmed, smiling in an appreciative way. "You'll be comfortable here."

She pointed out the bathroom facilities down the hall, then described the routine for her twice-weekly cleaning and once-weekly laundry service that came with the cost of the rent. Then she left me alone to unpack. I'd forgotten to ask about my money. Her letter said she had a safe that all residents used, overseen only by her. I peeked into the hall. She was gone. Tonight, I would sleep with the purse tucked beneath one half of my pillow, and its strap wound around my right wrist.

I could barely walk in the room, given the trunk took up the entirety of the free space of the floor. Once I emptied it, it'd go to the attic for storage. I scooted sideways to the door and latched its lock—I wouldn't leave myself open to strangers. Men might be in the room next door.

I lowered myself on the end of the narrow bed, and it was neither too hard nor too lumpy. That was comforting.

There was an electric lamp softly lit on the bedside table and a chest of drawers to its right. Mrs. Sturgeon had left a lidded chamber pot for the middle of the night or for when the bathroom was otherwise busy. And there was a washbasin on a stand—and a small pitcher with water and a glass.

I brightened a bit as I poured a drink. Evelyn would say I had everything I needed.

Everything but her. I hadn't expected to miss her so soon. As a girl, I would sometimes tiptoe into her bedroom, cuddle up with her beneath the sheets. Sometimes I was cold. Sometimes I was scared. Sometimes I just wanted to hear her voice and laughter.

For tonight, I was exhausted. It was as if I'd slept with my eyelids taped open for weeks. My pinkie toes were sore from hustling across grand marble floors. My back ached from sitting upright in one position on the train. I would unpack only necessities tonight and the rest tomorrow.

I unstrapped the leather belts of the trunk and unlatched the locks. I lifted the heavy lid and dug down into a layer of clothes. Folded into my nightgown were two pictures. I unwrapped the flannel and removed the frames. My dear Evelyn. I brought her face to my lips. Next, I picked up the photograph of my parents, posed in the Frankfort studio several years before. Mother was seated and Father stood beside her, both dressed in their Sunday best. Father had a thick mustache in those days, and Mother had an hourglass waist.

They each had had a hand in who I was. From here, I was in charge of who I'd become.

As I lay my head on an unfamiliar pillow in a clean, crisp case, I wondered who'd slept in this bed. A young woman who worked in a typing pool? A man who was an iron worker? I wrinkled my face to think of anyone sleeping here before me.

I longed for my own bed. And this, I decided, was what homesickness was. I'd never had the disease before.

Thank goodness diseases could be cured.

I would send Mother a telegram in the morning, though, telling her I was safe.

My adventure had begun.

CHAPTER 9

Melanie

Frankfort, Kentucky
July 2018

Today I was going to meet up with Brian. To clarify: I would meet the cute car guru guy *with my mother*. Yikes. She had insisted she tag along so she could do one more pass through Violet's property before the appraiser showed up on Tuesday, and she would leave him a key in a lockbox he'd already hung on the door. Brian and I had emailed after the women's bourbon event I'd hosted. Thanks to him, within two days, I had a specialized storage unit reserved—one that had the right humidity, lighting, and security to preserve vintage cars—and Brian had lined up a crew to come tow the car. He'd made it all so easy for me, I'd be forever be grateful.

If only I could survive the drive to Frankfort and back with Mom, things would be grand. Violet's journal entries were so touching—the love she had for her mother. The support her mother showed her. Couldn't Mom and I be more like that?

Half an hour into our forty-five-minute drive, it seemed she and I were on our best behavior. We talked about her recovering ankle; the latest on her mother, who lived in Florida; Dad's firm acquiring another small accounting firm; and my current gym routine.

But I hoped that when she saw Brian, she didn't think he was more than an expert coming to assess the car and oversee the towing crew. He wasn't a love interest of mine. I peered over at her at the wheel of her four-door BMW. She'd pulled her medium-length ponytail through the back hole of a Hunting Creek Country Club ball cap. She looked more like forty-four than fifty-four. Her face was still cute. Yes, cute. Among the moms in my friend group, mine was the only one we called *cute*, rather than *pretty* or *beautiful*. She was like Sally Field, whose face was sweet as a flying nun no matter how old she got. And Mom had a petite body to boot. She carried off the warm-up-jacket-and-black-leggings look well. Mom was the epitome of studied casualness.

"So this guy Brian," I began, "is, like I said, an expert in old classic cars."

"The one you met at some kind of conference for car enthusiasts."

"Right." It was called a *cruise*, but close enough. "I'm just gonna warn you, this guy is hot."

She craned her head and gave me an "oh really" stare. I barked out a laugh.

She faced the road again, and I could see the mechanizations of her brain's cogs clicking. "He's someone you're interested in?" she asked.

"In an ideal world?" I said. "Maybe. But I don't reside in an ideal world, Mom. My career is goal one. I'm over men."

She nodded and pursed her lips. I took a gulp of Smartwater. I might need extra electrolytes for when she asked about Jason.

"And what about Jason?" she said right on cue. She glanced my way again, and it appeared her hands gripped the wheel more tightly. "You're saying it's too soon for a new relationship?"

"Five months since breaking up would hardly constitute a rebound," I said but controlled my tone. "But when I say over men, I mean over men."

"I'm sure that's best," she said. "You don't want to play around with your heart yet."

She had to use the word *yet* as if in time I'd change, as if I'd fall in love again or, even better, save myself to take Jason back. She liked how he played golf with Dad on Father's Day; she adored his well-to-do family; she loved how he promised her grandchildren. But if I wasn't able to trust *him*, *my chosen one*, to accept me for who I was—a bourbon girl who would never leave Kentucky—I couldn't trust anyone.

I kept calm, trying to convince myself that Mom's need to throw up the yellow lights of caution was just her being a mom.

We arrived at Violet's house on West Campbell Street thirty minutes before our scheduled time with Brian. We mounted the seven wide steps to the front porch. Mom had the slightest limp remaining in her left foot. The porch swing that was once suspended by chains was sadly gone. Memories returned of Aunt Violet waving to me from this spot, and I got sentimental all over again. Mom and I moved to the century-old double doors that had thick-glassed windows covered inside with white sheers.

"It's weird to see the appraiser's lockbox on the handle, isn't it?" I said. It was a concrete sign of things going away, almost like being at Violet's funeral all over again.

The ornate stained glass window above both doors—the only one in the house, designed to impress guests—was majestic in colors of blue and green and gray and yellow. I followed Mom inside, where midmorning light shone through the windows, and dark hardwoods were everywhere . . . the planked floors, the elaborate moldings, the original staircase. I got a whiff of lemon oil on the walnut. When I was a kid, I doubled up on thick pillows and slid down the steps on my butt, bumpity-bump-bump. A toboggan. It was Violet's idea. She did it as a girl.

Renters had moved all their stuff out, and with no rugs and no furniture and no lamps or books, the rooms felt stark. I noticed it when

I was here the week before, but now, with the lockbox out front, a foreboding sense of finality followed me from room to room like a ghost.

In the parlor, Mom said, "Violet used to primp this room all up for the holidays, didn't she?"

"*Mm.* Sure did. I kinda hate that someone else is going to own those Rookwood tiles around the fireplace."

"I can't keep this house forever," Mom said wearily.

"I know." I'd change the subject, aiming to maintain harmony.

But I'd like to see more remorse in her—the kind I was having over the Jordan, where something kept niggling at me to keep it while knowing the practical thing to do was sell.

⁓

Brian pulled up five minutes ahead of our slated time, which was a half hour before the crew was due to arrive. He didn't drive his 1932 hot rod. He drove a little red Corvette convertible. Top down. I could almost hear Prince singing. Even Mom raised her eyebrows, like *whoa*.

He hopped out and resembled a construction worker with his faded jeans, weathered T-shirt, and what appeared to be steel-toed, lace-up boots. I was dressed equally casually, ready for the task of showing him the car and staying out of the way of his guys and tow truck.

Mom and I met Brian in a patch of dandelions. "My car expert has arrived on duty," I said, lighthearted.

"Pleased to be at your service," he said congenially. "Cool old house."

Mom shook his hand and said, "I'm Angie, thank you," with a professionally courteous tone she'd use with a cable TV guy.

When I opened the carriage house, Mom walked in and said, "Well done, Melanie. You did a major transformation on this garage."

She patted my back. It was nice of her to say.

"Thank you," I said. The stink of the place was virtually gone, too.

"Check. This. Out," Brian said, going to one side of the Jordan.

He ran his hand along the smoky red paint. It was as if this car called out to people to stroke it like the fur of a kitten. Brian soon marveled at the tool kit, the rag top, the motor, the wheels, the styling.

"So what do you think?" I said.

He said, "Let me put it this way. This car was never the intricate, high-performance vehicle equivalent to, say, a modern-day Benz. It was more like the 1923 version of today's Jaguar—hot, sporty."

Mom said, "This car was meant to turn heads."

Yay, Mom. It did that, especially, I thought, *with a flapper behind the wheel.*

"It's even got the factory hood emblem made of cloisonné?" Brian said. "This car is fleek."

Mom looked at me quizzically.

"Like perfect," I said.

A breeze blew my hair into my face, and I brushed it behind my ears. We meandered to the rear of the car.

Brian's eyes were bright. "A collector would love this."

"What if I were the collector?" I said. "What about customization and all that?"

"What do you mean?" Mom said. "Why would you keep it?"

I tried not to glare. I'm sure her question sounded innocuous to someone who didn't know my mother, but I knew her. I was running this show, not her.

Brian looked over the trunk at me with a serious mien. "Don't get me wrong, this would be cool to customize. But you might want to consider going original."

"Original?"

"Original color paint and factory materials or close knockoffs—make it look like it did off the showroom floor."

"No shaved door handles? No chopped roof?"

He laughed. "You remembered. But no, none of those."

"So who does that kind of work?" Mom asked. "You?"

He blew a stream of air from his mouth. "That's not really our specialty. We only do custom. But I can refer Melanie to the best."

"I hate to be so blatant," I said, "but any wild guesses for what 'going original' would cost?"

Mom nodded. She wanted to know the same thing.

"Not gonna be cheap, I'm afraid," Brian said. "Could run fifty thousand dollars."

"What?" I said.

"You're kidding, right?" Mom said.

"No, ma'am," Brian said. "I know it's sticker shock. But it takes special skill to put these cars back together inside and out. Collectors are paying for someone's decades of know-how. Refurbishing old engines. Finding rare parts or fabricating ones to fit."

I felt my whole body sag. Fifty grand was unreal. So now what? I guess that made my decision right there: I sell it "as is" and use the cash for trips and investments. Otherwise, what was I going to do? Hold on to the car in paid storage for another ten years?

I rubbed my forehead. I wouldn't add this to my worry list right now. I had enough weighing on me with work.

"That's a steep number, Brian," Mom said. "Melanie, you could get your MBA for what that costs."

Really? She just landed the annual jab in the ribs about my going to grad school? Here? Now? My getting a master's had long been one of her dreams for me, not mine. Mom accomplished getting one herself. Would she never let it rest where I was concerned? I'd been about as patient as I could be today. But that one irked me.

It almost made me want to restore the car just to spite her. To show her I was my own woman.

"Ray's Restorations does original work," Brian said, "if you want to get a solid quote. Don't hold me to that price. It's like someone asking how much a wedding costs. All depends on how expensive the flowers and band are." He chuckled.

Mom and I exchanged glances. Brian had unwittingly hit on another nerve. The day I watched as Mom called the wedding venue and photographer to cancel on my behalf was a low point for me. It was also a rare time that Angie Barnett had the gray pallor of defeat. She hated that Jason, who'd become part of our family over three years, was suddenly going to be gone. But the save-the-date postcards had already gone out, too, so she'd also be embarrassed with her friends.

"Can I get in?" Brian asked.

"Sure, please do." *And*, I thought, *it would change this subject.*

Brian climbed into the passenger side and slammed the door. These old doors were heavy.

"Mom, hop on in the driver's seat," I said, trying to quash my irritation. "I don't think you've ever been in it."

"I haven't." She got in and said, "It's a lot smaller in here than modern cars, isn't it? And why aren't there any windows in the doors?"

Brian explained that cars had "window curtains" back then—plastic coverings that snapped in and out. "It's another one of those specialized kind of parts that restorers would have to make," he said.

"Looks like the tow truck's arriving," I said.

The rollback truck, as Brian had termed it, was slowly backing down the driveway making a loud beeping sound. He'd said an ordinary tow truck would not do.

Mom started directing the driver with her arms the way a road crew did when painting yellow lines on new pavement.

"Mom," I said, so Brian wouldn't hear, "remember, they're reporting to Brian. Not us. And he's on it."

"Okay, but I don't want tire tracks four inches deep in the yard."

I rolled my eyes. "They'll do their best."

Brian's guys had the truck's whole long flatbed lowering, tilting toward the concrete slab by the open bay door. He guided the workers in attaching thick straps to my Jordan. The car got pulled on, and the flatbed rose up to its horizontal position.

I walked inside Violet's carriage house and made a circle. It felt hollow in here now—like my parents' living room when Dad hauled off our Christmas tree. Only lonelier.

As the truck drove out of the driveway, something tugged on my heartstrings, worse than I'd even expected. First the house. Now the car.

"Brian, what can you tell us about selling the car?" Mom asked.

Tell *us*? I would make any selling decisions, not her. Why had I agreed to let her come?

"He's nice. And cute," Mom said when Brian was gone and we got in her car. "He's very helpful, but—"

"No buts, Mom. I don't need counseling."

I glared out the windshield. I'd really been trying not to get ruffled today. But I wasn't up for her needling.

"Wouldn't it be best to just sell the car and be done?" she said, unable to let things drop.

"What, and use the money to get an MBA? Please don't ever suggest that again. I'm not a freshman in high school anymore with you ruling over my every choice of elective. I'm twenty-eight years old and on my own track."

She huffed, rounding the corner. "You're really thinking of keeping it then?"

I groaned. "Grape Aunt Violet left it for me. And I got it out of *your* space, per deadline." My voice was definitely tight. "I might very well sell the car. I might not. But it's my decision that I'll make in my own time."

When I graduated from UK, my heart led me to bourbon—inspired by Violet's stories, like when Kentucky distilleries converted bourbon production into war alcohol during WWII, which was used for making synthetic rubber for tires, plastics for airplanes, and antifreeze to help win the war. I didn't let go of her tales and history.

But then, did I get a job doing marketing in that field? No. I listened to Mom, who bragged up a position at a Fortune 500 insurance company where her colleague could pull some strings.

"It's higher pay at entry level," Mom said.

As a twenty-two-year-old just getting out on my own, that did hold appeal.

"And, of course," she went on, "you'd get a great benefits package. You'd work in the company headquarters, too, Melanie."

I was young and decided to take the job with its impressive bullet on my résumé.

Our department developed publications for promoting to corporate clients. I didn't hate the work. I learned a lot. But to me, our product—insurance—was something everyone needed but nobody wanted.

After a year, I left. I could've gone to a big spirits corporation—one with several brands of bourbon and other liquors. And maybe one day I would. But when I found Goldenrod, it felt right to me. When I told my parents, it was Dad who said, *We support you, honey, no matter what.*

"And you know what, Mom?" I said now as she drove west. "Where my life is concerned, I'll do whatever makes me happy."

"Okay, Melanie," she said. "I just thought, as busy as you are with work, you don't have time to—"

"You're the one who bought me a Franklin Planner when I was fourteen," I said.

It'd been a birthday present. It came in a zippered faux-leather case. And as for my hectic schedule, even when I was in middle school, I often overheard her speaking to friends.

"Melanie runs track, plays in concert band, takes art lessons, gets straight As, is on the summer swim team, active in church youth group, and babysits."

She wore my "busy-ness" in the way a sheriff wears a silver star badge. As my mother's only child, all the eggs in her mothering basket fell to me. I was her project. I had to perform. I had to achieve. I had to make her look good.

There was one thing I wanted to do as a kid that I hadn't gotten to do—one extracurricular that I wanted but that Mom discouraged. Yet I wouldn't dwell on that sad case right now.

Mom was right about one thing. I was stretched thin. Work. The car. Dealing with *her*. And coping with life's disappointments. The car was now off to an environmentally controlled storage unit. It gave me reprieve to wait to decide its fate if I wanted to.

And I would decide without taking her wishes into consideration.

CHAPTER 10

Violet

Detroit, Michigan
July 1921

I jumped from deep sleep at the stomp of footsteps and coarse coughs outside my door—and I had to orient myself as to where I was. The boardinghouse. Oh yes. I rolled over, away from the window's dawn light. I prayed I'd get used to this ruckus. I hadn't known I'd miss the soft patter of Mother's feet outside my door. But I already did.

Soon, I scurried to pin up my hair, put on a day dress, and swish tooth powder around in my mouth with a brush. I mustn't be late for breakfast, or I wouldn't get to eat at all. Butterflies fluttered in my stomach as they had on the first day of school when I was a child. But I followed the smell of bacon, eggs, and coffee and the sounds of conversation to the dining room.

"You can sit by me," a pretty young woman with red hair said. "I'm Sarah."

I sat at the large oval table, and others gave friendly hellos. I introduced myself, and only one person asked where I was from with my accent, but everyone else nodded.

Sarah said, "I've got to eat and run to prep for my second graders. But it's nice meeting you."

"You're a teacher?" I said happily as she stood. "My mother taught."

"Mine, too. I look forward to spending more time with you, Violet." That was nice.

Hannah, a Polish woman who'd followed her brother to the States, sat on my other side. We conversed, mindful, I thought, to understanding each other's speech that was new to our ears.

"My brother works the line at Ford," she said. "I'm a tobacco stripper at a cigar factory."

"I wonder if Kentucky tobacco is used in your cigars," I said.

I had new friends on day one. I began to relax. Mrs. Sturgeon appeared and set plates before Hannah and me. There were no grits, but the food tasted better than I'd feared. I enjoyed the zwieback toast.

Afterward, I found the landlady alone in the kitchen.

"I've got only a few minutes," she said. "Cleaning day, you know."

"It's about the safe you have for residents?"

She pulled her agreement out of a drawer. "You can sign it and slip it under my door."

The agreement included blanks for how much money I had, and that I willingly gave it to her for safekeeping; that she agreed to return it to me at my request, in whatever increments I chose; and that we'd both keep accurate records. She didn't charge interest. Everything seemed fair. But how did I know she wasn't leeching off unsuspecting newcomers? Yet I'd learned she opened the house when her husband died of the Spanish flu, and I reasoned that her reputation would've suffered by now if she swindled people. So I trusted her to guard my emergency fund. I signed by day's end.

A resident told me where I could find the nearest telegram office. How I wished that I could telephone Mother instead. I would love to hear her voice. But long-distance calls could run two dollars per minute—while telegrams were two cents a word.

I kept it short: Arrived safe STOP All well STOP Miss you STOP Sending love STOP

~

On Monday, I left the boardinghouse half an hour ahead of my job orientation, though Oliver, an accountant who lived at the house, had said it would take ten minutes by streetcar at most. He gave me directions. I wouldn't take any chances on being late at the Jubert-Dufour factory.

I arrived early and strolled the block back and forth across the boards of the sidewalk. The July morning was muggy, and the exhaust from delivery trucks lining the street made me cover my mouth. It was a working-class commercial area. Men in newsboy caps nodded as they rushed past. I peeked in a plate glass window of a dairy distributor with its artful display of spotted cows and filled buckets of milk.

At last I opened the door and entered the small lobby space. It was drab, uninviting. No place to sit. No clerical girl to greet me the way I had greeted visitors at Labrot and Graham. And I couldn't name the smell of this place. Industrial. Or metallic. Harsh. I had tried not to dress fancy for this engagement, but certainly came clean and neat in my plain day dress and low-heeled shoes. But I wondered now if my hat that was on the prettier side was too much.

I was glad my dress covered my knees so no one would see them knocking. Mr. Adams, from Ford back home, had described to me what spark plugs did. Simply put, cars needed three things to run: fuel, air, and spark. Spark plugs were small but powerful components, working with a car's cylinders to help an engine propel a car forward.

A short, burly man with whiskers and wearing laborer clothes came through after a time and asked, "Who are you?"

"I'm Violet Bond to meet Mr. Giddens," I said. I wanted badly to make a good first impression. "For orientation as a new employee."

The gruff man glared. "You what? I can't understand a word you said except I know it's English. Better than some women around here."

"Beg your pardon?" I guessed my southern accent perplexed him, so I spoke more slowly. "We had an appointment. I'm the one who mailed my application, and my former employer from Labrot and Graham sent you a reference, too."

My old boss, Mr. Baker, had not written of my work in the sales office, but rather of my stint doing labeling on the distillery's bottling line. He'd given me a copy. *Miss Bond is one of the fastest learners on the line, with nimble fingers, precision in her work, and ability to keep up production.*

"Right," the man before me said. "I'm Giddens. Follow me."

I expected the factory to have more noise, more action, more energy in the way Robert Neumann had described the massive Ford plant the day we met. But what I found was a warehouse filled with table after table where women sat on what appeared to be little more than wooden crates without backs. But for quickly glancing once my way, they worked with their heads down and their hands up.

I felt out of place, shaky. But I had to remember why I was here. It was a means to an end: employment and freedom. Father had forbidden me to drive, and while he hadn't lived long enough to see it, one day I'd own my own car—one that might even hold the very spark plugs I made.

Mr. Giddens rooted through some bins and grabbed a fistful of pieces. There were ten workers to a table, and their tables were covered with open wooden boxes the size of those that had held Father's boots. This factory might be freezing come winter, but it was hot, stuffy, and had little circulation this summer. I removed my hat.

Would I be able to stand it in here for eight hours a day?

The working women were young like me and wore plain dresses with smocks or aprons. Their hair was uniformly pulled and pinned up out of their faces. Other long tables contained what I assumed were finished products lined flush end to end in row after row: white spark plugs about as wide and as long as the handle of my hairbrush.

The manager said, "See these? An insulator, a gasket, a shell, a terminal, some steel threads, and electrodes. You don't gotta know what they do. You just put 'em together like a puzzle."

"I can do this," I said with conviction, despite some doubt. But I had bills for the first time in my life: rent. I needed money. "Do you have a diagram? Of how the parts go together?"

"Oh, she needs a picture, does she?"

I could feel my eyes going wide at his manner. Mother had taught me never to be so rude.

"Sure, we'll draw you a diagram," he said. "When you start tomorrow." He pointed to the rear table of the room. "You'll sit back there. Josie will show you the ropes. You've got one week to prove you can keep up."

One week? Keep up with what? I didn't know I'd moved all the way here for nothing more than a trial period.

"How many spark plugs do workers assemble per day?" I asked. He'd already turned to go, but he paused and looked back over his shoulder.

"Smart girl, aren't ya? I've gotta get another box of insulators off the truck. Eight a.m. sharp, Violet from *Ken-tuck-y*." He mimicked my name and my drawl, and I felt a sting of hurt. "Bring a bagged lunch. We quit at five thirty."

"Thank you, Mr. Giddens. I'm excited to join the company."

I had gainful employment at an automotive supplier in the car capital of the world. As long as I met the quota, I wouldn't just be earning a wage, I decided, I'd be helping modern people be mobile. I would prove that I could keep up. But I'd have to deal with Mr. Giddens's coarse behavior. So insulting. I'd seen that Father had dealt with rude people, too—like his customer Mrs. Heaty who bought a pound of flour and returned half of it the next week, saying, *Mr. Bond, your flour is riddled with bugs. I demand a full refund.* Father subscribed to the philosophy that "the customer is always right" and put up with it. Here, I would subscribe to the philosophy that "the boss pays my wages" and put up with it.

I had a dream for my life, and I wouldn't let gruff Mr. Giddens ruin it. I wouldn't go back to Kentucky and be relegated to marrying like my sister had. No, I couldn't fail here.

Given the schedule, I had figured out that I wouldn't miss breakfast or dinner at the house. That in itself was worth celebrating.

I was so excited, I forgot to refer to Oliver's map to find my way back to the house.

The trip required a transfer from one streetcar to another, but I'd missed my stop. We were passing businesses I hadn't seen before—a high school, a motor garage. An uncertainty snuck up within me. An uneasiness.

No signage hung above the windows to help. I could check with the conductor, but I'd ride it a bit first. I'd stay alert, like a mouse scoping out cheese.

Then a little girl in the seat across the way smiled a toothless grin at me. Did she sense my confusion? I smiled warmly back. Her dolly was all dressed in lace and had skin as brown as hers. It continued to surprise me to see Black people on a streetcar with everyone else, unlike in the South. It was a good surprise. The girl cuddled into her mother whose arm was wrapped around her.

"I love you, Mama."

"I love you, too, Josephine." The mother kissed the top of her head.

It gave me a pang in my heart to watch. I hadn't known I'd miss my mother so. One minute, I rose defiant; Mr. Giddens wouldn't get me down. The next minute, I closed my eyes, remembering the contentment of Mother's arms around me, and the smell of her floral shampoo.

Mother was brilliant. She knew there are things in life that can't be taught—except by one's experience. I had her money in my pocketbook. I could hop a train home tomorrow if I chose.

But I would choose to stay the course. I was learning that independence wasn't all I'd imagined it to be. With rewards came risks and trade-offs and sacrifices.

The streetcar stopped, and the mother and daughter rose to get off hand in hand. I peered out the window again. Was that Jasper's Market I'd seen before? I stood to follow the others to the front to confirm. The mother and I nodded at each other in the aisle, friendly, and Josephine and I waved.

"Have a good day," I said.

"You do the same," the woman said.

"Goodbye," the sweet girl said to the conductor.

But he scowled at her real mean. I roiled. No one had ever looked at me that way. Then he shooed her mother down the steps as if she were an insect. I saw the profile of her face wilt.

I ignored the conductor's polite farewell to me and got off as fast as I could. My heart hurt for the small loving family. I wish I could've said something kind to them outside, but they'd hurried away too quickly.

CHAPTER 11

Violet

Detroit, Michigan
August 1921

I sat at the assembly table with nine other women, each of us wet as if we'd just come out of the river. This was sweat, not mere perspiration. It dripped from my forehead and nose onto the pieces I snapped together. I rubbed my forehead with the back of my arm, bare from the elbow down. It did no good. I had gotten used to the metallic smell of this place, but I'd not gotten used to the sweltering heat this first week, even with high windows wide open and electric fans whirling. But I kept humping to finish more spark plugs.

Today was the last day of my trial, and I was behind to meet my quota. I needed my pay. I needed this work. I needed not to fail.

The norm was one completed spark plug per three minutes—or 160 in an eight-hour day. That was eight hundred a week per girl. The best gals like Josie, who sat beside and trained me, completed one every two minutes and got paid more. No wonder no one talked while they worked. It'd taken me five minutes per product when I began the week, and though I'd gotten faster each day, I was scrambling to catch up by the end of Friday's clock. First-timers had a fifty-spark-plug grace period in week one, and even with that, I had to knock out forty more spark plugs today than norm. I was throwing finished parts in the bin as fast as I could, bearing in on two minutes per plug.

The tips of my fingers were calloused from snapping or screwing metal pieces together. The work wore on my eyes and on my back, too, but Josie said I'd get used to it.

"Time for lunch," she said.

"I'm going to work through lunch."

Everyone scrambled to their cubbies with no time to spare. We had thirty minutes sharp to eat and use the ladies' facilities and rest a few minutes with coworkers. I'd packed a sliced turkey sandwich, an apple, and water. And a molasses cookie. Mrs. Sturgeon provided food for lunch for an extra fee. But it would go home with me later.

Mr. Giddens passed me for the first time all day.

"How are you?" I said while I snapped and screwed, not looking up.

"I'd be better if the gaskets arrived in the shipment we need. Just got word they're gonna be late."

Oh no. I prayed there'd be enough parts for me to meet my quota.

"They were supposed to arrive Thursday, weren't they?" I asked.

"It's not Thurs*dee*," he said. "It's Thurs*day*. It's a day."

I felt his spittle land on my neck—quite a feat given I was already soaked. He huffed off and made a snide remark to one of the Polish girls, insinuating she was fat.

He was nothing like my old boss.

Communication was a constant topic. Two Polish women attended classes each night to learn to speak English, and the company paid for the course. I understood their accents better than most, as I had my friend Hannah at the house. She'd told me of her brother's attendance in Ford Motor Company's Americanization program at the big manufacturing plant. The Poles had sessions in language, personal hygiene, and civics. Then at commencement, Ford staged an immigrant ship. The pupils came down the gangplank and then into a giant melting pot. They came out wearing new clothes and waving American flags. I wasn't sure how immigrants as a whole felt about that program, but Hannah said only that she and her brother were grateful to be in a land of opportunity.

The Polish Catholic women here worked hard, but Mr. Giddens was even meaner to them than he was me.

Later, I dared to lift my eyes from my work to check the clock. Fifty-five minutes to go. I started another box. So far, the parts hung in for me. Bam. Another spark plug down. Bam another. I was in a rhythm now. My sister could sit down beside me and I wouldn't know it.

Four minutes before the horn blew, I threw my last one in the box. I was done. I was huffing so hard I thought I would cry. I crossed my arms on my workspace before me and rested my head atop. Josie was leader of this table, and soon her records confirmed. I'd met my first week's quota. I was too tired to be thrilled.

When I heard Mr. Giddens making his way around the tables with pay, I lifted my head. "Here's yours," he said as he went. When he got to me, everything faded away—the pain, the fear, the hunger, the insults. I collected my wages: 25 percent more than I'd earned at the distillery sales office. And that was just meeting quota, not going over.

My smile must've looked silly to others on the streetcar that night. I didn't care. I'd done it.

Mrs. Sturgeon's small group of residents disembarked the Belle Isle bus, a thirty-two-passenger open-sided bus where every seat had been filled. Weekend social outings didn't come along often for the boardinghouse group, but it was good for me to socialize despite how tired I was from work. For decades, this island in the Detroit River had been the largest park in Michigan. Sunshine and the scent of fresh-cut grass made me glad I came—with summer air in my lungs away from the factory floor. It felt good to dress a bit pretty, too. My leisure outfit included a box-pleated skirt, a cotton hip-length top, and a large-crowned hat all in cream. I wore summer gloves, because my fingers were nicked and I had one scab.

I scanned the vista laden with black-eyed Susans, yellow coneflowers, and red and purple zinnias, bringing to mind happy days with Father. He used to love flowers, and when I was a tot, he'd roll me around the yard in his wheelbarrow, pretending like he was going to dump me out, while I held tight and giggled all the way. He would've been entranced by this place.

"Mrs. Sturgeon," I said, "I've never set foot on an island before."

"There's a first time for us all. Look that way," she said, pointing to the northeast. "Across the river is Canada."

I would buy Mother and Evelyn postcards, letting them know that I'd already glimpsed a foreign country.

Everyone chimed in their favorite recreations on the Isle—the conservatory, the aquarium, a bicycle ride, a relaxing stroll down Central Avenue lined with trees.

Sarah and I moseyed to the picnic tables in the trees. There was a tall, striking man chatting with Mrs. Sturgeon now. Then he seemed to look right at me, with his hand shading his eyes from a shaft of dappled light. Robert Neumann? Was it him? This movie-star-looking gentleman whom I met when I was eighteen? So I was destined to see him again after all. Good. I couldn't imagine what he was doing here, but I'd welcome the chance to thank him for referring the boardinghouse two years back.

As Sarah trailed off to see Hannah, Robert took a few steps my way. My, but he was handsome—even more so than I remembered. More self-assured and mature than before. And would he think I, too, had changed? Though, I shouldn't have a care what he thought.

"Hello, Violet," he said.

He remembered my name? He stood with his hands in the pockets of his summer suit. A breeze caught his straw boater, and he raised his hand to steady it. "I learned only yesterday," he said, "that you'd made the leap to our city. I hope you're settling in well at the boardinghouse."

"Very well, thank you, and thank you for the referral," I said. The breeze now fluttered in my eyelashes and hair. "Your aunt's an excellent landlady. I was glad I'd kept her address."

So now the pleasantries were over. I should move on. I should help set out the picnic and mingle with friends.

"And you're working?" he asked, looking at me from beneath his dark brows. So attractive.

"Yes," I said. "As a matter of fact, I assemble spark plugs. So let me thank you again."

He laughed, and it was a welcome sound to my ears.

"And you?" I said. "Still on the road?"

"All the time. It's a wonder I'm here today." He looked around the place. "Auntie called to invite me. She and my late mother used to bring my brothers and me here as kids. We used to play stickball on the other side of the island."

I smiled, imagining him as a boy. Rough and rowdy.

"There's woodlands and water here. Ever hear of Frederick Olmsted? He designed the landscape for Central Park in New York. He had a hand in Belle Isle, too."

"Fascinating. I enjoy details like that." I loved getting the insider's take on my new city. "Well," I said, "good to see you."

I took a first step away. I didn't wish to lead him on—or worse, get other curious lips here flapping. Or incite a glare from his aunt.

"Wonderful to see you, too," he said, looking as if he wished the conversation hadn't stopped.

I took two more steps.

"Oh, and Violet," I heard him call lightly, though I hoped none of the other revelers would hear him above their laughter and telling of jokes.

"If you'd like to go rowing in a canoe today, it'd be a nice diversion. We could float by the great conservatory designed by Albert Kahn. It was inspired by The Crystal Palace of London."

The Crystal Palace was from London's Great Exhibition of the mid 1800s. And wouldn't I love to see the conservatory he mentioned? Mother would, too. She had toured us girls through widely varied attractions. The lovely grounds and structures of Louisville's Cave Hill Cemetery. The glorious Seelbach hotel with its decor fashioned after fancy places in Europe. I did so enjoy interesting places.

Robert kinked his head left. "A canoe ride could be a *Treasure Island* adventure."

I managed a laugh. He had taken me aback—and not for the first time. He remembered the novel I'd been reading when he arrived at the office long ago.

"I do hope you're not afraid of the water," Robert teased.

"Never," I snapped back, defiantly but friendly. "When I was a girl, my grandfather took me fishing for smallmouth bass at Elkhorn Creek. We'd cast our lines from seats on mammoth rocks, and sometimes I'd wade in to my knees."

"Impressive. Given you are an official newcomer to Detroit," Robert said, "if you change your mind, I'll rent a canoe. We'll each have our own oar, and I'll expect you to hold your own." He winked.

"Ha! Thank you, but I'll be taking a nature walk. With the girls."

Again I turned to go. And this time I didn't look back.

Sarah was waving me over. It was time to dig in to Mrs. Sturgeon's picnic of fried chicken legs, triangle sandwiches filled with chopped boiled eggs, and sliced canned pineapple.

I made sure to sit at a table far away from Robert Neumann. I hadn't come all this way to the city to latch on to a man.

CHAPTER 12

Melanie

Louisville, Kentucky
July 2018

I hadn't come all this way to the city to latch on to a man.

I'd already worked a few hours from bed on my marketing plan for the Bourbon and Books program and other projects, but it was Sunday so I caught up on laundry and reading. Some entries—such as the streetcar conductor's treatment of the lovely Black mother and daughter—gave me a deeper understanding of Violet's later work in civil rights.

Her journal also made me think of my personal life: the way she thought Robert was so handsome but was adamant about keeping her distance was exactly how I felt about Brian. Now I wanted to decipher the significance of the *Saturday Evening Post* that she'd bequeathed to me.

Then an email notification dinged.

My buddy who works at the Fest enjoyed talking to you Friday, Mitchell wrote, copying our boss Cora on the weekend. Such a suck-up. You got him excited to have our brand on his lineup. I suspect there's room to negotiate—to knock the sponsor fee down by five grand. Thought you should know. Every dollar helps. See ya tomorrow.

I typed as fast as two thumbs could fly. He was either showing off or trying to show me up.

You think I didn't already ask him that, Mitchell? What kind of rookie negotiator do you take me for? I even asked for more than that, you effing big shot wannabe. Then I hit backspace, backspace, backspace. Delete. Maybe I should sound less spiteful.

I was ticked. But was it purely an annoyance, or something more? Was I afraid that I wouldn't measure up to my competition for the advancement after all?

It would do me no good to psych myself out.

Retype to Mitchell: Cool. I'm glad the progress I made had its desired effect. Cora and I discussed it earlier, and we both had a good feeling about the $7K reduction I asked for.

There. Done. Sent.

The only thing worse would be an email from Mom. Was I holding a grudge? I hated to think that's what this was. But I didn't like her controlling behaviors, her insinuations about selling the car or about Brian or Jason or grad school or anything else. Especially after I'd tried so hard to get along. She and I could continue to chill for a while.

I slipped the *Saturday Evening Post* from its protective sleeve for the first time. The clear plastic crackled with every touch. The cover had Rockwell's drawing of a farm boy standing upside down on one hand and balancing with his legs bent like a frog's. Why had Violet left this with her journal?

I smiled in noting how the 1923 issue cost only five cents. Yet it was larger in dimensions than a modern magazine—three or four inches wider each way and heavy, too. No flimsy, glossy sheets like today. I brought it to my nose, and the paper smelled musty, as if it'd been buried in an attic for generations. It made me feel closer to Violet.

I took in the pages with their old-fashioned ads for Del Monte canned fruits and Campbell's pork and beans. Those brands went back that far, huh? I came upon an ad for a "Buick Closed Car," black-and-white with a no-frills picture; it listed the various models and prices. Another black-and-white ad was for an automaker I'd never heard of, Packard. The copy claimed a "fine car free of the haunting thought of costly maintenance."

"The Sunny Side of Thirty," a short story with a drawing of a fashionable young woman, caught my attention.

> . . . if one is to have a big family of children, it is a good idea to make some sort of plan in that direction before thirty, especially if one belongs to the sex that bears the physical burden of the children's arrival.

This was a story of a woman's biological clock? It could be a story today.

I was twenty-eight years old, and I'd thought I had a plan. A man. A future. Jason and I agreed we'd have children—two, not an only child as I was. But with our split, that dream ended. The most important man to ever come into my life—my one-and-only forever man, my destiny, my betrothed, *my person*—had taught me that love and career were incompatible. I could have one or the other. Not both.

Aunt Violet led a wonderful life, free from love entanglements, fulfilled in her work and philanthropies. She didn't need a man even in an age when most women married. I didn't need one, either. Even if I had doubts, now she confirmed it.

What is this?

From between two pages, the pointy corner of something poked out. An envelope like I'd buy at CVS. I opened the magazine at the spot, and then I noticed the page that the envelope marked. JORDAN. It was jarring. The automobile's logo was in huge bold letters at the bottom of an ad for my car. I set the envelope aside. Was this what Violet intended for me to see?

The headline read: Somewhere West of Laramie. Intriguing.

The ad's artwork was a stylized colored drawing as if someone had sketched it out quickly using colored pencils, leaving the scene's edges jagged and fading. A rough outline of a mountain served as backdrop, but in the foreground, unlike in all the other car ads, a scene was in full motion: a cowboy in a blue-checked shirt rode horseback with one arm outstretched and his hat in his hand as he raced against a big car—a convertible doused in blue shadow and light.

And the car was driven by a woman.

The woman wore a flapper-girl hat snug to her head, and that's all we viewers could see—besides *her* scarf and the *cowboy's* bandanna billowing behind them in the wind as they raced.

She was leading the race.

Goose bumps tickled my arms. This historical ad for Violet's model of car showed a woman beating a man in a race. In 1923. Wow.

When I was a child, she said, *You know, this is a girl's car*. I was beginning to get it now.

I started reading the ad's considerable body copy, at first through the eyes of a marketer.

> The truth is—the Playboy was built for her.
>
> Built for the lass whose face is brown with the sun
> when the day is done of revel and romp and race.
>
> She loves the cross of the wild and the tame.

Ooh. Ooh. Ooh. Wild and tame? This sentiment was in an ad a hundred years ago?

Now I read through the eyes of a young woman almost a century before—through the eyes of my aunt.

> There's a savor of links about that car—of laughter and lilt and light—a hint of old loves—and saddle and quirt. It's a brawny thing—yet a graceful thing for the sweep o' the Avenue.
>
> Step into the Playboy when the hour grows dull with things gone dead and stale.
>
> Then start for the land of real living with the spirit of the lass who rides, lean and rangy, into the red horizon of a Wyoming twilight.

Damn. The word *damn* rang in my head as if it held two syllables. *Da-um.* I read the full ad again—every line aloud this time, to hear the sounds of the words play together. This writing was poetry and beauty and magic and seduction.

It was art.

I wished my aunt could've shared this magazine with me while she lived. I wanted to hold her in my arms now, to feel her bony shoulder digging into mine. I wanted to hear from her own two lips about the *wild* side of her life. I only knew her side that was *tame*. I wanted to ask her juicy questions. To see if her wrinkled face blushed. I wanted to hear her laugh with her silver-haired head thrown back.

But I smiled. I had her journal.

Perhaps Violet didn't have the responsibilities of family, but she still had flings with men in her youth. Would I read of her having one with Robert? Was it something else for me to ponder, say, with regard to Brian? A fling? I didn't know.

Something propelled me to google the ad. Article after article emerged in my feed. The Jordan Motor Company had forever changed the automotive industry's approach to advertising. A whole series of ads in the campaign promoted not the car's features but the spirit of the car and appealed to emotions. It ran in other magazines, too, like *Vanity Fair*. I read where *Ad Age*, the premier modern trade rag for advertising, ranked the campaign as one of the top thirty of the whole twentieth century—in the mix with Nike's *Just Do It* and Budweiser's *This Bud's for you.*

It pitched the car specifically to the young independent woman of the roaring twenties—the one who got to vote and smoked cigarettes and wore her skirts short.

Damn. Two syllables. This was my aunt.

The Jordan ad pioneered the work that marketers like me would one day do . . . understanding consumers and creating messages to reach them.

It hit me that I'd have to use the car campaign in the Cocktail Bash somehow. Creativity bred creativity, and I was having an idea on how to bring this campaign to bourbon women—to tie it to the historical period of the 1920s. I would flesh this out later in the week.

I hadn't gotten to the year 1923 in Violet's journal yet, and I wasn't going to skip ahead, but to her, I thought, the car must've stood for freedom or adventure. Almost a century later, she had never let it go.

I was sad to think of selling the car now. In fact, selling it felt wrong. Now I was sure. I'd have to keep it somehow.

I gingerly opened the flap of the envelope that was blank. There was an old black-and-white photograph. A caption on the back said: *A day I'll never forget 1923*. The year the Jordan was produced.

Two lovely young women stood in a wide sweep of lawn. In the distant background was a mansion that made Mom and Dad's country French two-story look like a shack. The women were posed as if for a modern Facebook post—squeezed in together and each with a hand on her waist, elbows out.

They looked fun—like girls my friends and I would enjoy partying with. Were they girlfriends? Or two beautiful young lovers? Or sisters?

One had to be Violet, though I'd never seen a photograph of her at this age. I studied it.

The taller had on one of those flapper-girl hats, but she had light-colored eyes and cheekbones resembling my aunt's. A knee-length, light-colored coat hung open on her—with fur trim despite the clear sunny day. And the slightly shorter woman was in a sleeveless top and a skirt with the waistline riding low on her hips. She looked as though she had wrapped a scarf into her dark cropped hair, like a wide makeshift headband. Her top had a monogram sewn at its center: *LH.*

I wanted to know more. My aunt had left her cherished objects for a reason . . . the car, the journal, the magazine, the photo. She'd taught me much that influenced my career.

What else did she have to teach me?

CHAPTER 13

Violet

Detroit, Michigan
August 1921

I scribbled numbers and expenses on my pad in my room.

I was finding my budget harder to manage than I foresaw. Little things added up. Postage stamps, telegram services, lunches for my break, and weekend matinees with the girls. But I'd splurged on a couple of dresses and a pair of shoes. There had only been just so much space in my trunk. At some point, I would go out for more entertainments, but this past week, my wages were gone two days before my next pay, even with my going slightly past quota. And I was already thinking about my train ticket to go home for Christmas.

I wouldn't dare touch my nest egg. That was for emergencies—and saving for things like a car. Though that would be far into the future. Even if I could afford one now, there were never enough empty spots to park on the street where I lived. So many Ford Model Ts in this town.

Perhaps the biggest surprise of late was that Ford man Robert Neumann appeared in my mind more than once a day since the Belle Isle outing. He was attractive, smart, sweet, witty. Trouble. At least for a girl like me.

I was thrilled to have a letter from home. Home was how I still thought of it. This house with my tiny room, comfortable though it was, and where I now lay my head, wasn't yet.

I sliced open a letter, giddy as always. I kept each one neat in a shoebox to reread when I was lonely. I heard Evelyn's voice as I read her words.

> Dearest Violet,
> I miss you! And I'm glad to hear of your outing at the park with friends from the house. Everyone here asks about you.
>
> Charles is busy with law cases, and I'm decorating the kitchen. Yes! Out with the green and in with the yellow. I chose this all myself.
>
> There is, however, something troubling that I must share. About Mother. I thought you'd want to know, but please keep this to yourself.

Please God, don't let Mother be ill. I couldn't bear it.

> I won't belabor all the details, but Mother has not been totally open about her financial picture. Yes, she's taken on six tutoring students now—and loves it, thank goodness. But it seems Father left her with more debt than we knew. Honestly, I think she held back, because she didn't want any worry to interfere with our lives. She point-blank told me: "Don't dare tell Violet. There's a reason I didn't tell her before. I wouldn't stand in her way of having her dream in the city."
>
> She says she'll make do. But the long and short of it is, the property taxes are weighing on her, and the

> life insurance monies won't last as long as she'd hoped. She actually pulled her back out (It's okay now! Don't fret!) lifting the birdbath to another spot in the yard. Can you believe that?

No, I could not believe a single word of this. I thought I might faint, though I was lying down flat.

> Mother fervently says she's done bringing in help for the house once a month. But rest assured, dear sister, Mother will not be attempting things that Father or you once did anymore. Charles and I will help her.
>
> My question for you is, might you devise a way to send her a little money each month? Just say that things are so swell that you had it in mind all along? Or some such.
>
> Do not worry. She hasn't sold off Grandmother's good china. It's not that dire. Go off and have fun. Like Mother said: you have only one life.
>
> Love,
>
> Evelyn

Now what was I supposed to do? I rubbed my head for its throbbing. Was sending Mother money enough? Or did she need me to come home—for good?

The next morning was Saturday, and Mrs. Sturgeon waved at me from the rear stoop. I'd gone for a walk to settle my mind and now sat under a tree. I would help Mother. I could definitely be more frugal, and pick up my pace with the spark plugs. But I would stay here. No more splurges on dresses and shoes. I could send Mother 10 percent of my earnings most months. A gift. I would do as my sister suggested and pretend I'd planned it all along.

Now I met my landlady near the clothesline where other residents' pants dripped dry in the sun. "It's a beautiful day," I said. "Not as hot."

"September will be even better," she said. "I was just talking to Robert on the telephone. He'd like you to call him. He's got something you might find of interest."

I didn't wish to appear anxious, nor insult his aunt by acting put off.

"Mind you, Violet," she said as warmly as ever I'd heard her. "My nephew has plenty of girls trailing after him. But he's not the marrying sort."

My eyes popped wide. That might've been the best news I'd heard all week.

"I am not," I said playfully but firmly, "on the marriage market, Mrs. Sturgeon. So I'll not be trailing after him. But thank you. I might give him a call."

"He's here," Sarah said, peeping between the curtains.

Had I lost my mind? No. This was not a date.

I'd read somewhere that no one called it *courting* since couples had been given free rein to go about in automobiles. Young people had complete mobility. Without chaperones. But with courting, a woman invited suitors to her home. Now, the male invited the female. There was something off about that.

On our call, Robert had taken two minutes to get through his pretense of cautioning me to steer clear of the crowds on the Detroit River over Labor Day weekend. The city was hosting an international boat regatta—and hundreds of thousands were expected. Rich people would have fancy tents with caterers. Others would hang from every ledge and dock to watch the fastest speedboats in the world race.

I thanked him for his thoughtfulness. Though the races sounded enticing, it would be best not to get lost in that horde.

Then he said the clincher.

"Do you like chocolate?"

"I love chocolate," I said. My defenses were down.

"I know the best spot in the city for chocolate. If you're free Sunday afternoon, I could take you. Show you some sights on the way."

What was the harm of going for chocolate?

"Okay," I said, with a tiny smile in my voice. "We'll have chocolate."

He and I were just going for dessert. Yet I'd selected my beige midcalf dress with its fringed floating panels that I'd packed with my pointed shoes with Louis heels.

Why had I said yes?

One, he wasn't the marrying sort.

Two, part of my coming here was to see the city, wasn't it?

Three, I missed my family. He was a friend.

Four, he wasn't the marrying sort.

Robert was on the road most of the time, and surely if he wanted a wife waiting at home, he would've snagged one in these last two years.

He came to the porch like a gentleman. I opened the door, and there was his smile that I'd kept going back to in my head for a week, much as I tried not to.

When we took off in his car that he had all shined up, I was at a loss for conversation. I fidgeted in my seat. What would Mother think of me now? Alone in a car with a man?

"We're heading to Woodward Avenue," he said, the main artery of the city, dividing East Detroit from West. "This was the first street in the country to be paved," he said. "Back in 1909, someone decided to try concrete."

We passed through the downtown financial district with far more skyscrapers than Louisville had.

"Cars line the street like a parade," I said, gawking out the window. "And look at all these department stores."

Not that I'd shop anytime soon, with my current money constraints. But there was Hudson's, Crowley's, Newcomb-Endicott, B. Siegel, and more. People scrambled everywhere like ants.

"This avenue makes Louisville look like a village," I said. "My sister would be dizzy."

Robert pulled into a parking spot in front of a store with a red-and-white awning.

"Chocolate?" I asked.

"Fair warning," he said. "Sanders is addictive."

My mouth watered like one of Pavlov's dogs to the sound of a bell. We sat on two swiveling, leather-topped stools at the soda fountain.

Robert told me of his three brothers, one of whom died in the war. We talked of my sister and Charles, of our mutual German heritage. We discussed Prohibition's effect on immigrant groups—taking away the culture of brewers and distillers. Neither one of us liked seeing liquor shut down.

We had no lulls in conversation.

"This is pure decadence," I said of my first-ever hot fudge sundae. It was served in a tall glass, with rich, bittersweet sauce in layers with vanilla ice cream.

"I'm glad you like it." Robert dunked his long spoon into his frosty ice cream soda. "Legend goes," he said, "that in the 1870s, the ice cream soda was invented here."

"Really?"

"The German-born owner had run out of fresh cream for cream sodas, while customers waited in line. He substituted a scoop of ice cream, and ice cream sodas were born."

"You do a nice tour. I like the details." He was sort of like Mother in that way.

"One more stop," he said as we left.

By now, I could've guessed that our next stop, the Highland Park Ford plant, would be the largest manufacturing facility in the world. No matter what it was, if Detroit did it, they took it all the way. The factory was the first to produce cars on a moving assembly line. The building was only four stories tall but spread out with almost a hundred acres under its roof—and it looked to me as if it had more windows than some small cities.

"This factory makes Jubert-Dufour Spark Plugs look as small as a key on a typewriter," I said.

"No tour would be complete without a nod to the home of automobile hysteria."

"Of course not," I said.

"Six years ago, before I worked here," he said, "Henry Ford announced his five-dollar-a-day program. Ten thousand hopefuls crowded the lots outside this building."

"Five dollars a day?" What I could do with that.

He nodded. "They came from farms across the state and all corners of the country. The going rate until then had been two dollars, forty-five cents."

"More than double their daily wage," I said. If my wages were doubled, the first thing I'd do would be to buy tickets for Mother and Evelyn to come visit. Let them see this amazing city themselves.

"At the same time," Robert said, "Ford reduced the workday from nine hours to eight. But there were stipulations to qualify for the higher wage," Robert went on. "Ford sent company investigators to where employees lived to ensure they had clean homes and bank savings accounts, and weren't prone to drunkenness or mistreating their wives."

"I had no idea," I said.

Robert smiled. "These steps all served to attract laborers, reduce turnover—"

"And to influence social reforms," I said.

"Exactly," Robert said. "But nothing is ever all rosy. I might bore you with more another day."

Another day? But he was anything but boring. I enjoyed spending time with him more than I expected.

I wasn't sure how I felt about that.

I'd no sooner put my hat and lunch bag in my cubby at work when I knew I'd have to write in my journal tonight. I'd been making entries about my life every few days, but this morning was not starting off well. As I stepped away from the cubbies, I said hello to Margaret, a fellow employee. She looked right at my face with blazing eyes, lingered a second, and ignored me. I liked to think I was a friendly gal, but that was an odd exchange.

Margaret had started her antics a couple of days before. I was going into the lavatory when she was coming out, and she ran straight into me—shoulder to shoulder. Whop. It wasn't my fault, but I apologized to be polite. Now, she was coming to sit at the lunch table I shared with Josie and a few others. An unusual spot for her.

I ate a bite of my deviled ham salad and went on as if nothing were awkward. Josie and I were talking about her upcoming Labor Day weekend plans to visit family in Muskegon. I crunched on a slice of green apple.

"Little Miss Tender-Hands has been getting a taste of real work," Margaret said in a way intended for me to hear.

I pressed my lips together but kept my sight on my food. But she had to pipe up again.

"Did Miss Bond's maids tire of her perpetual smile and sunny disposition and then up and quit on her?"

Muffled giggles followed, but I didn't even follow what she meant. When I glanced from the corner of my eye at others, their expressions showed empathy. They hadn't known what else to do at her remark.

Then my eyes locked with Josie's. She tilted her head ever so slightly to suggest to me this would pass. She'd worked here longer than anyone.

"Does someone have any hand cream for me to borrow after work?" Margaret said now. "Maybe Miss Bond would share hers."

Enough already. I glared her direction. She screeched her chair on the planks of the floor and got up with a boisterous laugh. No one else made a sound. I wanted to roll my eyes but didn't.

So I was perceived by her to be highfalutin. I'd been raised in a middle class family, the daughter of a merchant, perhaps a more moneyed upbringing than Margaret's. Mother had taught us to respect all others—and that's what I tried to do.

My feelings were bruised to be the mark of harsh comments in front of my peers, but I'd be more careful and get over it. What else would I do? Write to my older sister, whining that a bully hurt my feelings? No. When I was five, Evelyn chased a boy in the neighborhood with her snow shovel because he'd called me names like lizard legs. I laughed inwardly thinking about it. I was over Margaret. What kind of person targets another for having a sunny disposition anyway? There were worse crimes than being perky.

"Margaret O'Connor, looks like you're having too much fun," Mr. Giddens yelled to her, and I jumped. "Aren't you late to be back at your chair? Working? You'll get docked for that, you know." He sneered. "Or fired."

Josie said he'd once fired a girl for less than that—one who had a female emergency and ran to the toilet without asking permission. I went back to my box of parts to assemble, too. I wouldn't miss my quota. I was fast. And accurate. And I didn't get distracted with the parts in my hands. I needed to earn money.

Snap, click, twist. Snap, click, twist. For hours.

How I did miss my sister. I'd written her back with my plan to help Mother. That's what we did in our family, from near or far. It didn't sit right with me that Father had left her in a predicament. I was disappointed. But he had no idea he'd die so soon.

Snap, click, twist. Work here was work—not as fun as the old distillery.

Father was stuck in my mind.

The summer after my freshman year, I was helping at his dry goods store. Evelyn taught piano that summer before her senior year, and Father was off at meetings. I was the only one in the shop when my sister stopped to say hello before her afternoon lessons. I asked her to watch for customers while I ran to the storage room for a minute. I was going to get supplies to spruce up window displays whether Father liked it or not. I hoped it'd be a special surprise.

I stacked two crates on top of each other and climbed up to reach the top shelf on a metal bookcase where empty planters sat. I would fill them with knickknacks and fabrics, rolling pins and pots. When I reached for them, the whole case—four shelves high—wobbled and almost toppled over. I fell back but landed on my feet. But goods had spilled and were scattered in piles. Evelyn heard the crash and came running.

"What happened," she screamed. "Are you okay?"

I was dazed, but I was fine. The storage room, however, was not. Among other things, box after box of scissors had tumbled to the floor. The shop door rang out front with the bells. Father? I was in a frenzied panic.

"It's got to be a customer," Evelyn said. "Go. I'll clean this up."

"But—"

"But nothing. I'm quicker than you."

I helped the patron to a pound of oats and ran back to the storeroom just in time to see Father lording over Evelyn and half the mess. He'd come in the back.

"What in blazes have you done?" he said to her.

My eyes were glued to Evelyn's. He was angry. She shook her head minutely at me.

Father picked up a pair of sewing scissors, the tips dented, black paint chipped off the handles. "I can't sell this pair now. Look." He spread his hands out. "The whole box of inventory is ruined."

"I wanted to give my piano students a present, Father," Evelyn said. She held her head high. "I'm sorry. I thought they'd like the toy tops on the shelf above. It's all my fault."

"You'll pay all your money from teaching piano to help offset this loss," he said. "And you'll not go to the dance this weekend, either, young lady."

"But, Father," I said. "You can't do that to her."

My eyes pled with him and then her. She shook her head no. She was taking this one for me.

"Get back out and help the customers," he said, nodding his head my way.

My sister had lied, had sacrificed for me. She hadn't just sacrificed her money and a dance with a boy she liked. She'd let herself be seen in Father's eyes—Father, with whom she always curried favor, always tried to please—in a negative light.

Snap, click, twist. I scratched my head now with the tip of my pinkie, with metal parts still in my hand.

Yes, women in our family sacrificed for each other, like my sending money to Mother.

As I walked out of the factory to head for the streetcar, I thought about how independence was a trial. It was never going to be *easy*, was it? Never would everything go *smoothly*. Not with work; not with family.

I dodged people on the sidewalk, everyone anxious to get where they were going. The image of Robert Neumann's smiling face appeared in front of me. I was lighter of foot for it after the day I'd had. I wondered if I'd hear from him again. Did I hope so?

Perhaps.

CHAPTER 14

Melanie

Louisville, Kentucky
August 2018

I pedaled and pedaled on the bike at the gym, oblivious to the muted TV. I pumped and pumped and spun and spun. I had to release myself of work stress, a new guy's eyes that lingered on my mind, and the persistent mini–cold war with Mom. I just didn't need the hassle of communication. But she'd texted as though our row in the car coming back from Frankfort hadn't happened.

She said that a few days after the appraisal, the Realtor advised that the carriage house roof, bay doors, and upstairs balcony needed to be replaced first, for safety of prospective buyers—along with two kitchen appliances to improve value. Her message ranted that the scheduling was putting her behind two months. I had little sympathy to muster. I was inwardly thrilled that there was no For Sale sign in front of Violet's beloved house.

Another good thing was that my boss loved my Bourbon and Books program plan. It helped that Cora was in two book clubs. Tanisha would assist in kicking it off in November. Between the Jordan car's magazine ad and having attended the women's bourbon club chapter meeting recently, I was also bouncing around another new idea.

I slowed down the bike's speed. Slower. Slower. Slower. A cooldown before a coast. Deep cleansing breath. Sweat gleamed on my arms as if I'd smeared them with baby oil. If only I smelled closer to baby oil than I did an NBA locker room.

I gingerly got off the bike, bracing for rubber band knees. I grabbed my towel off the handlebar and saw Nicole coming. I hadn't noticed she was here.

"Hey!" I said. It looked like she was wrapping up, too. "Legs day? Or upper body."

"Legs. Ugh," she said. "But I wasn't hitting it as hard as you. Exorcising some demons?"

"How'd you guess?"

We strolled outside past the bocce ball court en route to our loft apartments. She said, "Is Jason hovering in that head of yours?"

"No, as a matter of fact. He's not." It was true. I'd gone, what, forty-eight hours without thinking about him? It both surprised and relieved me.

"Good," she said. She pulled her scrunchie out to readjust her hair. Even right out of the gym, she had long, wavy auburn locks like a shampoo model on TV.

We stopped at our favorite bench. "Whew," I said.

Nicole bent her knee to her chest and stretched her calf. "Maybe it's time you *finally* put your profile on some dating apps?"

"Yeah, yeah, yeah," I said. Nope.

Brian's handsome face came to mind. I'd been holding out on my friends about him. I hadn't wanted to get their hopes up with a new guy. They were supposed to have been my bridesmaids and knew how I'd suffered from the breakup. They had thought Jason and I were a great couple, but they couldn't believe he'd expected me to ditch everything for Silicon Valley.

The night it all came down with Jason and me was after a UK basketball game. There we sat wearing our Wildcat shirts in the parking lot of Rupp Arena. All the other cars had left, and the glow of a light post cast shadows on Jason through his windshield. "I'm not going," I said at last. "To California." Those were the hardest words I ever spoke.

Jason tilted his head like a puppy and said, "But I thought we were going to grow old together."

I had thought so, too. We didn't quarrel. It was just how it was. I slipped my engagement ring off my finger, opened his hand, and pressed the diamond into his moist palm. Even now, when I thought of getting out of his car and the sound of his door shutting, its echo rang like words: your life will never be the same.

I shoved the memory away now, not wanting to turn all gloomy. I smiled at Nicole.

I couldn't keep Brian a secret forever. I was already determined to save Violet's car.

The loan on my Honda Accord was paid off. I kept my credit cards to zero balances pretty much every month. I could call my bank and finance funds to invest in the Jordan. It'd be expensive, like buying a high-end car, like a Lexus or something, wouldn't it? The promotion at work would help me pay the loan off in five years.

It was yet another reason to land the new position at Goldenrod. I wanted that raise.

"Back to the dating apps," Nicole said.

There was no way around it. "Okay," I said. "Confession time."

I swigged my bottled water. I told her about the cute car guru guy while she sat with her mouth hanging open. Literally.

"Sooo," she said. "When do you ask him for a date?"

"In another life, I might've been interested," I said. "Not now."

"Why the heck not? A date here and there doesn't mean commitment."

"But remember, I live in this life. A life without men."

Nicole twisted a lock of hair around one finger, staring at me. "I get that Jason hurt you. And you're bucking for the promotion. But remember, my friend: it's best to rest your leg muscles on days you do your arms."

"Touché." She was brilliant to suggest I date a guy to actually help my job.

"Oh," she said. "Casey's big 3-0 is coming in like a week. Let's plan a get-together one night?"

"Sounds cool. Maybe at Nach?" Nachbar was a fave neighborhood dive bar within walking distance of the lofts. "But I won't be bringing a date."

CHAPTER 15

Violet

Detroit, Michigan
September 1921

I did hear from Robert again, and I welcomed it. I'd been diligent in staying away from Margaret's hostility at the factory and had been scrimping to send money to Mother. There was no denying it this time: Robert called for a real date. And I was itching to have fun.

Mrs. Sturgeon steered clear of my comings and goings with her nephew. He said maybe we'd go to a film, or maybe out for a bite. But our destination shifted in the car.

"Remember when we spoke of our dislike of Prohibition?" he said. I nodded. "If you're inclined, we can join the crowd and go try a cocktail."

He sounded so tentative, but my first reaction was *yes*.

"Why not?" I said. "An adventure." Isn't that one reason I'd come to the city?

We had to park blocks away and take the streetcar and then walk a couple of blocks more. The early fall air was crisp with an evening breeze off the river that flowed in its parallel line across the street. Trees in the city were turning a cheery red or brilliant orange. But their color was not visible, for the sun had set two hours back. We passed but few people here on Jefferson, at a point farther east on the avenue than where I'd been before.

When Robert took my hand, it felt naturally comfortable and yet so new to me, I had to get used to it.

I hoped he liked my dress. It was perfect for fall, a pretty coppery brown with a sheen. I'd brought it from home. It fell inches above my ankles, and the bodice was blousy with a boat neckline and no sleeves. A sash tied just above my waist, and I wore rayon stockings of beige with beige beaded shoes. Sarah had spent an hour teasing my hair and tying it into a lovely chignon.

"This is it," Robert said in a tone so low I could scarcely hear him. "Little Henry's. No relation to Henry Ford." He chuckled.

There was no signage. This was a residence, a house with barely a light inside. The house was old, like something on Wapping Street in Frankfort: symmetrical brick in the Federal style, a row of shuttered windows. I would never pick it out off the street to be a speakeasy.

We stepped around to the windowless door of the unlit back porch. Robert knocked four times. He tapped his foot anxiously on the wooden plank before the door finally opened a crack. He flashed his business card and in we went, hushed.

We entered a dimly lit space where tobacco smoke rose in clouds, making my nose itch. I followed Robert around a sharp corner where my eyes began to adjust, and I caught hint of a light and the faint sound of voices. As we descended the narrow, creaking steps into a brick-walled basement, the smoke became thicker but a dim glow brightened in equal measure. The low-ceilinged room was now loud and thick with revelers standing as close as Robert and me. I felt a thrill of discovery. A new experience.

To my right were men who might've worked in factories, with their newsboy caps of wool. To my front were two men dressed in black tail-coats with exquisite jeweled women at their elbows. As Robert led me through the crowd to a bar, everyone smiled and dipped their heads in friendly hellos. It was as if one's social class didn't matter here.

Everyone shared one mission in common: to drink despite the prohibitions of Prohibition.

Robert swiveled to me and smiled. "Hear it? The phonograph playing?"

"'I'm Forever Blowing Bubbles,'" I said, recognizing the faint sound of the peppy orchestral melody behind the buzz of the crowd.

Robert's eyes glistened in the dimly lit room with its golden light casting on walls and turning them into yellow bricks. He said, "I'm going to have a gimlet. It's gin. And what for you, my dear?"

My dear? How a place like this did let down one's reserve.

Robert was so handsome. His fine suit was a soft brown with high lapels and slim tucks at broad shoulders. His tight pants were cut above the ankles, and crisp short cuffs hung over spit-shined Oxfords.

"May I get you a drink, miss?"

I pivoted to the man at the bar. He was one of three without a coat standing behind the bar that had no stools. Behind him were ceiling-high shelves loaded with bottles of illegal liquor. He wore a white shirt with puffy sleeves and cuff links of nickel. Black-colored bands cinched in his sleeves at his upper arms.

I looked to Robert as if I were a kindergartner having never before seen a chalkboard.

"She'll have something sweet," Robert told the man with a wink.

"I've got just the thing."

Another server pushed Robert's cocktail across the bar's smooth, tightly pulled hide top hammered with brass upholstery tacks.

The barman mixed my drink, pouring clear liquor out of a dark bottle into a silver metal container. He added assorted liquors or juices. Using small tongs, he tossed in a chunk of ice and vigorously shook the drink as ice made a racket on the metal.

"For you," the bartender said after pouring the drink in a stemmed glass with a flat, rounded globe. "We call it a pink lady."

It was a gorgeous cocktail, dark pink in the light of this room. Father had only drunk beer or bourbon. Mother rarely indulged, so it wasn't as if I had someone to emulate.

I took the cool rim of the glass to my lips. Its frothy white foam had risen to the top and teased my skin. Then as the pink drink slid down my throat, I saw a flash of Mother forcing nasty cough syrup into my mouth. I managed not to gag and smiled pleasantly. I squeaked out, "Delicious."

A bare-shouldered, rotund woman beside me dressed in festive blue said, "I see you have the pink lady? The first time can hurt a little, and later it takes away your breath. Isn't that the case with everything?" She laughed. "Only the good gin here. Or at least, the best of mixers to cover up bad gin." She cackled. "There's apple brandy, lemon, and the white of an egg. And a splash of grenadine syrup."

Oh! I had much to learn if this was part of being a modern woman.

Robert cocked his head toward the back of the room.

Half of the women I passed and most of the men balanced cigarettes between their fingertips. One woman's cigarette was tucked into a long, skinny black holder the length of a pencil or longer. It matched her filmy black dress, her raven bobbed hair, and striking eyes the color of Kentucky coal.

Robert and I squeezed on by. I dodged others at right with my shoulder and at left with my hip to avoid a spill or a burn. He found an empty area in a corner. He dug into his pocket, lit up a smoke, and offered the lit cigarette to me.

"I'm still getting used to holding my cocktail." I tittered. My hand-crocheted reticule dangled from my wrist as I sipped. "Maybe later?" I had never smoked before.

"Sorry there are no seats open," he said.

The few sofas and leather chairs scattered on the concrete floor held twice as many partygoers as they ought, with everyone draped every which way. Stockinged legs swung. Men's arms wrapped around bare shoulders. Heads bowed low in private conversation.

"I'm wonderful," I said. I was having fun. I felt I had a stamina to go on all night.

Robert's taut thigh pressed my leg as we talked. Due to the crowd? Or was it on purpose?

"Violet," Robert said, his voice husky.

"Yes?" I felt light-headed from the gin. Or from him casting a spell on me?

"You look so pretty. The loveliest lady in the room." He sipped his gimlet, his eyes narrowing over the rim and boring into mine.

I blushed—no, rather, my face became inflamed I was sure. Loveliest of all?

Again I saw behind him the woman wearing black, and the V in the back of her dress was as stunning as its straight neckline had been in front—a dress made to be viewed while surrounded in a room like this.

But Robert had eyes only for me.

"Thank you," I said, looking up at him from the corners of my eyes.

And I began to get a taste for a modern woman's freedoms. It was like when I six, and Mother let me cross the street without holding her hand. I had arrived at a turning point and couldn't wait to see what was around the bend.

~

I ascended the last step of Little Henry's mahogany staircase and turned toward a dim light, approaching the third door on the left for the ladies' lounge. The door swung open and released five or six women, each of them carrying themselves in a listless debutante slouch—their hips pushed forward and their shoulders back to accentuate their long, lithe bodies.

They wiggled their fingers at me in a wave as they passed, and one said, "It's all yours."

I found myself in an ordinary yellow master bedroom. Though heavy, dark fabric obscured the windows to dampen any light from the street. There was one small glass lamp.

I went to the narrower door in the room that was open by a fraction and where another light leaked from beneath at the rug. At last, the water closet.

"Oh!" I said, slamming the door shut tight. I'd opened it to find a woman sitting atop the pot. "I'm so sorry!" I said through the six-paneled door. "I thought it was vacant."

"Come in!" her voice called, and I flinched, but she opened the door immediately, fully clothed.

"You didn't find me in an embarrassing situation," she said, and my shoulders relaxed.

Her fragrance—at once exotic and decidedly youthful—clung in the air like a bouquet. Her striking dark eyes weren't brown, but black.

"I was on the commode's lid to try to fix my stocking," she said. "Not that it would bother me if you had caught me. Why, at college, three sorority sisters and I once crammed into a bathroom smaller than this at a party. I took the toilet, one took the sink, while the other two waited their turns."

At once I inwardly recoiled at the image of those girls, while I was entirely amused that they did not conform to their grandmothers' primness or properness.

This woman's hair, lashes, and brows were even darker than her eyes, and she lifted her stylish uneven hems and swung her foot to the edge of this sink without inhibition. She caught my eye in the mirror.

"Don't worry. We girls found some Boraxo powdered soap and cleaned that sink well."

Her elfin foot atop this wide porcelain sink was fitted in the most exquisite double-strapped shoe, dark gold with clear glass beads. This was the woman in the black dress I'd seen earlier in the throng. The V of her dress was high on her back now. She pulled her hems up above her right knee—and the sweep of the feathery fabric fell to where her leg bent at her hip. The frilliest garter emerged, and she released her beige stocking from its decorative elastic ring. She tugged on the stocking high and low, twisting it all down her leg this way and that.

"Damn," she said, startling me again. "It's of no use. This ghastly hole has caused a run."

The runs in the silk multiplied with her every tug. Perhaps a hot ash of a cigarette had caused the hole on her shin?

"Good news is," I said sincerely as she resecured her garter, "no one will ever see the damage. The crowd is too thick, the hole low on your leg, and the basement is dark."

The woman dropped her foot to the tiled floor with a clack and looked squarely into my face. Again she smiled warmly. "Thank you."

Her skirts swished at midshin, the stocking's hole in all its glory with runs clear to the top of her foot, edging even under the straps. In a glance, then, I took in this woman's ensemble.

Her dress was not pure black after all, but a shimmery gunmetal charmeuse. It epitomized everything of today's latest fashion: a dress with lines that could fit a schoolgirl's body—flat through the chest and boyish through the hips. The fabric's airy cut was made for letting a female's body move. The front of her bodice was loose and under it an opaque slip of light gold. Fine embroidery adorned the skirts with leaves of golden threads. Her dress was what models or movie stars or wealthy wives would wear.

Her dangling, sparkling green earbobs were a surprise—shockingly placed in ears that'd been pierced.

"I'm Lela," she said with her lush black lashes fluttering as if eyes could smile.

"I'm Violet." We shook hands.

"Violet. Pretty name for a pretty girl."

"Thank you. I like your earbobs," I said, sounding stiffer than I wanted.

"My birthstones. Emeralds. I was lucky enough to have been born in May. Join me for a cigarette out here?"

I nodded but motioned to the toilet beside us. "Perhaps I'll meet you out there."

"I'll wait, and we can return to the bar through the smoky maze together."

I opened my drawstring bag, prepared for an emergency like the Campfire Girl I'd once been. I would not be caught with ripped stockings on the first official date with Robert.

"First, I happen to have a spare pair of stockings," I said. "Not your color exactly, but—"

"I couldn't possibly impose on you for that." But her face looked open to the idea.

"I don't mind." I lifted them out in their white tissue wrapper. There was plenty of room in my reticule. I had a lipstick and a compact—no cigarette case and no flask of liquor.

"I'll pay you." She promptly went about replacing her stockings.

Lela then slipped out a quarter from her vanity bag of ring-mesh—not a full-size bag like mine, but a beautiful accessory with a cathedral dome–shaped frame. And attached to the bag by a thin braided chain was a small compact engraved with the letters *LH*.

"You see," she said, frowning at her discarded stockings. "I have an after-party to attend with my boyfriend. I don't care to be the only flapper there with a run."

She laughed again, and I laughed, too.

"No, they're my gift."

I bit the inside of my jaw. Kindness was ingrained in me by my mother, but now my budget was tight. What a fool I was. But I was overwhelmed by Lela—the epitome of today's woman, the one I wanted to be. But if my generosity left me to buy another pair of stockings myself, I'd have to go without lunch. For three days.

"I'll simply purchase another pair or two and have them couriered to your house," Lela said to my relief. "What's your address?" She tapped her forehead. "I never forget names of places or addresses."

Before I could change my mind, I gave her the Saint Aubin Street number, hoping she was true to her word.

"I'll meet you for cigarettes out here."

After I used the facilities, I returned to the bedroom and found her lazily lounged on a divan, one leg crossed over the other. I mustn't take long. Robert was buying another round of drinks and would be looking for me.

Lela was already holding a cigarette out. "The only two left in my bag."

She kept the one that was slightly bent. And I confessed to her that if I were to learn how to smoke, now would be a good time, without an audience downstairs.

"Would you and your date care to come along to the party? It's just north, past where Jefferson turns into Lake Shore Road. Not far from my house at Grosse Pointe."

Grosse Pointe? I'd heard of that from Oliver at the boardinghouse. Grosse Pointe and Grosse Pointe Farms—there were some four or five Pointes in all, where Detroit's richest residents lived. *Old money. New money. Everything money,* he said.

"We couldn't possibly, but thank you for the offer."

I didn't know about Robert, but I'd be too intimidated around all that wealth.

Lela's smile radiated as I leaned in toward the flame of her silver-plated lighter. I drew on the cigarette's tip and remembered Father telling Mother that men don't inhale the smoke of cigars. They savor the taste of the smoke and then blow it out. Was that how one smoked a *cigar-ette*? That's what I did, and the smoke went straight up my nose. I turned to sneeze three times.

"You have to inhale into your lungs like this," Lela said.

She took a drag off hers. She didn't use her long holder that I'd seen earlier near the bar. Yet she blew the smoke to the ceiling and puffed out three circular rings. Astonishing.

"See? You might cough once or twice. The first time can be rough."

Another young woman swept into the room and quickly shut the door to the water closet.

"You know," Lela said, "my friends could listen to your lilting voice talk all night."

"That's funny. Some people get frustrated because they can't understand me at all."

I puffed the cigarette in the manner of Lela and other women in the basement. My nostrils stung. I couldn't finish the cigarette, but it was a start. One day, I'd hold my own with any woman in the crowd. I set the cigarette in a dip of the glass ashtray the color of butterscotch candy, and I let the tobacco burn down.

"I'm afraid I'll have to practice some more another time," I said.

"Yes, best to take it slow. And I'd better get you back before your date worries," she said as she snuffed out both of our cigarette butts. It was like something my older sister would say.

We stood and her eyes sparkled. "It's been a true pleasure meeting you, Violet. I'll not forget the stockings."

It was well past midnight with the starless night's air chilly against my bare arms making me feel less tipsy. Robert removed his coat and slung it around my shoulders like a cape.

"Robert. Thank you for a perfect evening." We'd had another cocktail and shared a cushy leather chair that'd freed up. Cozy. I'd taken a few puffs of his cigarette.

Outside, we returned the way we came, over flat stepping-stones that ran adjacent to the house. But he put his hand on my back so we'd pause. I leaned back against the weather-roughened bricks in the dark. He raised his fingers to my cheek with a feathery touch, and I didn't stop him. I tilted in to that touch. My lips felt puffy. I could scarcely control my breathing.

"May I kiss you?" he whispered.

I wanted him to. I'd read of necking and petting in magazine stories and novels. And Evelyn had described some of her wedding night. But I had never before been kissed.

"Yes," I said.

My mouth watered as his came to mine. I brought my hand to his hair, and I marveled at its silkiness. His lips touched mine, exquisite, soft, gentle, warm.

He lifted his face and looked at me again in the dim light. Then he kissed me again in delicious tension of the pressure, our mouths melding together with force. These kisses were intense and wet—and, was that Robert's tongue? He pulled me closer and I let him. There was an urgency to our kissing then that I had never imagined existed.

When our mouths parted, I swallowed and tried to catch my breath.

"You have utterly captivated me," he said, huffing softly.

I kissed his cheek, assuring myself this was just fun. No more.

And then we made haste with my feet nearly skipping to keep up block after block to the streetcar. I had to get back to the boardinghouse.

CHAPTER 16

Violet

Detroit, Michigan
September 1921

By a week after my heated embrace with Robert outside the speakeasy, we'd talked twice by telephone, me whispering from the alcove how much fun I'd had. But he was going to be on the road for several days, and I was glad. My head had been like the metronome on Evelyn's piano—first swinging one way and then swinging the other. I wanted to see Robert again. But I worried it was too much. What would come next? My feelings for him were changing. I didn't know what it meant any more than I'd known what a pink lady cocktail would taste like. But he was on my mind every day when I awoke and when I turned in.

Hannah and I sat playing a round of checkers. Her red pieces had more crowned kings than my black ones. The phonograph was silent for now. Our luncheon was over. My hair was washed and set and it was a beautiful day outside, but I was going nowhere. I didn't have money to spend. No matter what, though, I didn't want to go home and give up my independence. If I couldn't attend a matinee or take the streetcar to a park or send a telegram to Mother instead of a letter, I just couldn't. I was working harder at the factory to knock out a spark plug every two minutes, but that extra income went straight to Mother.

Yet she had sent the loveliest card with her monogrammed stationery, writing:

> Darling girl, I'm so proud of you . . . up there living your dream, supporting yourself. So responsible. Had I had the opportunity to do so, I would've. You know that, right? Thank you for the gift. I'll spend it wisely, my dear. Love forever, Mother

The pleasure it gave me to help her was as nice as a big, warm hug. And the joy I had in her pride in me was like fresh-churned butter on toast. As if that wasn't enough, my sister followed up with a note saying, "I'm proud of you. You've become quite a young woman."

I would stick it out. Keep my budget tight to the bone.

"There's an automobile out front," Oliver said as he let the curtains fall from his fingers with glee. He'd been reading the newspaper. "And a movie star is walking up to our porch. Her dress is as green as her car."

Green? Cars in our neighborhood were black. Most cars in the city were black. And a movie star?

But there was a knock. Oliver rushed to open the door. "Hello. May I help you?"

No doubt he was hoping so. But she was probably just lost. I moved a piece on the checkerboard.

"Hello yourself," a sparkling voice of a female said. "I'm looking for my friend named Violet."

A current of confusion shot through me. I shrugged at my game partner and rose. "I'm sorry. Excuse me."

"No problem. I was two moves away from beating you anyway." Hannah snickered and collected the checkers.

"May I say who's calling?" Oliver asked the stranger as I rounded the corner.

"Tell her it's Lela."

What in the world was the woman from the speakeasy doing at my boardinghouse? I never thought I'd see her again. But I had fond memories of meeting her—and learning how to smoke.

Oliver turned, and I said, "Thank you. I'll take it from here."

The expression on his face was pure bewilderment. Rather than invite her into our home—which might cost less than the machine she drove on the street—I stepped onto the porch and pulled the door shut.

"Lela," I said, grinning. "You remembered my address, just as you assured me you would, but—"

"Yes," she broke in. "Rather than calling a courier, I decided to deliver your stockings myself."

Wonderful, I thought with relief filling me. I wouldn't have to spend the money I didn't have. I was down to one pair of stockings left—washing the feet out in my basin each night, hanging them on a line in my room, praying I didn't get a run. I couldn't show up for work looking slovenly or the boss would be unhappy; I couldn't risk losing my job. And I didn't wish to incite more attacks from Margaret my coworker, either. But my appearance was also a matter of personal pride, something ingrained in Evelyn and me by our mother.

Lela held aloft a bag from Siegel's, one of the high-end department stores on Woodward Avenue, where Robert had driven me on tour. But this bag was larger than would be required of a pair of rayon stockings.

"You didn't have to do that." I felt a tinge of pink seep into my face.

"But I did," she said. "Besides, I wanted to. You were so sweet to help me in a pinch."

I accepted the bag graciously, and indeed, it was heavier than warranted. With the sweep of one arm, I suggested we sit on two porch chairs.

"Open it," she said eagerly, just the way my sister might've when giving me a present.

I pulled handfuls of tissue from the bag. A mild breeze rustled the filmy paper as Lela bunched it up in her lap. I dipped inside the bag and removed three packs of stockings—silk, not rayon, in the colors of beige, black, and brown.

"Thank you," I said. "But you're too generous."

She lifted her chin good-naturedly. "Go on. There's more."

"What's this?" I asked, merrily holding up a french-blue blouson-style dress to my body. "It's lovely."

She seemed so pleased. "I can never resist a sale," she said.

"It, well, I. Well, Lela, I don't deserve this."

No, I didn't. But what a godsend this was in my financial situation. Father would've said, *Don't look a gift horse in the mouth.*

"Don't be silly," Lela said. "Tell you what, if you don't have plans, run and try it on. Make sure it fits. Then let's go for a spin. It's a beautiful day."

"Put the new dress on . . . now?" I said. It truly was a gloriously beautiful day.

"Why not?" I said. Why couldn't I be spontaneous?

"I'll wait in the car," Lela said. "We'll have girl fun."

Was there really anything to stop me? No. I didn't reside with my parents anymore. I could fly off with someone rich whom I barely knew any day I wasn't working. So what if the house would be abuzz with whispers? No more so than when Robert came for me.

When I scurried out of the house, Lela was unfastening the last snaps of the plastic window curtains on the car doors. She tossed them into the rear passenger compartment.

"We'll let the breeze blow in as we go," she said. "The dress looks darling on you."

I glowed. "I have to admit, I love it," I said.

"Well, your sharing your stockings that night was an act of kindness, I thought, like a sister might've done. But I don't have a sister."

"Yes, a sister would've done that. I do miss my older sister."

I rounded the car. Two polished headlamps with ornate cut-glass lenses astonished me. Their cases were nickeled and held tiny brass plaques. I wouldn't embarrass myself by bending to read them, but they struck me as being hallmarks of a fine artist's ware. And the spokes of the wheels were thick and green as the car's glistening paint. The only thing marring the car was a splatter of mud on the running boards and tires caked in dirt. But that was so normal no one would notice.

Lela seemed to live the life I wanted, had everything, yet she was so unaffected by it. Not haughty.

"And we won't even care," Lela said with a laugh, "if the wind musses our hair."

With her stylish black bob, though, she hadn't spent an hour before a mirror that morning with a brush in one hand and hairpins sticking out of her mouth.

I slid into the black leather seat, and she started up the engine. Unlike a Model T that needed to be cranked, this car had an electric self-starter. Lela pressed a button on the floor with her foot. I saw the name on a dash instrument—Packard, the most luxurious American car made.

We were off, and I never glanced back to see who was watching.

Goodness, though, Lela did shift the gears and drive with uncommon speed. The tires chugged through dips and bounced over ruts in the packed-dirt side roads as rough as an old-fashioned washboard. I reached up to secure the pins of my hair tighter.

"Can you believe," Lela began as if we'd been friends forever, "we'll be voting for president in five more weeks? Five!"

The first presidential vote. If this young woman had not already charmed herself into my admiration, her opening topic sure did. She was far more glamorous and worldly than me, but some issues were common to us both—as women.

"My mother said she'll be first in line," I said, "but I'm not yet twenty-one."

Lela twisted to look at me, stunned, making the car jig sharply right. I grasped hold of the lip of the door with one hand and the seat cushion with the other. Lela righted it and my tension eased.

"I turned twenty in July," I said, soon finding myself enjoying the speed when Lela was driving straight. Mother had never let Father speed.

"Isn't that a damned shame?" Lela said. "You're missing the first women's vote in history." She shook her head.

"Where have you a mind to go?" I asked with no idea of what "a spin" in a car for "girl fun" entailed. A fifteen-minute ride? A whole day?

Then she bore on the brakes near a crosswalk, and the car screeched. She'd come within inches of the car in front of us. I hugged the seat, but I was getting used to this.

"I had a mind to visit my stockbroker but then remembered it's Saturday," she said. "All the days are a blur. But I like to drive for the fun of driving. Even with nowhere to go."

Driving for the fun of it. She just put words to something I'd longed for.

"You're an investor?" I asked.

"I dabble. Well, maybe I do better than dabble. Daddy thought I'd be a spendthrift with my graduation money. Boy, I proved him wrong. Investing's the only job I hold, despite my college degree."

I wouldn't inquire more of her private money matters, especially as we barely knew each other. But Lela continued to astound me. She was the modern woman in all its manifestations. How lucky I was to have met her.

"What university did you attend?" I asked, thinking of Evelyn quitting college to walk down the aisle. Lela and I were of very different minds than my sister.

"Michigan," Lela said, and her voice insinuated it was the only choice. Then she barked out a laugh. "Daddy sent me so he could brag to his fellow Packard execs that his offspring attended the finest—even if she wasn't a son." She rolled her eyes emphatically. Turned out her father was a vice president for the luxury automaker. "Mother sent me to hook a husband. But I'm not ready for marriage."

Again, something we had in common: the yearning for freedom. I hoped she and I'd be friends. It felt as if we already were.

"When I wasn't studying first downs and touchdowns at college," she said, "or going to first base in a broom closet of a frat party, I did a little studying." She giggled and winked at me.

Then, more solemn, she said, "I'll miss Ferry Field when the football season kicks off in October."

"You can still go to games."

"Oh, and I will. But it'll be different, you know?" In her profile, I saw a hint of wistfulness. "Some experiences in life we can never re-create."

"How true." It was something Mother might've said.

Lela was smart. Not just that. Wise.

We drove without a destination, a new and liberating concept to me. My hair was escaping its confinement and blowing into a tangle. Who was to care?

"My hair used to do that," Lela said. "Blow in every which direction. I'll never go long again. But what I wouldn't give to have your thick curls, even with a bob."

"Really? Well, I've broken more teeth off combs than I care to admit. One of these days, I'll get it bobbed." When I could afford it. I thought of Mother having to put her foot down with Father just to let me take it to barely my shoulders.

"Oh, you simply must! Oh! Let's go now. My barbershop's not far away." She wiggled in her seat, doing a little dance clear up to her shoulders while steering the wheel. I'd never seen such behavior in a car.

"Today?" I had money in my purse but couldn't afford to spend it. "I'm hardly prepared," I said.

"What's to prepare? Just imagine how much time you'll save from all that washing and towel-drying and setting it before bed." She glanced my way with a wicked little expression. "And it's easier to pull yourself together after being with a man, if you know what I mean."

She was so nonchalant about relations with a man, I had to bust out laughing.

Maybe I could continue to see Robert. If we had heated embraces, it didn't mean I was promised to him for life. It didn't mean gold bands on ring fingers. Besides, he wasn't the marrying sort. Between Robert and Lela, I was beginning to feel like I'd finally arrived: I was here, becoming the modern woman.

This was what "girl fun" was all about. Why couldn't I get a bob? I would be extra frugal next week—skipping lunch at work three days, stretching Mrs. Sturgeon's lunches to two days instead of one. Or I could take a tiny bit from my savings instead. Yes. This wasn't a frivolous expenditure: a new style would proclaim the new emerging me.

You have only one life.

"On to the barber!" I said.

Lela maneuvered the car into a parking spot on the street. I walked with a spring in my step on the block to Hal's Barbershop. I recalled passing by my father's barbershop and peering into the window. Neither Mother nor I had ever gone in. Never had I seen a woman inside at all. It made me want the haircut all the more—to do something that neither my mother nor my late grandmother would *think* of doing.

"Hal!" Lela said as we entered the shop that smelled a mix of spicy-clean and burning tobacco.

Then everyone stopped—the barbers with their shears midair, the customers telling tales. The men were all frozen in place with their eyes set upon us.

"I've brought a friend," Lela said.

"Welcome, gals," Hal, the owner, said jovially. "Take that chair right up front, miss."

The barbers resumed their work and chatter, but two gray-haired customers sneered at us. One of them said under his breath, "Have young women today lost their minds?"

Had Hal meant for me to take the chair in the front window? I sat down and rested my feet on the metal bar. A family walked by, gaping at me in the window and pointing. I could just hear the wide-eyed children chanting, "Look, Mommy, a woman is getting her hair cut at the barber?"

I would've said the same thing at their age. Yet here I was.

The floor had black-and-white squares that, on the diagonal, resembled diamonds. Every station had a barber in a hip-length jacket in neat, starched white. There was a mustached man reclined in the seat beside me. A young and handsome barber had a long, wide blade and was shaving the man's neck whiskers with quick, short strokes. Another patron was getting thick globs of cream brushed onto fat cheeks. On one wall hung a large calendar with a picture of a bird-hunting scene—two men aimed rifles at hawks in the sky.

Lights strung on thick cords hung from the old tin ceiling. I removed my pins and let down my hair—gazing into the mirror one last time at my frizzy locks that fell loosely along my breasts. A hint of nervous fright suddenly hit me. What if I hated it? But Evelyn would say, *It'll grow back if you don't like it.*

Lela and I had a smoke, and when my turn arose, Hal draped the oversize bib around me and fastened it behind my neck. His fingers were cold as they tapped my skin. The bib dangled about my thighs and arms and sides. He swiveled me around to face the room and adjusted the height of the chair.

My back was to the mirror. Hal gently tugged on ropes of my hair, and it began to drop in small handfuls, sprinkling the tiled floor like spilled sugar. As each bit drifted down, I lost a day of my youth.

Hal clipped and fluffed and parted and smoothed my hair with cream. Then with the rims of his flattened hands, he pressed firmly at my jaw on two sides. He began to hum. Lela stood watching, mesmerized as if Hal were a sculptor at his stone. Hair was his art.

"I love it," she said, her voice light as a fairy. Was she just being kind?

Then without giving warning, Hal spun me around to face the mirror.

CHAPTER 17

Melanie

Louisville, Kentucky
August 2018

"Girls Just Want to Have Fun" played on the piped-in music, and birthday girl Casey was getting into the vibe with her shoulders wiggling to match the beat.

I was where I needed to be as of this moment at work. I had a plan to get a loan to keep Violet's beloved car, and that felt right. And her journal reminded me that girls worked hard—but they deserved some fun, too.

"Damn, grrrlll," I said to Casey. "You're lookin' fine for someone who's over the hill."

We cracked up. "I'm three decades old," she said, "and I feel like a spring chicken, as my granny used to say. Now, let's partayyyyy."

Nicole joined us and said, "You don't look a day over twenty-three."

Nope, Casey didn't look her age. Practicing law as a fifth-year attorney agreed with her. Tonight, she wore form-fitting white cropped pants, strappy heeled sandals, and a midriff top in tomato red. That shade was perfect for her complexion, too, her skin a warm, natural brown—and her loop earrings sparkled against the thick brownish-black coils of her hair. She wove herself through the crowd now.

Our growing group gathered informally on the enclosed rear patio at Nachbar, a total hole-in-the-wall in Germantown, but beloved by all in our neighborhood. The patio had well-worn picnic tables lined with ashtrays; flower boxes that hadn't been watered in weeks hanging on the privacy fence; and a triangle wood-burning stove for parties come fall. A bunch of us had walked over from the lofts early to save some tables, and liquor was flowing freely. Cheap vodka, bottom-shelf bourbon, and one-dollar PBR beers.

I was still on my first no-frills margarita, no salt. I wasn't nursing it; in fact, a friend had just stopped with a pitcher to top off my plastic cup. Did that make this round *two*? No, still round one.

By the time Nach's live band—a three-piece combo with a 1980s and 1990s list—warmed up under the awning for their first set, it was ten o'clock, the crowd was getting thick, and it was time for round two. I lifted my cup high in the air, and the server in a Reds ball cap nodded.

"Hey, Casey's looking for you," Nicole said a few minutes later, nudging between two smoking guys—guys smoking cigarettes, that is, not smoking hot.

"Thank you, sir," I said as my cocktail arrived in my hand.

"Did you hear me?" Nicole repeated over the noise. "Birthday girl is looking for you." Nicole tossed her head toward the back, away from the music speakers, and her wavy auburn hair went flying. That girl mastered a curling iron like no other.

I wormed my way through a bunch of tipsy hipsters and ex-hippies and saw Casey waving her hand above everyone's heads.

"Hey."

A man's voice? An all-too-familiar man's voice? I swirled left and my eyes bulged.

Jason.

"Hey back," I said, surprised that my tongue even worked. I felt like someone just lit a cherry bomb inside my body—a rush of hormones invading my chest with nerves.

He was home from California? We hadn't spoken since he moved away in March. Wait. Was he home visiting, or was he home as in "back for good" kind of home? If I were strapped to a lie detector and asked if I hoped he was here to stay, the machine would've short-circuited. It wouldn't be able to read me. Part of me still held bitterness for how things had gone down. The other part felt pumped to see him.

I tried to crook a little smile to match his. He held up his beer in a mock toast. I twisted my head around and caught Casey giving me the "I tried to warn you!" look.

I turned back and lifted my head to face my taller-than-tall ex.

He looked good. Smelled good, too. Same sporty aftershave. He smiled again, close-lipped, and even with that, his dimples could not be denied.

What am I wearing? Think, think. A super-casual but sassy new summer dress I've only worn twice. *Something he has never seen. Yay.* I was vain enough to want him to think I looked pretty. And if I read the subtleties in his eyes, I thought that he did.

"I hear there's a birthday party," Jason said, speaking loudly enough that I could hear over the crowd and the music.

"Yeah, we're hoping the band will sing to Casey."

He shrugged as he said, "I didn't know about it until I got here."

"That's cool. Everyone's welcome."

Had he slid by Nach, hoping to find me? He wasn't turning to leave after saying hello. His eyes didn't waver. There was an old hint of light in his hazel irises. He was warm but somehow detached. I couldn't quite figure him out.

What would I do if he asked to see me privately while in town? I hoped he didn't. He'd made me choose between my career and him. It hadn't been fair. It wasn't even fair for him to be standing here, on my turf, by my friends, on a night we were all having fun. I was still recovering from losing him, a toddler on unsteady feet. Why was he here?

I nodded to Jason's oldest friend. "Hey, Kev," I said.

"How's it going?" Kevin was as friendly as ever, as though nothing had happened.

He would've been Jason's best man. A spike of fresh pain shot through me, imagining our wedding party as I'd once envisioned it—the guys in slate blue, the girls in champagne. Now a dream in the dust.

A couple more of Jason's buddies nodded at me.

Finally, I asked Jason flat out: "Welllll . . . What are you doing home?"

"Dad's birthday's tomorrow. Out with friends tonight."

Ah. Two thoughts struck me at once.

First, not having known he was coming home required an adjustment, despite how I had no right nor need to have heard in advance. Second, for years I'd celebrated his family birthdays with them. I had a twinge of feeling left out . . . left out of watching Jason's father, he with his dimples to match his son's, as he blew out all candles on a cake—one for every year—with a single big breath. I would miss his grand performance.

"Looks like you got some sun," Jason said, his eyes affixed to my chest.

My dress had spaghetti straps and a swooping neckline that showed off the blushy rays I'd gotten while working on my laptop outside today. The dress gave a little peep below, too, but as Jason would know, I was moderate in the "stacked" department—like all the women on the Bond side of the family. But he'd never seemed to mind.

"There you are," said a pretty, long-haired brunette as she shimmied in and gave Jason's right bicep a squeeze. "That restroom is sketchy." She laughed, and more girls joined their group. "Clean, but wide as its one toilet that sits right in front of a full-length mirror. And that sink! It's the size of a cereal bowl placed outside the door in the open of the bar."

Who was this girl? A bass drum seemed to bang in my chest. Bang, bang, bang. Had she flown home with him?

Jason looked at me sheepishly, and I glanced at Kevin without rotating my head. His expression said, "This is awkward."

I lowered my head to see what I could of the flat concrete pavers; not much, given the crowd of sneakers, sandals, and one pair of red stilettos. I slowly inched my head back up, having composed my "I'm okay, this is normal, and the fact that her bra size is 38C doesn't bother me a bit" look.

Just as I'd been vain enough to want Jason to think I looked pretty, I hated that I was jealous enough to wonder if he'd rather I'd been busty like this girl all along. And was he falling for her? Did he leave her sweet notes? Jealousy sat in me like a tumor.

"Hi," she said in her plunging, low-cut top. "I'm Taffy."

Taffy? As in . . . sticky, sickeningly sweet, pull-it-all-the-way-apart and open your mouth wide *Taffy*?

"It's short for Tiffany. That's what my twin brother first called me, and it kind of stuck."

Sticky, just as I thought.

"I'm Melanie," I said with great diction, though I could see from the blankness of her eyes that she had no clue who I was. That kinda stung. Had I thought Jason would spill his entire history—including the great love of his life—to every girl he slept with? I really was delusional.

"You guys take care," I said, forcing a smile. "I'm off to see if the band plays 'Happy Birthday.'"

Then Taffy turned to her friends, who were drawing her into a debate about *The Real Housewives of Orange County*.

Jason leaned toward me with a semiserious look. "She and I aren't together." He shook his head. "She's just with a bunch of friends of ours. Not that you care, but just so you know." He bit his lip. "I hope everything's going well for you. Good seeing ya, Mel."

He was the only one who ever called me *Mel*, and the sound of it struck something in me: a sentimental chord, like in an old movie I once watched with Mom, *The Way We Were*. Jason and I were like the stars of that film: the woman had her principles and stayed strong to them in the end. Love wasn't enough.

Yet as he and Kevin headed to the exit, I felt like a fool. A sad, silly fool.

I crossed my fingers that Mom wouldn't hear he was here. I'd never tell her of this encounter and have her launch into how I should've handled it, or how he probably wanted me back. But for her couple of texts, she and I still hadn't talked since towing away the Jordan.

~

That night at home with nothing but a pillow beside me, I couldn't help replaying my encounter with Jason. Memories made me well up in tears in the dark.

It was a Tuesday in November last year when Jason let me into his apartment. He took my hand and walked me along a path on his floor lined with Hershey's Kisses. The silvery chocolate trail wound to his bedroom, where fragrant red roses were arranged in a cut glass vase. There was a pink envelope on his bed.

"Open it," he said. His face was as pink as the envelope, and one eyelid had kind of a tic.

I thought to myself, *This is the day*.

No public spectacle at the Derby. No audience with cameras poised at a fountain. No showy banner floating in the sky from the back of a biplane. That wasn't our style.

I tore open the envelope to find a handwritten note:

Melanie,

Now that I've kissed the ground you walk on, will you marry me?

As I lay in my bed in the present moment, my pillowcase now damp, I thought it was a beautiful memory. I guess I would always think it was. No matter the outcome.

Then our ending in a parking lot came flooding back, too—my pushing my ring in his hand and the sound of shutting his car door. It echoed again: your life will never be the same.

I'd made my decision. I'd stood up for myself. Women's careers weren't subordinate to men's.

CHAPTER 18

Violet

Detroit, Michigan
October 1921

Robert waited in the boardinghouse parlor. I practically floated down the stairs. With him being on the road so much, I hadn't seen him since the night of the speakeasy. I hoped that we'd kiss again tonight.

First, he would see my new look—but I hadn't told him about my afternoon with Lela at the barbershop. It would be a surprise.

I'd loved the new style from the instant Hal spun me around to the mirror. When I took exercise outside in the air, the lack of thick coils and pins felt freeing. I felt as if this was a stage in my own metamorphosis—like a caterpillar becoming a butterfly. I was now more the woman I yearned to be. Modern. Independent. Somehow, it reinforced that I was in the right place, not back home following the path of my sister.

"Violet," Mrs. Sturgeon said as I stepped to the first floor. "You're radiant."

"Thank you, Mrs. Sturgeon," I whispered, raising my brows in excitement.

I'd selected a skirt and an embroidered coat smock in a color called sunset tan. It had big buttons down the middle, a deep rounded collar, cuffs and patch pockets, and a loose buttoned belt of matching cotton fabric. I'd borrowed Sarah's cloche hat. Its evergreen color picked up on a thread in my top's embroidered pattern.

Residents had assembled in the parlor, no doubt primed to gauge Robert's reaction to my new look—and my reaction to his reaction. Would Robert be the kind to support the change, or would he be like the cronies in the barbershop?

Voices quieted the second I entered the room. Robert stopped mid-sentence as if Oliver weren't standing beside him in conversation. His eyes became large, and it seemed to me he tried controlling his grin—as though he wished not to appear like Little Red Riding Hood's big bad wolf with his tongue wagging out.

But he liked my new hair.

I could tell.

"Hello, Robert," I said casually.

As he moved toward me, I imagined I could hear his brain's calculations. It would be ridiculous for him not to acknowledge my new look, but how far should he go, given the audience?

"You look like you just stepped out of *Photoplay* magazine," he said. "Everyone at the theater will think you're the star."

And the glint in his eye seemed to cast sparkling light my way, too. That light singed my skin as if it were a real beam. He made me feel like a star.

The next day at work, Mr. Giddens was fuming because gaskets weren't delivered as promised.

"Damned supplier," he said. "What are you staring at?" he said to me with a snarl.

Thankfully, I wasn't within spitting distance.

"One of the tables has got to go home," he called out to everyone. "Gotta cut back on production till tomorrow."

Hands stopped moving. Mouths shut. We all wished it wouldn't be our table, but knew someone else would suffer. It meant no hours for ten women. No earnings for a whole day. Maybe no food for a baby brother or no medicine for a grandma. I needed every penny myself, for my living expenses—and now to send money to Mother.

"You." He pointed to the right and then hiked his thumb toward the door. "This table goes."

He chose the table with several Polish immigrants. Their faces dropped, and along with them my spirits. They were women who met quotas and who never were late. They were grateful to be here and worked hard.

"But I owe for my rent," whispered one named Ethel Nowak as she passed. "I'll lose my home." Her eyes told of despair. They walked to their cubbies, and even the bully Margaret who'd taunted me before looked downcast for them.

I wanted to help—to be charitable like Mother had taught. Ethel could have my spot. But no, losing a day's wages would be tough on me. I looked at Ethel again, so forlorn. At least I'd still have a place to live. I could sacrifice—find somewhere to cut my budget or assemble parts faster tomorrow—for someone whose circumstances were worse, couldn't I?

I stood. "Mr. Giddens," I said respectfully. "I can go home today, so Ethel can work my seat."

"What'd you say, Miss Bond? You *ca-an* go home? It's *can* go home and *can* work, not *ca-an*," he said, embarrassing me. "You and Miss Nowak can both go. Don't bother coming back."

My body inflamed. I glanced at Josie. My friend's face looked mortified. She'd taken it the same way I did. Ethel and I were fired? But why?

"Mr. Giddens," I said, looking from him to Ethel and trying to keep my hands from shaking. "I'm not sure I understand."

I hadn't known a laugh could sound so cruel.

"Welcome to the club. I can't understand you, either," he said.

He stormed off to his office and slammed the door. He'd berated me in front of everyone, and I wanted to hide under my work table. I scanned their mix of angry and empathetic eyes. I was let go while they'd watched. But worse, I needed my money, and I needed work.

And I wouldn't go back to Kentucky. Especially not when I was just opening my butterfly wings.

Mr. Giddens couldn't do this. Not to me. Not to Ethel.

I asked her to come and we filed to his office, our heads hung low like schoolgirls being sent to the corner. I tapped lightly three times on our boss's door.

"What do you want." It was a statement, not a question.

Having nothing to lose, I grasped the dingy iron doorknob and opened it a crack. Then an inch, then two. We padded in. I would stand up for myself. For us.

The room smelled like sweat and metal. Mr. Giddens sat behind the big wooden desk that was sloppy with spare parts and binders.

"Mr. Giddens, I came to apologize. I meant no harm to you or her." I gestured toward Ethel. "I intended only to help a coworker who would be equal in production for today only. The company would be covered. I'd like to come back tomorrow, to work. Both of us. Please, sir."

He tapped a pencil on the two inches of clear surface left on his desktop.

"Who's the boss around here? Me? Or you."

"You are, Mr. Giddens."

"Who decides the schedule, runs the whole factory, decides who comes and who goes?" he said.

"You do," I said. My hands were wet with stress but my mouth dry. "I was only trying to help you and her both."

He laughed at me again. "I don't need your help, missy. You're both fired. Get out."

Ethel went running, wailing as she went. I hated it. Next to Father dying, I couldn't think of a time I hated worse.

"Mr. Giddens," I said. "But I must respectfully request the rest of the pay I am owed. Three days' worth. Please."

"Here you are again, telling me what my job is? How many times do I have to tell you to get out?"

"I will get out when I am paid!" I shouted and was sure everyone must've heard. "I demand my fair compensation."

I had never struck anyone before, but I wanted to slap the smug look off his face.

No wait. He really could do it. What if he stood and cast a blow to the side of my head? I quaked, but I would not back down. He took his keys from his belt and unlocked a drawer on the left. The smell of this room and the rattling of his keys was making me sick. *Breathe.* He pulled something out.

"Here," he said and shoved some bills in my hand. "One day's worth for your trouble. And don't be asking for a character reference, Miss *Ken-tuck-y*."

He opened a manual and feigned deep study. Unlike Robert, who made me feel a star, I didn't exist to this man. What would happen to poor Ethel?

Would Mr. Giddens have treated a man this way? Would he have treated a table full of native-born women this way? Robert told me that Henry Ford had been the first to hire Black people in the automotive industry. He found jobs for others who had difficulty getting work as well, like ex-convicts, men without a leg or a foot, the deaf and blind, and epileptics. But Robert, though he was loyal to the company that employed him, had also alluded that for all his good, Ford wasn't a saint. Not with everyone inside or outside his company.

How many managers in industry treated their employees the way Mr. Giddens did?

When I exited the building, I planted myself on the rippled wood boards of the walk. I looked to the sky, and its puffy arrangement of clouds might've been the tops of mountains in the distance, their rounded tips covered with fresh-fallen snow. But on this Indian summer day, a searing heat baked my cheeks.

What was I to do? Back home in Kentucky, when Mr. Baker let me go from Labrot and Graham, it was with the utmost caring. And there was a reason for the dismissal: the distillery could produce no bourbon. Here, the factory would be one day behind and then have to catch up—faster and faster. But Ethel might lose her home. And I couldn't think straight to fully assess my damages.

I ran for blocks toward my house until I could run no farther. Then I walked. Better to save the streetcar fare. When I got home, maybe I should stuff my clothes in the trunk, retrieve my nest egg, hug Mrs. Sturgeon goodbye, and take Mother's money for a ticket and flee to the train station.

After all, what was I doing here? My yearning to accomplish big things with my life must all have been a pipe dream. Maybe I had deluded myself into thinking I could be independent.

Had I truly overstepped my bounds with my boss? Embarrassed him? Or was it that I'd showed compassion for someone Mr. Giddens thought was different or beneath him? I would never know. Ethel's face would haunt me always.

When I arrived at Saint Aubin Street, the arches of my feet ached and I could tell a blister had bubbled up on one pinkie toe. As I slowly mounted the steps to the blue boardinghouse, I thought: *No, I cannot go home. I have to fix my dream and live it.*

I should've kept my mouth shut—and worked. Then Friday, I could've paid Ethel some money that she lost. Without raising a stink.

Without subjecting myself to being berated in front of coworkers. Without an innocent woman being punished, too.

I got to my room without Mrs. Sturgeon seeing me. Everyone else was on jobs. I silently closed my door and wished I could bawl on Mother's shoulder—or, even, to my shock: on Robert's shoulder.

But Robert was in Missouri or Illinois or Ohio. What was I going to do?

I would wait my turn for the newspaper that night and scour the wanted ads. I would ask Oliver the accountant if he knew of any openings. I'd find a new job as fast as I could before I lost more money. Two days? Four days? Five? I was already out two days' wages that I was due. Damn that Mr. Giddens.

No money could be sent to Mother. I couldn't bear for my family to be so disappointed in me. And what of her bills? Would she keep coal reserves so low that she'd freeze in the house come winter? I choked out a sob, muffled into my pillow.

Days ago, I'd been riding free in the wind with a new friend named Lela. She didn't judge me for the way I talked or where I'd come from. On another recent day, I'd been kissing Robert Neumann and losing myself in his heat.

Had I thought that life would all be so easy? Now look at me.

That night, I awoke with a start at fifteen past three. I was sweating with my jaw clenched so tight the back of my neck burned. I'd been dreaming a horrible dream: I appeared to be in Father's dry goods business that was now long gone. My top right tooth had come loose—but I was not a child still with my milk teeth. I was the age I am now, and soon the bloodied tooth dropped into my hand. Then each incisor and molar fell loose from my gums in their turns . . . with my sister running between bolts of fabric and racks full of yarn picking up my teeth and ramming them back in my mouth while Mother watched on, chained to a desk, crying.

A nightmare. My body shuddered with the fear it ignited. I pulled my covers up under my chin and ran my tongue along my top and bottom rows. All teeth were firmly in place, but still I felt tense.

Suddenly, I understood the dream's interpretation. By coming to this city on my own, had I bitten off more than I could possibly chew?

If all I had left at the end of all this was Mother's money for a train ticket home, so be it. For now, I wouldn't crawl back to Kentucky without first giving myself every chance. I hadn't secured employment yet, but I'd talked to Lela by telephone.

"You'll find a job," she said. "They're plentiful right now."

Even if I started work tomorrow, it would take a month to catch up and send money to Mother. "Looks like I'll be tapping into my reserve funds," I said. "My nest egg."

Lela went silent on the line. Then she said, "Come with me to my broker. Invest! It's almost a sure thing."

She had piqued my interest with her investing before. Lela didn't even hold a regular job. Could I really spend my savings on a risk? Maybe, if I at least sent a bit to Mother first. I couldn't sleep otherwise.

"Just come with me to my appointment," Lela said. "My broker can discuss financial options with you for supplementing your income. Let your money work for you, not you just work for money." She giggled.

More money sounded grand. "I suppose it wouldn't hurt to listen," I said.

Maybe it was just what I needed at just the right time. Maybe my dreams of independence weren't over after all.

Now my friend and I were in the financial district. Shadows streamed over her Packard from the height of the skyscrapers around us.

"Unfortunately," Lela said, "this firm has no women brokers like one or two firms on Wall Street have. But I trust my broker."

I slammed the car door and bent my head back to the point my neck strained. I was like a toddler, letting my gaze travel up. The towering Dime Building with its twenty-three floors reached clear into the clouds. The building was home to abundant banks and financial services. It was magnificent in neoclassical architecture of white terra-cotta. The structure got its name when erected less than ten years prior, Lela explained.

"The name made people think of the power of money," she said. "It worked."

By the time we entered the brokerage office on floor nineteen, I'd been dazzled by the shiniest tiles and more elevators than I could count. So many bells dinging and businessmen coming and going. Lela let the receptionist know she'd arrived and took a seat by me. The lobby was all clean lines. It smelled of lemon oil and coffee. Photographs of Detroit in shades of gray lined the pristine walls in heavy custom frames.

The receptionist circled, offering cups of hot coffee.

"No, thank you," I said.

Though it smelled richly brewed, I didn't need anything in my hands. I bordered on nervous, in the way I might when visiting a doctor whose expertise far outweighed mine. But the cure the broker could potentially provide excited me more than medicine.

Lela and I waited among clients dressed in tailored suits with costly fabrics, listening to what she called "the sound of the ticker tape spitting out someone's futures." Numbers came across every few minutes, announcing the values from the New York Stock Exchange. On the ride up, she had detailed how her portfolio was now 50 percent bonds and the other half shares.

"Some for stability and some risk for high return."

While much of this "ticker tape" talk sounded above my head, some of it resonated with me. I was no novice when it came to numbers or absorbing complex material. I did it every day at Labrot and Graham. Then there was Mother, who shared with us girls the inner workings of the bonds in her Liberty Bond Drive. Someone would buy a bond for a set amount, and after a preestablished term of time and rate of interest, the federal government would repay the person's investment when the bond matured—with a modest degree of profit. It was guaranteed. Americans had effectively loaned Uncle Sam the funds to win the war. I'd never forget our parents taking us girls to the Great War's victory parade to see the company of doughboys Mother's efforts had helped save. It was 1918 and I was seventeen. The boys marched down the brick street in their "tin hat" helmets and long great coats, with rifles propped against their shoulders. I could still hear the beats of the drums.

Today, the larger world of investing was here for me to explore. I'd learn of avenues I didn't yet understand.

"Mr. Jackson will see you now, Miss Hill," the receptionist said, jarring me out of my thoughts as Lela stood.

My knees felt elastic as I followed her.

Within an hour, Lela had reviewed and signed her papers, and the broker asked if I might need assistance as well. My mind was clogged with echoes of AT&T securities, railroad bonds, insurance stocks, industrial shares, interest rates, and margins and bears and bulls.

It was more overwhelming than I'd supposed. I was unsure if I could do this after all. The dream of my lost teeth made my gums ache all over again. But it buoyed me that Mr. Jackson had spoken to Lela on his level, and not from his nose in the air. Father never spoke of financial matters to us girls—and rarely even to Mother. Here, it was different.

"This is all somewhat new to me," I said, trying not to stammer. "More importantly, my funds are meager."

"You'd be surprised how many women invest," Mr. Jackson said. "It's not all bears and bulls. We help lambs with modest amounts, from widows to shopgirls. They don't all have pin money or inheritances. I often see women like you begin with bonds before taking the leap into shares."

"I see," I said.

Lela sat patiently, crossing her legs and smiling.

Mr. Jackson jumped back in. "Tell you what, I've got a binder with a glossary, overviews of the basics of investing, ways to tap into money through credit, and articles on ordinary women investing as far back as the 1880s. They're not all female tycoons like Hetty Green. But many are quite astute. This'll give you an orientation."

He handed me the three-ring binder. Its weight was daunting and stimulating at once.

"There's a whole section that deals with taking risk. Return it in a few days and ask all the questions you like. Any friend of Miss Hill's is a friend of mine."

I shook the broker's hand. "Thank you."

Back at the house late that afternoon, I got my turn with the newspaper. I rushed through the pages to the wanted ads again, marking anything remotely relevant. Sales Clerk Wanted, Clerical Assistance Wanted, Wanted: Shop Girl. Into the evening I prepared my applications for delivery the next day. I still had both clerical and production character references from Labrot and Graham.

I would not stop until I secured a position. Robert was on the road, and if I wasn't job hunting, sleeping, or eating, I was studying Mr. Jackson's manual.

CHAPTER 19

Melanie

Louisville, Kentucky
August 2018

The morning after Casey's birthday party, my mouth was pasty dry. My eyes felt bloodshot and puffy. My head was . . . still questionable. I'd take a couple of aspirin.

But first I'd click to open a text that'd apparently come in the night before.

Brian.

For a second I wished it were Jason. Had I really been that self-absorbed to think he'd gone back to his parents' place and pined over me? It was as if I wanted him to still want me, but I didn't want him to want me. Or I wanted him to want me even if I didn't want him. Or on some subliminal level I plain wanted him, period. I stared up at the ceiling fan spinning over my bed, trying to ground myself. But even if I wanted him, I wouldn't have him. He'd hurt me too badly before.

I shifted to Brian's message:

> Hi Melanie. Something tells me you're still up. Short notice, but wondering if you want to get together Sunday? Maybe dinner?

I have a Louisville supplier to visit that afternoon and again on Tuesday, if that's better. We can talk more about next steps with your car. Let me know!

His words lifted my spirits, maybe even excited me. Brian was a good guy.

Maybe I should go. Like a business dinner—one evening in the middle of a week after work. I could swing it. Again the idea floated in my head about getting a loan. He and I could talk options for restoring the car. But maybe the evening could be about more than business. I didn't have to sacrifice my job to a man any more than Violet sacrificed her independence to Robert. I could go just for fun, couldn't I? And word might leak to Jason that I wasn't sitting around waiting on him. I should've listened to my friends all along.

But eight hours from now would never do. The contents of my stomach swished and gurgled with the mere thought of doing anything as vigorous as washing my hair. I'd be lucky to get two hours' worth of work done for the Cocktail Bash today.

I texted Brian back: Sure, let's get together. Tuesday's much better.

Brian: You pick the place.

I crawled out from under my comforter, brushed my teeth, and pulled up my marketing plan on my laptop.

I had barely settled into my cube at the office when it felt like the kind of Monday that gives Fridays their own acronym: TGIF.

My rival, Mitchell, was preening through our cubicle environment, his peacock plumage fanned out in full color. He'd just landed Cora an interview with the premier podcaster in the whiskey space. The interview would be recorded and go up on YouTube, too. She'd get to talk about the rise of rye whiskeys today—their allure for those whose palates wanted a bit more spice—and she'd put in a plug for our product launching in November.

Score another win for Mitchell. Ugh.

But I was thrilled for Goldenrod. Any press that made Cora look good made our brand look good.

As I was staring at my in-box on my left computer screen, an email from the vendor for the etched-glass bourbon sets popped up. Subject line: Urgent Update.

That could not be good.

I scanned down through the message quickly, my pulse going up. The vendor couldn't get the glasses. Their own suppliers of the glasses fell through. WTF. I should invent a new acronym for Mondays like this: WTFM.

I'd have to find someone else to produce the sets now? On a rush deadline for delivery to the Cocktail Bash's VIP suite? I could always scrap them. Choose a different swag gift for members of our Connoisseur Club. But that would be a major headache, and after the great reception I'd received from the team during our midyear meeting—and my promise of the sets then becoming the most high-profit item in our online store—I was even more annoyed.

I had no time to backtrack. Even the smallest blip in my performance was bad when so much rode on my promotion—including my potentially financing the Jordan. With Mitchell chalking up more wins, I had to secure a new vendor and fast.

Coming in second place was hardly in my DNA.

My mom hadn't reared me as much as hewn me, like from a hunk of oak—I was chiseled and shaped and fashioned into a sculpture by Mom the master woodcarver. On birthdays when I was in grade school, she would rise at five in the morning to prepare healthy crinkle-cut carrots with tiny yogurt dips. I wanted pink cupcakes like other kids. And she didn't believe in "prefab Disney vacations" or coloring books with lines that stifled a kid's creativity. If Dad didn't intervene, I would never have watched TV once a week and even then, I never saw movies with superheroes; Mom said I might turn aggressive. If I got a B in a subject like math, she hired a tutor on the spot. I was carted to summer camps for everything from robotics to chemistry. Never culinary arts like I'd pointed to in the brochures—with pictures of children wearing chef's hats and holding platters of chocolate éclairs.

Visiting Grape Aunt Violet for a week had been a reprieve, one where I need not perform or report my success to my mom. I could just be a kid. Yet in my aunt's own life, she had lost two jobs and went on to accomplish great things in her career. She had fortitude. I wasn't a kid anymore. I was a grown-ass woman, and second place wouldn't cut it.

I pulled up my internet browser to find a new supplier who could give me an even better deal on beautiful glasses—and I'd negotiate to achieve higher profits.

CHAPTER 20

Violet

Detroit, Michigan
October 1921

I shifted my heavy bag on my shoulder and walked the two blocks from the streetcar. In the autumn chill, the wind whipped up my legs in my coat. It would not be a good walk in January nor in April's showers. But I'd manage. *Please, God, let this interview go well.* Schmidt Gauge and Valve supplied speedometers for auto manufacturers and pressure gauges for assorted industries. But I wouldn't be in production. Only three days had passed since my dismissal and I already had an opportunity as a filing clerk. This job would be something I enjoyed more—and a stepping-stone into advanced clerical positions that could pay more than the factory. I'd take a bit of a hit on the wages at first, but I had devised a new plan for that, too.

The lobby was clean, and the floors smelled of Johnson Wax. So different from the spark plug lobby. A woman at a typewriter stopped tapping and said, tersely, I thought, "May I help you?"

"I'm Violet Bond."

"Oh yes. I'm Miss Baxter. Follow me."

We walked down a hallway and into a room where six other women sat typing, their fingers flying too fast for them to look up. Miss Baxter indicated I should take the open seat at the end. "You'll be tested on typing first," she said.

I was confident. Mother had taught me well. Despite Miss Baxter's subtle sneer, she never balked at my accent.

Within twenty minutes, her boss, Mr. Miller, said, "You're hired. Miss Baxter will show you the filing room where you'll spend your days. You begin tomorrow. Be precise, I must warn you. Our accountants and customers expect labels to be accurate and files accessible."

"I promise," I said, and I smiled broadly. "I'm good with details."

Miss Baxter was chilly as she escorted me to the door. But I didn't care.

I couldn't wait to tell Robert I got the job. His city truly was the place of opportunity. I was proud of myself, too, for forging ahead when life didn't go my way. I didn't want to return to Kentucky, destined for a life like my sister's. But I dared to admit to myself something else.

I wanted to spend more time with Robert.

I wanted to feel his gaze rake over me, to hear him say sweet things, to have him maybe touch me. Tonight I would fall asleep thinking of his lips on mine again. For now, I was off to my next stop of the day.

Soon, the windows on skyscrapers in the financial district sparkled in the sunlight. My bag felt heavier by the minute on the streetcar. I kept it and its precious contents tight to my torso. I had the binder to return to Lela's broker—and more than half of my nest egg, too.

I was going to be an investor.

I'd finished poring over Mr. Jackson's materials late the night before. Bonds, stocks, how to read statements, the cycles, and shouldering risk. Between Lela's encouragement and one particular article in the binder, I was enthusiastic. "From secretaries to gasoline attendants, people around the country are making money every day," the piece read. "Wealth isn't just for the rich anymore." I didn't need to be affluent, I just needed to get ahead. Before I turned out my light, I decided. I'd do it. My reserve in the safe at the boardinghouse was for emergencies after all. This situation counted.

I'd use a bit to cover what I was shorted by Mr. Giddens and still send money to Mother. I wouldn't buy a single thing for myself all winter; I'd make my stockings last until Christmas. By investing, I could yield much more income. But unlike some other "lambs" who start slow, with only bonds, I would invest in shares right off. I took a risk to board a train north like Phoebe Snow . . . though, at Mother's request, I'd waited interminable months before embarking. This time I wouldn't wait.

Men ignored me on the elevator up as they talked of stocks and steak dinners. I looked like a secretary, dressed as I was. When I entered the brokerage firm, the familiar smell of lemon polish welcomed me, and I was so high from landing the filing job that my nerves felt barely noticeable.

I told the receptionist, "I'm here to see Mr. Jackson. To set up my investments."

"You don't have an appointment, Miss Bond," she said after calling the broker's office. "But he'll see you in ninety minutes if you're able to wait."

"I'll be glad to," I said, hoping it would be the most lucrative hour and a half of my life. Based on what I'd studied, within one year, I could have extra earnings and savings back, too.

"Tonight, we celebrate," Robert said. He got back from the road late last night, and I told him about my job crisis on the telephone this morning. "You deserve to be spoiled after suffering that Giddens monster. How about dancing?"

We arrived by boat at an island on the Detroit River, but in the waters of Windsor, Ontario. Boblo's dance hall was the second largest in the world and held five thousand dancers. The gigantic room had gleaming wood floors, a balcony for viewing, and an orchestration system that Robert said would please Apollo—the Greek god of music and dance.

I sat at a table behind the railing at the side, and he brought me a glass of Vernors ginger ale made here in Detroit. The fizzy liquid bubbled in my mouth, with a mild taste of ginger and vanilla.

"Thank you. So tasty!"

Lela had insisted I borrow a special dress for the night: it was black crepe with a long row of tiny button heads down its front, and the skirt panels had embroidery in metallic gold and blue. The music was energetic—fast-paced in a way that exuded the postwar, postflu feeling of optimism. Here, young people like us escaped.

When a waltz played, more couples flocked to the floor.

"What do you think?" Robert said. "Shall we give it a whirl?"

He pulled me close, and our bodies met chest to thigh—like they had that night outside the speakeasy. Never had Billy Probst in high school ignited a flame in me on a dance floor. This was what I'd been yearning for. Closeness. Robert's touch. It felt heady. We glided in a forward two-three step and then a backward two-three. He led in a gentle sway back and forth and then straight in a walking step while our postures and bearings relaxed. We grinned at each other as we floated across the floor, intermingling with other couples, and it was magical.

I forgot about the week's ordeals and triumphs. I saw only him. Something had shifted in me again. Something not physical, but deep inside.

***

December 1921

The tiny back office where I worked was cozy warm, and I had fewer paper cuts than I'd had nicks from spark plug parts. Though the work was equally mind-numbing and lonelier in my isolation. Rarely did I interact with the full-time typists, where more of the chatter was found. Miss Baxter, I'd learned, considered herself above us all, as our boss's personal secretary—and his mistress. I relished knowing that when the company closed for a week at Christmas with pay, I'd have my finances under control and a ticket south to see family. It'd be the first time I'd seen them since moving. Mother promised my favorite gingerbread and Evelyn's favorite fudge. For today, I was with the two people dearest to me in Detroit: Robert and Lela, who were meeting for the first time.

We stood at the edge of the rink at Belle Isle where we had the summer picnic. Winter froze the lake in front of the pavilion, turning the water into a glistening sheet of ice. Banks of snow bordered the rink, and ice-covered trees in the background had limbs like crystal lace.

"Violet, you didn't tell me that Robert looks like Douglas Fairbanks," Lela said as snowflakes caught in her lashes.

"I think you must surely be mistaken," Robert said jovially, and I could see his breath in puffs as he spoke.

I'd told him that Lela drove too fast, that she liked to dance, and that her parents had a marvelous house at Grosse Pointe. She knew he was a Ford man from a hardworking German family—and that I was utterly smitten. Couldn't get him off my mind. It was heartwarming to have them together.

I wore a pair of Lela's skates and her two-piece suit for winter sports. It was made of gabardine, a fabric that repelled both water and wind. The trousers were in a jodhpur style—fitted from the knee down, and wide through the thighs like for riding horseback.

I'd done my share of roller-skating in Kentucky, but never had I worn skates with metal blades. My bendy ankles were still getting used to the boots here at the edge of the ice. Lela was the seasoned one—the princess of the rink in her dress made for figure skating. Its skirt was fashioned of pale-green velvet with white fur trim. She was first to glide out onto the ice and immediately leaned into a long, slow ride on one foot, with arms out for balance and her left leg stretched straight behind her.

"Look at her," I said to Robert. "Such a graceful thing. And I love her beret."

Robert looked handsome in his warm felt hat, midlength coat, and long, wooly red scarf. He owned his own skates, too.

He led me by the hand onto the ice, carefully avoiding other skaters. I felt as I must've when I was one, first learning to walk. I was wobbly and almost fell twice. But soon Robert detached from me and I took a few sliding steps on my own—teetering but keeping my balance in check. Robert glided out with graceful strides, his hands joined behind him, and then returned and held my hand.

"You remind me of a skater in a print of Currier and Ives," I said, and he bowed.

Lela whizzed over and stopped with a sharp cut of her skates. "Come on out to the middle, Violet," she said.

Robert frowned. "She's still getting used to the blades," he said. Then, directing his next comment to me, he added, "The spinners and speed skaters are out there, darting in and out. Let's make sure you're steady before venturing that far from the edge."

Lela shrugged. "She may be more adept than you think, Robert, whether skating or investing or what have you." She smiled and sailed back onto the ice.

Robert said as we skated a ways, "Lela has had a lot more experience on the ice. Don't feel pressured to keep up."

From his expression, was he cautioning me about more than just the skating? I felt like Goldilocks, with one bowl of porridge too hot and another too cold. I was somewhere in the middle.

"And," Robert said, "you're investing?"

"Yes," I said, feeling my cheeks turn cherry red if they weren't already from the cold.

"How long has it been?" he said.

I thought back. "About the time I got the new job."

"Investing's becoming a fad, isn't it? Watch yourself." He kissed my cheek. "There are risks."

I chafed at his fatherlike warnings. After a while, we all got warm by the bonfire at the pavilion and smoked cigarettes until almost dark.

"I've enjoyed being with you," Lela told Robert. "One day, we should all go to Times Square for New Year's Eve. New Yorkers ring in a new year in a style unlike anyone else. The ball drop and all."

We hugged her goodbye.

After Robert and I changed clothes in the pavilion, he said, "I know you're going home, but I wish you could spend New Year's with my family. We'll play games and music, and Auntie will fix a big German feast."

Now I felt as if I were in a Dickens story, but rather than seeing the ghosts of Christmas past and future, I saw before me the two halves of my life—with Lela the modern adventuress and Robert the homey traditionalist.

And even as my feelings for Robert grew, I began to wonder if he was *too* much like home.

I giggled nervously and poked a curl up under the front brim of my hat. We'd just left the park.

"Mind repeating that?" I asked Robert.

"Up for another adventure?"

"I'm an adventurous girl," I said, curious.

"My brother Alvin and his wife are visiting her side for the holiday in Cleveland. I'm staying at their place, watching their dog."

Their sweet boy Max? Robert had spoken of the German shepherd often. My mind raced. I didn't think their house was far off. What was

Robert *not* saying? I felt a blush. But I would prove to him I was no traditionalist.

"Why not let me help you. With Max."

One glance into his eyes and I could see the fire and surprise.

"All right," he said and picked up speed in the car. "Just what I wanted."

Am I really doing this? My decisions were mine alone. Heat prickled the tender skin of my chest.

We drove in sociable silence the rest of the way to his brother's, my mind abuzz with possibility. Kissing. Touching. Touching some more. Then Evelyn's face appeared without warning. However little or however far I would go with Robert tonight, I wondered, would my sister sense the change in me all the way from Kentucky? Would she think ill of me if she knew?

I wasn't a bride, nor did I wish to be. And I hoped that Robert would get that.

He unlatched the side door to the bungalow, and Max barked and wagged his tail fiercely.

"Hey, buddy," Robert said. "Uncle Bobby's back."

"Bobby?" I said. "Like the up-and-coming golfer?"

Lela had mentioned Bobby Jones of Georgia. A friend she knew had met him.

"Mother used to call me Bobby," Robert said.

"That's so sweet."

The little house was homey with plants and pillows and framed family pictures. Robert showed me his brothers, including the one who died in the war. We stood inches apart beside the brass torch lamp with its creamy glass glowing dimly.

"Smoke?" he asked, pulling his Camels from a pocket.

"Sure," I said. My nerves seemed ready to sprout through my skin, and I hoped a smoke would calm me.

Yet I put my arms around his neck, and before we had the cigarettes lit, we were in a crush with hands everywhere and us breathing heavy. He smelled of leather and spice. His lips parted mine. Then his tongue.

He tossed my hat onto a chair. I wanted him to want me. And maybe . . . I felt something else less definable—like a boulder tipping off on a hill that would pick up speed, unstoppable. For a flash, I felt afraid of where the rock might land. I didn't want to be in the valley of homey tradition.

"Your hair has been driving me wild all this time," Robert said under his breath.

His words reassured me, and I leaned in to the instincts of my body. His fingers raked through my short, wavy locks, his thumbs grazing my jaw.

"I think I'm falling in love with you," he said.

Stunned, I wasn't sure what to say, so I said nothing. This might be love I was feeling, but that scared me. I wanted us to be like Lela with her boyfriends. Just fun. I could have marriage or I could have independence. The latter was always for me.

Robert brought his fingers to the cloth belt at my waist and unbuttoned the two buttons that held it. Again, the surge of lust inside me set my fears aside. The loose ends of my belt dangled apart. Then he began at the top of my collared coat smock and released each button in turn, slowly, meticulously, with fire smoking in his eyes. He reached to slip the top off my shoulders, and I bloomed before him with the soft plum of my silk bandeaux and the bareness of my arms at his sides.

By the time the mantel clock on the shelves in the guest room struck nine, I was his through the pain and he was mine through the bliss and we were living in the moment, together.

CHAPTER 21

Violet

Frankfort, Kentucky
December 1921

On Christmas Eve I awoke to luxurious, comforting quiet. How had I ever gotten used to the hubbub of the boardinghouse? I arrived by train the night before, and the first words out of Evelyn's mouth were, "I love your hair!"

The second thing she told me—by only a whisper in my ear as we hugged—was, "Don't tell Mother, but I think I'm expecting."

I squeezed her tighter. "I'm happy for you." And I was. It was what she'd always wanted.

An announcement of a new baby at Christmas would be Mother's best present, too. And I would love Evelyn's baby with all my heart. I would. I'd hold it, rock it, kiss it, and let it coo. What an aunt I would be. But the *institution of marriage*, as it was called, felt like latching a wire door on a cage—a reminder of all I had in Detroit. And all I didn't have there: like no strings. Marriage and motherhood, though not vile to me at their core, were incompatible with being a modern woman.

Mother looked older, I thought. Not old, but older. Her skin had less luster. The lids of her eyes were more hooded, I supposed from missing Father. But she already had her homemade noodles cut and dried in the pantry. She would stew them in broth tomorrow to serve with traditional goose. Tonight, we'd gather around the piano with her eggnog in Grandmother Bond's delicate cut glass cups. We'd sing "Jingle Bells" as my sister played and I flipped her pages of music . . . followed by Mother's favorite German carol, "O Tannenbaum."

I confess, I did not feel stifled in this house of my youth. It was peaceful. I knew our holiday customs to be beautiful and sacred, each one. I would envelop myself in their warmth and love for our time together. Yet the key thing was this: I knew I had the freedom to leave here. More adventures awaited.

For now, we two sisters were baking. "Pass me the cutter in the shape of the star," I said.

"No," Evelyn said in fun as if she were four years old and I two.

Our aprons and hands were covered in flour. I held the rolling pin, but she was boss of the cookie cutters. We were making sugar cookies in shapes of stars, bells, and mittens. Mother was taking a bath.

"Tell me something true," Evelyn said, recalling a game we'd played as girls.

I could tell her about my investing. I'd already told Mother, who said, *It's a different time. Perhaps I might've done the same at your age.* She took my shoulders in her hands. *You have a good head on these shoulders,* she said. *But my girl, do remember: moderation in all things is prudent.*

Moderation in all things.

I'd hold off telling Evelyn for now. She knew I had a new job from my letters, but I relayed instead my saga of getting fired.

Evelyn said, "Mr. Giddens is not only an idiot, but a bigot. You're best to be rid of him."

"Exactly. Yet I still feel bad for Ethel Nowak." I loved how Evelyn took my side. "Now your turn," I said.

"Hmm," she began, and I heard a hint of melancholy in it. "I had a false alarm," she said.

"Huh?" I was confused.

"I got my monthlies this morning," she said, her gaze fixed to a bell shape she was cutting. "I was three days late, and I had gotten my hopes up." Then she bent her lips into a grin. "Charles wants a baby as much as I do. He says we need to practice more."

"What?" We giggled. It was hard to envision straitlaced Charles saying that.

I was sad for Evelyn. After all, she wanted motherhood in the way I wanted freedom. "There's plenty of time for you and Charles," I said. "You're so young!"

"Violet, tell me more things that aren't in your letters. Have you and Robert kissed?"

I stopped rolling out cookie dough, and I felt my face flush. I'd done more than kiss.

"Yes," I said, looking to make sure Mother was nowhere near us. "Outside a speakeasy."

Evelyn lifted her head. "You've been kissing *and* drinking with him?"

"A cocktail or two with him or my friend Lela. It's not abnormal."

Evelyn quieted. Then, "What else, Violet? There's more, I can tell."

I pondered. Maybe we could swap stories. After all, Evelyn had said something suggestive about Charles, and we'd laughed.

"I've been with Robert," I whispered. We were sisters, and I wanted, I thought then, for her to know but not judge me.

She slid a baking sheet of cookies into the hot oven.

"*Been* with him?" she asked, turning with pot holders on her hands.

"Yes. I'm no longer a virgin."

Evelyn screeched as if the reference to my deflowering had offended her Puritan ears.

"Shh," I said, putting my finger to my lips.

"How could you?" she hissed in a whisper. "You're not married."

"You're not really going to scold me, are you? You never even had a petting party with Charles before you wed?"

"Yes, I'm going to scold you."

"Why?" I stood there with my hands in the mixing bowl, wishing I never said anything.

"This is what happens when you've been away in the big city for a mere six months?" she said. "Did you . . . take precautions?"

"Of course," I said, feeling my chest redden. "Robert took care of that."

"How do you know he doesn't have diseases? And what of your reputation?"

"Who are you," I said. "Father?"

She had loved my hair, but now she was disappointed in me, and I couldn't bear it.

"Evelyn, please. Let's talk about something else. Mother will be along soon."

"Mother has to do her hair," Evelyn said. "Are you going to get married?"

"You know I don't want to get married," I said, feeling my temper flare. "Modern women do these things all the time, Evelyn." I carried the bowl to the sink, defiant.

"Maybe. But not my baby sister."

"I'm an independent woman," I said, staring out the window with my back to her. "Not an appendage to your person."

The roof of the carriage house had icicles dripping long and pointy as giant carrots. But then I swung to my sister's next question.

"Do you love him?" she said, sounding less critical.

I paced to the table and stubbed my toe on the chair leg. "Damn," I muttered.

"What did you say?"

"I said I think about Robert endlessly when I'm alone. I want to see him and kiss him again. Soon. I want to please him. Is that love?"

"Maybe," she said. "What else are you doing as a *modern* woman, besides drinking and having relations?" she said. "I saw you eyeing Charles's cigarettes last night. Wishing you had one?"

"Yes," I said, sounding rebellious. "So there."

"What!"

"*Shh!* Do you want Mother to hear?"

"Violet, I'm concerned. Going to Detroit was bold. But these illicit behaviors?"

"Calm down. Everyone does it."

"Not everyone," she broke in. "Though it does happen everywhere. Shorter dresses, shorter hair, later nights. Smoking, cursing, and drinking. What if you get arrested at a speakeasy?"

"Prohibition isn't fair," I said. "Mother taught that the Eighteenth Amendment is the only one to take rights *away* from citizens instead of *giving* rights to us. More people drink now than they did before." It was true.

"Violet, promise me you'll look out for yourself. Guard yourself, I mean it," Evelyn said. "Especially where that man is concerned."

That man? "Oh, I promise." I sighed.

Had my sister always been so pure and judgmental? Certainly she'd always been bossy. But then the nightmare of my teeth sprang into my head, and I shivered.

What if she was right? About my being more careful.

Mother's footsteps sounded on the stairs.

"You promise me in return," I told Evelyn, placing my palm over her mouth. "You'll not blab to Mother about all this."

I let go.

"I promise," she said, and then she pressed a cutter in the shape of a mitten into more dough.

CHAPTER 22

Melanie

Louisville, Kentucky
August 2018

Per my plan with Brian, we each took an Uber to Royals on Tuesday night to get sandwiches so we wouldn't go to the evening's main attraction on empty stomachs. More important, if cute car guru guy didn't meet me somewhere first, he might never find our ultimate destination. Inspired by the old journal entries, I'd known exactly what to choose for tonight: a place conjuring the spirit of Violet and Robert—a place for a modern woman having fun with a man. No attachments.

Our main event would be at Hell or High Water, a contemporary speakeasy that evoked the past and that didn't post a sign.

Despite my excitement about tonight's plans, I almost canceled to stay home and work. I still hadn't found a new supplier for the glass set after the WTFM debacle on Monday. And Mitchell landed yet another PR hit this morning: a premier bourbon blogger with thirty thousand subscribers would feature a tasting of our new rye when it released. But as Nicole had said at our gym, you're stronger when you rest your legs on the day you do your arms. And a girl had to eat. I'd attack work tomorrow, early, to make up for what I missed tonight.

Brian and I now walked along the sidewalk, with me as one half of a duo. Not a couple. It was little things I often missed about Jason . . . holding hands, cooking omelets together, watching *Game of Thrones*. But tonight wasn't about my job or my ex, either.

I forced my brain to focus.

"The place is right along in here," I told Brian, examining the display windows as we went. We were on the street down a ways from Louisville's Whiskey Row, a block-long entertainment district that included a few distilleries.

"We want to see a round, white light in a window, and on it, the words *Hello Curio*."

"Hello Curio? That's the cover-up for this hidden place of debauchery?" Brian said, playing along good-heartedly. He looked so cute in his collared golf shirt and jeans—and that thin beard, meticulously trimmed to look scruffy.

"Mm-hmm. There." I pointed.

One would think it a private gallery of collectables or curiosities. But no. I pushed the inconspicuous doorbell, and soon we were admitted.

A hostess with blonde hair cropped into a real bob and wearing a red beaded headband led us down steel steps underground to the intimate space and the bar. At the last step, I looked over my shoulder, and Brian was soaking it up. The exposed brick walls, the dim, glowing light.

"Let me just say," Brian said, "if my drink is half as tasty as this place looks, you'll be picking the places from here on out."

Did that mean he was thinking in future terms? I was taking a big step, but I couldn't think past five minutes from now.

It might still be daylight outside, but in here the ambiance was dimly dark as if it were midnight. Okay, the place was a tad romantic. The building was a hundred years old, and the ceiling had ancient wooden beams, an iron fence on a mezzanine, and concrete floors with oriental rugs. A crystal chandelier contrasted with metal industrial lights. But what my friends talked about was the button-tufted leather seating—and the curving red velvet couches. On a Saturday night, this place could get as crowded as Little Henry's in 1920s Detroit. Without the smoke.

"Is this okay?" the hostess asked.

"Perfect." I'd reserved one of the red velvet couches, which were really built-in banquettes. Each one snaked in a U-shape around a low round table.

"After you," Brian said.

The hostess laid down menus beside the flickering white candle. The bar's logo—HOHW, for Hell or High Water—was on the front in stylized letters with an art deco vibe.

I sank into the thick cushion, leaning against tufted crushed velvet that ran higher than my head. I'd poured myself into my Seven7 jeans, and I thought that Brian noticed. He sat close—not on-top-of-me close, and still not we're-holding-hands-now close—but close.

"So what do you recommend?" he said, perusing the menu. He sat with one leg resting atop the other at the knee.

"You'll see that drinks are broken into categories. One of the main categories, the Hell section, has your drinks that are stiffer."

Stiffer? Really? A Freudian slip.

"Stronger. Cocktails," I said, sure I was blushing. "Stronger than the High Water selections."

He said, "I'm actually feeling the section on HOHW Standards. I'll be ordering the old sport."

A Gatsby reference. I flipped to the page on HOHW Standards. The old sport had a single barrel rye, cognac, orange, coriander, dry curacao, and absinthe.

"Man, that looks like one I'd love," I said.

I glanced toward the bartender, a full-bearded man in a white shirt, with sleeves rolled up past his wrists, suspenders, and a tie. And he was wearing a cool brimmed hat.

"Brian, you won't believe this, but I'm feeling a drink that I don't see on the menu. I might have to go rogue." I told him about my aunt Violet's journal and her first stop at a speakeasy in the 1920s. "Half the fun of coming here is tasting each other's drinks."

"I'm down with that," he said. "I'm sure the bartender here can make anything you want."

Ten minutes later the server delivered our drinks. She said, "The old sport for him. And the pink lady for her."

"Awesome," I said. So they'd had the grenadine, apple brandy, and of course, lemon, gin, and egg whites. It was a gorgeous drink in a long-stemmed coupe, and I channeled Aunt Violet as I took my first sip.

I swallowed, but barely. My face wrinkled up. "Yuck."

Brian cracked up. "That bad?"

I assumed that Violet had struggled to adapt because it was her first drink ever. I held the glass out to Brian.

He looked at me as if to say, *Do I really want to do this?* He sipped.

"Nasty," he said. "Tastes like Pepto-Bismol."

"You nailed it." Our gazes held overlong. This hadn't happened with me since Jason. But I wasn't going to look away.

He let me sip his drink. "I'm switching to what you're having," I said as the server headed our way.

"I don't blame you," Brian said.

"Oops!" I said. My hand accidentally brushed his firm, warm thigh as I brought it back to my lap after returning Brian's drink to him. This might've seemed forward on my part. "Sorry!"

"Never apologize for touching my leg," he said, and his movie star good looks took me aback. It was a cute thing to say, I had to admit. And it had an effect on me physically.

In fact, I had to admit . . . he was tempting.

My replacement drink arrived. Brian lifted his own old sport in the air. "To your aunt."

"To Grape Aunt Violet."

Conversation flowed easily. Brian was interested in my Bourbon Craft Cocktail Bash. He spoke of his little red Corvette. Every Corvette in the world was manufactured on the west side of our state. That meant something to him. He'd left the sports car with his dealer today for its routine tune-up. He wasn't going back to Lexington until tomorrow.

I was surprised at how I was feeling. Jason wasn't looming at this moment. Brian was the fun guy—the Robert in my scenario. I imagined stretching out on the red velvet couch right here—posing naughtily for him. Or taking him home for tonight and posing on my own blue velvet. No. No way was I going to hook up. Call this a date? Yes. Spend the night together? Not happening.

Work was beckoning, and I had to get back on it, fresh-eyed, by five in the morning. I had deadlines and a worthy contender I wanted to beat. I needed this promotion to prove something to Mom. The raise that came along with it would help if I was going to preserve Violet's car in her honor.

"Any further thoughts on what to do with the Jordan?" Brian asked.

"I'm going to keep it." I smiled. "The more I read in Violet's journal, the more it pained me to even think of selling. I, uh, I'm actually considering getting a loan to have it restored."

"Wow." He grinned. "That's a big decision. I heard from my contact at Ray's Restorations," Brian said. "He'd love to take on your Jordan, if you're interested."

"Wonderful," I said. "He could give me a detailed quote?" I hoped it'd be less than Brian's guesstimate.

"If you like," he said, "I'm happy to take Ray over to your storage unit and let him write it up."

"That would save me over an hour for a trip to Lexington. But I couldn't impose on you for that!"

"I'm excited for you," he said. "He and I see each other all the time. It's no problem."

"We'll add your time to my tab," I said, teasing.

"How's your mom doing?" he asked. "Nice lady. I enjoyed meeting her."

"She's fine," I said. "Super busy with her job and all. You might've noticed she's very driven—no car pun intended."

He chuckled.

Yesterday, Mom had texted me saying she had "something special" to give me the next time I "dropped by." I thought it was a gesture to mend our cold ruffled feathers. I was certainly curious. Though "something special" to her might be about as special as a Franklin Planner to me. I'd neither seen nor spoken to her in a couple of weeks, since the day we towed the Jordan. I didn't want to be controlled or manipulated, and I wanted her to know it. I'd get my promotion—and earn her pride without relinquishing my independence. But I would accept the olive branch she was offering and slide by sometime to see what was "special." She was my mother. I wasn't disowning her.

After a while Brian said, "Dessert drink? They have ice cream." He wiggled his brows.

Ice cream. Cool cars. Sweetness. And hot. What a guy.

"An ice cream fan, huh?" I said, remembering an unopened jar at home: Sanders original hot fudge from Detroit. I'd had a craving after reading of one of Violet's dates with Robert and ordered it online. The name Sanders hadn't changed since around 1875. I had vanilla bean ice cream in the freezer, too. Brian and I could see if Aunt Violet's taste in sundaes was better than her taste in gin cocktails.

"Ice cream may be my one vice," Brian said, subliminally drawing me closer to inviting him home.

Our eyes were locked and I struggled. Play? Or work?

CHAPTER 23

Violet

Detroit, Michigan
January 1922

Tommy's was a blind pig that Lela and I hadn't tried before. No food. Just booze. Its building was more than fifty years old, and we had to stoop when entering through an old secret tunnel, arched and made of worn bricks. It'd been used for the Underground Railroad. Tommy served mostly near beer here, a cheap, watered-down pour that was legal. Marion Harris sang "Jazz Baby" on a phonograph behind us, and that alone was worth the stop. Lela mouthed along with the lyrics and bounced her head to the melody.

After a whole week at home in Kentucky and a few days back in Detroit—and an unpleasant day at work—I was ready for a night out. Girl fun. The traditional smells and sounds and tastes of home were lovely, but Kentucky had reinforced my drive to be in Detroit.

As I'd left, Mother had reiterated, *You have only one life.*

Her five words meant more to me now than they had years ago. She accepted my pursuits—my career, investing, and supporting myself. But she didn't know of all my "illicit behaviors," as my sister had termed them.

As Evelyn had put her arms around me to say goodbye, she repeated with an ominous tone, *Take care of yourself.*

So far as I could tell, she'd kept her promise, though; she hadn't revealed to Mother my confidences. But I feared we'd damaged our relationship. The coolness at the door as I left. My hesitancy to write as soon as I got back to Detroit. No letters yet from her, though Mother and I had penned them the very night I left—just to say we missed each other. I was still coming to terms with my sister's judgment of me.

The boardinghouse I'd returned to, however, was becoming intolerable—the sharing of one bathroom with a crowd again, rigid meal schedules, the noise. It wouldn't do forever.

Robert would be home on the weekend, and I missed him. I wanted to fool around again. Get naked. It didn't mean we had to wed. Again, I pressed my sister's admonitions out of my mind.

Lela and I sipped on some kind of rum concoction. Her hair embodied her trendy style in a finger wave with its soft, deep curves in the shape of an S that rolled from her head to her chin.

"So you were going to tell me about the fiasco at your filing job," she said.

"Right. I arrived at work early today," I said. "And when I entered my filing room that's no bigger than a bedroom in a servant's quarters, what do you think I saw?"

"Wait," Lela said. "Let me guess."

"No, let me tell you. Miss Baxter and our boss in a heated embrace."

Lela burst into laughter. "How juicy. Was her dress unbuttoned or hiked to her waist?"

"No," I said. "Nothing that indecent, but she smoothed the pleats of her skirt and scurried out like a rat."

"This is marvelous," Lela said. "But you shouldn't have to put up with it."

"No. So then Mr. Miller says, 'Good morning, Miss Bond, have a nice day,' as though nothing ever happened! I need a cigarette."

We lit our Lucky Strikes.

"You don't believe in the legend, do you?" Lela said.

"Legend?"

"How Lucky Strikes got their name? How the luckiest person would slip from the pack a cigarette laced with marijuana."

"That sounds silly," I said. "I can't believe you haven't told me before."

But Mother's warnings from my school-age days reared up. Might I soon be seeing hallucinations? She had warned that Co-Cola, as they called it in the South, had once been made with cocaine. We still never drank it at home. She had an open mind about many things, but narcotics was not one of them.

Lela rolled her coal-colored eyes dramatically to one side. She might've been a silent film star with that captivating face and dark cosmetics giving her down-sloping eyes.

"Personally," she said, "I think the legend's rubbish."

I wondered. If I did get "that lucky" to draw the secret cigarette, would I heed Mother's warnings there? Or smoke it down and get hopped up? Hmm.

"What are you and Robert doing this weekend?" Lela asked. "Besides hanky-panky." She tittered.

A shabby-looking man with heavy whiskers leaned between us then, sozzled. "Hanky-panky?" he said. "I'm game for both of you sweeties."

His breath smelled of fish and as if he hadn't brushed his teeth in weeks. I frowned, looking to a couple of guys behind him. His buddies?

One of them said, "You ain't got a chance with these lovelies, Moe. Move on."

But he didn't listen. He bent over me as if coming in for a smooch. I was about to smack his face when Lela drove the heel of her shoe into the side of his thigh. He jumped back in a wallop of pain, and his buddies hauled him off.

Lela's facial expression seemed to say, "Oh well."

"Thank you," I said.

"I grew up in a big house," she said. "My parents gave me everything money could buy. And love, too. But you know I always wanted a sister. That's what I'd do for her if I had one. I'd make any sacrifice."

What would my sister think of the man moments ago? Here's what I knew. Even if Lela hadn't stepped in, I was looking out for myself. Evelyn need not worry about me.

"So, Lela, you told me once you're not ready for marriage."

"I'll marry one day," she said. "When I'm too old to flirt." She cackled. "Why do you ask? You're not thinking of getting hitched, are you?"

"Nothing close."

Robert had said he had feelings, though. Love. But hadn't I long known he wasn't the marrying sort? His aunt had said so. Maybe I had feelings, too. Maybe even love. But I couldn't have both marriage and independence any more than I could have blue eyes and brown.

"For me," Lela said, "there's pressure from my parents to wed the right guy. Correction: the right family. But all that doesn't matter so much to me."

"What family would be right?" I blew out smoke from a draw.

"Mother would have me hold court like a princess of Sweden or Greece."

She went on to say how a Grosse Pointe woman who'd married a member of the Russian nobility—and became Countess Gwendolyn Tolstoy, now related by marriage to the famed Russian author—had attended their private event at last year's Detroit regatta. "Mother would prefer old money," Lela said.

"And your father?"

"New money spends as well as old money, Daddy always says."

Her own family's line didn't reach back to Detroit's French or Dutch settlers. Even the Dodge brothers, who'd been automotive tycoons before they died of the Spanish flu, were refused membership in the Country Club of Detroit. So Horace Dodge had built a palace on acreage adjoining the club in Grosse Pointe Farms. And then he'd bought his wife a pearl necklace that once belonged to Catherine the Great. Club members got friendlier when Dodge's daughter Delphine planned a wedding for thousands of guests.

Lela welcomed me into her life as a friend. It wasn't all about class to her. Anyway, no matter how far families went back, all "old money" had to have been "new money" at one point, didn't it?

"What about you, Violet? Any pressure to walk down the aisle?"

I squirmed. "Yes. From my sister. But for entirely different reasons."

"Do tell." Lela puffed her cigarette.

"Because of my sexual dalliances. To Evelyn, intimacy means home, family."

"Oh," Lela said.

When I was a girl, I wanted Evelyn's approval. She was my sainted big sister. These days, one minute I thought her opinions of me didn't matter anymore. But then I thought they did.

Fond memories of being back in Kentucky reared up in my head without warning. The candlelit tree, the freshly baked cookies, the music and eggnog and hugs. I did love them.

Lela said, "Far be it for me to dissuade you from an older sister's wisdom. But you know how I feel about that. Men are fun."

I thought of my upcoming weekend with Robert. Fun only. No expectations. I feared that I leaned more to Lela's way of thinking all the time. Not Evelyn's. What would that mean for our future?

Within days I got a raise at work, ostensibly because the company was in a growth spurt. But Lela said it was "hush money" due to what I'd witnessed. I didn't care what it was. I had a higher income. And I wouldn't have been stupid enough to blab to others and risk getting fired. But I thought I was valued for my work's accuracy and pace. They didn't want to replace me. Sending money to Mother now meant less angst when sealing a stamp. I'd already started saving again—this time, it would be bit by bit for my car—and I took new interest in advertisements in magazines and cars on the road. I was preparing for the day I'd have what Father said I couldn't.

On Saturday, Robert called to say he was running late, so he didn't come to the door. I threw on my coat and gloves and made my way to his car. As I crossed in front of it, I glanced at his face through the windshield. That dazzling smile.

He leaned over inside and opened the door for me. When I got in, our eyes met—and held like a moment suspended. It was as if fireworks had been lit up on the night of July 4. We hadn't even touched, but his eyes—raking my face and legs and body—were as palpable as if his hand grazed my skin.

"I've missed you so much," he said, all breathy. "Damn, you're a gorgeous girl."

When he spoke to me that way, I went light-headed.

He drove down the street. It wouldn't be dark for hours. I didn't care. I wanted him to find a spot right then and for him to pull me into his arms and bury his face in my neck. But it would wait.

Do you love him? Evelyn had asked.

You're not thinking of getting hitched, are you? Lela had asked.

Had I missed him more than I could admit? What of this yearning that had nothing to do with sex? It felt protective of him somehow. Possessive.

My mouth watered. I didn't know for certain what these feelings were, but I wanted to close my eyes and be engulfed by them, if only for the moment.

He held my hand as we wandered the collections of the Detroit Institute of Arts. People stared at us as we walked by. Old people smiled and nodded as if remembering the days of their youth, I thought. Young people eyed us and wished they had this power. Robert and I made a striking couple.

When we found ourselves in a small gallery alone, Robert nuzzled my ear. He ran his hand beneath my coat and up my back. I nipped at him with my lips on his cheek. He smelled so good.

There were French paintings by Claude Monet and art by old masters like Rembrandt van Rijn. As much as I loved the works—and even thought Mother would be bowled over by the collections—I only wanted to get out of there.

As soon as dusk fell, Robert found a private place to park behind a business that was closed.

We went at it as soon as he stopped the car. Hugging. Kissing.

"Remember how I said I'm falling for you?" he said with a growl. "I was wrong. I'm already there. I love you, Violet Bond."

Now I was falling. That was it exactly. This feeling. I was falling and had no idea if it would hurt to land.

CHAPTER 24

Melanie

Louisville, Kentucky
August 2018

I gawked at the unopened jar in my hand. Sanders—Detroit's finest hot fudge.

I hadn't invited Brian home after the speakeasy.

The idea to ask him had taken shape in my head. It'd amassed a huge size and swayed this way and shifted that way. It'd turned inside out and back again. I'd visualized feeding him a big spoonful of rich, dark decadence—hot fudge stringing from the spoon like hot cheese on a pizza. Sitting there in the dim light of the speakeasy on the red velvet couch, I had almost formed the words with my tongue: *Why don't you stay at my place tonight?* Then I froze.

I had to put work first. Not a man. My goal was to get the promotion, and I was on a crunch deadline. I wouldn't let myself down.

By a couple of days later, I'd lined up good leads on a new supplier of custom glass sets, and I was getting two proposals by this afternoon.

My folks lived in Louisville's suburb of Prospect. I'd gone to work early so I could take a little longer lunch: time to see the "something special" Mom had to give me—and to once again move forward as if no riled feelings had occurred. But I wouldn't take any crap.

Dad wasn't here in the middle of the day to play peacemaker. He was a partner at his accounting firm in the city, and he had to "bill those client hours"—or make sure someone else billed those client hours.

"Snickers!" I said as I came up to the pool in my parents' backyard. Our chocolate lab—the family dog we got when I was sixteen—ran to welcome me. "Have you been swimming, Snicky-doodle? What a good boy." I gave his wet neck a hug, hoping my clothes would dry before I returned to work.

"Hey, honey," Mom called out all perky from her lounge chair where she held her laptop.

It was a perfect seventy-five degrees with no clouds in sight, and for a sec, I longed to slip on my Ray-Bans and teal bikini. But I had to get back to the office, and she was heading to the airport in a few hours for business.

I bent to hug her.

I said, "You're living the life, aren't ya?"

This wasn't a bad office, here by the sparkling blue water of their gunite pool, surrounded by pebble stone decking. Small fountains at one end of the pool peacefully rippled. So feng shui.

"I'm glad you're here," Mom said.

So we'd made it through our greeting, playing our roles, with any surface awkwardness abated. I stretched out on the chair next to her, clothes and all.

Mom sported bold dark sunglasses, a big floppy hat, and a sleek black one-piece cut high on her legs. She pulled off that look as well as any middle-aged woman on the French Riviera. At least of her crowd with tummy tucks.

"Here," she said, handing me a bottled water. "But we'll have to wait until we go in the house for the little present I have."

"Can't you give me a hint? Besides, I don't have long. Duty calls."

She slipped her laptop into her beach bag. "It's best you see for yourself."

"The suspense," I said.

I really couldn't harbor a guess as to what it would be. A piece of art she was wanting to get rid of? A new novel just out? Gourmet cheese straws? These seemed unlikely to need all the lead up.

"I brought something for you, too," I said. "Though it's not a gift. I need it back."

Snickers ran and jumped in the pool. He swam to retrieve a stumpy rubber noodle in his mouth and then swam back to the side. That dog climbed up the wide, tiered steps, got out, shook the water off, and then jumped back in again.

I pulled from my shoulder bag Grape Aunt Violet's journal and held it up.

"Best not to let this get wet, but this is what I'm loaning you. I found it in the old car. It's like Violet's diary or journal. I think you should catch up reading with me."

The journal would give us something neutral to discuss—but she would also read of Violet's supportive mother and her declaration to stay single. Maybe Mom wouldn't bring up Jason again.

"A journal?" Mom said, frowning. "How surprising. I've got a four-hour flight to LA and a four-hour flight back Saturday, so good timing. But why are you just now telling me about it?"

"It's not like you're the history buff. And I really didn't know what to expect at first," I said. "Till I got into it. But it's quite juicy."

"A week ago, I would never have thought of Violet's story being juicy," she said.

"I know, right?"

She smiled. "Any more thoughts on the Jordan?"

I hadn't intended to bring that up, but dodging the question would be fruitless.

"I'm thinking of getting it restored."

She lowered her sunglasses and eyed me. "Really? You've gotten a bona fide estimate?"

"I talked to Brian again. He's getting it for me."

"Ohhh," she said.

I waited for her to say, *I seeeee. So you and Brian are a thing now.*

But she didn't. No lectures on protecting my heart. She was being good. I turned toward the row of high evergreens that bordered the yard at the rear. Such a peaceful place here, while the rest of the world worked.

"We'd better go inside," I said. "I have to get back to the ship soon. Besides, I can't wait to see what you have."

~

Black-and-white photographs were a jumble, spread across the end of Mom's banquet-size dining table. At the holidays, this distressed wood monstrosity seated ten guests with room to spare. Natural light drenched the dining room open to the kitchen and great room, highlighting the pale-sage green printed wallpaper. Miniature framed prints of birds adorned the walls, and roman shade valances hung above two sets of french doors painted creamy antique white.

"What are these?" I said, fanning one hand across the table.

"Remember the shoeboxes full of old photos? The ones Grammie left me."

"Sure," I said. Mom had been promising to sort through those for years.

"I've seen how interested you are in the car Violet left you. I decided to pore through the boxes in hopes of finding an old photo of it. No luck. But there are others you'll like."

This was sweet and unexpected. I knew how busy she was, but she'd taken the time.

"Mom," I said, rubbing her back over her swimsuit cover-up. "I'm moved that you would think of doing that."

I picked up one of the pictures. "It's your grandmother Gladys, right?" I said. "Evelyn's daughter? That's her old fireplace with the stockings hung."

"Mm-hmm. I see a lot of you in her, don't you?" Mom said.

It was hard to tell with the late fifties hairdo and cat-eye glasses. "I suppose in through her chin and lips maybe?"

"Yes, in the mouth," Mom said.

"And this one," I said. "A vintage wedding photo."

"Right. My great-grandmother Evelyn," Mom said. "I think it's a beautiful dress."

"Violet's sister," I said. "Gorgeous." I wished I'd gotten to meet her.

These pictures meant more to me now, having learned more of Violet's life.

The white dress from the late 1910s fell to Evelyn's shins, and she wore stockings and white or silver shoes; it was hard to tell in the black-and-white photograph. A headband of flowers adorned her hair, and a voluminous sheer veil fell around her body and puddled on the floor. The floral bouquet was as wide as her hips, dwarfing her waist, and streamers of ribbons hung from the blooms.

"There are two poses here. Take one," Mom said. "I'm going to have the other framed to set on our piano." Then, looking down, she said wistfully, "I should've had a picture of her out years ago."

Her baby grand was what Dad bought her when they built this home. Mom had played as a girl.

"I love that idea," I said. "From the journal, I know Evelyn played."

"But here's the photo I thought you'd like most," Mom said, moving on. She reached into the pile.

"I can see why you didn't want to spoil the surprise by telling me you found pictures," I said. "These are over the top."

Was she actually being this thoughtful? No hounding me? Maybe I'd gotten through to her after all.

"It's Violet," Mom said, handing the photo to me. "Youthful Violet. The one with the juicy story."

Goose bumps prickled as I took the picture. This was the young—wild and not tame—Violet Bond. The one who drank gin and showed off her gams. The shot was much more casual than the picture I'd found in the car. She was dressed in dark, shockingly short shorts and an even shorter light-colored sleeveless thing, slim through the waist and flared at the hips.

Mom said, "That getup reminds me of tennis outfits Chrissie Evert wore in her day."

"Yeah, like in the 1970s, not 1920s," I said.

Shoes with moderate heels accentuated Violet's shapely bare legs, and she held behind her a ginormous umbrella with big polka dots. She'd wrapped a scarf around her head, where little curls of hair escaped at her temples—and the length of the polka-dot scarf draped down long across one breast.

"I'm wondering if it's a bathing suit?" Mom said.

"Ha! Hadn't thought of that."

The picture's setting was sunny, like by a lake or a river nearby. Or a pool. Did they have pools back then? Well, Gatsby had a pool. Perhaps Violet was on the same estate as the photo I'd found in the envelope. She didn't look directly at the camera, but rather from the corner of her eye like a flirt. Yeah, she was a total coquette.

"I totally love it," I said. "Thank you."

There were photos of Bond House with the trees before they'd matured. A shot of the carriage house in its heyday. And newer pictures, too. Mom and Dad on a date. Dad holding me as an infant. He had a true look of pride even then.

“Look at you in this one,” Mom said. “You were around four and just adorable.”

Adorable? I grimaced. It’d been my first ballet recital. Not a happy memory.

Mom had stretched an onionskin-tight hair bun on the top of my head. She sprayed on a cloud of hairspray in which I swore I could smell its chemicals. Then in my dance class’s second number, I dropped my big bouncy ball prop, and Daddy jumped from his seat in the front row to place it back up on the stage, smiling, encouraging—while Mom tried stifling her look of horror. Even at my tender age, I sensed that she thought: How could *my* daughter do *that*? And it wasn’t just her. Another girl’s brothers in the auditorium laughed and pointed at me.

“Mom, I can’t believe you think this picture’s cute. I felt embarrassed that day, a complete and total flop.” I’d never done ballet again.

She frowned. “Now that you mention it, I do recall you sniffling on the way home in the car. I’m sorry, I saw this and thought you were the cutest thing in the world.”

“I had disappointed you.”

“What do you mean?” she said.

“I mean . . . Oh, never mind.” I had to get out of here.

“Honey,” Mom persisted. “I assure you, you didn’t disappoint me.”

How could she say that? It stood as the first, pivotal moment of my understanding that she held high expectations for me. There were standards—and I was certainly never to be the worst of the group.

“I literally dropped the ball, Mom. I saw your horrified face in the audience. I saw it.”

Her face turned crimson.

“You misunderstood,” Mom said tentatively. “What had gone through my mind when your daddy had to put the ball back onstage was something else completely.”

Yeah right. “Like what?”

"Like wondering what kind of sadistic dance instructor forces four-year-olds to toss balls above their heads, catch them, and then spin around? Weren't pliés and pirouettes in pink tutus enough?"

I didn't know how to respond. That was certainly the kind of thing that would go through Mom's head. I wouldn't be surprised if she sought the teacher out afterward to correct her, but with Dad holding her back. Had I misjudged Mom? I was only four at the time, after all.

But no. Mom's image-conscious trait got worse as I grew older—clear up to when I didn't get to wear cords for the highest GPA in college. I was magna cum laude, not summa cum laude as her best friend's daughter in Chicago had been. Mom tracked things like this on Facebook and made a point to tell me.

But what was the use in throwing all that in her face today, with a short time clock?

"Let's forget it," I said. "Thank you for the photos. I've got to get back to work and prep for the Cocktail Bash; you've got to get on a plane."

Her look of concern had barely subsided, but she said, "What about the journal?"

"Oh, right." I gave it to her.

Mom held the brown leather tome in her hands with the reverence it deserved. She took it to her nose.

"It smells so old," she said.

"Yes." I suddenly felt remorse for letting it out of my sight. I said, "Whatever you do, don't lose it."

CHAPTER 25

Violet

Detroit, Michigan
March 1922

I spun in my new dress in my room at the house. It had blue-and-cream checks and a V neckline. The hat was adorable, wide brimmed with two feathers, but it was the shoes that set everything off: leather with wide straps that buttoned around my ankles.

"Robert will love your new outfit," my friend Sarah said, admiring.

"Thank you. But I bought it for myself." It'd been on a rack sale, and I loved it.

"Are you and Robert getting engaged?" she said. "Everyone's talking."

"No," I said, swinging toward her and sounding as if the question were absurd. "Who's everyone?"

"Oliver, Hannah, Mrs. Sturgeon," she said. "I wouldn't be surprised if you were getting married. You never date other men." She eyed me, looking for signs.

"I don't know why Robert's aunt would speculate in that way," I said. It hurt my feelings that my landlady talked about me behind my back—especially given she herself had advised that Robert was not the marrying sort.

"Violet, I'm not the only one who sees how he looks at you," Sarah said. "But maybe you're right. Have a fun evening."

I was beginning to feel under siege. Since Christmas, Evelyn's letters had come not weekly, but every two or three weeks. Sadly, I looked for a post from her nearly every day, despite our disagreements. Her latest had asked (again) if I was getting wed. Funny how some people like Lela called marriage getting "hitched"—tied together like a horse to a fence. But my sister had also thanked me for keeping up on Mother's payments. And she said weather was turning to spring back home. Yellow daffodils. Pink tulips.

The relationship between Evelyn and me wasn't entirely severed. But I would ignore her question of marriage when next I wrote. My independence was hard-won, and I didn't wish Robert to jeopardize it.

"Where are you taking me?" I asked him when we got in the car.

"A surprise." He gave me a sideways glance.

I wasn't in the mood for surprises, not after the surprise of learning my friends had gossiped about us. It was none of their business. I was living my one life.

"We're heading west?" I said. The sun was lower in the sky.

He patted my knee. "I'm taking you somewhere I hope you'll love."

In time, he turned into a newer neighborhood. Some homes were still under construction.

He pulled up to one that was complete. There was no lawn as such. But the house was built right down to the porch lamp.

"Who lives here?"

He looked to me with a marvelous smile and said, "Me."

I pointed. "You own this adorable bungalow?"

He nodded. "Let's get out."

It was a cute, quaint house with a blue nearly the shade of turquoise, white trim, and a red accent around the windows. The porch had two Craftsman pillars—one on each end.

"How exciting, Robert. You bought this?"

"Yes," he said, and his humble pride that I'd detected the first day we met overtook him. "My father was sad to see me go," he said, "but happy for me, too."

We entered the little living room. There was no furniture yet, but a functional fireplace and walls with cheery blue paint. White curtains already hung from rods. The place was absolutely adorable.

"There's two bedrooms, the kitchen, and bath," he said, beaming.

I thought I'd love spending time with him here, just us two.

"I'm hoping you'll help me decorate," he said. "Furniture, pictures for the walls, what have you?"

That gave me pause.

Of course I was ecstatic for him to be a homeowner. A newly constructed home at that. Robert's Ford business expanded by the month. He already had a larger territory.

But this was not my home. I was a visitor. If it were important enough to Robert, he might've asked me to help choose it, not just choose the trinkets. Then I felt a sting of my own hypocrisy. The fact that this was *his* home, not mine, lent itself well to my independence. I needed to keep it that way. So while I would generally love selecting fabrics, pillows, clocks, and rugs, I'd do so with caution. I had to navigate my clash of desires.

Mother's and Evelyn's lives were the examples so common in society. Marriage wasn't bad in and of itself. I'd seen good in my parents' relationship, too. But to wed and raise families sabotaged our power as females. It was a truth that a modern, independent woman could have love with marriage—or she could have freedom with her own governing choice. Not both.

Robert's new home scared me now. What if my friends at the boardinghouse were right? He might be the marrying sort after all.

"Do you love the kitchen, Violet?" he asked.

"Mother would say there's abundant light, plenty of workspace, and nice cabinetry," I said straightforwardly.

His expression was nonplussed—as if he'd purchased a gift for me, watched me open it, and I'd been milquetoast at best. Did Robert wish to hear me say, *Oh, how I'd love to get in here and whip up a nice meal?*

"Let me show you my bedroom," he said, and he led me by the hand through its door.

"Oh!" I said, shamefully considering that our necking wouldn't be limited to his car. We could be alone anytime we wanted. "You already have a bed?"

"Well," he said, "a man's got to have a place to sleep before he has a wing chair to read the paper."

"True enough." I smiled slyly.

"Violet, you know I'm wild about you, right? It's more than a crush."

"Yes." And when he looked at me that way, I was wild about him, too. I felt something inside me just from his eyes.

He brushed my hair away from my forehead.

"I'm in love with you," he said, drawing me close with his arms. "You might as well accept it. It's plain as can be."

"I have feelings for you, too, you know that," I said, and I was at a loss for how to reconcile them with everything else.

Over the last several months, my investment broker had shown me the numbers and a chart where a red line went up and up to the right. I'd borrowed on credit, put in the bulk of my nest egg now, and taken some higher risk. I was earning money even as I stood here doing nothing. And it wasn't giving me paper cuts like with filing. I had money left over each month, a reserve fund building again. I was becoming more independent, not less.

Robert lightly pressed his forehead to mine. We rubbed noses.

"One day," he said, "I hope this house will be yours, too."

There it was. It was generous and honorable. But my muscles contracted. His idea was not revolting to me, but I was nowhere near ready.

Robert led me to the bed and we slowly, with no rush, no one to pester us, took our time together. And it was special because it was here, and he cared for his every touch to please me.

Was this love? Maybe. Was it enough? Yes, for me. He didn't press for more that night. But now I'd watch him more closely.

***

Two months later, May 1922

May Day was beautiful. Robert brought me back to the park at Belle Isle where we stood in a crowd of festive admirers watching the girls. They were ten or twelve years old and circled a maypole carrying streamers from its top. Blue forget-me-nots bloomed in the shade. Birds flew overhead. After the park, we would head to a Detroit Tigers baseball game. Robert had tickets near center field where we'd get the best views of Ty Cobb catching fly balls. Spring felt rejuvenating—and with it my wish to have a great day together, a day of light and fun.

We walked hand in hand away from the pack now. We found a flat, grassy spot under a large sycamore tree and sat down. I was careful to slide my legs to one side and bend my knees, my feet crossed at the ankles. With spring in full force, his business had picked up—and so had my investments.

When Robert was away, I spent more time with Lela, and if I had a late night, I cared less and less what the boardinghouse residents thought. I even spent the night with her at her parents' place a time or two—all the better for the residents to get used to my being gone overnight. On any given weekend, they didn't have to know if I was with her . . . or taking the streetcar to meet Robert.

He stayed on the road a few weekends, digging into time we had left together. During those times, though, I was diligent in monitoring his every word since he bought the house. One time we were there, and we awoke together. He said, *I wish we could be like this every day, forever. You waking up in my arms.* It was a tender thing to say, but somehow his loving arms felt at once as if they gave me life—and like a vise, squeezing me. I craved being surrounded by him, hearing his gentle breathing, feeling his soft breath on my shoulder. But his words rang too shrill of permanence.

I thought in an impulse that I might leave him. But I didn't. Within minutes, I decided I'd overanalyzed what he said. I cared about him. I let it pass.

"I have a present for you," he said now beneath the tree, and surprise swam across my face like water.

Whatever it was, it was small, because he hadn't carried anything in. I was nervously curious. And when he pulled a jewelry box covered in black velvet from a pocket in his coat, my limbs went limp. I was glad to be sitting down. Jewelry? A ring?

An engagement ring?

For many young women, this would be one of the best days of her life. A proposal on a glorious spring day. Evelyn would be overjoyed for me. No doubt she scrambled to open all my letters in hopes of learning that I would conform.

"For you," Robert said. "Open it."

I forced a smile. Could he tell?

The velvet felt soft on the tips of my fingers. What was happening to me? I wanted him, but a forever promise made me jumpy. I had the luxury of looking down at the box and not into his eyes. I took a breath and lifted its lid.

A bracelet. "Oh, Robert," I said, my eyes meeting his now and feeling a fool. "It's lovely!"

And it was. The prettiest piece of jewelry I would own. A sterling chain scarab bracelet had five pressed glass beads in the Egyptian style. Two reds, a black, a green, and a yellow.

"Help me put it on," I said. "I truly could not adore it more."

His face said everything. He was so glad. His larger fingers worried the tiny clasp of the chain, but he managed to get it hooked. Then he lifted my wrist to his nose where I'd sprayed a mist of perfume, and he said, "You smell so good. Like flowers."

"Thank you."

The bracelet fit gracefully around my right wrist, just loose enough to move and dangle a bit. I modeled my wrist for him, and he laughed. Then, not minding the people out on this splendid afternoon in the park, I kissed his cheek. With my thumb, I rubbed the faint print of lip color off.

"Thank you again," I said.

"I love seeing you happy," he said.

We walked the distance to his car, my relief making the sunshine feel brighter. I wouldn't have to leave him. I wouldn't have to feel an emptiness. A weight lifted from me. I could stop analyzing his every word like a warden. My feelings for him deepened in that very minute.

Robert knew me after all.

CHAPTER 26

Violet

Detroit, Michigan
August 1922

Lela and I lounged by the pool on a scorching summer day at her parents' place. They had a gorgeous home on Beverly Road in Grosse Pointe Farms. It was designed by her father's friend Albert Kahn, the same architect who'd designed the groundbreaking early Packard plant—with the first concrete walls and pillars to ward off fires and that had revolutionized the auto industry. Lela's parents were gone to Boston, and she and I tipped a little hooch. We wore our scanty bathing attire with our umbrellas that matched our suits; mine was a pretty polka dot.

The bracelet Robert gave me glinted in the sun, making me think of him even more while he was traveling. During the summer, he was on the road more weekends than he was home.

"I don't know how Robert and I ever managed before he had the bungalow," I said. "At least when he's back we get to be alone."

Lela gave me a nod. "But if Robert should ever propose," she said, "well, I just can't imagine a woman would want to be stuck in a house all alone with the birds and nosy suburban neighbors. No nightlife."

Robert understood me, though. He'd proven that, and I felt no need to convince her. I enjoyed being in his pretty little house some days. He and I had everything we wanted, just as we were.

"You and I should get an apartment together in the city," Lela said. She'd mentioned it more than once of late.

That idea was appealing. Robert and I could have private time there, too—and I'd get out of the annoying boardinghouse. I'd rise for breakfast when I wanted to eat. I'd have a bath without waiting turns for Sarah or Oliver to get out of the tub. I'd read a paper that didn't have square holes from ads snipped out of it by fellow residents. Between my recent raise and my investments that were trending up, in a few months I'd be in a financial position to move.

I would buy my own car, too, finally. I'd have a place to park it. It would be another big step in my grandest independence, something I'd wanted since I was sixteen.

"Father," I had said years ago, on another hot summer day back home. The two of us were in his Ford, headed to his dry goods store. "Won't you teach me how to drive?"

He looked aghast. "I most certainly will not."

"But why? Mr. Thompson lets his wife and daughter drive his Buick." Granted, that family was unusual.

Father parked the car and shut it off. "Violet Dorothy Bond, I wouldn't send you into combat at war, and I won't let you drive. It's not safe. You could get stranded, or, or—"

"But, Father, it's a new age." I bit my tongue. Perhaps progress was not the right petition.

"Do you think Mother and I will let you gallivant about town? In my Model T that I spent hard-earned money on? And am I to think you have a mind to wander outside our sights?"

Father glared at me with one eyebrow arched.

"No," I said. "But I can stop at the market for Mother or pick up your polished shoes." *And*, I thought, *I could simply drive around the block, alone and free.*

"Driving is not for females. So get that idea right out of your mind."

He climbed out of the car then, leaving me festering and wanting to break free. He never spoke of it again.

⁓

That night Lela and I set out on another evening of dancing. We couldn't get enough of the fox trot, though other animal dances like the grizzly bear and bunny hug had been passé since the war. Last night we made a splash at the Addison Hotel's Florentine Room with a dozen or so friends among four hundred lively souls. I'd worn a little number with a handkerchief hemline, all the better to jump or bend to the tunes of the big society band. Those horns!

But unlike last night—where girls danced with girls, guys danced with guys, and girls and guys danced together innocently—tonight at the Palais de Danse, Lela and I sat at a table with Joe, a guy from college she ran into, and a guy he knew named Lawrence. Lawrence was on summer break from law school in New York.

It didn't feel right to leave Robert out of a foursome. Not that I was promised to him, but we didn't seek other company. Sitting here made me feel edgy, something inching toward disloyal.

I bit my bottom lip. I wished he were here instead.

When these boys first arrived at the dance hall and introduced themselves to me, Lela shot me a look to suggest, "Well, I *thought* they were bringing their gang with them."

Lawrence was a gentleman. "Violet, you have the name of my mother's favorite flower. Nice to meet you."

"Thank you. You as well," I'd said to be polite.

Lawrence was well-heeled, and it showed in the fit of his jazz suit jacket. His octagonal cuff links were of black glass trimmed in white enamel and gold, with half pearl centers. He was handsome, too, in a prep school sort of way. His collar was expensive—high and rounded and pristine white against his skin lightly bronzed from the sun—and his hair was the color of what I imagined sand to be at the Hamptons. Was he a golfer? A boater? Probably both. But I didn't sense Joe's brand of arrogance in him. Lawrence wasn't constantly looking around to check who might be noticing him—or to see who else in the room was worth noticing.

"As long as we're at the Palais de Danse," Lela said for all to hear, "how I wish I could drink something French, maybe a French 75."

Instead, with her arms covered in shimmery long gloves, she parted her slit dress on one of her thighs and slipped a hip flask from her garter.

This dance hall was in Electric Park at the entrance to Belle Isle. I would've loved to drink an aviation right then—to lose myself in a speakeasy cocktail of gin, maraschino, and lemon. But I pulled out my flask, too, and sent it around the table with Lela's. I'd gotten accustomed to sipping pure gin.

"If you girls get a taste for a nip of whiskey . . ." Joe opened his coat and pointed to his sleek silver flask. Most everyone came prepared to these joints.

Tonight's seventeen-piece band was astounding, better than the wildly popular Paul Specht band from the night before. It was an all-Black band led by Floyd Hickman. But, of course, the crowd wasn't of that race, and I wished the world was different.

Lawrence tapped my elbow and I jumped. "Excuse me," he said agreeably. "Ever seen a high-wire act?"

"I'm sorry," I said. I'd scarcely been paying attention; I wasn't feeling right about this night. "But to answer your question, no."

"Despite my being the daredevil that I am," Lela said, "you wouldn't catch me holding a parasol and skipping across a rope strung between two New York skyscrapers. No way. Why would Bird Millman have left Ziegfeld Follies to do that?"

"Doll, let's go cut a rug," Joe said then, dragging Lela to the dance floor with her long strands of pearls swinging and her face seeming to say, "Oh well."

Lawrence offered me a cigarette. I leaned in for a light.

"One thing that puts me off about places like this, candidly," Lawrence said as he puffed his cigarette, "is the segregation. It's bunk. Why not let the band's own race come have a good time?"

I'm sure my eyes were round and wide as autumn persimmons. Other than my family, few had spoken so freely with controversial opinions, and never upon a first meeting.

"I couldn't agree more," I said, matching his tone. I was compelled then to tell him something of my family.

"My great-grandfather died fighting for the Union—fighting for a cause he believed in. He was shot by a man who'd once been his friend. Both had run retail shops in our Kentucky town. But the other man had sided with the rebels."

Lawrence nodded. "My great-grandmother had an Underground Railroad stop in Ohio. And my cousin with the Red Cross helped provide relief in Tulsa last year."

"Oh my, yes, the race massacre," I said, and he nodded. Homes and businesses of wealthy Blacks had been burned across more than thirty square blocks. "So terrible—the deaths, countless injuries, and destruction of property."

I remembered the little girl named Josephine and her mother on the streetcar shortly after I'd moved here. I thought of the Black business district in the town where I'd grown up. Tulsa had families just like the ones in Detroit and Frankfort. Those in Tulsa were shattered. I shook my head.

"Tragedies like that should never happen," Lawrence said.

Lela and Joe returned from the dance floor.

Lawrence smiled at me and said, "Ever gone to the Palms? It's very different from this place."

"Can't say I've heard of it," I said.

"I'm up for going slumming," Joe said snidely. Slumming? What did he mean by that? "If that's what Miss Kentucky wants to do, we'll do it."

"Slumming? And Miss Kentucky?" Lela said as a sax wailed in the background. "No one talks to my friend that way."

Joe reminded me of Mr. Giddens, making fun of where I'd come from. Lela had taken up for me, and it wasn't the first time. It was like what a sister would do.

But even Lawrence looked off-put.

"Slumming, Joe?" he said. "I'd hoped you'd changed. But you're still judging people by the color of their skin."

Joe's eyes met mine.

I jumped up and said, "I'm ready to get out of here, Lela." I was glad Lawrence put Joe in his place, but I didn't care to hang around.

"Gladly," Lela said.

She scooted her chair across the tiles, neither of us glancing at Joe again.

Lawrence escorted us to the exit. "You gals be careful. I'm cutting out for the night, but I hope our paths cross again, under better circumstances."

CHAPTER 27

Melanie

Louisville, Kentucky
September 2018

It was September, and that meant one month until the Bourbon Craft Cocktail Bash. It sent a rush of adrenaline through me. Tanisha and I were meeting in one of the smaller offices on the floor to ensure we were in a good place with the event. We had already surpassed last year's registrations for the cocktail competition, but I wanted to be sure we weren't missing anything.

"I've got confirmations from the mixologists on what charities they support if they win," Tanisha said. "And I've rounded up contact info of each charity's PR people. We can co-op some media with the one that receives the donation."

"Good thinking," I said. "Mitchell should be informed, too."

"Got it."

She and I discussed the reminder eblast going out in two weeks to current registrants; the social media campaign for a push for new registrations; the status of flyers in liquor stores statewide; and the handwritten note cards to be sent to the Connoisseur Club about the VIP suite. We would spend hours writing them, but most people appreciated a personal touch.

"What about the branded glass sets?" she asked.

"Covered," I said.

I went round and round with the two final suppliers who made proposals. After an eleventh-hour negotiation where I thought I'd pull my hair out, we had a deal. I had to order more quantity to get the discount, but I could charge part of the stock to next year's budget.

"Our deadline is set," I said. "If they don't meet it, they pay a penalty."

"But if I know you, you won't rest until the stock has shipped," Tanisha said warmly.

"You do know me." I laughed. "In fact, I won't rest easy until the boxes are delivered. What about the volunteers lined up to man the suite?"

"Close," she said. "I lack a couple of shifts. I'll be sure be our VIPs aren't left hanging."

"Great. And I have all the bottles of bourbon and accompaniments ordered for competitors to use onstage."

"We're where we need to be as of this moment," Tanisha said and winked.

I felt good.

Mitchell's star had seemed to dim a bit lately. No more big, boisterous hits.

But I wasn't naive. For all I knew he was keeping something confidential, ready to pounce when I least expected—like a trick play in the red zone of a football game.

Brian called after Labor Day weekend. He'd been gone for a week on an extended holiday at a rustic cabin with buddies, fly fishing and golfing.

"Hey, Melanie," he said.

"Brian, it's great to hear your voice." I wasn't into "relationships," but I wasn't turned off to fun if work would ever allow. And then there was the car thing hanging out there.

"I've got news you'll find interesting," he said. "About the quote."

"The numbers came in?"

"Yeah. Ray will be in touch in the next day or so with specifics. He says the car's in great condition. The quality of the carriage house storage wasn't the best, obviously, but the car rested in place. So the body is in good shape, never been wrecked."

Maybe the cost wasn't going to be as high as I'd feared. "You have my rapt attention, Brian."

"And the bulk of the important parts are there," he said. "The downside is, the restoration cost overall is still high. I'd underestimated it."

"Oh no. Well, that's okay," I said kindly, but I was internally losing it. "You'd made it clear that I shouldn't hold you to the fifty-thousand-dollar guesstimate."

But he'd started this conversation by saying he had *interesting* news.

"His quote came in closer to sixty," Brian said.

"Oh my gosh." I shook my head.

That was certainly "interesting." That figure was not going to work. Even if I could get a loan approved, I wasn't going in that deep. Now I felt as if I were letting Violet down.

"On the upside," Brian said, "I suggested some things to lower the cost that Ray jumped on."

I kind of laughed. "Oh! Okay."

"He wants to work with you, because it's such a rare automobile. It'll be a hundred years old in five years. Your car will be good for him to get more business for older models like that. Not just the ones in the 1930s and up."

"Aha. So what's the plan?"

The wheels of my marketing brain kicked in.

"If you agree to let him trailer it and show at three national car conventions—I'm talking the biggest shows, like those at Hershey, Pennsylvania, and Amelia Island, Florida—and agree to let him seek publicity in the national car trade media, he'll give you a discount."

"Now you're talking my language. Any chance he'd want the car to be featured on one of those car guru shows on cable TV?"

"Yes, ma'am, he would."

"Awesome. I'll do it. Well, wait. What's the discount?"

"He'll do the job for 40K."

That took my breath. That number was 20 percent off Brian's guesstimate.

"Brian, it's like the best news ever."

I thought I might even be able to swing it without getting the promotion, though it'd be tight. I'd have to recheck the numbers. But the car was a new mission. It was like I owed Violet for all she'd done for me. There her car had sat for almost a hundred years, waiting for me. And I would answer.

"I thought you'd be pleased," Brian said. "If you pay Ray a deposit, he can rearrange some other projects and get a crew started right away. He'd like to have yours done by Christmas."

"Thank you, thank you. I'll apply for a loan as soon as I can. I'm jazzed."

"Me too," he said.

Then there was a pause—a pause so pregnant it was a pause expecting twins. This was where one of us would take the next step, if there was going to be one.

"Well," he said. "Better let you go. The rest is up to Ray. He'll get the Jordan towed to his shop and all."

So Brian and I were done? Another pregnant pause. This time it was triplets.

Was he brushing me off? Or, after a couple of texts since the speakeasy, had I left him thinking he was nothing more than a car guru to me? A "future," as defined by many, wasn't in my stars. But we could enjoy being together some, couldn't we?

"Hey, when the work's in progress," I said, "I should run over and check it out, right? Maybe . . . you and I could go together? Then maybe get a bite?"

I thought I could hear his smile though I could not see it. "Let's do that. Name the time."

As I later turned to Violet's journal, I felt all sentimental or something about the car. Like, I was making her happy. It was weird to think of a dead person being happy.

But there was something else stirring inside me. I liked this guy.

I hadn't thought of Jason in, what, two or three days? But I thought of him now. His dimples. How he might've spent Labor Day weekend. How he always called me Mel. I closed my eyes. There was his surprise proposal with the pink envelope and silver kisses. Would I ever truly be over him? I didn't know.

I opened my eyes. I did know I looked forward to going to Lexington soon.

CHAPTER 28

Violet

Detroit, Michigan
September 1922

I strolled down the aisle on Robert's arm in Orchestra Hall. In the six months since he moved to his bungalow, I'd helped decorate the living room with two cozy chairs, a sofa, and prints of wooded scenes by a river. I'd be lying if I said I hadn't loved every minute. But no matter how it made the house feel a bit more mine, and no matter how strong a pull it was, my fear of losing my autonomy was equal to it. Robert was a clever man; he hadn't pressed about my role in his life or a plan for the future. Nor did he hound about my outings with friends. He had his job. I had mine. And when we met in the middle, we were . . . content.

Yet since last month at the Palais de Danse when I walked out and Lela followed, I missed Robert more when he was away. Perhaps he knew all along that the best path to my heart was through patience.

Tonight Orchestra Hall was indeed the "cat's meow," just as Robert had intimated the day that we first met. He ushered me now into a seemingly endless row of red cloth seats. Soon the auditorium would fill with more than two thousand spectators, including those up high in loge boxes. He and I were among the earliest to find our seats toward the rear of the floor and admire the walls and ceiling with their rich shades of gold and classical trims in silver and ivory.

"I listened to the 'little symphony' this week," I said, "at the house, on the radio in your aunt's parlor."

"That group has made quite the splash in its inaugural year, hasn't it?" he said.

Sixteen of the ninety-member symphony played live nightly—the first such ensemble in the world to be organized specifically for the airwaves.

Now I looked left and craned right. People were dressed in evening wear with sparkling jewels as they converged in the rows like uniformed armies filling battlefields. My attire was modest by comparison, but I treasured Robert's lovely bracelet on my wrist. The lights dimmed, once, twice, except for the stage. I quickly glanced at the printed program. Then the conductor stepped into his place.

Following a thrilling performance of a piece composed by Beethoven, the symphony played a Ketèlbey melody. It'd come out the year before and opened with solo bells that were followed by woodwinds and strings.

Robert leaned to my ear and said, "The acoustics here are all they're cracked up to be."

Yes. A repeated effect of the chimes set in my mind a belfry in the distance, maybe in a French village. But my vision of the meadows—taken from the title of the song—reminded me of land in Kentucky, of home, and family. My pulse built with the louder ringing of joyous bells and then slowed when bells faded in the end. I wished Mother were here to hear it with us. And Evelyn, too, regardless of our ongoing chilliness. One letter was signed *Ever your sister*. She didn't even sign it *love*. It hurt, and I put it in the back of my shoebox of letters, determined not to reread.

Part of me wanted to be near my family, the warmth and comforts of home. I loved Bond House. But then, what of all the expectations there? What of my leading my own life here?

Here, I had Robert, and tonight was special. I wouldn't ruin it.

"Bravo!" the audience cried, clapping. "Bravo!"

Robert and I still felt on high as we drove the few blocks down Woodward to the Hotel Tuller. He'd reserved a room for us near the top of its fourteen floors.

We swept the window treatments wide on their rods, leaving us open to city lights. We stood in front of the window as Robert slipped the arm of my dress off my shoulder with a chill and a warmth both at once. He nibbled me there, and I heated at feeling his teeth.

Then he kissed my ear and whispered, "I love you."

"And I love you."

It was the first time I said it. It was so natural. Like breathing. Love blossomed inside my heart and came out as sound by my lips.

Robert drew his head to where he looked into my eyes. The glow of lights passed the bridge of his nose and his cheeks in turns as headlamps of cars streamed beneath us.

He took my face in his hands. I adored the rough, manly feel of his palms.

"How I've longed to hear you say those words," he said. "I'm a happy man."

I pressed my lips to his. Here, in this place, I could have a man I loved and a life of my own. We could just live in the moment.

We were carried away then by echoes of cellos, violins, and flutes.

~

The next day we awoke in each other's arms. My first words were, "I love you, Robert." I couldn't stop smiling, and nor could he.

After lunch we ambled along Grand Circus Park. Woodward Avenue ran right through the middle, separating park grounds shaped into two pieces of pie—one piece on the east and one west of the thoroughfare. We were surrounded on this temperate fall day by our hotel, skyscrapers, and a Methodist church with a towering steeple.

The east and the west sides of the park each had a monument of a past mayor. Both mustached men sat powerfully in heavy chairs on raised pedestals. The statues faced each other, symbolically, from across the acres.

"These men were enemies," Robert said. "One favored the rise of private corporations, and the other thought they were threats."

I cuddled closer into Robert with our steps. "This outing reminds me of our first tour of the city." A fond memory. I liked his details.

He smiled. "When citizens complained of new horseless carriages speeding through streets at twelve miles per hour, one mayor saw a way around an ordinance that led to letting cars have free rein."

"To think," I said, "had that change not been made, this might not have become the automotive capital of the world."

"True."

I led Robert to a bench where we sat to enjoy the soft breeze. Winter would come soon enough. Families and couples happened by us in turns, nodding or waving. A little girl in a green felt coat ran by, giggling, with her father pretending to chase her. I remembered fondly my father playing with me at that age—rides in the wheelbarrow or hide-and-go-seek. The mother of the girl in the green coat looked on, relishing the sight as my mother might have. Would I be in that position one day, myself?

I looked up at Robert, and he might've been thinking of his own childhood, too, but that's not what I read in his eyes and the tilt of his head. Whereas I had a passing thought about family, what I saw in his face was longing.

As ridiculous as it may have been, I felt threatened. Longings were too heavy for me. But maybe I misread him.

We shared a cigarette, and then Robert put his hand on my thigh covered by a lightweight wrap.

"Violet," Robert said. "I once thought I'd never wish to settle down. But you've changed all that. I yearn for permanence. Family."

He smiled with his eyes. So I was right. I felt numb.

"You're the only one for me. I want to make you my wife. I want you to bear my children. Isn't it time we got married?"

My limbs turned statue-like. I had to say something.

"Darling," he said. "I know, I know. There's a matter of a ring. But I love you. You love me. Let's go to Miller's Jewelers. Right now. You can pick out whatever you want. You decide."

I wanted to decide more than a choice of sofas or rings. I didn't leave Kentucky to be a wife. Or a mother. Robert made it sound as if I would be part of him. His wife. His children's mother.

Was I being rash? I turned to face the ground and thought of lovely times back home in Kentucky that I held so precious. Fishing with my grandfather. Making biscuits with Mother. Sitting on the porch swing out front watching fireflies. Home. Could Robert and I create that same hum, that same wooly blanket, that kind of warm life? Even the starlets of the old film series I watched as a girl fell in love at the end of the story.

But I was unsure.

Robert had just asked me to marry him. If I said no, I'd lose him just as I realized I loved him. There'd be no more us. Could I do that? Oh, how I would long for him. My chest felt heavy.

But what of me?

He caressed my leg some more. "Violet?"

I faced him and smiled. "You've clearly taken me quite by surprise."

When I was sixteen, I lay in my bed in my room at the back of the house. In the dark I would imagine myself choosing my outfits, driving my car, having a key to my own place. I never envisioned a wedding or a baby carriage, at least not yet. In all these months, I'd worked and sacrificed and barreled through obstacles—and picked myself back up when I fell. I'd made myself proud.

I was almost there now, to where I'd dreamed of being.

I did Robert the honor of gazing right into his eyes as the laughter of children and voices of mommies rang out behind us. I would tell him the truth. His lips looked pale. I'd taken too long.

"My dear Robert," I began. "You are the one. As a modern woman, I do see our future together . . . but not in that way. Can't we go on as we are? I'm so happy."

He sighed heavily.

"Do you understand what I'm trying to say?" I asked as caringly as I could.

"I understand. You don't want to marry me." He lifted his hand from my leg, and now it felt cold.

Visions filled my head like a colorful merry-go-round: Father dying with Mother knowing little of their finances. Evelyn serving her role in her home and deferring to Charles on matters. My sitting alone Monday through Friday in a suburb while Robert traveled from Saint Louis to Kansas City and Toledo to Akron.

Where would my adventures be? My important decisions? My name?

"It's not that," I said. "I mean, it's not you. I don't wish to be married at all. I *do* wish us to be together."

In the silence, we both rose in unison as if cued by an orchestra conductor, and I wondered for the first time if love was enough.

We held hands as we walked the rest of the way back, not warmly, not coldly. It wasn't over between us. But it had changed. I was struck, then, by how we were like the two statues on opposite sides of this park: he had his view and I had mine, though how different they were.

We got to his Ford. We said not a word on the way to Saint Aubin Street. He parked in front of the boardinghouse, cut off the engine, and faced me. The mere inches of leather in the seat between us felt as wide as a mile.

His crystal-blue eyes lowered, not meeting mine. "Violet, I have to know if the day may come that you *will* be ready to marry." His eyelids lifted. "I need the answer now, before I drive away."

The weight of my head leaned toward nodding yes. What if this was the last time I'd see him? Robert could pull away and never return. Of all the things I didn't want, I didn't want that, either.

"Yes," I said, "that day may come." And I felt it then, earnestly.

"Then I'll wait for you."

Three weeks later, October 1922

I ripped open Mother's letter, anxiously awaiting her response. I'd invited her, Evelyn, and Charles to come to Detroit for Thanksgiving. I'd grown weary of the distance between my sister and me. I wanted us to be good again. I read as fast as my eyes would take me.

> Dear Violet,
> Charles gave his blessing after Evelyn practically begged. It'll just be us girls! He's happy for her and me to come spend needed time together. He'll be with sisters, nieces, and nephews. We could not be more excited! We're off to get our train tickets.

If I knew Mother, she exaggerated Evelyn's degree of excitement. But I didn't care. Oh, this was wonderful. They'd arrive on Wednesday, the night before Thanksgiving, and I had Friday off all for them. They'd travel home on Saturday. I couldn't wait to tell Robert when he returned for the weekend.

I wanted him to meet my family. I wanted them to meet him. I wanted them to see this exciting city. I held my faith that Evelyn would drop her judgments and see that Robert and I were fine as we were.

Since my outing with him at the concert and the park—those days combining bliss and burden—we'd been cautious. But when we made love at his place, it melted away our tensions. Things were feeling good.

Lela said when we talked by telephone, "Either you have him wrapped around your little finger, or he has you wrapped around his."

Whatever that meant. She and I then went on to further discussions of sharing an apartment—I brought it up myself. We set a goal for spring. Over the next few months, she'd do the legwork to find some places we liked and check out the rent and availability. She knew my budget. Of course, hers was bigger. But I had to have a new place to live before I could get my car, so I'd have somewhere to park it. I could scarcely wait. I'd make my own house rules. I was done with the boardinghouse life. Done! And Lela was done living with parents.

"Even though we can go two days without running into each other," she said of her folks and their large house, "and their club's so convenient to me, I, too, want to get out on my own, with no one asking where I was the night before or why I looked so tired." She laughed.

At my suggestion, we agreed to keep our plans to ourselves for now. It wouldn't be right for news to reach my landlady's ears too soon, or the gossipy residents.

By Saturday when Robert and I sat at the Sanders chocolate counter—an ode to our first unofficial date—I was beside myself with joy.

"Robert, dear," I said. "Guess what? Mother and Evelyn are coming for Thanksgiving."

"That's great news. I'd love to meet them, if there's time."

I beamed. "There's time. It's my sincere wish that you'll tour us around on Friday after."

I hadn't seen a smile so big since I first told him I loved him.

"I'd be honored," he said.

His humility shone from his eyes. He was a good man.

"Where do you have a mind to go?" he asked.

In between bites of hot fudge, we talked about the many places to see. It'd be hard to narrow them down to one day.

"Mother loves art and science and history sites," I said. "She's easy and so is Evelyn. As long as they see the skyscrapers and the river, I leave the rest to you."

He pretended to bow. "I am your humble servant. I'll make sure we work everything in."

"I'm thrilled!" I said. "Thank you. Now, if only they could meet Lela, too. But she'll be in Ohio with her grandparents for the holiday."

Robert's expression stilled.

"What?" I said, puzzled. "Of course I wish they could meet my best friend."

He kind of laughed. "You may be doing yourself a favor by not having her meet your mother," he said jokingly, though I wasn't amused.

"Why ever not?"

"Well," he said. "She's a bit fast, right? She might alarm them."

Maybe he had a point. Truth was, though, as elated as I was for family to come and spend time together, if I had any hint of hesitation at all, it wasn't about Lela meeting my kin.

I hoped Evelyn wouldn't give Robert the third degree. I hoped he'd win her over and she'd get past her concerns of my "illicit behaviors" with "*that man*."

CHAPTER 29

Violet

Detroit, Michigan
November 1922

Mother and Evelyn arrived at nearly midnight the night before Thanksgiving. Between the two women, they managed well to secure a Checker Cab and wind their way here.

"So this is it," Evelyn said, smiling. "Your home for more than a year."

Perhaps I'd jumped to conclusions about Evelyn. We'd had a heartfelt hug when she'd come through the door. We were sisters.

Her and Mother's eyes darted around the parlor—the upright piano, the game table, the handmade doilies on the fresh-polished tables.

"It feels warm, cozy," Mother said, and I knew this gave her comfort.

We all were the only ones up. Mrs. Sturgeon had given me her apologies, but she would rise before the sun to fix the turkey feast for those few residents who weren't traveling themselves.

I showed Mother to her room—Sarah's room. My friend had offered, given she was leaving. Evelyn would stay with me.

Mother said, "We have two days before heading back on Saturday. Let's rest up. Besides, I'll help your landlady in the kitchen tomorrow."

I lifted my brows. We'd see how that would go.

In the quiet of my bedroom, I longed to hear Evelyn say, *"Eeeeee!"* as she'd done for fun when we were alone as girls. Yet though I'd been afraid that there would be a distance, seeing her made me want our bond again all the more.

"When do we meet Robert?" she asked as she pulled her nightgown over her head.

"Friday," I said. "He'll be our chauffeur for a tour of the city."

"That sounds grand."

This was good. She didn't follow it up with any nosiness. My bed was only a single, so it was tight. Our knees touched. Our faces were inches apart in the dark.

"Even after fifteen hours on a train at her age," I said, "Mother looked fresh and happy and well."

I loved seeing her that way. Last Christmas, she'd looked a bit pallid.

"She is well," Evelyn said. "It's been four years since we lost Father. She's active in everything from church to tutoring. She's content."

I missed Father, but this was the best news I could hear. I was proud of Mother. Even if she needed a little help with the money I sent her, she had reclaimed her independence as a woman. She was pursuing her dreams—on her own, without a man to direct her. I felt in that moment that Mother and I were kindred spirits.

"And you?" I asked Evelyn. "You're prettier every time I see you." It was true.

"Thank you. I'm well," she said. "Nothing's new, but for Charles's law practice being quite in demand. I'm the wife of a rising star."

I heard the pride in her voice. That's one of the things she wanted, to shine in his light. I didn't understand it, but I could celebrate it for her.

"So exciting," I said. "I'll be able to say I knew him when."

"There's one thing," she said, sounding less enthused.

Was it a baby? Since I last saw her, only one letter referenced her "hoping to be pregnant soon." It felt too invasive for me to ask outright.

"Here we are again," she said. "No baby."

"But Mother, as you well know, was married five whole years before you came along."

"That comforts me to a point," Evelyn said. "But all my friends have broods of two or three already. And I'm at four years of marriage and counting."

"Exactly. Only four years, so why not quit worrying?" I said. "Who knows? The night you return to Kentucky could be your magic night." I truly wanted her to have one so she could be fulfilled.

The following morning, my sister and I padded into the kitchen to the scent of onions cooking.

"You don't make corn bread dressing, then?" Mother asked Mrs. Sturgeon good-naturedly.

"Dressing? Pshaw. It's *stuffing* of sausage, onions, and soaked stale bread."

"Different than we do in the South, but I look forward to tasting it."

It was seven thirty in the morning, and Mother was wearing one of my landlady's home-sewn aprons and glowing like a schoolgirl.

"Violet," Mrs. Sturgeon said, "your mother's pumpkin bread is the best I've ever eaten. Slice yourself a piece. Breakfast is on your own." She stirred and stirred with her wooden spoon.

It was nice of Mother to bring her a gift. Evelyn brought jars of cranberry jelly, too. The women put us to work peeling yams and baking pies. It was truly fun and heartwarming, all of us together for the holiday.

By the time we all gathered around the table—and Mrs. Sturgeon had assigned Oliver the job of carving the bird—she and Mother were debating which was best: the breast or the legs. Mother thought the latter.

"This stuffing is delicious," she said, and Mrs. Sturgeon beamed. "I'll have a second helping, please."

I loved seeing Mother be so spirited. What a blessing they had come.

~

At five minutes until eleven on Friday, I waited with my family for Robert to arrive. My stomach felt as if it had a brick lodged in it—a dense block of nerves, heavy as fire-baked clay. Would Evelyn judge us? I thought not anymore. Our visit was everything I'd hoped so far. We were family.

Mrs. Sturgeon peeked between the curtains. "Robert's right on time."

He let himself in, and when he wandered into the parlor, displaying his dazzling white smile and offering warm handshakes, I could see my sister soften.

Today was looking up. Evelyn barely blinked when he pecked me on the cheek.

Robert was the quintessential gentleman, opening doors left and right in the rear and the front right side for me. He held Mother's bag while she climbed in, though I was sure she hardly needed it. He smiled so pleasantly with every word they spoke.

"You're too kind, Robert," Mother said.

"Robert, it's so good of you to take us on tour," Evelyn said.

Indeed, I'd had no reasons to worry. They oohed and aahed from the shopping district on Woodward to the river that separated Detroit from Canada. The highlight of the day would be the aquarium at Belle Isle, which was new to me, too. We were almost there.

Robert and my sister chatted on the way to the entry door. He made her laugh. Mother strode along with me, saying low, "He's such a nice young man, Violet."

"He is, isn't he?"

Funny how I saw him through new eyes—or through my old eyes all over again, like the day he walked into Labrot and Graham. There were no bad memories of feeling pressured by him wanting more. He was marvelous.

We entered the building under a massive carving. "Neptune," Mother said. "Roman god of the sea."

Robert led us into a long, domed structure. Its ceiling was fitted with tiles of green glass, giving us the feeling of being underwater. And lining the sides were gigantic tanks with aquatic life in both fresh and salt water.

Robert said, "Architect Albert Kahn had a vision for the fish to be viewed at the sides, like walking through a gallery with beautiful hanging art."

Mother's eyes glistened at the notion. I locked gazes with Robert. He'd listened to me. He knew what Mother would enjoy: art and science in an interesting presentation. I wanted to hug him.

We all chitchatted in the Ford on the way back to the house. Mother said her favorite exhibit was the mammoth sea turtle.

"Robert, where do you live?" my sister asked.

Oh no, here came the interrogation I'd feared. I glanced sideways at him in the front seat.

"I purchased a bungalow on the west side a few months back," he said as if it were nothing. "No longer living with my father and brother."

Was it my imagination, or did the sound get sucked out of the back seat? My family now knew he lived on his own. It was something I'd never written about.

Mother said, "How impressive to own property so young."

That was kind. The subject dropped.

Then I asked myself what I could've long before: Why should I be so concerned with what she and Evelyn thought of me and Robert, anyway? I wanted my sister's approval. But I was gainfully employed. I had investments and friends. I was making it on my own and sending money home.

And one day, I'd have a car.

That evening, Mother, Evelyn, and I gathered in Sarah's room. We had tea, and we girls sat on the bed and Mother in the rocker. Our visit had flown so fast.

"Violet," Mother said. "When are you and Robert going to tie the knot?"

My skin prickled at my collarbone. I hadn't seen that coming from her.

"It's clear you two are close," she said, not waiting for my response.

What did Mother mean by *close*? My vision cut to Evelyn, who held a mischievous smile. Or was it a triumphant one, her glee in knowing Mother was about to say everything she'd been saying for months? Had my sister betrayed my confidence about my *being* with Robert after all?

When Mother took a sip, I glowered at Evelyn who then mouthed, frantically, *I never said a word!*

"Violet, I can read your face," Mother said. "It's abundantly obvious. And with Robert having his own place. Again, are you going to marry?"

"Mother, I, well," I stammered.

Why was this so important to her? She was independent herself. She lived a fine life without need of a husband. We were alike in these periods of our lives.

"Mother," I said. "I'm not done being on my own."

She pondered that. Evelyn's eyes again radiated surprise that Mother was so pointed.

"And how do you know how close he and I are, anyway?" I boldly asked.

Maybe Mrs. Sturgeon had said something. I burned a bit warmer, remembering the gossips at the house included her. I hoped she couldn't hear us through the walls.

Mother said with the tone of a teacher, "Do you think me so old that I cannot recall the beating heart of youth? You're a modern woman. I know what goes on. Speakeasies. Dancing all night. I suppose you smoke." Evelyn gasped. "Just because you haven't told me, Violet, doesn't mean I don't know."

Evelyn went dreadfully still. I did not.

"How do you feel about it then, Mother?" I asked.

I'd grown up seeking her approval, but . . . I wasn't a child anymore. "How do you feel about it?" I repeated.

"Since you've asked . . . I think you should marry a man whom you love and whom you're intimate with." I winced at her word *intimate*. "But you have only one life. And it's yours to decide. I assume you and Robert are smart enough to protect yourselves. Society isn't so forgiving."

Evelyn pressed her hands to her mouth. I slowly nodded.

Only one life, indeed. But I wanted this matter closed.

"Perhaps it's time to get packed," my sister said awkwardly to redirect us. She rose.

"Girls, there's something I want you to know."

Mother's vision shifted from me to Evelyn. My sister sat back down.

"The youthful beat of a heart is not only for the young."

My face turned ten shades of crimson. Evelyn touched her fingers to her forehead, and I thought that she might faint.

"I've met with Dr. Keller on two occasions." She faced my sister. "I can see you're surprised. Well, you both are first to know. He and I are to take things slowly. Respectfully."

She perplexed me. Shocked me even. Was this why Mother had been practically skipping through the house, cooking and laughing like a schoolgirl? She was smitten?

"So, my daughters, I foresee taking my own advice. By this time next year, I'll likely be wed."

"A wedding to look forward to!" Evelyn said, having awakened from her daze.

I felt apart from them in that moment. Did this news leave me the sole modern woman of the family?

CHAPTER 30

Melanie

Louisville, Kentucky
September 2018

It was six thirty in the morning, and Mom and I were FaceTiming. Both of us had our terry robes on and hair pulled up in clips on our heads. Dad was at the gym. Besides Labor Day weekend when Casey and I'd swung by to get the journal for my turn, it'd been benign texts between me and my mother—ever since the photo extravaganza in her dining room with our opposite views of my ballet recital. But Mom said she "missed seeing my face," and now was the only time our schedules fit.

"Can you believe Aunt Violet?" Mom said. "A real flapper."

"I know. And her mother being so open-minded about Violet with a man?"

This was like a water-cooler conversation about *The Bachelor* on TV the night before.

Yet the truth was, my own mom scrutinized my life choices worse than Violet's mother did hers. I wanted Mom to be proud of me . . . and I also hoped that one day our perspectives on my independence would align.

"So you'll keep reading ahead and then get the book back to me?" Mom asked.

"Yup. But now I'd better jump in the shower," I said. "Gotta get to work."

Mom raised her hand. "Wait. What's the latest with the car?"

I had contacted two lenders while I slammed down a salad yesterday at my desk, and it seemed the loan was harder to secure than I foresaw. I'd been referred to two more hopeful sources.

"Oh, right!" I said, summoning the excitement I'd had when Brian told me the final estimate and my knowing I was honoring Violet.

I quickly told Mom about Ray's assessment of the car, having a date to get the restoration finished, and how I was looking to take out a loan. Her eyes kept getting bigger and bigger. She downed her coffee.

"And—" she started.

"And . . . the best part is, Brian negotiated on my behalf for a twenty percent discount."

It was more than that if we counted the actual quote being higher than Brian's guestimate. But I didn't have time to dicker with her. Not with Mitchell on my heels at the office.

"You'll pay 40K then?" Mom said.

"I know, it's still high. Think of it as an investment. The restoration guy wants to show it all over the country at conventions."

"Impressive. So when do you see Brian again?"

The sneak attack first thing in the morning? Even if I didn't wash my hair, I didn't have time for twenty questions.

"No date set with Brian yet, Mom. I gotta go."

I had to say *yet*, didn't I?

"Melanie, just remember he's in the car business. You can send Brian referrals in the future, too, for the customizations he does. It's networking. You don't have to date him because you feel some obligation for all his favors." She scratched her chin. "And do you think that getting a loan that high is wise?"

I was surprised only that she didn't call the Jordan the "old jalopy." She was selling off Violet's house, but I didn't want to sell off the last personal possession of our beloved aunt.

I'd been having heartburn for the last twenty-four hours, though, about getting the money. Turned out, loans for classic cars were different than getting a loan on a new car or even a regular used vehicle. Interest rates were higher and the term of the loan shorter. Even with the required down payment, which would eat up a chunk of my savings, I wouldn't be able to afford the monthly payments *unless* I got the promotion.

If I got the loan, I *had* to get the raise. Had to.

All of a sudden, the promotion was about more than my reputation in the department. It was about more than making Mom proud. Her questioning my decisions made me want to lock in a loan over lunch to spite her—a way of asserting my control, not hers.

In fact, I'd do what Violet did: I'd take a gamble. She had risked her nest egg on the stock market and turned out fine. I would secure the loan, confident in my ability to land the promotion. And Mom would finally see that I was a capable pilot of my own life.

That included relationships with men.

"Mom. When it comes to Brian, I've got this. I'm being, like, the most cautious, circumspect, guarded woman in the effing world." She could see me scrunch my face. "Brian is a genuine, nice guy."

"I know," she said, but her words didn't match her worried face.

"What do you have against him anyway?" I blurted.

Why, why did I have to go down that road? I wasn't supposed to be caring what she thought. I was supposed to be squirting body wash on my legs in the spray of warm water.

"Nothing," she said innocently.

"That he graduated college at a small school in Lexington instead of UK, or, or, somewhere Ivy League? That he doesn't have an *MBA*? That his job isn't in a big corporate headquarters on the twenty-fourth floor?"

She'd set me off, and I got louder as I went.

"Melanie, please stop." She feigned total calmness. But there had to be something.

"Or is it because Brian isn't Jason?"

Mom looked as if she'd been caught stealing apple fritters from the grocery store's help-yourself bakery. That was it. I'd suspected it before. Now I could see that for some reason, she thought we'd get back together.

"Do you still hold out hope that Jason will leave his new job and come crawling back to me in bourbon country? That we'll reunite?"

She didn't know about the fiasco at Nachbar when I'd seen him at Casey's birthday. He wasn't moving back here. I felt pangs in my chest that I wished I hadn't.

I looked deeply into Mom's virtual eyes. I knew she and Dad had cared for him. Maybe she went as far as to fantasize about Dad in a tux, escorting her into the Medallion Ballroom of the Seelbach hotel in her gold mother-of-the-bride gown with a live seven-piece band playing "Only You."

"It's not happening, Mom," I said. "Me and Jason."

"Honey, please," she said, "let me get a word in edgewise."

"You want me to be late for work when I'm gunning for the most important promotion of my career?"

"No," she said, but she held up her index finger as if to suggest she'd have the last word. "I urge you to be careful with love," she said. "Decisions made at life's crossroads can hang with you for a long time."

Her gaze dropped, her lashes shielding her eyes. Then she said, "I know all too well."

I felt off balance. Was she referring to my decision to part with Jason? Or did she mean her own past decisions?

I didn't have time to be her shrink. I wished we hadn't even talked. "Have a good day, Mom. I'm signing off."

Bleep went the screen.

CHAPTER 31

Violet

Detroit, Michigan
January 1923

I heard Robert coming in from chopping wood for a fire.

The holidays with people in Detroit and winter storms had left little time for us to be alone. It was hard enough just getting to my job, and there were times Robert couldn't get back to Detroit by train nor to his aunt's to pick me up. We had ten inches of snow over twenty-four hours in December. And that was just one day. With the sub-freezing temperatures raging on, snow kept piling up past my knees. Crews had to shovel the walks and the streetcar tracks. But their piles and drifts on the sides of the roads and walks climbed up as high as my neck.

Tonight, another blast was expected, but I was already here, with him, ready to hunker down for the weekend. We'd been to the market the night before, and tonight I would cook dinner for us for the first time. Mother having deferred to me decisions for my "one life" at Thanksgiving, including intimacy with Robert, had been reassuring. Yet it'd also been disconcerting . . . the revelation of her own need to loop back into marriage where she'd lose all her independence. I hadn't reconciled how she and I weren't kindred spirits after all. She and Evelyn were.

But one good thing happened. My sister had seemed to be over obsessing about me. We parted beautifully, and she sent the prettiest card, thanking me for having them.

I tightened the ties of my frilly apron. It's not as if I didn't enjoy cooking. I did. I just wanted to do it in my own time, my own way. It didn't mean I had to be a "little Mrs." The day was coming when Lela and I would move in together, and I'd have a kitchen of my own. I'd have beef roast on Saturday instead of Tuesday if I wished. No more of Mrs. Sturgeon's rigid schedule.

I stood in Robert's quaint kitchen and started hand-stirring a batter for muffins. I'd assembled all the ingredients, including graham flour, molasses, and sour milk. My menu included deviled eggs, Mother's marmalade ham, and duchess potatoes. I'd already mashed the spuds and rubbed them through a sieve, and stirred in beaten yolks with seasonings. I'd piled them in pretty little pottery dishes to bake and brown before serving.

"Sure smells good in here," Robert said. He hadn't stopped grinning since he unloaded my groceries from the market. "Anything I can do to help before I build the fire?"

He was so sweet. In the times we had spent together since Thanksgiving, there'd been a comforting peace between us. Connecting him with my family had brought us closer.

"I've got it all under control," I said. Then he pecked me on the cheek.

I set two candles and matches on the table and set our places to dine. Soon, the muffins were rising nicely in their tins. I carved some ham into thin, juicy slices. Mother would be impressed. I hoped Robert would, too. The sound of the crackling fire floated in from the living room.

For a second—or maybe a whole minute—I imagined myself as his wife in this house. Could I get used to this? Mrs. Robert Neumann?

I had it within me to create a nice home.

But what of my decisions beyond choosing menus and pillows? And my earnings and freedom to come and go as I pleased? Especially after I'd buy a car. As a husband, Robert might be like my father.

The cold winter nights alone in my room at the boardinghouse had provided me time to peruse the stacks of residents' magazines. Six-cylinder cars. Eight-cylinder cars. Those that were dependable. Those roomy for hauling a pack. Buicks and Chevrolets and Dodges and Fords. I'd concluded I only needed a two-door coupe.

A roadster would be all the better, Lela had recently said.

Roadsters had two seats with a top that folded down. I could feel wind in my hair as I had with her the first time, two girls without destination.

My investments were strong. Though even if I couldn't afford a roadster by the time Lela and I became roommates, I would one day become a true motoriste. Something Mother never was.

As Robert and I cuddled before the fire after dinner, he repeated, "You've spoiled me. That dinner ranked up there better than my mama's finest."

"High praise, I'd say, 'Bobby.'"

We tittered. I wondered then. Once I had the car for a time, might I be ready to wed? After all these years, with my goals accomplished, might my dreams shift to a brand-new picture? Could I have both—marriage and independence—after all?

I once told Robert I thought I'd be ready . . . one day. Perhaps that day was closer than I realized.

As soon as that thought lodged in my mind, my guttural fear kicked back in. Would Robert "allow" me to keep my independence? I would stick to my original plan. I'd grow my career—or work solely with my investments for the long term.

For a moment, I was light-headed, intoxicated without as much as a sip.

The spell of love and a cozy fire almost got me sidetracked. But I wasn't my mother or sister. No, surely I wasn't.

Robert leaned to kiss my ear, a precursor of things to come. I was content right where we were. *We* were content right where we needed to be.

~

Three months later

Spring was in full bloom, and I was ready for the move that Lela and I'd planned. Today I'd tell Robert. I worried he'd be lukewarm about the news, as he preferred my friends at the house to Lela. But my move shouldn't affect him, or us—except for us having fewer prying eyes and two places to spend nights together instead of one. Nothing would effectively change.

"Robert, I'm glad you're back," I said on the telephone with extra cheeriness. I'd made sure no one in the boardinghouse was near the telephone alcove. "I have news."

"Oh yeah?"

"Exciting news," I whispered. "I'm moving out. Leaving the boardinghouse."

"Really?"

"I'm getting an apartment."

"Where? Does Auntie know?"

Underlying his every word was support and skepticism. I could read the layers of his tones like lines in a book. I pictured his one hand going to his chin. His brows furrowing.

"An apartment with Lela," I said.

At first I thought the telephone line had gone dead. Maybe not. I went on.

"It's a fabulous place in a high-rise. The Pasadena apartment building."

"You can afford that?" he said.

"I'll spend the same amount I do here." That wouldn't count food and laundry, but I had a plan to manage. "I'll be closer to work. I'll have more autonomy."

"I see."

He sounded more cynical than I'd feared.

"Don't get me wrong," I said. "Your aunt has been wonderful." I might even miss her. "But I'm ready to move on from the stringent schedule. The rules. Sharing private facilities with men, for Pete's sake."

"I certainly understand that."

"Just think, Robert, I'll be able to cook us dinner at your place and my own place sometimes. And best of all, we won't have peering eyes of Oliver and Sarah every time you pick me up."

"All good points," he said evenly.

"Glad you agree."

But I suspected I knew what was bothering him. Lela.

"I thought when you left the boardinghouse, you'd move in with me," he said, throwing me off kilter. "As my wife."

I reared back and looked to the hall, hoping no one had snuck up. How would I respond? I hadn't thought this would be about marriage.

"Had I gone to college, I'd be finishing my fourth year," I said, thinking fast. "Then going out into the workforce. Out on my own."

"When will you be ready to marry me, Violet?" he said, ignoring my comment and sounding monotone.

It hurt my feelings. His throwing this in my face. I told him in the park that one afternoon that I thought I'd be ready one day. Now he was pressuring me for a date?

It's the Jazz Age, Lela recently said. *Today's woman doesn't need a band—at least not one on her finger that's gold.* Then she laughed as music played, lifted her skirt, and took out her flask.

"Robert, I know how you like to take charge. You're successful in work because of it. But in this, must I put a month or year to it?"

"You make it sound like a chore."

It wasn't that as much as how I feared his pressures would infringe on my freedoms if we married. I massaged a spot between my eyes growing tighter. Then one of the newer residents passed by. This was not a conversation for here.

Yet if I didn't answer to Robert's satisfaction, he might be done with me. Could I go on the rest of my life without him?

I felt again that sense of being like Goldilocks, tasting of two bowls but wanting the one in the middle. A blend. Togetherness or independence. Love or freedom. Submission or choice. Was there a perfect middle?

My stockbroker reported that my earnings were on the way to making me a wealthy woman. I was considering quitting my job. Did I really need the security of it? The hassle? I wouldn't go another winter hiking in the snow for the filing job. That was for sure.

Yet how I loved the warm, cozy nights and intimate mornings with Robert. Cooking, reading, or going on tours. Visions of home in Kentucky resonated, too. The smells of food, the light of candles, the warmth of smiles from people who cared.

How would I decide? A home with Robert or my one life. I had longings, two incompatible longings.

He spoke again. "Do you think Lela is going to be so much easier to live with than those at the house? Parties? Boyfriends? More late nights?"

This was more the objection I thought he'd bring. "I think Lela will be great to live with. She's my best friend."

"What if I told you," he said, "that your partying and late nights with her sometimes trouble me? And now you'll be with Lela more than me."

I drummed the tiny desk with my fingers. "Trouble you how?" I said, feeling a spark of anger, but I'd give him the benefit of the doubt. "You fear for my safety?"

"That and, I don't know. Lela's so free with men."

Only when Father was about to admonish me did I feel such mounting discomfort in my gut. No, this was worse.

"You mistrust me?" I said, twisting to ensure that no one here heard.

But Father's voice boomed in my ears, back to the time I'd asked to drive. *Do you think Mother and I will let you gallivant about town?* I'd never even done anything untrustworthy.

But I also recalled the night at Palais de Danse with Lela, when I felt uneasy with her and two men at a table for four. It was one of several reasons I'd gotten up and left.

Still . . . *I* wasn't untrustworthy.

"I assure you, Robert, I'd never step out with another man."

"I didn't mean to suggest you would."

"Frankly," I went on, "you're the one on the road all the time, alone in strange cities. How do I know what temptations you face? Women in dining cars on trains? Women in your hotels? And, while we've never made a formal promise, I've always believed we were true to each other. Perhaps I was wrong."

"I'm sorry," he said. I heard him breathing. "I am loyal. I'm sure you are, too."

I hoped he was. I couldn't bear to think of him with another woman's hair brushing against his ear, or his fondling the skin of her hips. I shook the images away. Robert was struggling with my decision. I cared about him. I should be able to do better than this.

"Remember how you felt when you got your own place?" I said. "Can you try to sound a little happier for me?"

"You're right," he said with a note of tentativeness. "You need help moving?"

I laughed. Lela's father was handling it. But Robert was trying to meet me halfway.

CHAPTER 32

Violet

Detroit, Michigan
June 1923

I was relaxing on the sofa of the apartment, lazily turning pages of the *Saturday Evening Post.*

Lela and a guy named Gil were off for the weekend to Saugatuck, an art colony with entertainments on Lake Michigan. Robert was hung up in Nashville. And on this late Sunday in summer, rain showers fell, but I didn't mind. I had my home to myself. Quiet. Solitude. Except for Mrs. Sturgeon's breakfasts and soups, and a few friends at the house, I didn't miss the boardinghouse. True to my word, I hosted Robert my first week here for an intimate dinner of fresh perch, baby carrots, and boiled potatoes with parsley. I baked a pineapple upside-down cake in a cast iron skillet, and he said it was now his new favorite.

The living area here was nearly the size of the whole upper level at the boardinghouse and gorgeous. The walls, the rugs, the furniture, and the objects of art were all straight lines, modern, in colors of purple and gold. No frilly curtains. No floral prints.

I sipped lemonade and then turned another page. I got goose bumps at a colored sketch of a car. It so caught my attention, I sat up: an advertisement with the headline Somewhere West of Laramie. A flapper was racing a cowboy—and winning. I clutched the magazine tighter and read every word, my body pulsating.

> The truth is—the Playboy was built for her.
>
> Built for the lass . . .
>
> It's a brawny thing—yet a graceful thing for the sweep o' the Avenue.

After months of following advertisements and a few visits to nearby dealers, I thought I'd found the one.

My car.

I'd call for prices, assess my savings, and meet with my broker for options.

I wrote letters to Mother and Evelyn, telling them for the first time my dream. And as I thought of the homey house on West Campbell, and Mother with her beau Dr. Keller, the oddest sensation returned to me. The words "Mrs. Robert Neumann" formed in my mouth.

Perhaps after a time here with Lela, I'd be ready to move on. Me and my Jordan. Might I marry the man I loved when all was said and done? His bungalow driveway had a space for my car. I wouldn't be stuck there when he was gone. I had become the modern woman. Was there such a thing as a modern wife?

I got up to refresh my drink. I looked out the window above the sink and saw a pastel rainbow over the city.

July 1923

At Robert's bungalow a couple of weeks later, we made love for the second time that day. The sheets were damp. I snuggled into his armpit and rested my head in the dip between his chest and shoulder. He kissed the top of my head.

Unlike with my getting an apartment, I would announce this news in person: I would soon accomplish one of my highest aims since I was a girl of sixteen. I knew that this time, Robert would be thrilled to hear it. I'd worked hard. I'd saved money. In fact, it'd been almost two years since I first invested and three weeks since my latest boon.

And I didn't have Father to tell me I couldn't. There was nothing to stop me.

"Guess what," I said, tracing a little circle on Robert's chest through his hair. "I'm going to buy a car."

"Wonderful. An adventure." Robert's head turned closer to mine with a huge smile.

"Thank you," I said. "I knew you'd be happy for me."

"And one of the best things is," he said, "I can help every step of the way."

My body tensed. I was in charge of this.

The Jordan was my first choice. I'd already purchased shares in the company. The MX Playboy model was so popular with young women in the country, I had to wait for new shipments to reach the Detroit showroom.

"You've got to get a Ford," Robert said jovially before I got to speak. "I'll connect you with my best dealer in the city."

"I've considered all domestic makes," I said, rising up on one elbow.

"Don't you think you should support the company that provides my livelihood?" he said, and his lips stayed open as if he wished to add, *and a company that provides for our future family's livelihood.*

What of my own income? As far as car manufacturers were concerned, I'd already invested in stocks with Ford's competition—General Motors and more. I hadn't mentioned it; Ford didn't even sell shares.

I forced a laugh now. "You don't mean that as an order, Robert, surely. You're fine with whatever I buy. Right?"

"Buying another automaker's car is like taking money right out of my pocket," he said, sliding the covers to get up. "I sell Fords."

I saw his point. But his insistence was snatching a decision out of my power. I hadn't come all this way to have a man dictate my choices.

Father's voice from years ago pounded in my head so loud I wanted to plug my ears with my fingers.

Do you think Mother and I will let you gallivant about town? In my Model T that I spent hard-earned money on? Driving is not for females. So get that idea right out of your mind.

I would do as I pleased with *my own hard-earned money*. And I wouldn't let Robert stop me from choosing what I wanted.

When I got home to the apartment, Lela was mixing us cocktails. A Tom Collins with gin she'd gotten from Gil Ratliff, now her new official boyfriend. A former medic in the war, he was born rich and had everything he wanted.

I vented about Robert's insistence that I buy a Ford.

Lela handed over a drink in a tall glass with chipped ice and gaped at me.

"Violet, you know that you're more than a friend. You're the closest I have to a sister. And with Evelyn far away, I hope you'll consider me your sister in spirit here, too."

"Always," I said as we headed to the sofa.

"Robert is the best stock of man," she said. "Kind. Ambitious. And not bad to look at." She giggled and then took a sip. "But it's as if a bomb is waiting to drop. He wants marriage. You've resisted. I wonder when the spark will ignite and this will all blow up."

Her cynicism triggered a spiraling sense in my chest that hurt. What did this have to do with my buying a car? And what about my secretly reconsidering marriage? Like Mother. The spiraling sensation twisted tighter.

"You think he and I are over?" I asked. "But for a formality of making it final?"

"Maybe. Or maybe it's time for you to go be with him. Don't worry about the apartment. Think about yourself. What do you want? Independence? To make your own choices—to come and go as you please? Do you wish to do things like buy your own car without a man's permission or, nearly as bad, setting forth a decree on what you may pick?"

She sipped her drink again, and I was at a loss for how to respond. She made some good points, but that spiraling feeling inside me wasn't ready to give Robert up.

Was it?

"If what you want is not being his bride," she said, "then isn't the right thing to do to let Robert go? Let him lead the life he wants, too?"

"Well . . . ," I started.

"Or," Lela said, butting in and more serious than normal. "If you want the car of your dreams, go get it. See what happens?"

Father's voice reverberated. *Driving is not for females. So you can get that idea right out of your mind.*

"Um," I said. I took another sip. "I'm going to go see the Jordan automobile when the model arrives at the dealer in a few days. Then I'll decide."

I was hesitant at first to touch it, stunning though it was. If I touched it, I'd buy it. And though I had a couple of thousand in my envelope purse, I wasn't sure I was ready. I fiddled with the sash that hung low at my hips on my dress. The Jordan dealership showroom was large with a square tile floor. There was a wall of plate glass with plenty of light, but more lights dipped from the ceiling on cords. Rug runners ran between at least a dozen cars in several models, for the walking comfort of buyers—many of whom were women in heels, here to fawn over the Jordan MX Playboys.

I'd called my broker and bought a ton more shares. Jordan's sales were soaring. And I felt in my veins that this was the car of my choice: a girl's car like in the *Somewhere West of Laramie* ad.

But if I bought it, Robert and I could be done for good. His ultimatum would create a standoff. I was in charge of my one life.

Now in the showroom, my pulse seemed to slow to a stop. I looked to Lela with a barely contained smile and a long, slow blink of my lashes.

I lifted my hand.

Gold and silver bangles clinked about my wrist as my fingers ran along the door—the driver's side door, not the passenger's side. I heard the salesman's breath catch. He adjusted the knot of his tie. He knew he had a fish on the line.

Lela's perfect Cupid's bow lips bent into a smile.

I felt my face flush.

I glided my flat palm along the back of the car where the swanky stow-away top could be folded onto metal strips. I'd never touched anything so cool, so smooth, so tempting as the slick red paint of this red-hot machine. Saliva gathering in my mouth could mean I might be sick after getting my edge on with last night's gin fizzes—but no, it was from my desire to fully possess this Jordan MX.

"Take it for a spin?" The salesman's deep voice jarred me.

He'd already been so attentive. He'd pointed out the tiny compartment equipped with a small set of hand tools (and which might be used, as Lela had noted, to store our beaded headbands). He'd said the engine would roar if I pressed the pedal to the floor outside the city. As if I hadn't known. I glanced at the salesman who now seemed to sense that my purchase would come without as much as a test drive. He ignored two nearby men clad in summer suits. They were talking while examining the pamphlets on a rack. They were lookers, not buyers. They probably favored Fords.

Ford. Robert's face flashed before me again. I'd have to try to ignore it. This purchase was my decision and mine alone. I wouldn't let visions of his glorious smile dissuade me.

When Mother voted for president the first time, she said that I'd have the power to do things in life that she never could. Now I knew, I had the power to want things, too, that she had never wanted.

"I'll take it," I told the salesman, unfastening my purse for some cash. His grin compared only to Lela's.

To me, this car was more than a half-ton piece of machinery. I was becoming a true motoriste—a word practically synonymous with the height of *independence*.

I was today's woman.

The salesman dangled in front of me a key on a short metal chain, one bearing the Jordan brand name and iconic arrowhead emblem.

"What's that noise?" Lela said, suddenly looking to the ceiling, her flawless face wrinkling into a frown. The salesman moved for the windows at a brisk pace.

Then I heard it as well—a great roar as if coming from the skies over Detroit. I flinched. We made for the dealership's door and saw the chaos. Cars jammed the street, and people were climbing out of them, scrambling around and waving their arms in the air. Even the streetcars seemed to have stopped. An airplane was causing all the commotion—and the smell of exhaust fumes about made me cough. A barnstormer over Woodward Avenue in the heart of the city? Unlikely. But horns were honking and people were cheering for this daring fly boy. We girls packed onto the sidewalk as the plane swooped over again, dropping treats to the ground by the hundreds. Maybe thousands.

"Baby Ruths!" the crowd cried. More people charged out of businesses lining the street—the bank, the boutiques, the eateries. Children swarmed on the sidewalks to scoop up a stash in their fat little fists. Two old men had a tug-of-war over a candy bar, too.

The salesman caught two Baby Ruths falling midair in one masterful grasp. Lela and I squealed and clapped. Each bar was tied with a rice paper parachute. It was the latest marketing gimmick. Candy bar drops had begun in Pittsburgh and had been surprising city after city ever since.

"For you, ladies," the salesman said and winked.

Though I'd not discerned it before, he was a handsome sort. Then he handed one bar to my friend as if he were a suave cake-eater for the ladies, not a man bent on a sale.

"How gallant of you," Lela said, flirting. The long, thin lines of her dark brows were a tease beneath the brim of her white cloche hat.

I took my treat from the salesman's hand and ripped open the end of the wrapper. I sank my teeth into milk chocolate, roasted peanuts, and creamy caramel. Delicious.

Then I noticed something else. Among the automobiles crammed in the street was one with a sign on its bumper: Don't Shoot, I'm Not a Bootlegger. Newspapers told of violence following smugglers, but seeing this was a first for me.

Lela licked the last of her chocolate off her thumb. Then her lips widened into a mischievous grin.

"Violet, can you believe," she said, "that the sky rained candy on the day you bought your car? Candy bars actually fell all around us." She wiggled her upturned hands. "Isn't it a swell world?"

It was.

But Robert returned to my mind's eye . . . pulling me close to dance a waltz, taking my chin in his fingers. I still wanted that, too. We had love. Wouldn't that be enough?

I clamped my new car key in one buffed and manicured hand. I owned it. Lela's smile was infectious. I couldn't help but toss my head back and laugh in agreement.

We were young. We were free. We were friends having fun.

CHAPTER 33

Melanie

Louisville, Kentucky
September 2018

Bad news, good news, and news I couldn't label—all within twenty-four hours.

It was TGIF at work, and I was headed to the ladies' room when Mitchell Fox came sauntering out of the office of the founder of Goldenrod Distillery—the latter of whom was patting my adversary's back. I ducked into the restroom without being seen, but an alarm was sounding in my body like a code blue on a cardiac unit. I considered myself a strong woman with fairly thick skin . . . one who withstood a type A mother and losing the love of her life. But this actually made me eke out a sob. What were those men doing together? I locked myself in a stall and sat on the commode, pants and all, rolling out reams of toilet tissue to stuff to my face so as not to be heard.

Had Mitchell been in there brownnosing the founder? Was he announcing another big win—one so important he went over Cora's head? Was the directorship already decided, and he was being congratulated? I wilted, wondering if my dreams of earning the promotion were already over.

Oh no. My car loan! *Shit.* I'd signed the papers the same day Mom and I had FaceTimed. Now, without the raise, I wouldn't have money to pay it. My mind spiraled and spiraled until I saw myself defaulting on payments and screwing my credit score. Or even landing in bankruptcy court. What a mess.

And . . . would I have to tell my mom that I'd lost the promotion? Lost everything? I spun around, dropped to my knees in the stall, and puked.

Get yourself together, girl. Your mama didn't raise no weakling. And Aunt Violet didn't stay down for long after she'd gotten blown out of a job. Twice.

I sucked back phlegm and flushed the commode with my shoe. I would splash cold water on my face and refresh my lipstick. Then I'd breeze my way back to my cube and keep my ears perked for a rumor. If Mitchell Fox had anything good going on, he'd be sure to spread it so loud I would hear.

There I sat, trying to concentrate on my work, with one ear attuned. But Mitchell was silent.

Oh no, I thought. Any minute, the boss could come around my three-quarters-high wall and wiggle a finger for me to follow—or worse, tell me I'd not gotten the job within earshot of everyone else.

I agonized until it all came out. Mitchell bragged in the lunchroom as if he and the founder were best buds. They were both grads from Big Ten schools, not the SEC. Now I knew I was still in the running. But Mitchell's personal connection could help sway the decision. I had to stay confident that my performance and longtime track record would override everything else. I had no room for error.

That evening at home, I discovered an email from Ray's Restorations. Ray had my Jordan for less than a week, but the car was dismantled, and if I wanted to, I could come see what they discovered and weigh in on the color of paint.

Paint color sounded important.

I would keep my word to Brian and invite him to join me in seeing my car's work in progress—it was just happening sooner than expected. I could slide by there tomorrow morning, if he could, but with my workload this weekend, dinner was out. I was halfway into drafting new text for a section on the website targeting women, inspired by the Jordan ad and Aunt Violet. I'd found some old photos of women working a bottling line in the 1930s that I thought would appeal to women who loved bourbon, appreciated its history, and admired the pioneering women who'd come before us.

I texted Brian, all excited. I had something to look forward to. The car. Seeing him. Getting away for an hour or two.

I threw myself on my couch to immerse myself in the journal, having mixed an old-fashioned cocktail. I poured it with Knob Creek Single Barrel Reserve, aged nine years and 120 proof. Sometimes I had to test-taste competitors' bourbon, and this was a fave.

Three hours later, I was on a roll with the journal—Violet's tiny cursive writing was now second nature to me. Still no word from Brian.

The more I read, though, I closed my fist and pressed my knuckles to my mouth.

For pages, Violet was torn. Independence, or marriage? Robert pushed against her decision to choose her own car—her life's dream. She was on the brink of buying the very automobile I'd see again tomorrow, knowing that they might be through.

I couldn't read any more. It evoked memories of Jason that I didn't need. His forcing me to choose.

It all gave me second thoughts about being with Brian tomorrow, too. Maybe a girl couldn't just "have fun" with a guy after all? Feelings got in the way. Eventually, a guy would want more. I'd learned firsthand; for me, marriage and career didn't mix.

Right then Brian texted Let's do it! 😁

Ugh. I'd have to get through this.

The next morning, I pulled to the rear of Brian's driveway as he'd suggested. He had a quaint modern farmhouse in a neighborhood with airy lots. Very nice—like he had this whole homey, domestic side. We agreed I'd toot the horn and he'd come out. The auto garage was minutes away, and if we rode together, we could debrief afterward on what I learned before I headed home for work.

I wouldn't go in at Brian's place. Aunt Violet's experience had shaken me. I'd keep some distance.

He climbed into my Honda, all smiles and scents of aftershave. "Good morning," he said, bright as a morning songbird.

"Hi," I said, feeling like a fifth grader with a crush on a boy who'd just picked me for his dodgeball team at recess. Oh no.

Within ten minutes we entered through a big bay door at Ray's. The space was filled with tall metal toolboxes on wheels and equipment I couldn't name with hoses and cords and electrical switches. There were drills and vises and sanding equipment along the walls. The aroma of chemicals—paint or something acidic—would wear on me if I spent hours here.

A silver-haired, thickset man in his late fifties or so came my way.

"This is Ray," said Brian.

"Hi, I'm Melanie."

The lines of Ray's face were like roads on a map for cars he had fixed. His crew in the background looked more like in their twenties or thirties.

"Pleasure to meet you, Melanie," Ray said. "Here she is." He waved his hand.

It took me a second to realize the "she" was the car, not a woman and not me . . . and that the vehicle he pointed to was mine.

The Jordan's basic body was up off the floor, mounted on a stand of some sort that was five or six feet high. I moved closer to study it.

"That's a rotisserie," Brian said. "The stand rotates horizontally, so the crew can work from any angle. Goes higher or lower as needed."

The car's wheels and doors and fenders and windshield were all off. Nothing was inside, either, just the bare floor. To see my aunt's prized possession so naked was shocking—like how I looked in a salon mirror with my hair all greased up in goop with foils. I couldn't wait to see the car look normal again.

Ray pointed his finger for me to home in on something where the driver's door used to be. Brian and I bumped shoulders to get in for a peek, and I twitched.

"We know from Jordan Motor Company records the original color was called scarlet red," Ray said. "But see here? This spot in a hinge of the door well is smaller than a penny, but after combing the whole car, it's the only clue we have to the body's true color."

Brian and I exchanged glances. This was fun.

Ray went on, "The paint right here didn't suffer wear from the elements. It's as close to showroom color as we're gonna find."

He motioned for us to follow him to a metal workbench off to the side. "Based on my experience," Ray said, "I think one of these two formulations will be about spot-on."

"May I?" Brian said.

Ray handed him the two paper samples that had smears of red color on them. Brian held them between the two of us near the light. His face was cute with his lips pursed in concentration.

"Any preference?" he asked me.

Gosh, this was hard. One was more fire engine–like and the other so close, all I could tell was the light hit it more brightly.

"This one," I said, notating the brighter one.

He smiled. "That would be my pick."

Ray said, "Mine, too. Looks like we have a color."

I swallowed hard. I didn't want to get emotional in this shop with all these car gurus. But I couldn't help thinking of Violet. This car represented her freedom. She was willing to give up her man for it—the same way I'd given up Jason for my job in bourbon country.

I was doing the right thing by her. Restoring this car. I had to get the promotion. The raise.

"Cars get under our skin, don't they?" Ray said, warmly, wisely.

Ray was part car expert, part historian, part therapist.

Before Brian and I left, Ray showed us another car that was in progress. It, too, was up on a rotisserie.

"A '34 Ford," Brian said.

How he could tell just by looking was amazing to me. It was the color of coppery putty.

"This coat is primer," Ray said, "where your car will go later."

The primer was a sealing layer before the crew would spray on the paint.

"Similar to priming a bedroom wall before adding wallpaper," I said, recalling Mom decorating my room when I was a girl.

"Exactly," said Brian.

He and I soon headed out. My Jordan was completely torn apart. Barely recognizable. Much like me with my fight for advancement, my battles with Mom, my war with Jason. But that's what it took to put things back together good as new.

On the way back to Brian's, I regretted not using the restroom before we left Ray's. I'd guzzled water all the way to Lexington in the car, and I had to go bad before heading back to Louisville.

This was an awkward personal emergency. It was the first time I'd been to a single guy's place in forever.

Brian had beautiful flower beds bordering his patio and house, with yellow mums and some dark purplish-brown blooms.

"What are those?" I swear I detected the scent of cocoa.

"Chocolate cosmos," he called them. He extended a hand for me to enter the house. "After you."

Inside, I smelled the aroma of Windex and coffee. His comfy kitchen was out of an episode on HGTV. He had a rustic table with distressed wood, stainless appliances, and a center island.

"Welcome to my humble abode," he said. "Cup of java?"

"No, thanks. I need to get home. But your place is a magazine spread."

"Can't take credit. I hired most of it done," he said. "I may not be in this house forever, though. I like old houses, too, from Victorians to late 1950s ranches."

"Old cars. Old houses," I said.

Brian wasn't boring. He led me through the living room where giant framed photographs of sexy cars shot in exotic locations hung—beachside, mountain view, and one with a castle behind it.

"These cars all your work?"

"Nah. Just cool photos for a motor head."

He had car photos the way golf buffs had pictures of holes at Augusta or Saint Andrews. Like Dad. I followed my host to the nearest bath.

"While you're here," Brian said, "I'd love to show you pictures of work that I did do. Won't take five minutes."

"Sure," I said, thinking, *As long as they aren't hanging in his bedroom.*

I came out of the bathroom expecting to see a photo album, but he took me up wide stairs leading to a bonus room above the garage—his man cave, I supposed, with a big-screen TV and a pool table at center. I could imagine a party with music or football in the background. Along one wall was a series of family photographs.

"This is you?" I asked. Various pictures showed Brian in a red toy motor car around age three; one in his first car in high school, a Dodge pickup truck; and one with him and his father in a garage, both bent over an engine under an open hood.

"Here's the first car I customized myself," he said, pointing to another picture. "A'66 Ford Mustang." He said the picture had been taken ten years before, when he was twenty-two.

"Look at you." He was such a cutie. His muscles still rocked it. "You really are a car guru, aren't you?"

He laughed. "Motor head. Gearhead. Tinkerer. I answer to many names."

My dad would like him. When not golfing, he tinkered, too, only on old furniture, staining and stuff.

"You've got your Vette now, but you like your Ford, too, don't you? In my aunt's journal, the guy she dated worked for Ford," I said. "Some pages back, I also read of Henry Ford paying higher wages and being the first in the industry to hire Black people."

"True," Brian said hesitantly. "Ford was an enigma, though. Did some good. Some bad."

"Bad? Like what?"

"He was an anti-Semite, for one. In the 1920s, he wrote articles slamming Jews. He supposedly later apologized, but was that really enough?"

"That's awful," I said. "I had no idea."

Brian nodded. I hadn't heard of the repulsive side of Henry Ford. It would forever change my view of him.

Brian and I took a couple of steps over.

"And I'm guessing this is a photo of you and your mom? She must be a car guru, too."

He laughed. "She loves old cars. And she's always been in favor of our father-son exploits. But she's got her own gigs, too."

"Oh?" I was curious. "What does she like to do?"

"Interior design. Her team helped with this place."

"Nice," I said.

"Yeah, it's nice. The older I get," he said, "the more I admire how my parents support each other's work, each other's passions."

Unlike Jason. *Mark another checkbox for Brian,* my friend Nicole would say.

Brian laughed sort of nervously and said, "I didn't mean to make this visit all about me. Like I'm a freakin' museum."

"Honestly," I said, though maybe I shouldn't have, "I've enjoyed it. And I appreciate your help."

He placed his hand on the small of my back to guide me to the other end of the room, but his touch seared my skin through my lightweight summer top. My body betrayed me.

Brian started to say something, then stopped. Shook his head.

"What?" I asked, suddenly sensing the thoughts going through his mind. Something had reached beyond my skin, thoughts of him circling my mind, too.

But under no circumstances would I stay longer than five more minutes. I couldn't let things happen. I couldn't risk another Jason . . . or a Robert.

Brian shrugged shyly. He looked left and then back to me, his hands in his pockets. "I was thinking that . . ."

He paused, and the connection we had said the rest. It was in the eyes. In our breathing. Maybe pheromones or something else I couldn't see. His hands came out of his pockets.

My mouth tilted up to reach his lips. We kissed softly, tenderly. My hands went to the sides of his warm waist. His arms cupped my back. He pulled me close. I opened my mouth and let him in.

After a moment, I drew back slowly, and his hands rested on my waist.

"I like you," he said, and his enchanting smile was an exclamation point.

"I like you, too," I said quietly, with a playful grin. Then, more seriously, looking down, I said, "But I'm not sure about all this." I didn't know what else to say.

He must've assumed that I had a recent relationship.

"I've been there," he said. "We don't get to be thirty-two like me, or late twenties like you, without having a past. I haven't wanted to be with anyone for quite some time. Until I met you."

This guy. I kissed his cheek. "I'd better go." We held gazes and it was combustion. Fire.

"When you're ready," he said, "you know where to find me."

But it wasn't a matter of when I'd be ready. I'd never be. It was a matter of principle. My career and a forever-man didn't work. And now, with Violet's story, I feared I couldn't even risk having "fun."

CHAPTER 34

Violet

Detroit, Michigan
July 1923

Robert was finally back in town.

Lela was out, and we'd be alone. I had a letter from Evelyn, but I would read it after. I was saving it, hoping it was a second thing to cheer me. I'd already called the dreadful Miss Baxter and officially quit my job. My investments were good. But I might look for ways to volunteer in the community with my time.

I powdered my face with my fluffy white puff. I dabbed some rouge on my cheeks. I lined my lips with his favorite shade of red. I sprayed a mist of perfume at my clavicle and wrists. I tidied my hair and smoothed my skirt. Maybe this would turn out well.

After all, he loved me.

With the sound of the doorbell, I tightened the belt on my dress and padded to my living room with its sharp geometric shapes.

I opened the door, and he came in without words and hugged me. We held the embrace, wordless, for a longer while than normal. His arms and chest felt so good.

"Glad you're here," I began. And his soulful blue eyes held mine.

The swelling in my throat came so quickly. A pain before I'd even begun, and I struggled to eke out a word. I had faith in us, but at the same time fear.

"Just tell me," he said.

"I bought the car, Robert. It's a girl's car, and that's what I want."

He puckered his lips. "So you've had your way."

My head reared back. So this was how it would be?

"I've made a decision for myself. It's my prerogative. Had you not insisted I buy a Ford, you wouldn't be thinking of this as *my way*, or that you didn't get your way."

My father once said owls could hear a mouse's heartbeat from twenty-five feet away—but I felt as if I could hear Robert's and my heartbeats loud as drums in a band.

"I love you," he said, and it felt incongruent without his magnificent smile.

"And I love you," I said. My fingers were woven together.

After a time, I asked, "Do you have any more to say?" I hoped he'd relent.

"You knew how I felt."

"Mm-hmm. I'm just not ready to defer my choices in life to someone else."

I'd made my decision. I would not back down.

Sadness filled my whole being like a bruise. I felt an age-old tug between my head and my heart. These difficulties of love were the stuff of which sonnets were written.

"And I know you want to settle down," I said. I shook my head. "I'm not there."

"I'll not stop loving you," Robert said.

Pools of water gathered in my eyes. I need not hide them. And it was as if a film reel spun in my head complete with clicking-snapping sounds bringing forth our every moment. Meeting at the distillery lobby in Frankfort. Our tour of Detroit and hot fudge sundaes. Making love the first time at his brother's house . . .

But this was the final wound to us both.

"I'll always love you, too," I said.

We have our love, true love, I thought. *But is love enough in this world?*

We didn't say the word *goodbye*, after all.

Instead he said, "Thank you."

I startled. Thank me for what? Then I thought: *For being us for a time. For days and nights we'd never forget.*

I said, "Thank *you*."

These were our final words. As Robert walked out the door, he gave me one last glance. I closed my eyes to the sound of it shutting. Click. I changed into my robe and reclined on the couch. I would take his bracelet off, but not until tomorrow. I wept long and hard and hushed, almost like when Father died.

I would never see Robert again.

I felt gutted like one of Grandfather's fish—gutted, scaled, and deboned. I had asserted myself as a woman. Stood up for my rights. But I'd thought, somehow, Robert's love for me would win out. I was wrong.

~

An hour later, I opened Evelyn's letter to distract me. Something happy.

> Dear Violet,
>
> I write with disturbing news. I've been to the doctor, one that Mother's beau recommended. A specialist at a hospital in Louisville. It seems there are "fibrous tissues and scarring" on the inside of my body that may be preventing me from conceiving. I've wanted a baby so much. Charles, too.

Mother says there's still hope. But I've been married five years, as long as she was.

There's nothing you can say to mend my feelings. I just needed you to know. Charles is taking me away for a few weeks. To the Grove Park Inn in North Carolina. Some mountain air might do me some good.

Your loving sister,

Evelyn

How sad that she didn't have the choice—not as I'd gotten to choose my own fate. But how ironic, too, that both of our fates came with pain. I vowed I'd go be with her after she returned. I'd write her tomorrow to say so. And I'd agree with Mother's assessment.

I had to believe there was a chance for Evelyn. If not for me.

CHAPTER 35

Violet

Detroit, Michigan
July 1923

Lela knocked and padded into my bedroom. It was well past noon, but my drapes were still drawn. Only a sliver of light shined through the crack where the fabric panels met. My friend placed a goblet of water on my bedside table.

"Drink plenty of fluids," she said.

Mother would've said the same. But I wasn't ailing from nausea or intestinal problems, nor headache or fever. I had a rotating list of problems that circled my mind like hands on a clock gone haywire.

Evelyn was worried about her future. Robert and I were done; my heart was raw. Then an hour ago, my broker called.

"Miss Bond," Mr. Jackson said. "I wanted to make you aware that some of your stocks have taken a dip."

"A dip?"

"It's the natural course of things. Highs and lows. I didn't want you to be alarmed when your monthly statement appears."

I envisioned the red bar to the right sliding like a slope of a mountain already climbed. "I'm losing a lot?"

He described the particular parts of the portfolio that were weakened. My loss of funds would not be catastrophic, but it would be a pinch—a big pinch, given I'd quit my job and bought the Jordan.

I did some rough calculations in my head. With the interest earnings remaining, I could pay my share of the rent and afford to eat modestly. There'd be no buying of clothes or new cosmetics. No movies or shoes. No extravagant dinners out. I would have to withdraw from my tiny remaining nest egg in my safe to send Mother her next monthly stipend.

How long would the drought on investments last? I had to seek another job.

"I recommend," the broker said, "a few adjustments. I've been studying the market and here's a plan of course."

He outlined what portions of my shares to sell and some promising ones to buy. I hoped he was right. Lela said some of her same securities outside of automotive had suffered.

"There's only two choices of action when things don't go our way," she said. "Stay in bed moping. Or get out in the air and have fun!" She wiggled my shoulder. "It's time for another driving lesson. Your tank is full of fuel. I suggest you get up, get dressed, grab your key, and let's go." She sounded like a military officer.

As I pulled on my clothes, I had a serious talk with myself: I was exactly where I'd wanted to be. Independent. The owner of an automobile. Released of the pressures to wed. Living life in the city where, if I had to cut back for a time, it wasn't a death sentence. Tonight I'd scour the wanted ads. I was not lazy. Lela was right about one thing, being bedridden wasn't the answer.

I was living my one life.

So why wasn't I happy?

No one ever said that a modern woman's life was perfect.

We climbed into my Jordan, and before I even started it up, I felt better. This I had. This was mine. I wouldn't let anyone take it away.

I headed out.

"You're getting the hang of it, my friend," Lela said as I jerked both our heads into near whiplash. She held on to the dash. "Smoother, smoother."

As long I was driving straight with no stops, we were fine. It was the braking and the taking off that were hard with the gears. But she was right. I was getting better at shifting. And the most fun of all was glancing out the windows to see everyone watching us. There was nothing like two young women in a hot red roadster. I was cheered.

We'd no sooner gotten back to the apartment when the telephone rang.

"Helloooo," Lela said, picking up. "Gil. Uh-huh. Uh-huh. Yes, Violet and I are both free."

I frowned at her and waved my arms, mouthing, *no, no,* a hundred times. It did no good.

"Yes," she went on. "We'll be ready. Looking forward to it."

With her click of the receiver, I said, "Darling, I didn't move in here to have a new Mrs. Sturgeon or Mr. Giddens or a new father or husband setting my schedule for me."

She laughed high and long. "I'm sorry."

"I mean it, Lela. What have you committed me to?"

"You recall that handsome man named Lawrence? We met him around a year ago, at the Palais de Danse, I think it was. Yes, the Palais de Danse. I always remember places and addresses."

"You mean the guy who was with that jerk named Joe?"

"I promise you," she said with her hand on her waist, "he never saw him again, just like we never saw him again."

Lawrence was a law student if I recalled correctly. A nice guy upon first impression. But I wasn't interested in going.

"The other thing about being down in spirit is this," Lela said. "When nice men ask for dates, we go. We won't have to spend a cent. They're picking us up at eight."

I should refuse to join them. Scan for jobs. Be the responsible one, not the hedonist. I could have an egg sandwich instead of a steak. The drive was all the fun I needed.

"Don't let me down," Lela said. "I double-promise never to commit you again."

I sighed. Against my better judgment, I put on one of my sparkling dresses and headbands for a night on the town.

~

A year ago, I hadn't noticed Lawrence had a cleft in his chin to round out his sporting good looks. But when the light hit just right—like when the candle flickered on the table for four at a tiny Italian trattoria—the cleft was deep.

"We should go dancing after," Gil said.

I stiffened. Was I ready for this?

"Let's do the Palms," Lawrence said as I took a bite of spaghetti with red sauce. "The place I mentioned briefly when last we met. It's a black and tan."

A black and tan? I raised my brows to convey I was at a loss.

"It's a club where we'll get the closest thing to authentic jazz you've ever heard." His eyes lit up. "They have all Black musicians like the Palais de Danse had that night. But no one is barred. Everyone gets in."

Black and white people mingling in society? It was a shock to envision. This is what the uppity Joe had called *slumming*? I bristled. But it made me like Lawrence all the more.

In retrospect, maybe Lela's insistence that I come tonight had been best. I gave Robert up on principle. It was right. Maybe I'd get past the pain of it by distracting myself with someone else on a dance floor.

"Let's go to the Palms," I said, looking from Lawrence to Lela, who grinned.

Gil said, "The Palms is darb. I'm in one hundred percent."

We heard the thrumming timbre of the bass and the lively meter of a piano before we ever entered the door. The lights of the Palms were dim, the atmosphere tropical, and the crowd cosmopolitan. I adjusted my headband with its glittering rhinestones. The dance floor was a mass of dark skin and light skin and skin in every shade in between.

Everyone was enjoying themselves and ignoring their race and their class. Music was art, and art was the glue.

We navigated our way through the standing-room-only throng, bumping elbows and smiling. As we got closer to the stage, we could scarcely hear each other speak.

Gil and Lela found an empty spot on the dance floor and danced a Texas Tommy, a swing dance. Lawrence leaned in toward my ear.

"What do you think?"

"I think I can't believe I haven't been here before."

"Well," he said. "Not everyone knows about it."

"Give it up for the Bart Howard Syncopators!" a man soon announced. "They'll be back after a short break."

Two Black couples squeezed by us, laughing. I waved at them, and they waved at me amiably in return. Lela and Gil rejoined us.

"I'm glad you like the place," Lawrence said. "Now, may I just say, I love your accent?"

He didn't hate it, the way Mr. Giddens had?

Lela giggled. "Told you so."

After a while, Lawrence took my hand as the band started back up and said, "Let's go tango."

Tango? I'd never danced that before. Not even with Robert.

I could tell from Lawrence's gentle grip of my hand and one arm around my waist—not resting on my back—that he had experience. He pulled me closer. Never should daylight show between dancers; that was the rule. But this felt more personal. I smelled a mix of cigarettes and cinnamon on his breath. He led me across the floor in the dance in the way sultry Valentino led his partner in *The Four Horsemen of the Apocalypse*. Primal. We didn't take mere earthly steps. We did rhythmic, lunging dips from the knees forward and backward, hugging the floor and immune to the crowd as if we were the sole planet in a solar system.

It was a dance I'd not wish for Robert to do with another woman. But of course, I'd given up rights to an opinion. He would lead his life. And I mine. But I didn't grow out of feelings, I learned, the way I'd grown out of clothes as a child.

Soon Lela and I stood in line with jaunty ladies awaiting the lounge.

"That was some hot tango," she said, doing a little shimmy.

"Candidly," I said, "I enjoyed it."

"Good," she said. "Men can be fun for fun's sake, without all the other . . . shall we say, complications."

Perhaps she was right.

"Oh, that Bart Howard can pound the keys, can't he?" said a rosy-brown woman wearing a gorgeous black dress. We all agreed. "And a cigar between his teeth the whole while."

"Mm-hmm. This isn't Chicago or Harlem or New Orleans," said her friend with a nip of giggle water, "but it's the jazziest piano I've heard."

"He had a doctor cut him right here," Lela said, pinching the webbed skin between her thumb and forefinger. "To widen his reach on the keys."

"You don't say," said the woman with darker brown skin, her irises wide. "That's the berries!"

The place closed at four in the morning.

By the time we left, the two women with brown skin, Molly and Helene, had taught Lela and me a dance we'd never seen—the Charleston. Lawrence later said it had roots in South Carolina and probably Africa before that, but then it'd made its way to Harlem, evolving as it went.

"You swing your arms this way," Molly said. "And twist your feet and kick your legs. Then put your hands on your knees and knock 'em together to and fro."

Lela and I laughed till we cried, trying to get all our limbs and hands to work in unison, despite how we'd not nipped the gin in hours. "Thank you," she said to our new acquaintances. "I predict this dance will become a new American craze."

We all hugged.

Molly said, "This has been fun."

"Yes," I said, "so much fun!"

Outside, Lawrence bent and pressed his lips to where my jawbone met my ear. A delicate spot.

He and I'd had a meeting of the minds—on our view of society. It was more, too. But I couldn't imagine slipping off my clothes for a man besides Robert to take me.

We got in the car, and Lela's giggling in the rear seat was all that I heard from up front. Then Lawrence stopped. At Gil's place in the city? Lela had mentioned this apartment complex to me, though he had a place in Grosse Pointe, too.

Being here made me uneasy.

Lela said, "Me and Gil are getting out." She kissed my cheek through the window. "See you tomorrow."

I knew the freedoms she enjoyed. But now I was stuck in the car with Lawrence and wishing I was stuck at home after all. I should've stayed there searching wanted ads. What was I doing here? I felt sickened inside.

He made casual conversation along the way. Music, theater, art. It was pleasant, but how did I know what detours he might take? He had the wheel. He seemed a wonderful guy, and he'd had only one drink at the Palms. I didn't know terribly much about him, though, considering I was alone with him in a dark car in the middle of the night. What if he stopped and tried to yank my dress up? What would I do? I didn't like the feelings I had then. And Lela should've stayed with me. But then, why? Had she not the right to do as she pleased, too? She probably would say she went to Gil's to avoid having both guys come up to our place. Then I'd really have been hemmed in. Had she done me a favor?

"So you're out of law school now, Lawrence?" I said, finding the noise of our voices better than the voice in my head. Sometimes it was Evelyn's voice.

Take care of yourself.

"Yes," Lawrence said. "I'm starting my practice next month with a big firm downtown."

"Congratulations."

When at last he pulled up outside my apartment building, I said with some distress, "I'll get out here."

The statement suggested that he shouldn't park. This was my way of ending the evening.

He skipped around to open my door, and I thought this was good. There were lights but few other people about. He'd make sure I got in the building safe.

"It was a nice night, thank you."

But for Lela stranding me up, it was a good night. Dinner. The Palms. Lawrence was nice company. But the fun didn't feel as fun as before.

His eyes held mine, and it seemed a question formed. Would I invite him up? I didn't speak. Being with him alone would be going too far.

"Can I see you again?" he asked instead.

CHAPTER 36

Melanie

Louisville, Kentucky
September 2018

I would take a pass on meeting for Mexican with my girlfriends. They'd just have to wait to hear about my tantalizing kiss with the cute car guru guy in his man cave. I was worn out when I packed my bag to leave work at seven. I'd updated my budget for the cocktail competition and met with Tanisha a couple of days before, and she'd sent reminder emails to our star mixologists with detailed itineraries for how timing on the big day would shake out. The VIP glass sets were still on track. But at home the night before, I hadn't turned out the lights until late, immersed in Violet's journal.

I would text Mom tonight to give her the scoop before hitting the sack. Violet had bought the car and split with Robert. She'd held her own, like I had with Jason. But she and I both suffered the consequences to our hearts. I felt Violet's ache from across a century.

As I hung my purse on my shoulder to check out, that's when Mitchell Fox said, "Take a quick look at the last press release before it goes?" It was one of several for the upcoming events.

I sat back down and took the stapled pages from him. It wouldn't take long to peruse the press release.

Blah, blah, blah. The usual publicity. It looked good. But when I got to page two, a big question mark scribbled itself in the matter of my brain.

"Wait," I said. "What's this?"

"What's what?" he said as if aggravated for having asked me to check it. "A typo?"

"No." I reread the paragraph from the start.

"Where's my fourth mixologist? The biggest celeb on my cocktail competition panel is missing?"

"What do you mean?" Mitchell said. "He canceled."

I shifted my weight and frowned. "Does Cora know about this?" She was on location with a photo shoot for the new product bottles all day, and we hadn't spoken.

"Of course. You and everyone else got the email."

"Show me." I turned my computer back on in a daze.

"Well," he said. "He actually called first."

"Called who?"

"Calm down, Melanie."

If there was anything a woman hated, it was to be told by a man to calm down.

"Your panelist left a message with the receptionist. And then an email went out."

I searched my in-box for emails from the receptionist. None. I searched for the mixologist's last name. Nothing new here. I searched his publicist's name. Again, everything I saw was old news.

"Mitchell, exactly what email are you referring to? I'm not finding it." Frustration was making my head throb.

"My email," he said casually. "From this morning."

Now I was really annoyed.

I swiveled back around and typed a new search. *Mitchell Fox.* Every key-click could probably be heard from two cubes away. His email from last Thursday appeared. That was all.

"I see no—"

"Hold on," he said with a sigh.

I followed him to his cube. He searched his in-box. "Okay, so here's where Cora responded. And here's where Tanisha responded."

I perused the chain.

"Subject line: Mixologist Bites the Dust?" I glared at him with so much fury, it might've burned holes through his shirt. "And, Mitchell, do you see where I was copied?"

"Oh." His head moped like a dog that just barfed on the carpet. "I'm so sorry," he said with no hint of remorse. "I must've blanked out. Didn't copy you."

The panelist's wife delivered their baby boy early. It was understandable that he had to back out. I opened my mouth, but no words were uttered. Why had Mitchell cut me out? Because of the promotion. This was fighting dirty.

"The worst that can happen," he said, "is you have three on the panel instead of four."

But Mitchell had undermined me in front of my peers. And that email's subject line: Mixologist Bites the Dust? Seriously?

Did he want Cora to think I was too much of a slacker to respond? That I'd wasted a whole day without searching for a replacement? Similar to my mother, I didn't like to lose face. But I couldn't mess up in this final stretch. I had a lot on the line—including a big fat bank loan.

"It was an honest mistake," Mitchell said.

Was it? Had I misjudged him?

Grape Aunt Violet used to say that distillers had five grades of corn to choose from, and her distillery used only the top three. Mitchell was feeling like a low-grade grain to me right then—one ruined with mold and not fit for consumption.

"Tell me," I said. "How do you leave out the one person who's in charge of the event?"

"You're really coming unglued, Melanie."

Maybe I was. All the way home, I agonized.

The cocktail competition event was not some run-of-the-mill banquet luncheon with rubber chicken. And it was more than a platform to help position me for advancement. It was a highlight of the premier extravaganza in the bourbon industry. All the players would be there: distillers, distributors, collectors, bartenders and other influencers, the trade media—and the everyday women and men who sipped bourbon on their screened-in back porches with friends. The real everyday people who picked up our bottles in stores.

This event had to go well. But there was always Mitchell, the wild card.

CHAPTER 37

Violet

Detroit, Michigan
August 1923

Despite the unseasonably cool, windy day, I looked forward to today's soiree at the mansion on Lake Shore Road. By comparison, the great house made Lela's parents' grand place resemble a dollhouse. For one thing, it was on the waterfront on Lake Saint Clair—the most prestigious address old money could buy.

Knowing there'd be a breeze off the water, I'd slipped a dress over my head and added a full-length coat—lightweight but with fur collar and cuffs. Sable from Lela's closet. But she bared her arms no matter the temperature. Her monogrammed top was embroidered with *LH* in its center. Within fifteen minutes, we'd flown from downtown to Grosse Pointe in her newest Packard, a powder-blue one, as though speed was no question and gasoline unlimited. Of course, my budget was tighter than hers. In the last week, I'd applied for three employment positions, but so far no luck. I wasn't sleeping well from my money worries—and from thinking about Robert. Some days I thought he'd call and apologize for the ultimatum. But no.

This would be the first time I'd see Lawrence since the dance club. Lela promised she wouldn't ditch me this time. We'd stay together regardless. Lawrence had called me once but had to leave a message with Lela. I'd been at the library checking out books for free. But when I tried him back, we missed each other. Lela thought he'd been traveling a bit and then digging into his new role at the law firm.

I'd met Thomas Pearce, who owned this house, while I was with Lela at a couple of summer parties. He was nice if not particularly handsome, but girls had trailed on his heels until Sylvia Manchester snagged him. Some still trailed after him. Today would be an intimate affair for a boat ride. We'd cruise before dark and return to the house for dinner.

Lela pulled into the imposing circle drive on the garden side of the English Renaissance–style estate.

"It looks so much bigger up close," I said.

"I know. Has forty rooms and cost 'em two million bucks."

That sum baffled my mind. The family's previous generations hadn't come over on the Mayflower, but they'd made their fortunes in lumber or steel or plate glass or something else industry needed. I couldn't recall. I was dazed by the great stone manse that King Henry VIII himself might've built—with steeply pitched roofs, abundant large windows, and tall chimneys climbing to the sky. There were decorative balconies and awnings galore on windows overlooking a side-yard pool.

A servant opened my car door, and I stepped out. I wasn't cold, but I gathered my coat up under my chin for something to do with my hands. Gil and Lawrence were already here. Gil's 1922 Rolls-Royce Silver Ghost was parked in front of Lela's car, his a dark gray color with a polished alloy hood that blinded me as rays of sunlight caught it. The car had six matching wheels—including dual side-mount spare tires. It had running boards with toolboxes, large Klaxon horns, and polished nickel road lamps. It was quite a vision of art.

Lela and I approached the glass porte cochere entry of the house with its wrought iron door. Mother had trained me not to drool when visiting a fine home. But she'd never visited one this fine. I wondered if children here played hide-and-go-seek. Evelyn and I would've enjoyed getting lost in this castle.

A butler welcomed Lela and me in. The great hall had massive twin staircases of hand-carved oak. There were tapestries and oils and bronze statuary. Lela had been a guest on several occasions and knew of its music room, the greenhouse, and the library where a portrait of Thomas's father took pride of place. As honeymooners, Thomas and his wife, Sylvia, had spent months abroad, collecting art for their home that took three years to build.

"Welcome, friends," Thomas said. "So glad you could come."

He led us through to the atrium and out to the waterfront terrace. The wind gently ruffled the fur of my collar and cuffs. Sylvia came to greet us. I adjusted my cloche and my curls peeping out.

"Lela, Violet, I'm sure you know Gil and Lawrence?"

"Yes, so good to see you again," I said. "Lawrence, I hope you'll share details of your new law practice."

"If your ears are willing," he said convivially.

Gil and Lela hugged. "How's that Packard treating you?" he asked her as a servant brought a tray of cigarettes.

"Best car in the world, *of course*," Lela said, sounding flirty.

"Of course." He winked as he lit up a smoke.

Some magazines had claimed otherwise, saying the Silver Ghost was the best. It got its name for, among other things, being so quiet when going as fast as sixty miles per hour. Though Lela said Gil's actually flew at eighty—thirty miles per hour faster than her car. The British Rolls company had started producing some cars in Massachusetts to appeal to the car-hungry market on the American side of the pond. Buyers could now avoid high import tariffs—not that money for a Silver Ghost was a problem for Gil Ratliff.

"Gil, Lawrence," Thomas said, gesturing to an outdoor setup as fine as any bar. "Pour yourselves a highball, my friends. We'll soon make our way to the dock."

"Lawrence," Lela said, though he was staring straight at me, not her, and it felt like a touch.

She pulled a camera from her bag. "Be a darling and take a photograph of Violet and me first, won't you? Stand way back there for a long, wide shot in front of the house."

I smiled brightly for the cameraman, as best as I could.

~

Lake Saint Clair was a glorious body of water at the top of the Detroit River and across from Canada. Our sunset cruise in the yacht had been short but scenic with grand homes along the lake's Gold Coast. There were geese, and I imagined their squawking, winged families preparing to fly south for the winter. As a girl, I'd seen geese fly over our yard in Kentucky in perfect formation. Thomas pointed out his neighbors' homes. One so-called "summer cottage" was fashioned after the White House in DC. A Beaux Arts–style mansion was inspired by the Vanderbilts' house in Newport. How had a girl like me ended up in a paradise like this?

I enjoyed a bit of this glitz. Yet the toasty-warm nights with Robert in his bungalow had been bliss. I didn't aspire to own a palace or chateau. I sometimes missed Bond House, too, with its garden and room for croquet—and memories of two little girls hunting clovers. I was anxious for Evelyn to return from her travels so I could hop a train to see her.

Now a bonfire was crackling in a pit near the dock, and it smelled of scorched hickory wood. The night air was chilly. Lela had a plaid blanket wrapped about her. Adirondack chairs encircled the blaze, and we all sat around chatting about everything from President Harding's recent death of a stroke to last month's film about a genie in a brass bottle. Sylvia's cook had prepared a scrumptious meal indoors after the boat ride—roasted chicken in cast iron skillets with butternut squash and sage—while Thomas's late mother in a giant oil portrait surveilled us from over a mantel. I'd done my best to hold my knife right and sip from the proper glass. But there was nothing she could do if I hadn't. Even now, my own mother had little control over my deeds.

We'd all downed another round of drinks and then another round of drinks, and Thomas passed a bottle around now.

Gil and Lela kept flirting. They might well inspire the six of us to partner off for a petting party. That would hook me up with Lawrence. Maybe it's just what I needed to get Robert out of my head.

Thomas and Sylvia went to check on their children. The nanny had tucked them in hours earlier. Lela and Gil strolled to the end of the dock, teasing and playing with each other. Moonlight reflected off the dark water, and I watched their forms kiss in its shadow, as if I were appreciating a fine silhouette.

"You're ravishing tonight," Lawrence said, his low voice startling me.

His gaze held on my legs, and I felt the heat of it. My coat had spilled open at my knees, my legs were crossed, and my hem had crept up one thigh past the roll of my stocking. Had I meant to let that happen?

Yes.

"Thank you," I said, my head lowered while looking at him from under my brow.

"You've got great gams, Vi." It rhymed with *my*. I tittered.

Then a terrible sound sliced through the night, and I jumped. It sounded like gunshots? Lela screamed.

I sprang up and turned to the sound of a motorboat, no, two motorboats—both smaller crafts, not yachts. Were they racing in the dark?

More gunshots tore through our peace in shockingly rapid succession. I doubled over in fear and confusion and looked for close shelter where there was none.

"Get down," Lawrence said, tugging on my arm.

"Lela!" I yelled, frantic for her. She was close to the water but running our way. I couldn't bear for something bad to happen to her.

"Get down!" This time it was Thomas, who'd just returned.

I lay on the ground, flat as I could, front side down. Lawrence lay atop me to protect me, and I felt relief—and vulnerability, for both of us shook with fear.

I lifted my head up inches to see Lela coming closer on the lawn with Gil.

The boats made hairpin turns in the lake, fantails spraying up wildly as one boat chased the other south toward the river until the sounds of their engines finally faded.

"They're gone," Thomas said, his voice quavering. "Damned rumrunners. Federal agents are just as bad."

We quieted. Slowly we each crawled to our feet.

What was I doing here? I was unsure of where I belonged. Here? Kentucky with my ailing sister? Robert's bungalow? The old boardinghouse or somewhere else altogether? I felt unmoored. Dizzy. I turned.

"Lela." I ran to embrace her. "Are you hurt?"

I couldn't bear for something to happen to her. She was my best friend.

"I thought I was going to die, Violet," she said, and I grimaced. "I didn't want to die, I didn't want to."

In the time I'd known Lela, I'd never before seen her cry. I held her until her shuddering sobs subsided. I began to question my choices. These places. I didn't want pain like this anymore.

After a time, we all gathered back around the sputtering flames. Thomas told of the smugglers—of how some nights they retrieved Canadian loads and used docks of his neighbors who only summered here. They'd unload cases and speed across the lake for more. Agents didn't care whose boathouses they destroyed in violent pursuit, often getting out and trampling gardens and property.

I rocked in my seat, silent.

"It's awful," Gil said. "The sons of bitches might've killed us. Those were machine guns, you know." Gil knew all too well from the war; he'd had to help those shot down.

The last sizzle of the fire was snuffed. "Let's return to the house," Sylvia said, as if she would bear to hear no more talk of this.

Lela was still shaken, and she'd had much to drink, so it was best we not be in the car. We decided to spend the night. As we made our way through the deep breadth of grass, I was glad for Lawrence's arm around me. I felt safer. Lela and Gil wandered off in the dark.

Lawrence stalled our pace and turned to me. Had it not been for the moonlight, I'd not have seen his hungry eyes or the cleft of his chin. He brought me close.

But what of Robert?

Robert was over.

A jumble of feelings whirled inside me now: my confusion earlier, my needing safety, my needing normalcy, my needing to be held. Needing, maybe, to be wanted—or maybe there was my own wanting.

Yes.

Lawrence bent his head, I lifted my face, and we met in a kiss that rivaled our dance of the tango. When I parted my lips, he tasted of smoke and whiskey.

When we came up for breath, he said, "I'm stuck on you, you know that?"

When he asked to come to my chamber that night, I almost said no.

Almost.

CHAPTER 38

Violet

Detroit, Michigan
Two weeks later, August 1923

It was a clear blue day, so I'd put the top down on the Jordan. Lela's voice rose up in joy as if we rode a roller coaster with our summer scarves blowing behind us. Pure freedom. Investments were ticking upward each day. Tick, tick, tick. A rebound. I'd secured a secretarial post at a big law firm, too, that would start next week and pay more than my last job. Mother had written that diligence would pay off. She was right. Lela and I were just out for a drive, nothing more—still craving normalcy after the incident . . . and after the call I got last night.

My old friend Sarah said she met a man, one she thought was "him." I squealed in delight for her. Then she said, "Robert came to the boardinghouse." Perhaps I should've expected that. "With a young woman. Thought you might want to know."

"Thank you," I said too quickly; I wasn't thankful. I felt my insides sink. Did he look at her the way he'd looked at me? Touch her in all the same places? But why should he not move on?

I had. Lawrence and I weren't in love, but Lela and I called him my boyfriend.

"Let's make a pact," Lela said this morning before we left the apartment.

She breezed into the kitchen wearing nothing but a silky fringed robe of pink that hung open to God and all. The fringe was a foot long, and for the first time I saw her naked body with round, jiggling bosoms. Only then did I realize the extent to which her bandeaux routinely strapped her in tight at the top—to conform to the fashion that matched short, boyish hair and waistless dresses that hung straight on narrow hips. Some women these days got breast reductions. Luckily, I was fairly flat-chested as it was. I could even wear dresses with nothing under and let my nipples ping through. Lawrence liked that.

"What kind of pact?" I said as Lela casually looped together the ties of her robe with no hint of shyness.

She said, "A pact that, beginning today and for the rest of our lives, we'll be devoted to happiness. Nothing sad."

My friend was watching out for me.

Now, I downshifted my car and steered around a sharp bend. We were two girls having fun. My Jordan and its freedom made me lose all my doubts—doubts on the night of the shooting, doubts about where I belonged.

I belonged in the moment.

"Yes!" I screamed to the wind, echoing our agreement that morning. "We have a pact. Lives devoted to happiness."

Lela and I laughed as we passed two old ladies coming out of shops on Woodward. I honked and we waved, but they scowled at us. Lela said, "Young women today are just sooo daring and sooo scandalous."

On we drove without destination.

As I steered the wheel past skyscrapers, I held up a few fingers, admiring my latest moon manicure. Lela's Cutex color nearly matched the scarlet enamel of my car. But the red was painted in a band at the middle of my nails—and left unpolished the crescent-shaped tips and the parts near the quick. I could do what I wanted, whether frivolous or daring.

I was in control.

A couple of hours later, we entered the massive gates of Beverly Road in Grosse Pointe. We'd driven and gabbed along the river and past former farms and new mansions, along lawns and colorful gardens. Time had flown, and now I had to drop Lela off at her parents' house. Her mother needed assistance planning a fall soiree. Then Lela and I and the guys would meet for an evening at a favorite speakeasy.

I pulled into the Hill family drive. Lela hopped out so she could grab her evening wear out of the trunk.

"Need help?" I asked as she loaded her arms with full hangers and small cases.

"Nah, I've got it."

Her evening dress unspooled as she carried its hanger—and the garment's metallic threads, crystal beads, and oversize sequins danced and twinkled in the sun. Embellishments were mostly gold but held unexpected tints of blue or white or amber or green depending on the movement of the dress and how the sunlight hit it. Lela would be film-star ravishing tonight.

"The Confectionary then," I said. "Nine o'clock?"

"Gil and I'll see you there. Love you!"

"Love you, too." I kissed her cheek goodbye.

CHAPTER 39

Melanie

Louisville, Kentucky
October 2018

Mom insisted on coming by for the journal in half an hour.

October had arrived with the turning of leaves, and Goldenrod was one week away from the Bourbon Craft Cocktail Bash. It'd taken me four days, but I'd filled the blank slot on my mixologist panel with a newcomer—one from an authentic revived speakeasy in Detroit. The wonders of the internet. Cora thought the fix was way cool.

Yet I hadn't forgotten Mitchell's treacherous email, his schmoozing with the founder, and his big PR hits.

Adrenaline seeped into my belly when I thought of the Cocktail Competition. The team and I had done everything to be ready for the big day. Preparation gave me confidence. But the event was my last chance to shine. I had too much to lose if it didn't go well. By next month, either Mitchell or I would be crowned director.

I spread moisturizer on my freshly washed face and body butter on my legs. I got all comfy in jammies before I planned to turn in; it would give Mom the hint not to hang around too long. She would pick up the journal for her turn to read. Mom was broaching our wide divide, but I needed a good night's sleep every night this week. Then Brian texted—the second or third exchange since I toured the "gallery" in his man cave.

The thought of our first kiss still lingered, and flutters filled me when dwelling upon it. But it didn't stop me from pulling back. No phone calls. Just texts. Kind of like the place where I was stuck with Mom until tonight. I wasn't up for anything as warm as communication with real voices. Violet's experience with Robert scared me. I didn't want to lean in to Brian only to be hurt later. I reminded myself that love and career didn't mix. But over the last week or two, he sent links to articles on collectors and shows. I thanked him promptly and added super-friendly emojis. Despite my holding back, truth was, somewhere underneath I enjoyed hearing from him.

When you're ready, you know where to find me.

Hey, check these out, his text read now. I happened to drop by Ray's. 😉

There were new pictures of my car's interior. A couple of them were shots of a man sitting at an industrial sewing machine; he worked on the seat's upholstery, sewing pleats in the new black leather. Brian said the guy was also replacing the cushion's stuffing in the old manner—with cotton batting, burlap, and horsehair.

The Jordan was getting closer to being back to original. I was kind of geeked for Violet and me.

I texted Brian back. It's so sweet of you to send these pics! Love them!

Then a knock came at the door.

Mom.

"Hi, honey," she said with a forced perkiness to match the forced cheerfulness of my "hello" greeting.

It was a start.

I supposed the proper thing to do was to offer a beverage or something.

"Want a cold-pressed juice?" I said. "With pineapple, beet, carrot, and ginger."

"Juice sounds great."

I grabbed two bottles from the fridge as Mom sat on a metal stool at my island. We both shook our bottles before opening.

"I'll look forward to hearing your thoughts on the journal," I said.

"First, how's the restoration going?" she asked.

I relayed the latest and showed her the pics. If she felt compelled to broach the Brian subject again, she must've bitten her tongue.

"How's work?" *That's a safe topic for most mothers,* I thought, but I cringed.

I took a risk to tell her about Mitchell Fox and the email debacle. "I got the problem resolved with the mixologist panel, though," I said, fluffing it off.

"I had no doubt," Mom said, sounding genuine. "In the eighties, some men put unopened rubbers in my desk drawer. It pissed me off and felt invasive, but it didn't deter me."

"That's abominable," I said.

I recalled then a while back, Mom saying, *Decisions made at life's crossroads can hang with you for a long time. I know all too well.*

She never divulged the sexual harassment before. What else did she know about life that she never told me?

She looked thoughtfully at me from across the bar. In the lighting of my pendants, the wrinkles of her face showed in relief, those in her cheeks above her jawline. Facial injections could only do so much. Staring at her, I thought, *That's probably what I'll look like in twenty-five years.* I sighed. Only it'd be worse, because I wasn't an injectable girl. Or maybe it'd be better.

Mom said, "Melanie, I know you're kicking butt to get this promotion, Mitchell Fox be damned. I understand innately how this promotion is important to you. But you know it'll be all right if it doesn't come through. Right? You'll get through it."

I gaped at her. *It would be all right?* How could she say that? It was like the total opposite of what she'd drilled into me all my life. Mom the woodcarver, and me the wood. I grew up never considering that being second best would suffice.

As for Mom asking about my work tonight? Filler talk. At heart, she couldn't care less about my distillery. She'd once called my career at a start-up "doomed."

I understood she came of age in the 1970s and 80s, when Kentucky fell from almost a hundred operating distilleries in the late 1950s to fewer than ten. She would recount how defunct distilleries, some dating back to pre- and post-Prohibition, decorated the landscape in the way Stonehenge or the pyramids filled old-world countries. Bourbon's decline had begun in the Vietnam era with the youth rebelling against everything their parents did, including what they drank. Vodka and other clear liquors rose to the throne.

Many factors led to the industry's revival. Bartenders embracing bourbon was one of them. Cocktails were instrumental—hence the significance of the pending competition I was in charge of.

I sipped my juice and had an aha moment. I got it now: regardless of my job or anything else, the only reason Mom said it was okay if I didn't get the promotion was because it wasn't important to *her*. It was merely something *I* wanted.

Or, on second thought, maybe she didn't think I was good enough.

When I was eleven, I wanted more than anything to be a cheerleader—to be cute and popular and have fun. I created my cheer for tryouts, practiced in the yard every day, dreamed at night of making the squad. Doing the splits was my superpower.

Dad took videos of me practicing and said supportive things like, *Great job!* Mom only watched me once. She never offered advice like she did for everything else; she didn't coach me. The night before tryouts all she said—as she peeled potatoes at the sink, not facing me—was, *Being a cheerleader is not that important.*

But it was important to me. Didn't she know that? In time, I realized that Mom thought I sucked at cheerleading. That was clear. Just like I sucked at being a ballerina and dropped the ball off the stage at age four during my recital.

On the day of my cheerleader tryouts, all the fourth, fifth, and sixth graders gathered on the bleachers in the gym, boisterous for having gotten out of class. They were the voters. I stood in line behind the other hopefuls, girls my age. I thought I'd throw up, so scared was I to go out there all by myself in front of hundreds of kids. Visions of the boys laughing at me in the auditorium at the ballet recital rose up in my head. But I wanted to make cheerleader. I wanted it badly—the cute little pleated skirt of the uniform and getting to yell in front of the crowd at basketball games like I saw the older girls do the year prior.

Now, it was my turn. I was up.

I positioned myself in the center of the gym. Sun shone through skylights in the ceiling. Kids quieted to a murmur. I began my cheer strong—*Go Raiders!*—but in a snap that I have no recollection of thinking about, I came down at the end on one knee in a stance—instead of nailing my better-than-everyone-else splits.

I didn't do my best. I didn't do everything I could.

Over the years since, I came to recognize that I created a built-in excuse for myself as to why I didn't win a spot on the team. I didn't do my splits. Now, I didn't want to live with that kind of regret again—or wondering "what if." What if I *had* done my best and nailed my splits? If I lost then, would it have hurt less? I would do everything now that I could to earn the new position at work because it was something *I wanted.* And no way would I let Mom undermine my confidence and sabotage me.

"Honey," Mom said now. "Did you hear me? Your career will be fine even if the promotion doesn't come through."

"I heard you. Remember the insurance behemoth where you helped get me a job? My heart wasn't in it there, Mom. Remember Jason, wanting me to move to Silicon Valley? My heart was here, in my own backyard in the hub of my chosen industry. Remember you pressuring me to get an MBA?" I said more snidely. "It could help me. I know. But these are things you or others wanted for me."

Mom tightened her bottle cap and shook her juice. Her neck was turning pink.

Maybe it was time that I didn't need Mom's evaluation or approval anymore.

I opened my mouth, and I didn't shut up until I spewed every painful drop of my childhood cheerleading trauma. She didn't speak. She barely blinked. I might never have seen her eyes so wide.

"Why couldn't you have encouraged me there?" I asked when I was almost finished, with the flats of my palms on the counter. "Told me to leave it all out on the field? Told me I did the best splits in the world whether you thought so or not? Pumped me up? Supported me the way Violet's mother supported her?" I took a heavy breath. "You could've told me to just do my best. But you thought I sucked. That I was *doomed* to fail. Right, Mom? And, and, and: because also, cheerleading was not an activity *you* picked for me."

I was too angry to feel relief. I carried years' worth of torment that'd built up, and right here, right now, no less—in a week before arguably the biggest day of my career—I flung it out. I felt like Frankenstein, a monster with bolts on both sides of my neck. Or maybe the Incredible Hulk, turning green with muscles popping and veins bulging.

"Melanie," Mom said. "I thought you were an awesome little cheerleader. I watched you more from the windows than you know. And Dad's videos, too. You were even *too* good in my mind. But I confess, I wanted more for you than standing on the sidelines cheering for boys. I've learned that sport has come a long way since then. Girls are athletes with competitions of their own now. But I came from an era where women were still having to fight for respect in the workplace. For getting their foot in the door, never mind getting a seat at the table."

That shut me up. But my shoulders were still heaving. Her eyes glistened with tears that didn't seem able to spill.

"You think you're the only one around here with a demanding past, Melanie? Do you?" Her voice crackled, making me jump.

"My great-grandmother Evelyn sat me down one day, oh yes, she did," Mom said. "She was in her eighties and I in high school. She pulled me aside at a family reunion at a park. 'You are my great-granddaughter, Angela. Do something I never did. Finish college. Then be the first woman in our family to earn a graduate degree. You'll have to sacrifice for it. That's what women do. We sacrifice.'"

I remembered Violet's journal entries of her sister quitting college to marry. Before that, Evelyn stood up for Violet in the dry goods store, to their father whom she idolized. Sacrifice.

Mom went on. "The fire in Evelyn's eyes set the fire in me. When she said I was her great-granddaughter as though she were the queen, I knew I mustn't let her down."

Mom hopped off the stool and started pacing, so unlike her. And I sat there as if watching a train veering off its tracks.

"The best colleges wouldn't talk to me, Melanie. My high school counselor said I hadn't achieved a strong enough GPA. I hadn't tried hard enough up to that point, you see," Mom said, "not hard enough to be Evelyn's great-granddaughter." Mom's hands balled into fists. "I attended a small state school as you know, got in the top ten percent this time. But Great-Grandmother had wanted me to be the first woman in the family to be first at something. Getting a grad degree."

Had Evelyn looked back on her life and had regrets about quitting college?

"After undergrad," Mom went on, "I watched other students from more prestigious universities—mostly men, mind you—land the best jobs. I didn't get hired at an impressive enough job right out of school. When it came to applying for the all-important master's program, the counselor at my school of choice said, 'Your experience working at a small, privately owned organization is likely not going to get you in here. Not with your competition.' I hadn't cut it, Melanie. But I got my grad degree somewhere else and yes, I made damned sure I graduated first in my class. First! By then, though, Evelyn was almost ninety with dementia and barely knew the difference. But I tell you, Melanie, I worked my ass off. I came through."

Mom took a swig of her drink with her rigid pinkie finger pointed up to denote I must not interrupt. I was feeling chastised. Her bottle came down with a bang on the quartz counter.

"Your father and I met and got together in grad school, as you know. What you don't know is that we broke up at one point. I had to focus. My grades came first, and I told him it was over. I can see from your face, you had no idea, did you? He waited for me, though. See? He believed in me. He 'got' me. And after I earned the job of my dreams where I could work my way up—because another *woman* who'd paid her dues saw promise in me? I came crawling back to that man who'd one day be your father. Yes, I did."

Mom let out a sob, and I was frozen stiff, mesmerized as she struggled to talk through her tears. A sense of remorse rose up in me. I had blamed Mom for so much.

"Your father picked me up—literally, Melanie, he picked me up off the floor and swung me around and around in his tiny galley kitchen and said it was the happiest day of his life. He knew what he was getting—an overachiever hell-bent on perfection. But"—she laughed now as she cried—"he never minded it."

So this all was why she made such demands of me. In her mind, she had to help me prepare for the rough-hardened world? I hadn't known about her and Dad, and it both broke my heart and made my heart sing all at once to think of him accepting her. Was this why Mom thought maybe Jason and I would reunite? Perhaps that was it.

But my parents' love story was not to be mine. My love story was more like Violet's.

"I'm sorry," Mom said, shaking her head as she stared at the floor. "I'm sorry I transferred all that baggage onto you." She barked out another laugh. "I actually thought your dad and I were the ideal blend. Him saying, 'Let's go get ice cream,' or, 'Melanie, you choose two school activities you like, you don't really have to do them all,' or, 'If you're going to get a B in a subject, just tell me it's your best effort and I'm okay with it,' or, 'If what you want is a refrigerator magnet from the souvenir shop at Yellowstone instead of a book about geysers, that's what you'll get.'"

Yes, I thought, *Dad had always been there.* I knew it. I closed my eyes and saw him retrieving the ball from the ballerina stage, his smile of support. But for some reason, Mom stood in my mind like the Statue of Liberty. Larger than life. A torch in her outstretched arm.

"Mom—" I tried to say now.

"I guess," she said, cutting me off, "my style overpowered you. I never thought of myself as a failure as your mother. Until today. All I tried to convey earlier was this: that you will be fine whether you get that promotion or not. You're strong. I meant only to be supportive."

Her words singed my ears as if someone flicked a lighter to burn the tips. Tears stung my eyes. I'd misjudged her.

I thought then of everything that she'd done—other things when I was growing up that I never took time to appreciate. She was room mother when I was in second grade and came to the parties to help the teacher pass out valentines and such. She was assistant Brownie troop leader, and chaperone on field trips—leading the games on the bus. She or Dad pored over my homework every night when she might've rather read a novel or had deadlines to meet. She never missed a teacher's conference clear through my senior year. She helped me with science fair entries, too—from first grade's "Using the Scientific Method: Which Raisin Bran Cereal has the Most Raisins?" to sixth grade's "Galileo's Law of Falling Bodies." No one had posters sharper than mine, and she'd grilled me on oral presentation. I won ribbons at state competitions.

No wonder she had no time for weeks off just to play as I'd done with Aunt Violet. Mom used up her PTO days doing all the things I took for granted.

All these things were *her* time and *her* energy . . . and *her* caring and devotion. Mom was home most nights, even when walking in late with her briefcase, but then she put food on the table. Because she insisted. Mom was beyond driven. She was a woman right out of a Helen Reddy song—or a 1980s TV commercial for a fragrance called Enjoli. I'd studied the ad in college.

And here I was, a grown woman acting like a spoiled rotten brat. *Oh, it's sooo bad that Mom set the bar sooo high. I had it so effing rough.*

"Don't apologize," I exclaimed with a sob in my throat. "I'm the one who should be sorry." My whole face was swollen with water ready to burst from my eyes. "You're a great mother. I'm blessed to have you. And I promise to be more appreciative."

Had I left her speechless for once? Then she said, "I love you, Melanie."

"I love you, too." I smiled. "So you didn't think I sucked at being a cheerleader?"

She chuckled. And I chuckled. And we hugged. It was a Violet and Evelyn kind of hug, the kind I'd read about early in the journal.

It was the kind of hug only a wonder woman mom could give me—a wonder woman complete with her stack of accomplishments . . . and all her weaknesses and vulnerabilities, too.

It was the kind of hug that reached all the way back to my youth and brought me through to today.

CHAPTER 40

Violet

Detroit, Michigan
August 1923

He had a highball with whiskey. And me? A bee's knees with lemon and gin. I didn't drink whiskey smuggled from Canada over the river; it reminded me of what Prohibition did to Kentucky. Gone were distilleries in the bluegrass with their smells of bourbon evaporating from barrels—the "angel's share" as it was called. I sometimes longed for those days, my family, and home. But I adored this splendid elliptical bar in the fastest-growing city in America. The crowd was affluent: automobile types vied with those of old money. The Confectionary had no address and sold no candy, but there were Tiffany lamps and green velvet sofas. A pianist played the hit "Dreamy Melody" on a Vose baby grand. Photographs of federal agents hung on the walls in gilded frames as if they were priceless art.

My boyfriend lit my cigarette in its long silver holder, and then he lit his.

"Had we known our friends would be late," he said with the cleft of his chin prominent, "we might've had time for—"

"There's always later tonight," I said.

I had enjoyed our romp the night before. But it'd taken me an hour to do my Marcel hair wave, and I hadn't wanted to mess it up before this evening began. No denying it, though, Lawrence looked dashing. I slid my palm along his worsted jacket of midnight blue with its matching satin lapels . . . yet for an instant, I thought of someone else. Robert. But I blinked that thought away. I peered up at Lawrence from the corner of my eye, my lashes thick and black from mascara.

"Your dress," he whispered now in my ear, "looks delicious enough to peel like fruit."

"Well, designers do call the color cranberry crepe." I grinned.

It was a stunning gown falling just to my shins with bugle beads of blue, gold, and red. Its sash of gold lamé rode low on my hips and glimmered in the bar's mellow light.

His fingers dropped to my crossed leg. I had dabbed Tabac Blond—with its whiff of carnation and leather, a fragrance designed for women who smoke—in the bend of my knees. As his fingertips teased my skin, it tingled. My thighs were bare, and I lifted my hems up higher. I'd rolled my stockings to below my knees on elastic garter bands. Then I'd rubbed a hint of rouge on my kneecaps, too, to make them look a tad rosy.

After a few minutes' more flirtation, I twisted to face the door. For a second tonight felt too frivolous. Where were Lela and Gil?

I checked my wristwatch: fifteen past ten. Perhaps they had some merrymaking of their own before leaving her parents' estate?

I took up the cool stem of my glass and sipped my cocktail slowly as the pianist began a tune my sister, Evelyn, used to play. I missed her.

Then people I didn't know stormed into the Confectionery, shouting. All heads turned to the man in black tails and a flapper in sparkling sequins.

Lawrence's blue-eyed gaze locked with mine. He secured his wallet inside his coat.

"What's the matter?" I asked him under my breath.

Then the strangers yelled, "A tip-over raid down the street."

Bartenders started stuffing bottles in cabinets and pulling out large jars of licorice twists and long, colorful candy sticks. A waiter rushed from patron to patron whisking our glasses into a bin.

"Violet, doll, looks like we've got to get out of this place. But we'll make our way out as though nothing's amiss."

There was no urgency in his low voice, so I wasn't afraid. Not at first.

"As long as we're gone before they charge in with sledgehammers," I said, suddenly having a vision of glass shards flying everywhere—and I wondered what I was doing here at all. I saw flashes of the night at the lake, my lying on the grass facedown.

I squeezed Lawrence's arm and walked more quickly in my T-strap heels than I had when we arrived. I felt quite frightened after all. Detroit's "tip-over raids" didn't require search warrants; enforcement officers couldn't arrest a soul. But they put owners out of business by smashing everything from chairs to booze bottles—yes, they broke the laws to stop the lawbreakers.

Outside in the dark, the streetlamps flickered and I felt a little less anxious. We'd catch the next streetcar back to my place and try to call my friend. But a speakeasy on the next block was in chaos—a confusion of cars and patrols and people angling to get away.

"The Apothecary is the one that got hit," said a woman with a purple feather in her headband.

I hated to think the Apothecary might be destroyed. It was another speakeasy we frequented. More people like us in their evening attire had gathered on the walks in clusters, despite the presence of police nearby.

But as the mass dispersed, the scene a block over emerged more clearly—in the way a master painter's floor-to-ceiling oil revealed itself when one entered a gallery.

I covered my mouth with my hands, but this didn't suppress my scream.

"The Silver Ghost," said Lawrence, pointing and sounding as worried as I was.

"Why would Gil's Rolls-Royce be there?" I asked. I tried to make sense of it. Where was my friend?

The car's dark gray fenders curved up and over its slick spoked wheels. The silver hood gleamed in the night.

Then gunfire roared.

I shrieked, and we ducked to the closest brick building and fell in an inlet of a storefront. Multiple rounds with machine guns came closer. Lawrence encased me with his body on the ground. But I thought tip-over raids didn't have shootings? My heart was pounding a million beats a minute. My fingernails dug into his arm. The haunting sound of guns over Lake Saint Clair echoed loudly in my ears. A car went screaming around the corner then, and a police car roared after it—with more shooting, shooting, shooting and bystanders screaming until the cars were finally gone. It all happened so fast but it felt so slow.

I had never in my life trembled so badly. I could barely stand on my own and continued to cling to Lawrence.

"We're safe," he whispered. "They're gone."

My legs were wobbly, but we both began to run. We had to get to Gil's car. Find our friends. My heel slipped on the curb when crossing the intersection, and Lawrence dragged me back up.

"Hurry."

A larger crowd now assembled, but we wormed our way to the front. "Excuse me," I said. "Excuse me, please."

And there in the center of the street were two bodies—or three or four, I didn't know.

"Lela!"

My scream was so shrill that even I gasped at the pain in its timbre.

"How do you know it's her?" Lawrence asked in a panic. "I don't see Gil. The people who are hurt are nowhere near the Silver Ghost."

"Her dress."

I hoped I was wrong. I prayed it was another dress with similar golden sequins. I pulled Lawrence along, and we got within feet of her but the crowd held us back.

It was like watching a horror movie with a cast of deranged actors. I moved as if in slow motion, and there was no sound. My mind blocked out the shouts and the cries and now the siren.

Then I did hear, "Stay back, miss," from a stranger as he yanked my arm.

"Who are you?" I yelled. "She's my sister!" The man let us pass.

Then Gil came staggering to kneel beside her. The tip of his ear was missing, and his hair was matted with blood while more blood trickled down his neck and jaw and collar. I felt dizzy.

Lela lay flat on her back, her face calm, her eyes open. I crouched beside her, too, sick to see her like this and oblivious to the audience and the stretchers being hauled to other victims. Gil tugged off his coat.

She was hurt but still breathing. *Thank God,* I thought. She was going to live. She wouldn't leave me in the dark. Lela would live.

"Lela, can you speak? Talk to me." Her eyes shifted to me, and hope soared from my feet to my heart. Her lips almost smiled. But she did not speak.

Her torso was grotesquely puffy as if her chest had inflated with air, her lungs like balloons. And her leg . . . one was in spasms with bullet holes on her thigh. Then blood began to gush from the holes in some sort of delayed reaction, and her chest began to deflate. Inky-red blood now pumped from her leg as if by the gallon, soaking her glittery dress and puddling in the street. I wanted to sop it up, stop the flow, swish the blood in my hands to put it back in her leg. I pressed my palms on the holes, my hands covered in blood.

Inexplicably, I recalled the gaping hole in Lela's stocking the first time we met. I wished so badly to go back to that carefree night in the speakeasy, our laughing in the ladies' lounge and smoking. I yearned to see her smile, to hear her laugh.

"She was hit by stray bullets," Gil said, now pressing his coat on her wounds. "I've got to stop the hemorrhaging."

Gil had been a medic in the war. He knew what to do.

Lela would live, I told myself. We'd celebrate. We'd do New Year's Eve in New York like she'd talked about long ago.

I wiped my hands on my dress and gently touched her forehead with the backs of my fingers, the way Mother would check me for fever as a child. Lela was neither warm nor cold. Another good sign, I thought.

"You're going to be fine, my friend. You're going to be fine," I said to soothe her.

I wanted to believe it. She had to be fine. This world of machine guns and shooting couldn't affect my best friend. That's not how life worked.

"Stray bullets," Gil repeated as he worked. "We were all bystanders."

"Lela," I said, and I smiled to reassure her. She'd escaped at the lake that night. Now, even if she lost a leg, I thought, there was no reason to think that—

"Will she survive?" Lawrence asked, his face contorted.

I snarled at him. How dare he ask that? Of course she'd survive.

"Her femur is shattered," Gil said. "I believe her femoral artery has been severed . . . and more."

What does that mean? I wasn't sure I could bear to hear it.

The long, thick lashes of my best friend fluttered, but when her eyes reopened wide, they shifted to look straight at me. She blinked. And her cherry-red lips parted.

She wanted to tell me something.

But then her lips closed. Her eyes shut, too. Nothing moved. Her emerald-green earbobs didn't dangle. With her body so still, the untouched sequins of her dress didn't sparkle.

Gil spoke, and it sounded muffled to me—something ridiculous, I thought, about a bullet, maybe in her back or her hip, making a trajectory inside her body and landing in a lung.

Was that why her chest had been puffy? I shuddered.

Echoes of the night at the lake whirled in my head: *I thought I was going to die, Violet. I didn't want to die, I didn't want to.*

"No," I cried now, so scared. I thought I'd spew vomit, or my heart would explode like a hand grenade. This wasn't happening. This wasn't happening. "No, no."

I hovered over her body draped in that beautiful, bloody gold dress. "Lela, this day was all about happiness, remember? Wake up!" I patted her flawless cheeks—and my fancy moon-manicured fingernails meant nothing. But the pull of the moon overhead raged inside me, a high tide, drowning me, drowning me. "We made a pact only this morning. Don't you remember? We had a pact!"

Lawrence caressed my back up and down, up and down. Gil bent to her shoulder and wept.

Two strangers in white moved in then. One checked her wrist for a pulse. He let go gently and said, "We're sorry, ma'am."

Lela had slipped away?

I cupped her left elbow in one hand and massaged her hand with my other, willing her to snap out of it. First Father left me, now her? I howled a frightening sound that went back years.

Why? I bent and kissed Lela's cheeks, leaving lipstick smudges by my blood prints while Lawrence softly repeated my name.

The men nudged us back to fit the stretcher beside her. I watched in disbelief, shaking my head as they raised a stark white sheet up over my friend's pretty face.

The guys and I sat like mummies in my apartment—my apartment, not Lela's and mine anymore. I wanted to fall asleep and wake up and this all be over, a nightmare so much worse than the one of my teeth. I looked around at the normalcy of the room. The clock. The lamp. The painting of a Paris scene. But nothing was normal. Three drinks sat on coasters, untouched, ice melting. And I'd forgotten how to breathe.

"Why were you late?" Gil said, slicing the silence with an oddly normal tone. "We waited for you, and then ran out with the raid."

"What do you mean?" That was Lawrence.

"You two were to have met us there at nine o'clock," Gil said.

"We were there," I said, perplexed.

"In fact," Lawrence said, "we arrived early at the Confectionary and watched for you from the bar."

And as the words slipped off his tongue, I knew.

Gil frowned in confusion. "Lela told me we were to meet at the Apothecary, not the Confectionary."

I was certain she and I agreed. That very afternoon.

I said the right place, didn't I?

CHAPTER 41

Violet

Detroit, Michigan
August 1923

On my third day alone at the apartment, the law firm where I was to work called. I apologized and resigned my secretarial position before it ever began. I passed through the living room to the kitchen and smelled Lela's perfume. Chanel No 5. For an instant, I forgot and thought she was home.

When I stepped into the tub, there was the bar of soap. I rubbed the wet bar all over my arms, as if I could feel her hug.

Later, the telephone rang, and my first thought was that it was her calling to say she'd spent the night with Gil. I was disappointed when it was him, calling to check on me—and to say he'd learned that the night of the tragedy, there was a separate chase by federal agents after bootleggers. It had nothing to do with the tip-over raid.

Still, I thought, had she been in the Confectionary with me, she'd be alive.

Then I heard a woman's voice laughing in the hall and burst out the door, hoping it was my friend's laugh. These neighbors I didn't know looked affronted at my disheveled appearance.

I padded through the apartment gathering up Lela's clothes at last—her shoes haphazardly lying near the door as if she'd just kicked them off, her pink silk robe flung over the sofa with its fringe, her beige lace camisole hung by a hook in the bathroom.

I missed her so much. *I can't believe she's gone. I can't believe it.*

Visions of her—in the street, bleeding, her lips parting to attempt to speak—made me wail in the night. And the word *Confectionary* replayed in my head over and over and over, no matter what I was doing. I could be staring at the tiles of her mah-jongg game or, like now, be searching for feminine pads in a cupboard for the last couple of days of my monthlies. Had my life of self-indulgence and parties made me reckless? Had I not been as focused as I should be? Had it made me tell her the wrong place? One minute I was sure Lela and I had been aligned. The next, I crumpled to the floor by the toilet in a heap, bereft.

Robert.

I needed to reach him and tell him what happened—tell him I lost my best friend. I needed to *see* Robert. I had to see someone I loved. That was him. I called with the receiver clenched in my sweaty hand, and his line rang and rang.

I ran to my bedroom, swung open my closet, and scrambled into the corner. I crawled beneath the hems and sequins of dress after dress to a shoebox. I threw off its lid and dug in: the bracelet. I cupped it in my hands and closed my eyes, and I was back in the park where he gave it to me—near the maypole and the girls and the sycamore and the birds.

I slept with the bracelet on for three nights. And following the third, when I awoke, though I did not open my eyes, it was Robert's face I saw first this time, not Lela's.

In the hours that followed, alone in my bed with nothing but water on a table, I learned something.

I wanted to be the modern woman. But the modern world had traps.

My sister's cautions echoed. Robert's, too. And Mother had once said, *But my girl, do remember: moderation in all things is prudent.*

Was it too late for me to change?

Lela was the closest friend I ever had—or ever will. She stood up for me. She shared with me like a sister. She never cared that I was not of her class. She never lied. She was smart and a wise soul.

But she had something I couldn't describe, something that I in my heart never had nor needed. A wild side.

I was tamer.

But that wasn't all. I thought again of Mother and Evelyn. I knew then that I was coming closer to calling them, too. I would divulge everything about the tragedy, even if it meant my sister saying *I told you so*. I would keep my promise to visit her this month. She needed things, too. One of them was me.

Being a modern woman meant what I foresaw for myself as a girl, untarnished: a career, making decisions, having freedoms like owning a car. But I realized now how much the people I shared my life with gave it value and meaning—how independence wasn't the same as glitz and glitter, going to parties, and having a good time. I'd somehow lost track of what was important.

And that included Robert.

I wanted him back. If he'd take me.

***

September 1923

On Saturday, Robert was finally home from the road, and I pulled up to his house. I once thought we'd never see each other again. I was wrong. I'd telephoned asking to see him in person.

His little bungalow looked the same on its corner, only someone had planted red mums in two big pots flanking the steps to the porch. Had it been him? His aunt?

As I stepped up, I felt nerves in my belly the way I had in high school when reciting a Whitman poem in front of the class.

The door opened without my knocking. Robert smiled—that same dazzling smile that captured me in the distillery lobby when I was but a girl. So long ago. Its effect had not diminished. Yet he was more. He may be flawed, but he was honorable. He tried to do right. He cared about me.

He welcomed me in, though he had a mere half an hour's notice. He smelled of soap and shaving cream and led me to a chair in his living room. "Coffee? Vernors?"

"Vernors, please," I said, recalling my first sip of the ginger ale at the hall on Boblo Island—the first time Robert took me dancing. A lifetime ago.

My chest grew hot. I wanted to go back to that night, swaying in his arms to the music.

"Everything okay?" he asked, taking a seat across from me, on the sofa that I'd selected for this room.

I knew I looked drained. Ghostly white, a pallor I might never lose. I'd hardly eaten or slept all these days.

"I could pretend that all's well," I said. "But. It's not."

Alarm darkened his face. "Your mother? Evelyn?" The lilt of his voice rang with sincere concern.

I almost smiled; he would've been Evelyn's brother-in-law, had we married. Why had I never thought of it in those terms until now?

"It's not them," I said.

Light and shadow marked the contours of his face, seeming to emphasize his concern. But the blue of his eyes radiated the love I knew he still had. He couldn't hide it. I felt its warmth. Yes, this was where I belonged.

I looked down to my fidgeting hands. "There's two things, actually, I came to tell you. One is about Lela," I said. I glanced back up and saw his inquisitive look.

"Go on."

I pressed my lips together for momentum to push out the words. "She died."

"Oh no," he said. His face went pale. "How?"

"She was an innocent bystander at the Apothecary."

"The shooting? I heard something about that one, though I didn't know any names. I was on the road at the time. Were you there?"

"I saw enough."

I closed my eyes now to ward off the vision of her in the street, of her mutilated leg. I looked again to the warmth of Robert's eyes. The compassion and safety they held.

"Her death might've been my fault, Robert."

"I doubt that," he said quickly.

Then I explained that afternoon as Lela got out of the car at her parents'. Her gathering her clothes.

"I thought I said the Confectionary, but thinking back, I'm unsure," I said, feeling ashamed. We'd gone from party to party for so long, my memories ran together. "I wake up in cold sweats. Confectionary. Apothecary. I can't be certain."

"Surely you don't think that means you're the cause." His knee began to bounce.

"The first night I met Lela," I said, "she told me she never forgets addresses or names of places." Recognition dawned in his eyes. "She showed up at the boardinghouse with new stockings a week later. I'd only told her where I lived once."

He reflected on this. "No one's infallible," he said. "She might've forgotten or not been paying attention. She was busy, right?"

"Right."

He inhaled deeply. "Listen to me, Violet. It wasn't your fault any more than it was my brother's fault that he was in France when he got shot down in the war. Things happened around him and to him, out of his control."

That almost made sense. Perhaps that's what I'd tell myself the rest of my life.

"Before my mother died," he went on, "she said there's a time and a place for everything. That was Lela's time." He inched forward on his seat and extended his hand.

It felt good in mine, and my eyelids drifted closed. He could never absolve me, but he provided something I yearned for: someone to know my pain. Someone who cared to say something, anything, to help bring me peace.

He said, "I hope you know I would never have wanted something bad to happen to your friend."

I breathed. "I know that about you. You are honorable."

Then I separated from him and stood. I paced from the chair to the dormant fireplace and back.

"Wait," he said. "There's something else, you said. What is it?"

I sat down beside him this time, a few inches away on the sofa. I swallowed what seemed to be a lump of pride and part of my heart.

"I still love you," I said, my breathing erratic, my eyes boring into his as they widened. I burned for him to douse me with his words.

His eyes searched mine as though he couldn't believe it were true. "I still love you, too," he whispered.

Inside, somewhere where my soul resided, I felt a glow.

His arm came around me, and it felt like the rays of sun warming the ground of its frost, like stars twinkling at night for the sailors. Both arms now. We kissed, and it was everything ripe and alive and physical and something else that only the bards can describe. Intangible. Love. I wasn't forgotten. His hand on my thigh inched between my legs.

"I shouldn't want to touch you this way," he whispered, his warm breath puffing on my ear.

"I *want* you to touch me," I said in a way to leave him no doubt.

The tender pressure of his other hand smoothed my back up and down, calming and electrifying me at once. I wanted to be one with him.

We took each other right there on the couch. Naked. In the daylight. Abandoned.

We held each other after—our bodies warm, damp, our breaths slowing, slowing.

We were together again. I was his and he was mine. This time would be forever.

"There's something I want you to know," he said. "I'm sorry about the car and all. I was a fool about you buying a Jordan."

His sincerity got me. "Thank you."

I rose higher on one elbow and caressed his cheek.

"I want to hold hands with you when skipping to a streetcar," I said. "To have you nuzzle my neck in an art gallery when no one's watching. To go for hot fudge sundaes, and discover new places. Together." I smiled for the first time since losing Lela, and I swiped one finger through the matted hair on Robert's forehead. "I want to cuddle with you every night and wake with you every morning."

A confusion—or no, maybe a hesitation—lit in his eyes.

"I am ready for you to be my husband," I said brightly, to clarify. Of course this would surprise him. "And I want to be your wife."

He looked away. He stood and slipped one leg into his pants, and then the other. He turned with his hand on his waist, as if pondering what room to go to next. He was frightening me.

"Robert? What are you doing? Say something."

Had I done something wrong? I felt I was going to be sick. I slipped my dress on over my head. He faced me again.

"Violet," he said. "I'll never love like this again."

"Wait." I heard tears in my voice though my eyes were dry. "Why does this sound like goodbye?"

He raked his hands through his hair. "Because it is. We got wrapped up in the moment. I'm sorry. And I do love you, still. But—"

"But?" I echoed him.

I felt as though I were sliding down a slope. When I first fell for him, I didn't know where I'd land. This crash I never foresaw. I felt as if my bones were breaking, my organs shutting down.

He put his arms around me, my own arms tucked between us in a cocoon, and he gently swayed this way and that.

"I'm sorry to do this when you're already hurting," he said, and his voice croaked. "But it's too late. It won't work for us."

I looked up and saw his eyes were bloodshot with tears. Like mine.

"What do you mean?" I said.

Then it hit me. Sarah had said he brought someone to the boardinghouse. Was it she who planted the flowers in the pots on Robert's porch?

Inside, I became a raging woman, a little girl being smacked, a ship without an anchor. I was a fool.

"I hope you don't regret what we did," he said.

What, our making love? Or was it regretting him ever telling me about Detroit in the first place. Or regretting our many days together—days that flew by, limited days, as Lela might never have known.

My regrets were many.

But if it weren't for him, I might never have known love. I dared to admit to myself that I didn't regret making love a last time. He'd been mine again for one minute.

"Tell me, Robert, so that I hear it from your lips." I tapped my finger to his bottom lip. "If you love me, and I love you, why is it too late for us?"

Robert wouldn't lie. Here's where he'd say there was someone else.

His face was filled with sorrow. "Because I asked you to marry me, and you declined. More than once. I can't get past it."

It was my fault that he and I couldn't reconcile. I'd wounded him.

The room began to spin, and my head felt heavy for its gravity. I pressed my palms to my skull to try to steady myself. I breathed deeply to get my bearings.

With my left hand, I clumsily unclasped my bracelet and let its warm, delicate chain puddle onto the table.

"You don't have to give that back," Robert said, sounding hurt or offended.

But I did have to.

He followed me onto the porch.

"Goodbye, Robert," I said from near the steps, the words making me weak.

"Goodbye," he said. "I wish you all the best, Violet."

Without looking back on the sidewalk, I kept going toward my red car, and I heard Robert's door close behind me.

CHAPTER 42

Melanie

Louisville, Kentucky
October 2018

This was the day. Do or die. All or nothing. Hero or zero. But I felt ready.

This event would land me the promotion and everything that came with it—Mom's pride and the financial backup for my commitment to Violet's car. I was like the Olympian at the top of the snowy slope, and this was the moment I'd been waiting for. It was my time to go for the gold.

People rolled onto the grounds of the Bourbon Craft Cocktail Bash. Early numbers suggested a record attendance on this glorious October day. I felt the spirit of Aunt Violet with the scent of bourbon in the air.

I strolled the midway of the Cocktail Bash. The bourbon barrel rolling contest was about to begin. At my suggestion—and inspired by the picture in the Jordan ad in the magazine—a cosponsor's tasting booth on Prohibition-era cocktails had set up a display with framed color photos of luxury cars produced between 1920 and 1933. The exhibit was fascinating with pictures of Packards and Auburns and Cadillacs and Cords. Pure art.

Our own distillery's booth in the sponsor area was a hit—fans loved our swag, and everyone signed up for the cash door prize.

As with any planned event, there were problems behind the scenes of events managed by host organizers. The lines to the portable toilets were long due to attendance; management rush-ordered more. Then they arranged more Drink Responsibly Shuttles, for free rides home. The popular Meet the Master Distiller event ran late as usual. These didn't affect my gig or performance. Good news was, for the first time since Prohibition, there was a woman master distiller. I wished Violet could be here with me to see it.

Overall, the event team and thirty sponsor distilleries had things running smoothly, but as time ticked closer to my show, I was tense: it was two hours until the craft cocktail competition. This event was important to me, and not just because of my job. Today, mixologists appreciated where bourbon came from and the story of its rise and fall and rise again. Bartenders had helped revive the bourbon industry after it nearly died in the 1970s and 80s. They appreciated all that it suffered from the world wars' constraints and Prohibition's drought and the sting of consumer preferences. Importantly, they appreciated how good bourbon could not be rushed; it was slow, unlike the hectic pace of our lives, and maybe taking things slow was what we needed. It was art. They helped our industry survive, and this event celebrated them.

Once the event was concluded, I could relax from the pressures and enjoy myself. I made my way to Stage F. Workers had set up three hundred folding chairs for the audience. Extras were stacked at the sides for walk-ins. Stagehands had assembled the four cocktail stations, effectively mini kitchens. Large video screens were mounted, so the audience at the rear could have close-up views of competitors.

I opened my iPad's cheat sheet of to-dos:

- Sponsorship signage was up, and our distillery logo looked awesome. Check.
- Tanisha and I tested the mics and sound system. Check.
- Caterers were on target to deliver the foods and bourbon to the chef stations thirty minutes before showtime. Check.
- Tanisha had sent the competitors special parking passes. They were to meet one hour from now in the designated tent behind the stage. Everyone had confirmed with my reminder email yesterday. Check.
- Glassware sets looked great and were delivered to the VIP hospitality tent. Check.

Then I heard a crashing sound of glass. *What was that?* And again, more breaking glass from behind the stage.

I ran toward the prefunction tent and whipped open the flap of the door.

Two event staff were bent over a sea of busted bottles of premium bourbon—the bottles to be used by the panels. The smell of the booze would clear the sinuses of an elephant. I might even get a buzz. What was I going to do with this mess? And get ready for the stage on time?

This shambles threatened my whole event. I felt my chances of getting promoted draining along with the bourbon.

"We're so sorry," the workers said over and over.

"It's not your fault," I said kindly.

A rented, portable table had collapsed. So many bottles. Each competitor on the panel was to have five brands of bourbon to work with. My limbs vibrated like hot wires.

I took stock of the mess. Even bottles that hadn't broken might not be safe to use. Stray glass splinters could get lodged in someone's hand.

One of the staff was bleeding as she tried putting large shards of glass in the bin.

"Please, no, you can stop. I'll notify the cleanup crew as soon as I call First Aid."

I grabbed a white cloth napkin so she could wrap her hand to stop the bleeding.

"I'm sorry," she said again.

Remain calm. "We've got this covered," I said. "Just stay safe."

I'd arranged to have these bottles delivered myself, planned weeks in advance. Yet this was the Bourbon Craft Cocktail Bash—there was lots of bourbon if I could get my hands on it in time. *Think, think.*

I scrambled to the sponsors' tent a distance away. Suzanne, the overall event manager, would have contact info for all the sponsor reps. Maybe we could push out an emergency text to them all, have them each round up two more bottles. Pitch in. A group effort? Distilleries supported each other in this industry. The hard part would be getting it done in thirty minutes. I dialed her number as fast as I could, my fingers jittery.

"Suzanne?" I said. "We've got an emergency . . ." I explained the crisis, and she said she was on it. "We have twenty minutes."

Shit. Mitchell was coming my way.

"What's up?" he said. He had the uncanny knack of appearing in my worst professional moments.

"A little hiccup. That's all." I tried sounding nonchalant. "What about you?"

"I had a hiccup, too."

"Oh?" I didn't have time for his shit, but part of me yearned to know. Had he messed up, too?

"Yeah. The media kits for the press conference didn't arrive. The shipping service can't find the boxes anywhere. They were to be at our booth with the rest."

"Oh no. What time does the press conference start?"

I could make him feel worse by reminding him how at our last team meeting in the office, we'd gone over everyone's "To Ship" lists and our individual "To Transport" lists. He had reported that he'd take some extra media kits in his trunk to be safe—and I thought about throwing that fact in his face. All the liquor magazine editors would be there. Huge PR.

I actually had the means to help him, because I'd stowed a few media kits myself. I could let him take a fall instead—and increase my own chances of winning. He had it coming after what he did to me. But without good PR, our whole distillery would suffer.

"Listen," I said in a rush. "I stuck some media kits in my car as backup, while I was grabbing extra name badges and a spare thumb drive of the PowerPoints. I'll run and get 'em once my stage is set. Hang tight."

"Brilliant," he said, visibly relieved. "Thanks for having my back, Melanie. I'm not sure I deserve it."

Was that his way of admitting he screwed me over with his email, "Mixologist Bites the Dust?" And everything else?

Someone tapped my arm. The sponsor coordinator. I braced. "What's the verdict, Suzanne?"

"Sponsoring distilleries are stepping up. You'll have your extra bottles onstage—and on time. It'll cost ya for the labor crew to cart it all over, though."

"No problem. Thanks so much for acting quickly."

I came close to budgetary limits when I added travel for the Detroit guy. And now this? My job was on the effing line here. Maybe I'd still come in under, since I allowed for contingencies. But I didn't have time to do mental calculations. Right now all that mattered was the crisis was resolved.

My boss came up to me after the show. I could barely hear her over the roaring applause.

“That. Was. Amazing!” Cora said.

“I’m sooo glad.” I wiped fake sweat from my brow. *Whew.* “They all did great, didn’t they?”

The panel had done riffs off classic whiskey sours and crafted original bourbon concoctions with everything from muddled blackberries to grapefruit juice to apricot liqueur. My Detroit guy used Vernors ginger ale in a recipe. In another drink, his pour included bourbon, elderflower liqueur, and lemon; then he squeezed the essence out of a lemon peel, rubbed the rim of the glass with the peel, and lit the booze of the drink with a torch. That was the art of the cocktail, and the crowd loved it.

Cora said, “I couldn’t believe you got his recipes added to the take-home packs in time. All that and thinking fast for plan B with the smashed bottles. Great work.”

“Thanks, Cora. I couldn’t have done the take-home packs without Tanisha. And I don’t mind admitting the broken glass freaked me out for a sec. Who knew it’d be a *bash* in more ways than one?” We laughed.

I slayed it on my big event. That’s all a girl could do. But I managed to help my teammate, too, even though he could be a jerk.

That’s what leaders did. That’s what Mom taught me.

If scads of media outlets jumped on our brand after the press conference, Mitchell would be a star. But I did the right thing. The distillery came first.

Now to find the rest of our gang at the VIP tent. I’d let them know they rocked it.

I spun around to go and— “Mom! Dad! What a nice surprise,” I said with a smile that could make my cheeks ache.

Dad said, beaming, “We didn’t want to miss your big day.”

“You’re a star, Melanie,” Mom said, her smile maybe bigger than mine. “I’ve watched you today—how you monitored every step of the event. How you interacted with the people who were here to attend, not just stars on the stage. Your face glows at connecting with these people who want to learn about bourbon, take home something to sip, to be entertained by the best." She hugged me. "The whole event ran like clockwork to any observer. But I know enough about these big productions to know you undoubtedly had some ordeals to manage behind the scenes. It never showed. Not in here, and not in you. Great work. I'm so proud of you. Not just for being so good at what you do, but for doing what you love."

Mom was proud of me and I hadn't even gotten promoted. She could see how being here fueled me—being around others who have a passion for bourbon, its history, its art.

"Thank you," I said, my voice syrupy.

I was filled with so much gratitude and happiness for having heard her words that I felt lighter—as if my feet might lift off the ground for me to float in the air like a kite.

Then Nicole and Casey ran up and hugged me and my parents. "That competition was so fun!" Casey said.

"You killed it!" my other friend said.

Then they were off for a session on how to make smoked drinks—to infuse a bourbon cocktail with the flavors of applewood or maple.

After we stopped by the VIP tent—where our club members loved the new glass sets, and a few even commented on our website's new pages about the history of women in distilling—my parents and I walked to the parking lot together.

Mom had brought Violet's journal back. She said, "You need to catch up to where my bookmark is."

"That interesting?" I said.

"Yes," she said. "I finally understand why the car was so important to her, and to you. You're doing the right thing by her, Melanie. Restoring the Jordan."

But if I didn't earn the promotion, how would I cover my debt?

CHAPTER 43

Violet

Detroit, Michigan
Two weeks later, September 1923

I remembered back when I got fired at the spark plug factory, how I didn't want to go crawling back to Kentucky as a failure.

But sometimes things changed. Sometimes decisions changed.

Sometimes people changed.

Living my one life wasn't necessarily a straight road. With the dissolution of my relationship with Robert, I understood now what I wished I'd seen sooner: true independence didn't mean being single and unencumbered. It meant I was free to make my own choices. Robert apologized for his ultimatum on my buying a car that wasn't a Ford. In the months leading up to that, we might've made our relationship work had I not rebuffed his proposals and instead had an open exchange.

To think, I could've had both marriage and freedom. It wouldn't have looked like Mother and Father's or Evelyn and Charles's. It would've looked like us. Robert and I could have been happy.

After leaving his house—a house that might've been mine—I folded him up like a delicate handkerchief and tucked him away in a vest pocket of my mind. His dazzling smile still crept back in, yes. Or the tender touch of his lips. But our final words did, too; they were unlike the time we'd parted ways before, when we had simply said, "Thank you."

This time was just, "Goodbye."

I was still suffering his loss and Lela's loss. But I had to go on. I had to be the heroine of my own story.

When I telephoned Mother long distance, we didn't have much time. But she said, "You're a Bond woman, Violet. I hate that you have to, but you will get through this." That's what she did when Father died. She got through it. She said Dr. Keller and she had set a date for a November wedding. Private at home, family only.

I was happy for her. Proud of her. She made her choices.

My sister was there, too. Evelyn told me, "My heart breaks for you and your friend who's gone, but Robert Neumann's a fool."

I chuckled every time I thought about her comment. That's what sisters were for. Evelyn withheld any hint of "I told you so." Neither of the women in my life made me feel a failure. I remembered the promise Mother extracted from me before I came to Detroit.

If things there don't work out—if they go miserably for any reason at all—or, if they do work out well but you just want to come home, come.

"I just want to come home," I said to Mother on the telephone.

It wasn't that I felt defeated. Independence didn't have to mean living on my own without family or community close by. I'd had my adventure in the city where I'd lived and loved and learned—and grown. And I was glad for it. But for the long term, I belonged in Kentucky.

I still had Mother's money for a train ride back. But I would return it. I would drive home in my own car. It was my choice.

I arranged with Mother to buy Bond House from her after the wedding. The newlyweds were to get a new place—start fresh in neither home of their former marriages.

In my weeks-long preparation for my departure, I drove to Detroit's Dime Building. I strode through the lobby with my heels clicking on tiles shined with wax. I rode up the elevator with three others—men—to my broker's office on the nineteenth floor, unannounced. He squeezed me in.

"I need you to sell all my shares. Today." I scribbled amounts on a page. I'd keep the guaranteed bonds. "This much of it in cash," I said, "and the rest in the Bank of Frankfort under the name Charles Weber." My brother-in-law would preserve my funds, given that as a woman, I couldn't open my own account. What rubbish.

Mr. Jackson said, "*All* your stocks?"

I could hear the ticker tape of his brain rattling. He thought I was being rash. But it was a good day for trading. Stocks were up. I would leave nothing behind in this boom town. And I wouldn't risk the red bar of the broker's graph dropping as it once had. I'd take my money. Now.

It took a week to arrange for Lela's things to be out of the apartment. I sold my own belongings but for some dresses, jewelry, shoes, and hats. Then I shipped three large trunks home by rail. I would cart some in the car on the road—along with my suitcase of cash.

The following day, I drove into my Jordan dealership. My former salesman had a map of the United States on his office wall, the size of two bed pillows side by side lengthwise. He pointed to the Dixie Highway, which ran from Michigan's northern border clear down to Florida. The Highway was a combination of current roads and newer roads that'd been built in the last few years. It wound through open land and tiny towns that served it.

"Here, please take this," he said. "It's this year's *Automobile Blue Book*. It outlines the Dixie Highway route for you to follow from Detroit all the way until you get off and go a short ways farther to Frankfort. See?"

He showed me page after page of exact instructions for streets I was to take, where to turn, and mileage to mark as I went.

"Thank you," I said. "I will guard this manual with my life."

The dealership's service center installed an automobile heater beneath my car's hood, too. It would blow some warm air into the interior. But I knew all too well to pack plenty of traveling robes and blankets. It was going to be a cold ride in autumn. I had to get home before winter.

Two days before leaving, I dropped by the boardinghouse and said so long to my friends. I hadn't been back since I moved out. But I was leaving Detroit for good, and somehow it felt right.

Mrs. Sturgeon said, "Violet, it's been a pleasure to know you. I wish you all the best in the world."

"Thank you," I'd said. "I'll miss you—and your hearty breakfasts."

Outside, when we were alone, Sarah said, "Before you go, do you want to know the latest on Robert?"

I tensed as the sun's rays made me squint and strands of hair blew across my face. No, I did not want to hear. But yes, I did. Had he divulged to his aunt or my friends that bright and dark day that he and I'd had? I gave one nod.

"That young woman," Sarah said. "He brought her here again. Seems they're getting serious."

So quickly? I hadn't wished to know this after all. A fresh wave of pain swept over me then. If finality could be forced on something already final, this was it. A red stamp of ink.

Within four weeks of my making the decision to leave town, I was ready.

I pulled into a filling station on day two of my journey. A man in a khaki uniform ran out for service.

"Fine automobile you've got there," he said.

I thanked him as I peered into the fuel tank on the outside rear of the car. The cork floater looked about halfway down.

"Fill it up, please."

I never risked going below half a tank. Father had done that once, and we'd had to drive up a steep hill backward, so the fuel had enough gravity to reach the carburetor and propel the car.

Ohio's two-lane roads were long, paved, and flat. I picked up speed past miles of golden farmlands and slowed in towns along rivers where smokestacks belched curling black smoke with signs of industry. There were pretty little town squares, too, with shady maple trees and monuments. My *Blue Book* showed where to "turn right with the trolley here" or "turn left at the school" as I went. I had packed crackers, raisins, and a thermos full of water to tide me over in between.

I would arrive in Dayton well before dark for my second night at a motor inn. Yet I'd been on the road for six hours already, and fatigue set in along with some dark thunderclouds. I was cold and shivered despite two layers of outerwear. My back ached. And I was nauseous.

I had to pull over and fast. I was going to be sick.

Soon, rain fell in sheets, so I stayed on the side of the road. I felt as if I were in a submarine under an ocean, and a mounting wave of nausea rose up in me again. I had to hold it off. Was it the eggs I'd eaten for breakfast? The oatmeal? Thunder clapped and I jumped. I checked my watch. It wouldn't be fully night for three more hours. I'd get to my next stop, surely. I bent my head back and prayed I wouldn't throw up in the car.

Wait.

Panic surged through me. Was I late? My mind was a jumble, trying to think back and count weeks since my last monthly cycle. Four, five. Six weeks? *Damn.* My last period was right after Lela died. Now I was two weeks late. What was I going to do? My limbs seemed to convulse in retaliation against me. With my grief and this trip's preparation, it hadn't dawned on me. I was carrying a baby. I had a hint of a smile, but then I pushed my hand to my mouth. Oh no. What had I done?

Robert hadn't protected himself that day on the sofa in the bungalow, which was half my own fault. We'd been urgent, reckless.

Was this some sort of poetic justice for my having lived in the moment? Fate laughing at me after all I thought I'd learned? What would I do now? How would I tell Mother and Evelyn? Questions spun like wheels careening off a road in my head. Should I turn around and run to tell Robert? But he'd told me it was too late for us. And he already had someone else.

I rubbed my hand across my abdomen. I was carrying a baby. Now more than ever, I had to get home. Safe.

The worst of my nausea and the storm finally passed, leaving nothing but a drizzle outside. But now I had to get to a ladies' lounge somewhere and relieve my bladder. I sat erect and tried starting the car. Nothing. I tried again. *Damn.*

Think. Think.

Cars need three things: fuel, air, and spark, Mr. Adams at the Frankfort dealership told me. Father once got under his hood when something was wet. I grabbed the rags I'd packed and got out and lifted the hood. Heavy water had to be the problem. It made sense. I knew the condition of my spark plugs was good, but the car wasn't getting the spark. The electrical current wasn't traveling to them.

Yes, I saw water had splashed onto a large coil and a cluster of yellow wires. A car breezed by, then another and another, one honking and making me jerk. Was no one going to stop and help me?

But I didn't want help. I would see this through myself, as surely as a heroine in the films of my youth. I would get this car running and prove Father wrong.

I gently disconnected the wires that led to the spark plugs and patted them dry to the tips, then reconnected them. I charged back to my seat, pressed my foot to the button on the floor. *Start, damn it, start.* Dead.

Back under the hood, I gritted my teeth and fiddled around, trying to dry more parts. There was a cap of sorts, brown, connecting the wires. I went back for the screwdriver in my tool set in the door. With trembling hands, I unscrewed the cap's two screws, lifted it off, and saw moisture inside. I blotted it dry and reattached it with my screwdriver.

One try to start the car. Two tries. Three tries and it started! I burst into tears, happy and heaving so hard, my hands firm on my belly, and then I bent out the door to vomit in the street.

On the last day of my journey, I approached the Roebling Bridge that led across the Ohio River from Cincinnati into Covington, Kentucky. The high bridge to Kentucky looked like a giant gate to a castle across a great, wide moat. The waters beneath me surged and along with them my heart.

I was a modern woman. I was a Bond woman. I would handle what was coming. I would make my own way.

I was living my one life.

Going home.

CHAPTER 44

Violet

Frankfort, Kentucky
Eighty-one years later, February 2004

I sat upright in my private, rented nursing bed set up in my bedroom at Bond House. The joints of my aged bones ached, but what else was new? I was more than a century old. I had heart issues, kidney issues, blood pressure issues, and more. The kind nurse named Amy rolled a narrow dining table that doubled as a desk across my lap and brought me a ballpoint pen and left.

With great effort I removed from under my pillow the journal I kept from all those many years ago. I managed to get up the day before and dig the book from the bottom of my dresser.

I turned toward the back of the journal to the first blank page after where I left off when Lela died. The rest of my story I hadn't needed to commit to paper.

Not then.

Now, I would leave my Jordan car and this journal to Melanie. I promised her that on her sixteenth birthday I would reveal to her the car's story—my story—and why I kept the Jordan all these years stuck in the carriage house. It got me home.

But I knew now from the doctors that I wouldn't live that long.

I rubbed my neck with my skeletal fingers. The words would come. I closed my eyes to let my thoughts drift back . . .

My great-great-great-niece visited last week. She's fourteen. A fine young girl. A beauty. Smart and caring, too.

We chatted about her friends and her grades and her track team meets.

"Remember how we used to watch *The Wizard of Oz*?" she said.

"First time you were, what, six? The flying monkeys scared you."

"They still kinda do," she said and giggled. "I remember your moral of the story, though."

There's no place like home.

I picked up my pen. I wrote about my last day with Robert, and my drive back to Kentucky alone.

In dredging up memories and choices I made, I felt the quaking in my limbs . . .

After a long while, I set the journal aside to rest.

I saw the rising and lowering of my chest with my breaths. It's a peculiar feeling to know one's breaths will soon end. Which rise will be the last?

Nurse Amy awoke me with a tray for my lunch. She set it on the swiveling table-desk. Cut-up lasagna and canned peaches—easy to bite, easy to chew, and easy to swallow. I took a couple of bites and pushed some food around the plate with my fork and was done. When Nurse Amy left, I rolled the pen between my thumb and forefinger.

I had to start writing again, to get everything out. I had so little time.

When I was done, I instructed the nurse on where to put the journal, the key, and the magazine—in the trunk compartment of my beloved Jordan, where Melanie could find them when I'm gone.

CHAPTER 45

Melanie

Louisville, Kentucky
October 2018

Mom came Friday night to sleep over. We hadn't felt this close in like, maybe, ever. Sometimes you have to get everything out.

At least we had to. And we were left the better for it.

I'd been a total couch potato last Sunday after the Cocktail Competition. Mitchell might still win the prize. But I did my best. No matter the outcome, I would have no regrets—unlike the little girl who wanted to be a cheerleader but wasn't. This was one way my reconciliation with Mom brought me peace.

Unfortunately, it wouldn't help my balance sheet if I didn't get the raise. *One day at a time, Melanie.*

Come Monday, our team went back to the grindstone, as they say. Our group geared up for the launch of Goldenrod 105 Rye—the label that I had proudly named—and the Bourbon and Books kickoff shortly after. These things still shined a light on me that couldn't hurt.

During the week, I took a couple of evenings to catch up on Violet's entries. So much had occurred. I ran my finger over the old photograph of Violet with her best friend, Lela. What a tragic, unnecessary loss her death was.

Violet's early entries concluded after that. Until she picked the journal back up in old age. Mom had seen the date and stopped, and so I had, too, per our agreement.

Even though I knew how Violet's story shook out in the end . . . her philanthropies, civil rights activities, her death in Bond House after a long life . . . I hated to see her entries end. I'd miss her voice. Her story had helped me evaluate my life and career—such an awesome feat from across space and time.

Mom came tonight so we could read the rest of Violet's journal *together*. It began from her deathbed in 2004.

Mom brought fresh mint leaves for juleps. I had the simple syrup and bourbon: a 100-proof Bottled-in-Bond selection that'd aged four years in a warehouse. This one was from Buffalo Trace Distillery on the river in Frankfort—formerly known as the George T. Stagg distillery—the distillery that'd been granted a license to sell medicinal alcohol in 1920, but where Violet couldn't get on. After the repeal of Prohibition, though, she'd built her career there.

It seemed fitting to drink this bourbon tonight.

Mom and I got cozy in my living room in our sweatpants and fuzzy socks, and she motioned for me to do the honors. I opened the old weathered pages in the way I did that first day in the carriage house. I took a moment of silent meditation.

Then I began to read aloud.

CHAPTER 46

Melanie

Louisville, Kentucky
October 2018

I was parched. All I managed to do was breathe. Mom's face was covered by handfuls of tissues. She'd been crying softly for a while. I chugged some water, not the mint julep, and read on. We chose to wait and chat later about Robert rejecting Violet and her journey home in the car. She was pregnant, and we had to learn what happened.

Violet's writing got shakier as it went, but I read on.

The night I returned home to Bond House, Charles had the carriage house ready. Even before I'd known I had a secret, I hadn't planned on townspeople hearing I'd returned. Not yet. I needed time to grieve and rest without watchful eyes and questions. Evelyn and I sat at Mother's round oak table in the kitchen—the same one where I'd learned to roll biscuits and she'd taught us girls about the paintings of Monet and novels of Austen.

"This looks delicious," I said as Mother set down two plates, apple pie for each daughter.

I took a bite, and the filling was just so: sweet and tart with apples from the tree in the yard. But my stomach churned. I prayed I could keep it down.

Then, resting my fork on my plate, I said, "Mother, Evelyn, I have news."

You see, Melanie, I had had a choice before me as I drove home from Detroit.

I could keep my baby—and become an unwed mother, risk this child having a stigma in society, perhaps risk my own mother's reputation and maybe her future with Dr. Keller. Or I could ask Evelyn—who had sacrificed for me years before, and who'd yearned her whole life to be a mother—to raise my child.

I hadn't been able to help Ethel Nowak in Detroit's spark plug factory. I'd not been able to save my best friend's life.

But I gave my baby to my sister. Her, I could help.

I paused and looked at Mom, staggered. "Evelyn wasn't your biological great-grandmother," I said. "Violet was."

She nodded, wiping her eyes and cleaning her nose. "I'm in shock. But this family," she said, her voice creaky, "is amazing. I'm proud to be part of it."

"Me too," I said hoarsely. "Violet was strong. And good. I miss her so much, Mom."

I missed Grape Aunt Violet like corn misses sun, like creeks miss water. I wanted to hold her right now, to lace my fingers through her thin, brittle ones. Now I knew why she'd kept the car in the carriage house all her life. It brought her home. It symbolized, I thought, her being a modern woman—and with it an independence to make big decisions that carry over all of one's life.

And I felt a change taking seed inside me—with a new view of what independence meant.

"Melanie, just think," Mom said. "Over the years, Violet must have watched on as Evelyn reared her daughter. Not planning the birthday parties. Not taking Gladys for her first day of school. Not nursing her scrapes when she fell and got hurt." Mom's voice cracked. "I can't imagine the moment she handed her infant all wrapped in blankets to her sister."

"Yes," I said. "Violet had sacrificed for others before. But not like this."

Mom and I sat quietly for a minute.

"There's three pages left," I said, lightly stroking the column of my throat.

"If you can't read to the end, let me."

I handed the journal over. Mom began.

Gladys was three when I saw how strongly she favored her father. Even Evelyn saw it. Gladys's blue eyes could've been Robert's or mine, but her dazzling smile was all him.

The night Evelyn and Charles took Gladys home, I had thought it was the hardest night of my life. Watching her go out the door in my sister's arms. Little did I know, it wasn't to be the hardest. But as Evelyn left, she'd asked Mother and me to promise never to tell anyone our secret. She asked that Gladys always would know her as Mommy. I agreed.

Now, Melanie, I want you and Angie to hear the truth, if only after I'm gone. I need someone besides myself to know.

Mom halted. "The page has a couple of tiny spots, as if droplets had gotten it wet. So that's why she never told us when she was alive? Because of her promise?"

I said, "Guess so. But what was the hardest day of her life?"

Mom read on.

My work with the distillery, charities, and civic efforts fulfilled me. Adventure and happiness take many forms. I could've found love again, too, but chose not to. Not after Robert. Once was enough.

Oh, there were men—one from Louisville, another from Lexington. We would periodically meet, like at the Greenbrier in West Virginia or the West Baden Springs in French Lick, Indiana. Yet these men meant no more to me than Lawrence had.

Mother passed peacefully in her seventies with Dr. Keller beside her. But in 1984 when Gladys died from cancer, neither Evelyn nor I could be consoled. Gladys was only fifty-nine. I'd survived the "roaring twenties"—roaring for the sound of machine guns firing, not just the jazz and the hedonism.

Losing Gladys was my worst day.

Mom stopped and looked strangled.

"Mom?"

"I'm okay," she said. "I came home from college to attend the funeral for Grammie Gladys. I remember, clearly, Aunt Violet weeping silently off to the side while Charles tried to soothe Evelyn next to the casket."

"How sad," I said, the picture of it piercing me. "Yet how strong Violet was. Mom, are you able to read on?"

She lifted her shoulders. "We've got to get through this."

Long after that loss, I wondered if I'd been wrong about love. I'd been wrong about things before. Living a life without a partner to share the good and bad works for some people. But what if I had let myself love again?

These aren't just ramblings of an old woman. I truly wonder. What if I'd opened my heart back up?

Six years after Gladys passed, Melanie, you came along. By the time you were three, indeed, you looked like a little brown-eyed Gladys. Your dazzling smile. It's remarkable how traits carry across generations.

My heart swelled every time you called me Grape Aunt Violet. So cute. Over the years, we had overnights. I taught you how to remove the crumb tray from the bottom of the toaster, and you were amazed. We debated whether maple tree seeds that twirled as they fell were called helicopters or whirligigs. You won. You puckered up when tasting rhubarb pie for the first time, but had taken right to weaving the strips of the lattice crust dough. You rode down the stairs on a pillow like I had decades before—the toboggan. And as you got older, you loved my stories of the distillery days.

I leave your mother my house, and to you, my only remaining treasure. My car. I hope you know, I treasured every single minute with you. Perhaps that's why this old body has endured as long as it has; I had a lot of "little girl time" left to experience.

Of the many things I've learned over a hundred years, this sums them up:

Though candy bars may rain from the sky, life will not always be sweet. Go on new adventures. Love and be loved. You can choose your happiness.

Mom paused and then said with more strain in her voice, "That's the end."

She handed me the box of tissues. One box may not be enough.

"Melanie," Mom said, patting my back. "I'm glad we did this together."

"Oh, me too," I said, trying to suck back an ugly cry. "Remember the day at your house, when we looked at old photos? You said I resembled your grandma. Gladys."

"Right. 1950s cat-eye glasses and all," Mom said, snickering. "It was in through the lips." More soberly, she said, "I am sure that losing her daughter was the worst day of Violet's life. Both mothers' lives."

"True," I said. "As I think back to Evelyn in her old age challenging you to push through, to be the first to earn a grad degree, I—"

"Yeah," Mom interjected. "Evelyn had emphasized how she was my great-grandmother. Makes you wonder now, doesn't it?"

I said, "Had Evelyn lived her life with the family Violet gave her, but with a shadow hovering over her? Like, maybe she felt unworthy?"

"We'll never know," Mom said. "It's terrible what women put on themselves. The pressures." She directed her sights on me. "That is, the pressures women put on themselves—*and* then pass to those who inherit them."

My eyes made one long, slow blink of acknowledgment. Yeah, we inherited some pretty bad baggage. Then I inwardly smiled. We women inherited good things, too.

I lifted Violet's note card from the table, the one she'd placed inside the journal. *Take from this story what you will, Melanie, and you can bury the rest.*

In her twilight years, Violet questioned what life would've been like if she opened her heart again. I reflected.

I didn't need men out of my life for my job after all. Modern women could have both career and marriage.

Like Mom.

Mom hoped Jason and I would get back together. But he just wasn't my person. We had incongruent goals for our lives.

Perhaps I'd call Brian. Take a chance?

Though candy bars may rain from the sky, life will not always be sweet. Go on new adventures. Love and be loved. You can choose your happiness.

Then it all hit me.

Mom and I both had descended from Violet Bond and her one great love, Robert Neumann. But more than that realization washed over me like waves.

Violet, my great-great-grandma, had written: *Sometimes things changed. Sometimes I change. Sometimes decisions changed. Living my one life wasn't necessarily a straight road.*

I knew I didn't want to let Cora or my company down. But striving to achieve the promotion had come more from my need to do my best at something without regrets—and from my need to prove something to Mom—than it had from the promise of the work itself.

To me, the bourbon industry was about the people. People like Violet. To those in the bourbon community, whiskey was more than a name on a label or menu. Bourbon was history. Bourbon was the earth. Bourbon was art.

The job promotion wasn't important to me anymore. I already had everything important.

As modern women, if we listened to ourselves carefully, we could choose new paths. It didn't make us failures. We were adventurers seeking the breadth of life's experiences.

And sometimes we came home.

At heart, I wasn't about being a director with leadership meetings covering PTO policies, capital expenses, new servers for IT, data privacy, and training for staff on phishing.

I was about events.

If it meant I couldn't afford the loan, I'd move to plan B—sell my Honda for top dollar, buy an econobox to drive, and use my surplus toward two years' worth of payments. Since Ray would keep the Jordan the first year for his shows, I realized I wouldn't have to pay for monthly storage or insurance. By the final year of the loan's three-year term, I'd have something else figured out.

I'd have faith in the same way Violet had when she crossed the bridge to Kentucky. I would take care of myself.

"Cora," I said, closing her office door behind me with a soft click. "Thanks for carving out time to meet."

"Of course. You were next on my list to call anyway."

"I'm pulling out," I said without preamble. Something tingled inside my nose, somewhere high, I thought, close to where tears were born. "I don't want the promotion."

She looked utterly befuddled. I could've announced that I'd been hatched from a dinosaur egg.

"But you already have it," Cora said. "The decision's been made. I was going to walk you down the hall just now and say, 'Welcome to your new director's office.'"

I already had the promotion? I'd been selected over Mitchell after all. My performance and drive had paid off, and I felt a prickle of pride.

But I looked to my lap with my hands cupped tight. In my gut, I still felt the same.

"Cora," I said, my eyes searching hers. "I'm so grateful for everything you've done for me, and your confidence in my abilities." I licked my lips that now felt dry. "I'm certain, though, the role isn't for me."

That night, I phoned Mom and told her everything.

"Honey," she said. "You followed your gut and your heart. I applaud you."

"Mom, there's one more thing," I said, knowing she wouldn't see it coming. "You'll soon sell Violet's house, and I want to buy it."

She fell silent. I sensed what she was thinking. *You can't afford that with the Jordan, especially without the raise.*

"You're the one who taught me," I said, "to think outside the box when challenges arise. I've done my research; we could have a rent-to-own contract. My lease is almost up at the loft, then I'd pay my monthly rent to you. This money would go toward my down payment on the house. In five years, or whatever term we set, I'd have to pay off the house for a price we agree to up front. When the balance comes due, I pay you off even if it means financing a conventional mortgage—or else I forfeit my investment and you sell to another bidder for full price."

She laughed out loud. "I see you're a chip off the old block."

That was her way of saying she'd do it.

EPILOGUE

Melanie

Lexington, Kentucky
December 2018

My fingertips glided along the side of the car with its smooth scarlet-red paint. I touched it in just the way my great-great-grandmother had done in a sun-filled Detroit showroom in 1923.

This Jordan was art on wheels. A girl's car.

I opened the driver's door as the crew who'd worked on the car watched. I zipped up my heavy coat and climbed in. The Jordan's interior had a new-car smell, part polish, part paint. But as I leaned back, the gravity of the moment overtook me: I felt as if I was little again, snuggling in Violet's lap, but in the same breath, I felt like Amelia Earhart settling into a cockpit for the very first time. This was it.

Brian skipped around the rear and got in on the passenger side. It was too cold outside to unsnap the plastic window curtains or to put down the stow-away top. And the car's type of heat wouldn't do much. Our eyes connected, and his had the cutest little crow's-feet when he grinned.

I wrapped my hands snug around the wooden steering wheel, just as I had as a girl. Violet had climbed into the car with me. I smiled now. And I prayed silently, thanking God that we'd had that day and other days together.

I glanced out the door to Mom, an invisible thread tying us together as she held her fingers to her face, watching. Nervous deep in my belly now, I followed Brian's instruction and used Violet's key to enable the automobile's transmission; there was a keyhole low by the gear shift for this purpose. Turned out the car key in those days didn't actually start the car. Who knew? I positioned my right foot on the raised round button on the floor. I pressed down hard and held it there, and the car fired up. The low, rumbling growl of the engine forced water to my eyes and dampened them.

I pumped the gas pedal, making the engine roar—and bringing to mind old ladies' eyes bugging out when Violet and Lela passed them, their scarves blowing behind them and horn blaring. I pushed the horn twice on the wheel, and its resurrected sound spurred me to bop up and down in the seat a little bit.

My little girl's voice rose up in my head: *Look at me now, Grape Aunt Violet. Look at me now.*

Brian gave me an empathetic nod. "Ready?" We would go around the block a few times, and then he'd jump out and Mom would hop in.

Having learned to drive a stick with my Camaro back in high school, I somewhat awkwardly shifted this car into gear. Soon, I was driving it out of the auto shop as the crew clapped and cheered. I dipped my head in a mock bow and then hung a sharp left.

"This car is not easy to drive without power steering or brakes," Brian said. We exchanged glances and he winked. "I'm impressed with your skill, and I don't impress easily."

I chuckled. So that's why the steering wheel was resistant to my turns and why I had to mash the brake pedal hard to get the car to slow down—not that it went that fast.

I relished steering the same wheel that my great-great-grandmother had steered.

But it was more than that. It seemed to me that as I followed her journal and restored her car, so too had my life been restored.

I took a new position, overseeing special events with one of the prominent established distilleries. It was based in nearby Versailles: the Woodford Reserve Distillery on the National Register of Historic Places. The lovely approach of its grounds toward a modern welcome center and historical stone buildings made me tingle; I could open my window to the smell of the angel's share in the air. And the distillery was among the first to recognize the contributions that enslaved men had made in the site's history of producing bourbon.

Distilling had begun on the Woodford site in the early 1800s as the Old Oscar Pepper Distillery. In 1878, some years after the Civil War, it sold and was renamed Labrot and Graham Distillery—where Violet got her start. The L&G initials were still emblazoned on the boiler stack that she saw. My great-great-grandmother met Robert Neumann at the Labrot and Graham Distillery's in-town Frankfort sales office, decades before Woodford took over. As Mom said when I interviewed, *You were born for this job*. My passion was helping to provide a place for people to come learn and experience great bourbon, and a place for celebration.

I'd also moved into Bond House—half an hour from the auto shop in Lexington—and with an easy commute to Versailles along green Kentucky bluegrass or snowy wide pastures and pristine brown fences of thoroughbred farms. Violet's dark woodwork was now a creamy, warm white. And the parlor was the palest matte gray with eclectic art in vibrant colors and my precious blue velvet couch. My first Christmas tree lit up the bay window in front, just like Violet's had when I was a child, and when she and Evelyn were girls.

There's no place like home.

Brian and I rolled back into the parking lot at Ray's. "Brian, how can I thank you enough for your guidance?"

"It's been my honor," he said. "But maybe you can make hot fudge sundaes again?"

"That would be a yes," I said, and we laughed. And I would kiss him again, too.

Before he got out, Brian bent to the floor where he'd hidden a gift. He grinned and passed to me a small hardcover book.

The Woman and the Car: A Chatty Little Handbook for the Edwardian Motoriste

"What?" I smiled. Violet had called herself a motoriste.

"The book was published by a woman in 1909," Brian said, "for women to be unafraid of automobiles, and to learn how to drive them in what was then called a 'great new outdoor pastime.'"

"Wow."

Violet wanted to drive a car around 1915, but her father forbade it.

"I love this," I said.

Mom tapped on Brian's door. "Guess I have to get out," he said to me in a teasing tone. He opened the door.

"Your turn," he told my mom, and she gave him a friendly hug.

Then Ray came over and stuck his head in. "Melanie, seems word has gotten around about your car. I just got a call from a collector. He wants to buy it. Says he'll pay eighty grand."

I heard the air suck out of Mom's lungs. Or was it mine? I felt light-headed.

"That's twice what you have in it," Mom said, dumbfounded.

Brian winked at me. "Looks like you made a sound investment."

And the value will only increase, I thought. I stroked the black leather of the seat beside me, remembering Violet sitting here with reverence when she was nearly one hundred years old. I turned to Ray.

"You can tell him thank you very much, but it's not for sale."

I was the collector.

Mom climbed in and slammed the passenger door closed. These old doors were so heavy. When I pulled out of the auto shop, I swear Mom said, "Woo-hoo!"

We were off. Two girls having fun.

ACKNOWLEDGMENTS

My heartfelt thanks go to Jim Lackey, the foremost historian on Jordan cars. I simply could not have written my novel without the help of his book, *The Jordan Automobile*, and our many conversations.

Michael Veach—a bourbon historian and member of the Bourbon Hall of Fame—was also indispensable in consulting with me. His *Kentucky Bourbon Whiskey: An American Heritage* remains a go-to source. I'm grateful to Mike for sharing his insider's knowledge on the history's big picture and on the lesser-known subtleties when I got stuck. I hope to sip bourbon with him on his porch again someday in Louisville.

John Willi, president of the Jordan Register car club, was also generous to assist me, and I'm so thankful. When my manuscript was under tight deadline, he provided quick answers on everything from how cars in the early 1920s got heat in winter to what might've made my character's car break down (and how she could fix it herself).

The Bourbon Women Association founded by Peggy Noe Stevens hosted virtual programs that were super insightful during my writing process. A big shout-out goes to members of the Atlanta branch of BW for their welcoming spirit that also influenced my story.

I'm ever appreciative for a bounty of other essential resources that got me through: period magazines, historical maps, and innumerable online sources that ranged from letters to academic dissertations to videos on Jazz Age dances. I studied more than one hundred books in researching this novel as well. The following seven were crucial in informing and inspiring my work:

- *Barrel Strength Bourbon: The Explosive Growth of America's Whiskey* by Carla Harris Carlton
- *Intemperance: The Lost War Against Liquor* by Larry Engelmann
- *Capital on the Kentucky: A Two Hundred Year History of Frankfort & Franklin County* by Carl Kramer
- *Ford: The Men and the Machine* by Robert Lacey
- *Whiskey Women: The Untold Story of How Women Saved Bourbon, Scotch, and Irish Whiskey* by Fred Minnick
- *Lost Girls: The Invention of the Flapper* by Linda Simon
- *The Changing Face of Inequality: Urbanization, Industrial Development, and Immigrants in Detroit, 1880–1920* by Olivier Zunz

I'm so grateful to my Louisville tour guides extraordinaire (and amazing hosts): Jeff and Holly Whitaker. Thanks also to Maddie Whitaker and her friend Casey Gray, for sharing key tips about the city that I could never have known. (And Hallie Whitaker, if I lived closer, I hope you'd have done my hair for my book launch!)

I feel so fortunate that years ago I met my historical fiction critique partners, Joy Kniskern and Betsy Crosby, in a novel-writing class. To connect with these friends every month—even via Zoom during COVID—has improved my writing and forever enriched my life.

Feedback from beta readers also proved critical in various stages of my manuscript. Abundant thanks to: Jenna Blum, Liv Radue, Grace Wynter, Kay Heath, Carla Gunnin, Mary Sutton, Sylvia Smith, Shelley Vallier, April Mojica Whitaker, Renee Bissell-Cole, Sara Samarasinghe, and Katie Woodruff.

Writing is solitary work, yet over the years, I've found I have cheerleaders in friends who've spurred me on. Thank you to Joshilyn Jackson, Travis Cole, Amy Anderson, Andrea Powers, Teresa Bult, and countless other current and former Constangy-ites.

And of course, my mother, Sheila Cole; my sons, Brolin and Justin; and my grandchildren, Evelyn and Lane, have my deepest, loving gratitude. I'm truly blessed that my family "gets" me.

Perhaps I could have no greater cheerleader than my husband, John—my own personal cute car guru guy. He's also the one who mixes our whiskey sours on Friday-night date-nights at home. Thank you to him for being my sounding board through difficult parts of the book's plot—and for inspiring this story with his passion for customizing classic cars.

What an honor and pleasure it's been to collaborate and become friends with the amazing, far-reaching book community that includes readers, Facebook groups, podcasters, bookstagrammers, bloggers, reviewers, booksellers, and fellow authors. Thanks to them all and to friends and loved ones far and wide for reading my work and spreading the word. I'm humbled.

My sincere thanks go to my wise and talented editors, Chris Werner and Tiffany Yates Martin, who could see the story beneath the clutter and pushed me to develop the layers, connections, and character arcs—all while never letting my writer's spirit waver. And what an honor it was to work with Danielle Marshall! I'm so thankful for the incredible Lake Union publishing team for everything from copyediting and cover design to proofreading and marketing. Thank you for making my work shine! And my books would not exist but for literary agent Katie Shea Boutillier who said *yes*.

My journey in writing this book has been so much fun for me. If only we could all toast with a round of bourbon or pass a tray of fine chocolates. Thank you, readers.

BOOK CLUB DISCUSSION QUESTIONS

SPOILER ALERT

1. Discuss how loyalty is portrayed in the novel—loyalty between sisters, lovers, mothers and daughters, girlfriends, and coworkers. And what of being loyal to oneself?
2. Some suggest that the Jordan car is a character in the novel. Do you agree? Why or why not?
3. How has product marketing evolved in our culture since the groundbreaking Jordan automobile advertisement, the candy bar drops, and the thriving department stores in the 1920s? How do you feel about the changes?
4. How did women's rights in the Jazz Age compare to those now? What are the differences between a modern woman then and now?
5. Art appears in the novel through architecture, fashion, and more. Before reading the story, did you perceive the styling of automobiles, the making of bourbon, or the crafting of cocktails to be art? Has your perspective changed?
6. How were Violet and Lela alike, and how were they different? What about Violet and Evelyn?

7. In the minutes before Lela died, what do you imagine her last words to Violet might've been, had she been able to speak them?
8. Do you think Violet ever regretted not marrying Robert when she had the chance? Do you think that on some level he loved her the rest of his life?
9. What recurring images did you observe as a reader, and what would their symbolism mean to the characters? Consider candy and sweets, teeth, birds, or others.
10. Was there something in young Melanie that Violet recognized that made their relationship easy? Or were there other factors that helped the two bond?
11. When it came to Melanie and her mom's differences, did you find yourself relating to one or the other of these women more? What reasons did you have?
12. Did you ever think that Melanie and Jason might reunite? How do you imagine Melanie's life will look in five years?
13. Discuss how the car is a metaphor for Melanie's personal journey in this story. Might a theme of restoration also relate to the bourbon industry over a century?
14. Did you foresee how Violet's life would turn out, or the secret she kept? What do you believe is her life's greatest legacy from the eyes of the women who came after her?

ABOUT THE AUTHOR

Photo © 2022 Greta High

Tori Whitaker is the bestselling author of *Millicent Glenn's Last Wish* and *A Matter of Happiness*. She belongs to the Bourbon Women Association and the Historical Novel Society. Her work has appeared in the *Historical Novels Review* and *Bookmarks* magazine. Tori graduated from Indiana University, is an alum of the Yale Writers' Workshop, and is recently retired from a national law firm where she served as chief marketing officer. She spent a decade in Detroit because of her husband's career in the automotive industry. The two now reside near their children outside Atlanta and have been married for forty-five happy years. Connect with Tori through www.toriwhitaker.com.